remember me this way

They tell her not to worry. Her sister, the police. They say it's only natural, when someone close to you dies, to see him everywhere, sense him still nearby.

But they don't know Zach like she does. How much he loved her. How he liked things just his way.

How far he would go to get revenge.

Sabine Durrant is the author of two more psychological thrillers, *Under Your Skin* and *Lie With Me*. Her previous novels are *Having It and Eating It* and *The Great Indoors*, and two books for teenage girls, *Cross Your Heart, Connie Pickles* and *Ooh La La! Connie Pickles*. She is a former features editor of the *Guardian* and a former literary editor at *The Sunday Times*, and her writing has appeared in many national newspapers and magazines. She lives in south London with her partner and their three children.

Also by Sabine Durrant

For adults

Having It and Eating It
The Great Indoors
Under Your Skin
Lie With Me

For teenagers

Cross Your Heart, Connie Pickles
Ooh La La! Connie Pickles

Remember Me This Way

SABINE DURRANT

MULHOLLAND
BOOKS
HODDER

First published in Great Britain in 2014 by Mulholland Books
An imprint of Hodder & Stoughton
An Hachette UK company

This paperback edition published in 2017

5

A CIP catalogue record for this title is available from the British Library

Paperback ISBN 978 1 444 76248 8
eBook ISBN 978 1 444 76246 4

Typeset by Hewer Text UK Ltd, Edinburgh
Printed and bound by Clays Ltd, St Ives plc

Hodder & Stoughton policy is to use papers that are natural, renewable
and recyclable products and made from wood grown in sustainable
forests. The logging and manufacturing processes are expected to
conform to the environmental regulations of the country of origin.

Hodder & Stoughton Ltd
Carmelite House
50 Victoria Embankment
London EC4Y 0DZ

www.hodder.co.uk

For B.S., J.S. and M.S.

'I am beginning to understand why grief feels like suspense.'

C.S. Lewis

Zach

I stood on the common and watched her up in the school library. The lights were on and she passed by the window twice. The third time, she leaned her elbows on the sill and looked out. She seemed to stare straight at me, though I knew I was hidden, my back pressed against the tree, my face concealed behind a web of branches. I had it in mind to step forward when a man came into view behind her, and as she turned, I saw her laugh, a chink of white throat. I imagined his lips then in the dip of her neck, where the vein throbs, her eyes closing, his hands on the swell of her breasts.

If I know for sure that she has moved on, that she has forgotten what we had, I'll kill her.

She has no one to blame but herself.

Chapter One

Lizzie

February half-term, 2013

A deep breath. Petrol, manure, the mineral tang of salt. I'm not that far from the sea, even here. My face is damp from the drizzle and the spray of tyres on wet road. I'm gripping the flowers in both hands now, like a bride. I chose hyacinths, though I wasn't sure – blue ones only. Zach told me you should only ever have one colour in a bunch. I've wrapped the stems in wet kitchen roll and secured them in a small freezer bag. Either I made the paper too wet or there's a small hole in the bag, because water is seeping out. It's dripping down to my elbow.

Over the road, I can see a slope of grass, a copse of blunt trees, the shadow of a hill behind. Above that, sky the colour of dirty sheep, darker patches, a dribble of falling sun in the distance as the cold afternoon closes in. I am concentrating hard on all these things, because I know that somewhere in the corner of my vision, across the carriageway and away to the left, is the spot. But I'm not going to look. Not yet.

It is Valentine's day, exactly a year since my husband's car crash, and I am two hundred miles from home beside an A-road in the middle of Cornwall. This trip is an ending or a beginning – I'm not quite sure which. It's time to move on. People tell me that all the time. I'm trying to believe them.

3

I pick my moment between the streaming cars and run. When I reach the far side, I look back at the lay-by where my Nissan Micra sits, rocking in the backdraught of the passing lorries. My dog watches me from the side window. I've had a feeling since I parked that I'm being shadowed. It's probably just the remoteness of the place; so many people driving past, no one else stopping. Or it's guilt – guilt about all sorts of things, but mostly that I should have come sooner.

It's conventional to visit the scene of a fatal accident, to leave flowers: all those lamp posts decked with cellophane where poor cyclists have been killed. It's less usual to leave it this long. The night it happened, when PC Morrow came to the door, she would have brought me here straight away. The patrol car was waiting. My sister Peggy stopped me. She told Morrow I needed to go home with her, not drive five hours to a wet, windswept Cornish roadside, to smoke and wreckage. It would be insane, she said. I could go another time. Zach was gone. There was nothing I could do.

And it wasn't as if I didn't know what happened. Morrow, fresh from her Family Liaison training, went over it again and again. I understood about the lethal combination: the sea fog and the wet road, the sharp bend, the soft-top roof, the bottles of his favourite distillery-only whisky on the passenger seat, the oil paints, the solvent-soaked rags in the boot, the thick trunk of the tree – the disastrously placed tree.

I kept putting it off. People understood. Cornwall was Zach's favourite place. He had a house down there that would need sorting out; they assumed I would get to it in my own time. But then, in the days and weeks that followed, I began to dread it – seeing the emptiness of his bungalow, feeling the loss of him all over again.

I feel a shiver up my back. The clouds are thickening. A gust whips my coat. I must hurry up, get this done, return to the car before it gets any darker. A motorbike, overtaking a lorry, howls. I step back. This thing that had seemed so necessary when I was two hundred miles away has started to feel mad, reckless.

I pick my way along the narrow crumbling shoulder between the white line and the barrier. One foot in front of the other. That's how you get through – everyone tells you that. One step at a time. I focus as hard as I can on the littered ground: a hamburger wrapper, smeared with ketchup; a used condom, oddly bright in the polluted grass. A polystyrene cup, lodged in the barrier, flips and flaps every time a car passes. As I near the bend, a horn blares – in anxious warning maybe, or perhaps in astonishment at the madwoman in the road with her hands full of flowers.

When I get there, I'll put the hyacinths down flat at the base. Is that right? Or do they need to be higher? Perhaps I should have thought more about it, brought Sellotape. Zach would know – though he'd hate me for coming. He would take it as an insult, not a tribute. He hated sentimentality. He didn't even like anniversaries. He'd think I was giving in to cliché, or to the advice of others. 'Who've you been listening to, Lizzie Carter?'

I can sense the tree's form now, its arms veined against the grey sky. I reach the frayed slash in the hedgerow. Pale green shoots on the tip of each twig. It's callous, the way this hawthorn has regenerated, the way it has bounced back. I glance behind once more and then I hoist myself over the crash barrier, and there it is: the tree, an oak, oddly dignified despite the deep gash in its gnarled bark.

Zach's tree. I reach out to touch it, to feel the rough grooves of the bark with my fingers. I rest my head against it. My eyes fill.

My friend Jane didn't think I should come on my own today. I made her laugh to prove I could cope. I put on a funny voice and talked about my 'ceremonial visit', my 'ritual deposit of floral tribute' – phrases from the self-help book my sister gave me. I didn't tell her the whole truth – how complicated my grief is, how murky; how, more than anything, this is about laying ghosts.

Is all grief so confused, or is it just my particular misshapen form of it? There are days I accept his death and I move through the world as if underwater. Ordinary tasks, like filling the dishwasher, or sending off bills, feel brutal and empty. I resent the pigeons nesting outside the bedroom window; the schoolkids at the start of the term in their new uniform. I can be sideswiped by the smallest of things. I saw a white bike helmet on the head of a man cycling down Northcote Road last week and a wave hit me with such strength, my knees buckled. I had to crouch for a bit on the pavement outside Capstick Sports. Other days, I forget. I am almost carefree, relieved, and then I am overcome by feelings of such intense shame I don't know where to put myself. I succumb to lethargy and depression. I put things off.

Standing here, I feel close to him in a pure way. This was the point of coming. His death feels real for the first time. I must let him go, hard as it is, because, despite everything, he was the love of my life. Peggy is right. He was the man I have spent most of my life loving – the most minutes, the most hours, the most days, the most time. I close my eyes, blink my tears away, and wonder if I can now let my restless thoughts lie.

Something crackles beneath my foot, and I look down.

Propped against the roots is a bouquet of flowers. Casablanca lilies, formally wrapped in cellophane, secured with a large purple ribbon.

I step back. Another accident in the same place: that's my first thought. A black spot. The curve of the road, and the unfortunate lie of the land. Another night of fog, perhaps. More rain.

I'm disconcerted. I don't know where to put my hyacinths. The lilies look so professional and important. I stand there, wondering what to do. I'm not sure Zach, despite his contempt, would want to share. So it's a moment before I even see the note. It's white. Someone has drawn a large heart with a name – I tilt my head: *X E N I A* – spelled out around it. And at the top, in big black letters, it reads: *For Zach.*

And for a moment, honestly, I think: what a coincidence. Someone else called Zach has crashed and died here. Did they, to use PC Morrow's verb, 'fireball' too?

And then, as the truth settles, I lay the flowers down meekly, to the side. I rise and, in a trance, pass again through the gap in the hedge, over the crash barrier, and I'm heading along the road the way I came, empty-handed, head down. It's only when I look up that I see another car – a silver SUV, right up close behind the Micra, tight against its bumper.

A knot begins to press at the top of my spine. I try to run back across the road but my legs feel weighted, drugged. Cars are coming from behind. A horn blares. My skirt is flapping, trails of scarf whip around my face. Brakes squeal, another horn sounds. A rush of air and spray.

I fumble at the car door, hurl myself into the seat, greeted by the dog, his wiry lurcher body, licking and wriggling and trying to get away from me all at the same time. In the rear-view mirror I watch the SUV pull out, catch the hunched form of the driver wrestling the wheel. He must have stopped to check directions, or take a call. Mustn't he?

Seen in the mirror, my eyes are red-rimmed. A scratch has appeared across my cheek. I rub the top of Howard's head, roll my fingers under his collar and dig them into the folds around his neck. I am trying not to cry.

7

A hand-drawn heart. Xenia. He never mentioned a Xenia.

I feel a sharp ache of jealousy, mixed with the old longing, but I am aware also for the first time of its opposite: a slipping of responsibility. Someone else loved him. I have a taste at the back of my throat, clean and metallic, and, despite everything, I realise it's relief.

The Internet played Cupid. I like to be upfront about that. My sister Peggy, who cares more about appearances than I do, decided early on that we shouldn't. Pretend it began with a chance encounter at the supermarket. 'Tell people you bumped into each other by the fresh fruit,' she said, 'reaching for the same Fairtrade pineapple or what have you.'

'Or at the ready-made meals for one,' I said.

'Picking over the Mr Brain's Pork Faggots,' said Zach. 'Or what have you.'

I was wary at first. I couldn't think what he saw in me. But at that moment, in Peggy's kitchen, watching him charm my sister, the 'what have you' already a private joke between us, I let myself fall in love.

Jane, happily married to her childhood sweetheart, had encouraged me to sign up. Since we first met at sixth-form college, apart from a brief period in my twenties she had never known me not single. We worked at the same school – it was Jane who put me forward for the job in the library – and she nagged every break time. 'It's not like it used to be,' she said. 'No stigma. You just need to pick a website attached to a broadsheet newspaper. You'll get the right kind of person there. You know . . .' She made a rolling gesture with her hands, spinning delicacy from snobbery. 'Educated.' Jane went to university and sometimes forgets that I didn't.

For my profile, I wanted to write, *Dowdy librarian, few qualifications, main carer for parent with dementia, very little*

8

romantic experience. Jane had other ideas. *My friends describe me as an outgoing and fun-loving world traveller,* she wrote, batting me away from the screen. *Equally comfortable in jeans and a little black dress.*

'I don't even own a black dress.'

She tutted dismissively. 'Who cares?'

Zach was my sixth date. An artist, he lived in Brighton, way beyond my prescribed five-mile radius, so I almost didn't meet him. On the phone, he suggested a walk. They tell you to avoid that sort of interaction; better to meet in a public place. He had already showed himself a rule-breaker. The others had engaged in a series of emails in which personality-revealing issues were debated – country life versus town, sexual excitement versus companionship. He just asked if he could ring me. Plus he used his real name right away, not 'Lookin'forluv_007', say, but Zach Hopkins.

In his photograph he wasn't skiing, or braced in front of a vintage car. He didn't have his arms around a German shepherd. His picture was black and white, out of focus, shot at a low speed, taken from above, his mouth half open, a slight frown; the puzzled concentration of a person deciphering a crossword. The picture looked artless, picked at random, though as I would find out, nothing was ever artless or random with Zach.

I said yes to the walk. I don't think I hesitated. His low, steady voice; his air, very slightly ironic, of cutting to the chase. Already I was enthralled, knocked off course by his certainty.

He caught the train from Brighton to Clapham Junction and I waited for him nervously outside the new entrance at the top. It was November, overcast, with a light chill in the air – but it wasn't cold. He was wearing a Russian fur hat and a heavy coat over a baggy linen suit. As we set off towards the common, me tugging at Howard to stop him leaping up at the hat, he told me it had taken a long time to choose his outfit. 'I wanted to impress you with my natural sophistication. You are, after all, a world traveller.' He gave a small bow. 'I was also pursuing a note of eccentricity, an oddity about which we could reminisce. I wanted us to be able to look back and say, "Remember that fur hat you wore on our first date. What were you thinking?" With the added advantage—' he paused to strike a pose '—I thought the trench made me appear more muscular.'

I found it hard to talk because I was so overwhelmed by how handsome he was. The breadth of his shoulders, the blue intensity of his eyes, the stooped height of him. Halfway through my previous date, a coffee in Starbucks with MrNiceGuy, a telecoms engineer from Crystal Palace, I had caught sight of the two of us in a mirror. Our rounded shoulders, our bland and yet vulnerable expressions. We looked like two turtles without their shells. I couldn't think what Zach was doing here. Or why he would waste any time with me. The way he spoke, too, the self-conscious theatricality and the slight nervousness behind it, the accelerated intimacy that might have been ironic or might not. He was the opposite of shell-less turtle, the opposite of bland.

'You seem quite muscular to me,' I said eventually.

We hadn't even walked as far as the traffic lights across the South Circular when he reached for my hand, stuffing it inside his pocket along with his own.

I remember that more than anything – the rough warmth of his fingers, the dryness I was to discover came from oil paint and white spirit, the cracks across his palm. I remember that more than his volubility, or the heavy overcoat or the ridiculous hat. He didn't hold my hand stiffly, either. He rubbed it as we walked, massaging it back and forth with his thumb as if testing the flesh.

Later, when I knew more about him, when he'd explained about his childhood, the problems he had with trust, when he had gazed so deeply into my eyes I felt as if my insides were melting, he told me it wasn't loneliness that had led him to the Internet. In the normal run of things, he met single women all the time. He was in search of a new beginning, that was all. He just wanted to start again.

I turn the key in the ignition and pull out. The traffic is heavy. It's the dull end of a Saturday afternoon, locals are heading away from a football match. Dusk is beginning to roll out across the fields. I still have twenty miles to drive from here and I promised Jane, who knows how much I am dreading opening the door to Zach's holiday house, that I would reach it before dark.

I keep going the long way – the Bodmin bypass and the main road into Wadebridge; two sides of a triangle. It's the route Zach used to take to Gulls before he discovered the short cut. A year ago, according to Morrow's analysis, Zach missed the junction and turned round at the next roundabout. Morrow said he'd probably been drinking. He would definitely have been tired, out late the night before with an art dealer in Exeter, a bad night in a B & B, and then a long day with his paints on the moors.

I think, before I can stop myself, about the last time I saw him – the morning before he died. We were in our small kitchen in Wandsworth. The radio was on, broadcasting the results of a by-election in Hampshire. I was late for work, wary of him, shrugging on my coat, finding a lead for the dog, stuffing on my hat. But as I passed by the door, he reached out and grabbed my sleeve. His pupils were smaller, the irises a lighter blue. His mood had changed. 'I love you,' he said intensely, tugging me closer. 'You do know, don't you?'

'I do,' I said. I never doubted that.

'Because I do,' he said. 'I do love you.'

He kissed me full on the mouth. I tasted coffee, and mint, and last night's whisky. I felt myself sink, yielding, as I always had. My stomach clenched. Tears began to prick. If he had moved his lips to brush the hollow of my neck, I'd have gone upstairs with him, however late I was for school, however scared I was.

I said: 'I'm sorry the chicken had mushrooms in it.'

His voice was soft. 'It's just I thought you knew.'

I said: 'I should have remembered. And I'm sorry I was late home. Peggy was in a state about the baby.'

'She's got you round her little finger,' he said.

Howard came up then and nudged my elbow. I scratched behind his ears. He hadn't been well and I put my hand to his chest, checking.

Zach looked away. 'You love that dog more than me.'

'I don't.'

He rearranged the coffee pot and his coffee cup on the table so the handles faced the same way. He aligned the teaspoon on the saucer. 'Do you promise?'

I'd been kneeling and I stood up, forcing myself to laugh. I had already decided to leave. I had written the letter and posted it. It would be waiting for him in Cornwall. I'd sent it there because I thought it would be better if he were a long way away when he read it. I was hoping this last breakfast would be normal. To my own ears my voice sounded too high, strangulated, the words squeezed dry on my tongue. 'I promise I don't love the dog more than you.'

I spoke to him twice before he died – once on the phone that night and once late the following afternoon. I wanted to hear his voice one more time. He was still on Dartmoor when I rang, at a point called Cosdon, painting a run of ancient stone tors. Bleak and funereal, he said, stretching into the distance like unmarked graves. He was after a dying light. He would reach the bungalow after dark. I told him to be careful on the last unlit stretch of road. It was the last time I spoke to him.

I pull off the dual carriageway, slow down, head over the bridge. The road narrows to a single lane. I put my lights on. I stay under the speed limit. I always do. Zach said I drive like an old woman. It's the sort of thing I try to remember, his fondness for a casual insult, the way his jokes could tip into something nastier. I hope it will make me miss him less.

It doesn't work.

You can love and hate someone at the same time. You can so pity them it's like a fist in your stomach, be so resentful you want to hit them. They can be the best thing that ever happened to you, and the worst. You can have thoughts of leaving them and yet the memory of their skin, the pads of their fingers across your ribcage . . . these can take your breath away, even after a year.

The letter will still be there at the house. It has sat unopened for a whole year. I imagine it buried under the pizza flyers and the TV licence reminders, the Electoral Roll brown envelopes.

Thank God he died before he read it. That's one thing to be grateful for. He never learned of my betrayal.

When I get there I am going to burn it.

I change gears for the hill. The car jerks. Howard, curled next to me, doesn't lift his head from his paws.

I have driven past the holiday park, and caught, through a hedgerow, my first velvet glimpse of sea, when I see headlights glaring in my rear-view mirror. Undipped, right up close. I am on a slight incline and I accelerate until the lights have receded. Stupid idiot, I think, but then the lights are back. Dazzling, flashing. The car is on my bumper. Its horn is sounding. I think of the silver SUV in the lay-by. Is this an

SUV? I can't see anything else, not the sea, not the banks, not the road, just these insistent, blazing lights, and I've started driving faster and faster, hurtling down the hill towards the village until I reach the farm shop. I skid into the entrance and screech to a halt.

The car zooms past and is gone. I wait for a moment. Howard has got to his feet and is nosing at the window. It is dark out, the vegetable racks loom like gallows, and suddenly everything is very still.

The self-help books with their formal stages of grief, they expect a standard trajectory: shock, disbelief, bargaining, anger, depression, final acceptance. I think I've got jammed. The one Peggy gave me, *The Flowering of Your Passing*, had a chapter on 'pathological grief'. It's when a bereaved person finds it impossible to move on. I think pathological grief might be what I've got.

No one is out to get me. It's pathological. Survivor's guilt. Leaver's guilt. Unfinished business.

If I had stolen the lilies, I could have them with me now. I would touch them, rub their dusty satin between my fingers, breathe their sickly scent and know that I hadn't made them up.

It's a short drive from here, along a web of rough roads that follow the contour of the hill. Gulls is on the outside of this network, close to the edge of the cliff where the properties begin to run out. I put on the radio and rattle the last pock-marked stretch of journey, singing thinly to Taylor Swift.

Chapter Two

Wheelie bins block the entrance to the studio Zach converted from the old garage next door. Rotten pears from last summer cover the steep pitch of grass. Decayed heads of hostas flop drearily along the path. The main limb of the climbing rose I tried to train across the porch two years ago has fallen backwards to the ground.

I approach the bungalow from the side, as you would a nervous cat. I never liked it here. It's too remote for me. This end of the cliff road is run down and desolate; the other houses look shut up and empty, even when they're not. Zach, who bought the house after his mother died, claimed to love the wildness and the isolation, but it felt like an affectation. I think it was what he thought an artist should say. The fact is he hated being alone.

The key snags and catches. I push gingerly against a pile of post. My letter will be under there. I'll destroy it as soon as I can.

The door gives and I stare into the gloom. No one is here. No one has been living here. Those flowers from 'Xenia', in a way are the proof I was looking for. He's not been hiding here. He's gone. There's a dank smell. Pieces of furniture stand in murky shadows. I step over the threshold and switch on the light at the wall. Not working. I cross the room, tripping over the edge of the rug, to turn on the lamps on either side of the fireplace. A yellow glow pools on to the dusty surface of Zach's cricket table. I rub the oak with the heel of my hand, leaving a smear in the shape of a tear.

How stupid it is to be scared by a house. I begin to walk around, switching on all the other lights, looking in all the rooms. A tap drips in the bathroom. In the kitchen, mouse droppings are scattered along the base of the Dualit toaster and a tendril of ivy creeps through a crack in the window frame. The row of ash-glazed jugs along the shelf are neatly lined up, the handles at the same angle; the natural birch washing-up brushes sit stoutly in their pot. Something acrid curdles in the air. It feels damp, that's all.

The bedroom is how it would have been left the last time we were here – pillows stiff, bare duvet folded like a body under the antique Durham quilt. The sheets are in the bottom drawer of the linen press – crisp, lavender-scented. I remember the last time we put them away: Zach's broad hands as he folded, the look of concentration on his face, the small dance as we came together, the drop, the laugh, noses above the sheets, a long kiss. Moments of perfect happiness – I can never deny those.

My legs feel shaky. I sit down on the side of the bed and lean my head against the wall. We didn't match, Zach and I. People used to wonder what he saw in me. His confidence, my diffidence. I'm nothing to look at. His were the kind of looks that drew the eye, that made shop assistants simper. What a catch he was. All my friends thought it. I'd lucked out – I could see it in their expressions. Jane was envious of the newness. But it was more about oldness. I felt tied to him, almost as soon as we met, caught at the ribs. Connections tangled beneath us, drew us together. He had been at school with my old boss. We had rented flats in the same block in Clapham, been unwitting neighbours. He voiced feelings I had had myself but hadn't put into words. He stood up for me – no one had ever done that before. And he had this way of speeding things forward ('How many children shall we have?';

'Where shall we retire to?') to the point where I felt I'd always known him, and always would.

And in bed, with our clothes off, we fitted. The things I'd read about in books turned out not to be clichés after all. I would melt. I didn't know where he ended and where I began. Whole nights would pass in a tangle of limbs. And he felt it too. I know he did, for all his experience. His hands in my hair, the breathless silence, the look of ecstatic anguish on his beautiful face as he came. His sighs afterwards, his weight pressing me into the sheets, the rasp of his chin in the crook of my neck. The small moan of satisfaction as he pulled me to him. I had my own power.

My eyes have closed, but I open them now and I realise I am staring down at a wire on the floor, trailing from a plug in the wall. I poke at it with my foot. It's a dirty white in colour, half coiled, with an adaptor halfway along. I bend down and, reaching under the bed to where the wire leads, bring up a silver laptop – a MacBook Air.

I try and make sense of it, turn it over in my hands, feel the coldness of the metal.

Zach owned a MacBook Air. He wrote on it all the time, poured down his ideas, notes for paintings, for projects. He was obsessive about it. He never let it out of his sight. He had it with him when he left London. He would have had it with him when he died. His was destroyed in the fire. So this isn't that one. This must be someone else's.

I open it. *Zach Hopkins* flashes across the screen, with a space for the password. The screensaver is the view from the clifftop – low cloud, rolls of Atlantic Ocean, Zach's favourite view. I snap the laptop shut and, hands trembling, lay it down carefully on the bed next to me.

Zach wouldn't let me touch his laptop. I lifted it off the kitchen table once, just to clean underneath, and he yanked it so roughly out of my hands it fell to the floor. He picked it up, checking it over, swearing at me, and I left the room so he wouldn't see my face. Later, when we made up, when he clung to me in bed, he apologised for over-reacting. 'It's just that my life is on it,' he said.

I stand up quietly now, trying not to make any noise. I pull out the drawer where he kept a few old clothes. I think a pair of shorts is missing, navy ones, and a grey sweatshirt, and a worn leather belt that is normally coiled in the corner. I kneel down on the floor and look under the bed. There should be a holdall – kept here as it's too bulky for the closet – but it's gone. I run into the kitchen. I search the oven and the cupboards, shake out the tea towels. From the cupboard, a torch is missing, along with a stash of emergency money, £40 or so, that was kept in an empty box of muesli. I go through the house, room by room, searching for evidence with a different eye, with a different set of assumptions. On the wall in the living room, a dirty square below an empty nail. A picture has been taken down. It was an early work of Zach's, an oil, simple, rough, of a woman in a doorway. His Hunter boots, in accordance with his strict sense of orderliness, should be in the hall closet, lined up in their usual place. My old blue Dunlops are there. But his – dark green, size 43, the left one chewed by Howard and mended by me in panicked secrecy with some special glue I bought online – are gone.

I sit down in the chair by the fireplace. My mouth is dry. I've started shaking. It's beginning again. I'm back where I started. People have told me I'm mad, and maybe I am. Perhaps I am imagining it. But I'm not. He has been in this house.

My letter.

The pile of mail is still lying by the front door. I pick it up and take it to the table, push through the brown envelopes and free newspapers and flyers for plumbers and electricians, gas bills and TV licence demands, then drop it all at my feet. There's no letter from me.

Howard is still out the front, in the garden. I move to the door and call him. It's a cold Cornish night, with a wisp of warmer Gulf wind. It's completely silent. He'll have gone further down the lane, on the nose of a scent, perhaps looking for Zach. I shout louder.

Phrases spool over and over in my head. *My beloved*, I'd begun. *I need space . . . a little time apart*: pat sentences, the kind of fake sentiments Zach hated, received ideas. I was too scared to write the truth. 'Be honest,' he used to say. 'Look at me. Tell me how you feel.' Panic rises within me, remembering that. Often, I didn't know how I felt. Sometimes, frozen by the ferocity of his desire to know, I didn't feel anything at all.

'You're everything,' he used to say. 'I couldn't live without you.'

You love that dog more than me.

Howard still doesn't come, and I go back into the house, into the kitchen. The bin is Brabantia, top of the range – Zach insisted. It has a vintage look to it. Details were so important to him. I click open the lid.

My letter and its envelope are scrunched up at the bottom.

'HOWARD!' I'm out the front, screaming now, too loudly, filled with trepidation.

My dog comes bounding, skidding across the dank grass, falling over his own feet. He knocks into my legs and then passes me into the house. His dirty paws, the white boards, the pale rug. The old panic sharp in my chest: I'll have to clean up before Zach sees.

In London, at night, I leave the light on since the accident. I don't trust myself. I double- and triple-check windows and doors. My brain is unreliable. When I am with people, I have a thought and then I don't know whether I have actually said it out loud. I repeat myself, Jane says. Other times I am unnaturally silent. I feel as if I'm waiting. My limbs turn heavy and uncooperative. If I'm not careful, I think, I will fall down the stairs, crack my head, break all my bones. I'm scared I might die.

I see Zach everywhere. I'll see a man in the street or along the platform on the Tube and my heart will stop. I'll run, pushing people out of the way and then I'll reach him, or he'll turn, and it won't be Zach at all, but a stranger with the same gait or messenger bag, the same floppy dark hair.

Peggy is always telling me to clear out his clothes. But it feels wrong. How can I get rid of his shoes, his shirts? He'll need them when he comes back.

PC Morrow assures me this is common. The brain needs to forge new synapses. It hasn't caught up with the heart. I am like a soldier, she said, experiencing phantom sensations in an amputated limb. It is neuropathic confusion. It will stop, she said, when I am more myself.

I am still waiting. But my mind seems to be getting more confused, not less. I sense his breath on my neck. Once, at work, I was alone in the library, putting books back on the shelves, and I smelt his aftershave. Acqua di Parma – Colonia Intensa (not Assoluta: I made that mistake once). The light in the room changed, as if someone were blocking the doorway. When I got there and looked out, the corridor was empty.

We had a break-in. I had a break-in. Although 'break-in' isn't quite the word. No busted lock or broken window; nothing left on its hinges. My handbag, the television, the loose change on the kitchen table, were untouched. They took Zach's iPod. 'It's all kids want these days,' Morrow said, 'small electronic gadgets they can sell on.' Even so. The front door tightly closed, the post neatly piled on the table in the hall – did I leave it like that? I couldn't remember. Morrow said I must have left the door unlatched. An open invitation. I make that sort of mistake all the time. Was it dread or longing that sent quivers up my spine, that made me imagine he had let himself in with his key?

At night I hear noises. A car pulled up in the street in the middle of the night a few weeks ago. Elvis Costello, 'I Wanna Be Loved', his favourite song, leaked from the rolled-down window. The car stayed there, engine running, right outside the house. The music was loud enough to reach me, even in the back bedroom where I sleep. By the time I got to the study window, the car had pulled off. I saw its lights at the end of the road.

I dream about him most nights. In the folds of sleep, my eyes shut tight, I think of his face pressed against mine. I put my hands between my legs and imagine his lips running across my neck, down to my breasts, his fingers around my nipples. A feeling of something weighing on me, under the sheets, my hands curled tight, the cotton sucked into my mouth. In the morning, when I wake, I think he crept in through the window and under the covers. I can smell him on my skin, see the dent of his head on the pillow. He has spent the night with me. It is Zach, I am sure, who made me come.

I don't tell anyone. They will think I am madder than they already do. Peggy says that when you lose the love of your life, you are allowed to lose your grip on reality, though I am not sure she banked on it lasting more than a year. Probably exactly a year. Peggy believes in absolutes. She doesn't do messiness.

Jane knows a little about my marriage, but no details.

There is darkness in my head, memories that burn – things neither of them know, that I couldn't begin to tell.

I destroy the letter and its envelope on the front step. I take a match to them both, watch them curl, and then sweep up the papery grey ashes and throw them out into the lane. Zach was here. I clean my teeth, gulping water straight from the tap – clay-red in its first gush – and sit upright in the armchair. I'm trying to think straight. I'd been so fearful of his reaction, so weak, I'd sent a letter to a cottage two hundred miles away. I spoke to him an hour before he died. Nothing in his tone told me he had read it. He was lying even then, suppressing his anger, working out what to do to me.

Darkness presses against the windows. Night noises – the wind rattling the windows, mice in the eaves. I think about running away, finding a hotel room, driving back to London, but I'm unable to move. I resolve to wait. If he's out there, let him come. I deserve it.

The truth is, I would never have left him. Zach could be funny and confident and clever, but it was his darkness that drew me. The shadows that crossed his face, the unexplained headaches, the snaps of anger (not directed at me; not to begin with). Once, after we'd been out with my sister and her husband, he ranted about how Rob had put him down: 'Did you see him smirk every time he mentioned my "art"?'. It made me love him more, things like that. His obsessions and his insecurities, the sensitivity to condescension: I knew where they came from. I've seen what childhood abuse does to kids at school – how withdrawn and angry they can be, how delicate their sense of self. His moods, I knew they weren't about me – the wrong food I'd cooked, the wrong clothes – even if he said they were. I knew that; I really did. By the end everything was so tangled between us and so intense, so absorbing, the loss of it, the hole he has left, has been almost too much to bear.

I think about Xenia and her heart-shaped note, let myself feel a clean, sharp jealousy for this unknown woman, this person I have never met, a wild, dizzying pain under my breastbone. Was she his lover? I let myself imagine him here, with me, a whiff of whisky on my neck, the feel of him against my thighs. Early on he told me he was touched by my obsession with his body. He said I was like a hatched gosling who had imprinted itself on the first living creature it saw.

The year is up. He has been biding his time, waiting for me to come to Gulls before he makes his move.

I am ready.

Whatever he wants, he can have.

I will stay awake all night.

Zach

July 2009

The way she chews plays on my nerves. Her mouth hangs half open, her small teeth crunch; there's a sucking sound as the two surfaces separate. She mops her lips with her tongue between each bite. I know it's unreasonable of me to mind, but I can't stop myself. It turns my stomach. The flat is too small, a bad conversion: I think that's part of the problem. I'm claustrophobic. Every time she shifts on the sofa, the springs twang.

Her eyes were fixed on the television. We used to call it a TV dinner. Now it's a ready meal. Count on Us. Four hundred calories or less. Salmon and wild rice. When she finished, she put her tray down on the carpet. A dollop of miso sauce from the bottom of the tray stained her skirt, but she didn't notice. She swung her feet up and laid her stockinged toes in my lap – except she was wearing popsocks. I could see the horizontal indentation where the fabric dug into her flesh. Her popsocked toes. I shifted my groin away. After a bit I moved her feet to one side, got up and went to the window to look out.

If only you could see the sea from here, that would be something. Instead, it's a run of red and grey roofs, the distant glass dome of the shopping centre. I don't get this about Brighton. Most of the houses shoulder the water when they could face it. Why would a builder worry about the wind, not the light? She likes the

24

warmth and practicality of this place – two square rooms, a single hop from TV to bed. One road up, now that's a place I could fancy – a Georgian parade, a wedding-cake sweep, with its own communal garden.

I sat back down, then waited for a raucous segment of the show before saying I needed air.

'Oh sweetie, sorry,' she said, jumping to her feet. 'Do you want to watch something else? I can switch it off if you like.'

I paused as if I were considering it, though I was way past that. Mentally, I was already out, pacing the streets, sucking up the ozone. I tried to make my voice sound considerate: 'You darling girl, you need your down time. I won't be long.'

I felt relieved as soon as I was out in the open, repentant because of the look on her face, but also liberated. It's her fault it's not working. I want it to work, or I used to. What's wrong with her? Why doesn't she see what we *could* have? She's a clever girl; for Christ's sake, she does psychometric testing for a living. She should have sussed out what would make us happy. She doesn't appreciate me, that's the problem.

Brighton in high summer. Bins spilled their contents on to the pavement, black plastic flapping. The rancid smell of rotting fruit mixed with fried food, the pungent tang of Chinese. Men on a stag, pushing and pulling each other, falling into traffic, the tragic failed camaraderie of a half-hearted sing-song. Down at the beach, a group of women lay on the pebbles in the still light, their red-and-white sunburned legs outstretched, the gleam of their throats, raucous laughter. Rihanna's 'Umbrella' blazed tinnily from someone's iPhone. 'Ella, ella, ella,' the girls shouted. Drunken hens. Or shoppers – Primark carrier bags behind their heads – tanked up from happy hour. The sea glimmered in the sinking sun like oil. Seagulls, fat and dirty grey, pranced and flapped along the boardwalk. Even the seagulls down here seemed unnatural.

Earlier I walked along the front towards the pier. It wasn't so much that I was attracted to the flashing lights or the high-pitched whirr. I just didn't want to take the backstreets and risk passing Blank Canvas. It would be like turning over a stone, seeing woodlice on their backs, legs flailing. Those three artworks – none sold last time I looked. No one wants them. People don't want heaviness, layers. They want small children with spades, the sky a shade to match their curtains. I don't know why I bother. I should stick with the casts. Jim rang earlier to say three more commissions came in today. A newborn's feet and two mothers wanting plaster representations of their kids' pudgy hands. The residents of Brighton really can't get enough of their own limbs.

I found myself outside Green's Wine Bar. It's far enough off the main drag to be quiet. Plus, no one wants solid, old-fashioned French any more – they want artisaned and heritaged and locally sourced. I thought about ringing someone but I'm not good company; it will be different when I sell a picture. I sat in the corner and the new waitress, dyed blonde hair and a heavy hand with the fake tan, perched on the edge of my table to take my order – grilled chicken with sautéed potatoes and green beans. When the food came, I divided it into sections, eating the potato first, then the beans, and lastly the chicken, smothering each mouthful with enough mustard to make my head sing. Sometimes I'll do anything to get sensation back where it should be.

It was dark when I got back to the flat, the TV off. Charlotte had tidied up the living room and was waiting for me in the bedroom. She had changed her underwear from the overwashed shapeless grey I saw her put on this morning, into a matching red-and-black nylon-lace bra and thong. I'd seen the La Senza bag in the recycling. I don't know if it was pity or the tackiness of her 'lingerie', but I felt aroused, despite myself. She told me she was sorry, but I don't think she knew what for. It's what I wanted, but *I* don't know what for. Either way, I felt hollow. I don't know what I'm looking for, but everything seems empty.

Afterwards I came back out here to the sitting room and poured myself a glass of Glengoyne. It seems to work when I'm feeling out of control like this. Out of the window is a purple-orange sky, white and yellow lights. Music throbbing from the nightclub a street away. Loud voices rising up across the rooftops. Brighton's wrong for me. It's not a good fit, literally. I'm too big for this flat; this town. The carpet is too static, the furniture too flimsy. The whole place brings out the worst in me. I should live in Cornwall. Perhaps I'll do that.

No – I need sweetness, naivety. I need someone to rescue me from myself.

I could be happy, I think. I could be good.

Something's got to happen. Something's got to give.

Somewhere out there someone is waiting.

Chapter Three

Lizzie

I wake with a jerk. My neck is stiff. Howard is on my feet. He raises his head, and then lies back down.

It is 8 a.m.

A branch scrapes the window.

I shift my legs and Howard stands up. A pale light fills the room. It's a day of flat cloud. I can't believe I let myself sleep. Nothing here has changed. The front door is shut; the pile of ravaged post lies on the floor where I left it.

I should feel relieved, but I don't, just a terrible deflation. I shiver and get gingerly to my feet. It's cold. I'm wearing the same clothes as yesterday – an old summer skirt of my mother's, from the back of my drawer. Zach wouldn't have liked it. Early on, he took all my old fleeces and jeans to the charity shop. He was only happy when I wore clothes he had bought. Once Peggy gave me one of her cast-offs, a swirly purple wrap dress. I thought it looked nice, but he said it didn't suit me and it disappeared from my cupboard.

In the chest of drawers in the bedroom, I find an old shirt of his – soft grey chambray, with a stain on the front. It was my fault, the stain. I rested a leaky ink pen on top of the ironing. He caught me trying to scrub it out, dabbing at it with a Stain Devil in the bathroom. I can still see him standing there in the doorway, a cold smile on his face. I jumped. 'Are you

28

scared of me?' he asked, and I said I wasn't. I forced my voice to stay steady. 'But I know this sort of thing matters to you. I'm just trying to avoid unnecessary stress for both of us. It's just a shirt.'

My tone surprised him; he looked confused, lost. He very rarely realised his obsessions were anything but normal. It was one of those moments when I experienced my own control. I felt a quickening low in my stomach, hooked my fingers into the belt of his jeans and pulled him to me.

I hold the shirt to my face, feel the threads against my lips. It smells of different washing powder – the only brand in the shop down here. I put it on with one of his old jerseys over that. I find an extra pair of socks in the drawer too. I catch my face in the mirror. I look old and pale. He liked me in make-up, but I haven't worn it since he died. That red lipstick he bought me, I don't know where it is. I sit on the bed wearing his clothes, and a wave of intense sadness and guilt surges through me.

Thoughts I have been keeping at bay begin to press. What if he read my letter and drove back to London to confront me? What if he had been drinking, was so crazed with anger that he wasn't seeing straight? What if he died on his way?

Am I losing perspective? Have I been too much on my own?

I've got to get out.

My Converse are damp from last night and I open the cupboard for my wellington boots. I stare at the empty space where Zach's should be. He must have been wearing them. Did he go for a walk when he first arrived, to blow away the cobwebs, and then come back and find my letter? I imagine him ambling back through the door, carefree, and then picking it up, and the thought is unbearable.

I grab my wellies then, knocking the fabric conditioner to the floor in my hurry. I put the bottle back on the shelf, in

29

alignment with the washing powder. The dustpan and brush I used yesterday have fallen off their hook. Or perhaps I was so anguished I didn't hang them up, as Zach taught me, just hurled them back in. I rehang them, thrust my feet into my boots, grab Howard's lead and unlock the front door.

The wind is stiffer this morning and I take my waterproof jacket from the back seat, pulling up the hood to keep the wind out of my ears, digging my gloves out of the pocket. My mobile phone is tucked in the plastic groove on the inside of the handle on the driver's door, where I left it last night. I don't feel like speaking to anyone, but I promised I would ring Jane, and Peggy.

I straighten up and shut the car door, and, as I do that, I catch a movement out of the corner of my eye. A figure on the other side of the lane, a girl with long hair, in a blue coat. She stares at me. I can't see her expression from this distance, but something about her body language, the way she's positioning herself, legs apart, shoulders thrust forward, is disconcerting. I wonder if she is lost.

'You all right?' I call and begin to walk towards her, but she doesn't answer. By the time I have crossed the road she has disappeared down the alley that runs alongside the bungalow opposite, and is gone

I take the same path, pocked with puddles from the recent weeks of rain. It leads down between a network of garden fences, along the boundary of the hotel, to the clifftop – the point where civilisation runs out and the swell of grassed cliff begins.

The sea: it's always a surprise. Zach used to say it was some sort of consolation, no matter where or when. You feel it coming, smell it in the air, sense the opening light, and then there it is – that great expanse, that stretch. Today it is riffled, uneasy, not rolling, but tufted like the hair of a terrier. It is coloured in layers, sage and granite, only a few white tips, a smudged horizon. Stepper Point, across the bay, is a patch-work of green and mustard yellow, edged with thin parings of sand. Seagulls yelp and wheel above my head. Behind, on the back wall of the hotel, polished jackdaws caw.

I'd never imagined the kind of happiness I experienced with Zach would belong to me. When I met him, I had got used to thinking of myself as an aunt and a sister and a daughter, not a lover. I had set my sights on average contentment. And yet within months I was striding along this clifftop, his hand in mine, gorse underfoot, the wind in my ears, the sea in his eyes. He told me when we were walking here one day that I was a source of constant surprise to him, that my humble delight in the world was infectious. I wasn't used to making a difference to anyone. When I wonder what he saw in me, I often think of that.

An elderly man passes with a black Labrador. I stand back. I'm having trouble breathing. I've got a tightness in my throat, an empty feeling in my abdomen, a need to sigh. I am biting my lip. This loss, this sense of emptiness, is worse than last night's fear. It's why I put off coming. The world seems blank. He used to ask me if I'd choose to die before or after him. 'Before,' I used to say.

I walk faster. There's a bench around the headland, below the large holiday houses, the ones with the telescopes and the balconies, the ones Zach used to hanker after, and I reach it and sit down. Below me, the sea swarms around the black rocks.

I fumble for my phone. There's a signal here. I ring Jane first, but she doesn't answer. Sunday morning. She and Sanjay are probably having brunch in one of the new cafés that have opened near their flat. She will tell me about it later. She believes in the comfort of food – the sunrise muffin, or the eggs Benedict, or the Turkish pide. I will tell her I'm fine, and she will pretend to believe me. She might mention Sam Welham, the new psychology teacher. She loved Zach – my knight without armour, she used to call him, my fairy-tale prince – but she thinks it's time I moved on.

Peggy answers. I stare at the sea and, keeping control of my voice, tell her Gulls is still standing. 'And yes, I am too.' Her Clapham kitchen, with its kids' drawings, its piles of washing, seems a long way off. She hasn't managed to visit Mum. 'You know what weekends are like.' She is preparing Sunday lunch and her five-year-old is helping. 'No, no, no,' she keeps saying. 'Careful, Alfie. Sorry, Lizzie. Are you OK, not too sad? *Watch out*. HOT.' Zach was always irritated by the way Peggy's role as parent spilled into every corner of her life, but I'm touched by it. 'I'll ring you back,' she says suddenly and goes.

I stand up. I've just got to reach the shop, buy a few things, organise for an estate agent to visit. It's not much. I can go through these normal motions. I walk around the last bend and the village stretches out below, a crescent of buildings around a deep bay, a glimmering stretch of beach studded with rocks. It's low tide, the sea pulling away in the distance. A scattering of sleek black-neoprene figures, leaning against yellow boards, disconsolate at the waterline. Several more bobbing a hundred metres out. Children scattered, people idly walking, more dogs. The mobile van's here – 'Rip It Up: Gary's Surf Adventure' – even if the waves aren't.

Zach loved it here. He actually grew up somewhere else, on a different coast, in a village on the Isle of Wight, but a girl he met when he was young had a holiday home here and he got to know the area through her. When his parents were dead, he sold their house and invested the money in property here instead. For him, it was a breaking of ties, but I don't think it was that big a leap – it's still the same small, tight world he grew up in: the middle classes in all their faded red-trousered glory. He just swapped one privileged sailing community for another.

South-London-on-sea, some people call it. It's funny, that,

how limited the imaginations of the wealthy few, how they all end up in the same handful of places on holiday. Lots of parents at my school have houses here or relatives in the area. Down here, in the summer with Zach, I was guaranteed to bump into someone I recognised. It made me uncomfortable, horribly self-conscious. I'd see them thinking, *What's that funny little librarian doing here?* I wonder, with an abrupt sinking feeling in my chest, if I will see anyone I recognise now.

I attach Howard to the lead and cross the last field to the path that runs down to the car park.

A river trickles from the hill, under the bridge and on to the beach, spreading and turning silver across the sand. On the rocky inland side, plastic bags tangle in the weeds, a supermarket trolley is upended. Three boys, bikes spreadeagled, are using it as target practice. Locals? I cross the bridge to the short row of shops. Outside the Spar hover two mothers with a gaggle of small children. Holidaymakers – you can tell from the warmth of their ski jackets: goose-down padding, fur-lined hoods. (The local lads with the bikes are in T-shirts.) They are peering at a peeling notice on the door – an appeal for help in the search for a missing person. 'God, can you imagine?' the taller woman is saying almost under her breath. 'Losing someone like that. Never knowing what's happened to them. You'd search for them, wouldn't you, everywhere you went?'

'Unimaginable,' the other woman says. She puts both hands on the shoulders of a small boy who has been trying to fit himself under the flap of the advert for Wall's ice cream. 'Do you think he's dead?' she adds over his head.

I'd planned to buy a few essentials, but the women are blocking the entrance. I turn round, pretending to admire the view. A café-bar, the Blue Lagoon, tops the surf shop next door. On a whim, I climb the steps, Howard right behind me.

It's too early in the year for the balcony to be in use. The white plastic chairs are stacked to one side and the stripy umbrellas tightly furled. I push open the door to a hubbub. Families mainly, in smaller and larger groupings, spilling between the tables. It is a big, open-plan place, azure walls and bleached wood, model seagulls on sticks – a self-consciously 'seaside' form of decor Zach found nauseating. There's a cloying smell of beer and slightly stale oil. Children are drinking hot chocolate. Somewhere a baby is crying.

I sit at the bar, my back to the room, and order a coffee. I should eat but I have no appetite. The young waitress brings a bowl of water for Howard and kneels down to make a fuss of him. She is from Lithuania, she tells me when she straightens up; her parents live on a farm and have lots of dogs. She tilts her head while she is talking and there is a certain look on her pale, pinched face, a look you see on kids at school sometimes, an openness, a vulnerability, that makes me want to hug her. But we don't talk for long because the owner emerges from the kitchen door. The waitress grabs a handful of menus and scurries off.

I rack my brain for the owner's name. Kumon? Something odd. When Zach came down to paint, the two of them would hang out, drink whisky, play poker.

He's seen me. He runs his hands through his greying surfer locks and then reflexively down the front of his pale blue sweatshirt. We both want to hide, but it's too late. His eyes have that glaze, the masking of momentary panic, I have seen a lot over the last year. I smile, because although people expect me to be sad, they seem to find it easier if I'm not.

'Babe.' He leans sideways across the bar, stroking his goatee with one hand. I don't think he remembers my name either. 'How's it all going? How *are* you?'

'Oh, you know, fine.'

He stares at me, making small, regular nods of his head.

'Kulon!' Activity at the door – new arrivals, voices raised, a big entrance. I look over my shoulder and turn back quickly. It's Alan Murphy MP. His wife, Victoria, is the old teenage friend of Zach's who introduced him to the area. They live in Winchester, I think, but still have a holiday house down here. It's been in her family for years. He's a Conservative rising star; she's a think-tank economist with a public profile of her own: local celebrities, not least in their own eyes. Zach loathed Murphy and he and Victoria had drifted apart, though we did once bump into them walking around Trebetherick Point. Zach was forced to introduce me, but I don't think Murphy will remember.

'Kulon!' The MP shouts louder this time. 'How the hell are you, you old devil, you!'

Kulon – of course, not Kumon. He raises his left arm high in a salute. He has already half swivelled, his expression shifting. 'Elena. Move some tables! Push these two together!' He turns back. 'Poor old Zachamundo.'

'I know.'

He shakes his head. 'Shit, man, I miss him.'

'I know,' I say again.

'Mind you, the bastard still owes me money from that last game, just before . . .'

'He owed you money? Oh God, I must pay you.'

'Nothing. Nothing. Peanuts!' He slaps his hand down on the bar. Relief floods his features. He has navigated the waters of my bereavement and, through this apparently generous gesture, come out the other side. 'Really. Nothing.'

The Sunday newspapers are laid out on the bar and I pretend to read. Alan Murphy MP has a group of people with him, but he's holding court, talking loudly, trying to lasso in anyone in the room who will listen. Since he became Minister of Culture, Media and Sport, he has become a big topic of conversation in the staffroom. Sam Welham says the whole buffoon malarkey is an act, that he's utterly ruthless. But Peggy loves him, or at least the persona he presents on *Have I Got News For You* – all bluster and blunder. He is said to represent a new spirit in politics, a return to *character*. Zach used to say he was a cock. What would he think now, listening to him work the room, brandishing his charm like a spotted handkerchief? 'How long you down for? . . . Isn't it heaven?'

It's hard to concentrate on anything else, but after a short while I notice two girls have started talking to Howard, cooing and rubbing his ears. I put the paper down. Their voices are familiar. Uggs, leggings, long blonde hair. I know them from London, from Wandle Academy: Ellie and Grace Samuels, twins in year seven.

Ellie looks up. 'Miss Carter!' she exclaims.

'Hello, girls,' I say. 'Having a nice holiday?'

Across the room, amid Murphy's entourage, I am aware of a plump woman in an outsize jumper and glasses rising and steering rather quickly past chairs to reach us.

'Yikes,' she says, making a face. 'Sorry. They don't call it South London on Sea for nothing! What a nightmare, coming all this way and then bumping into kids from school!'

'Doesn't matter at all,' I say. 'They're lovely.'

'I always tell the girls, if you see a teacher you should pretend you haven't.'

'No, really. It's fine.'

She tidies her hair behind her ears. 'We're staying with my parents in Padstow. We've just come over this side to spend the day with old friends.' She makes a small, dismissive wave in the direction of Murphy, clearly embarrassed to be thought bragging about the connection. 'Alan was at school with my husband. But am I right that you have a weekend cottage near here?'

'My late husband did. A bungalow, anyway. He used to come here to paint. I've come to put it on the market.'

She has flushed slightly. 'I did know about your husband, but I'd forgotten. I'm so sorry.'

'Thank you. Everyone told me not to make any changes for a year. The year is up and here I am!'

'You poor thing.' She puts her hand on my shoulder. 'You're too young to be going through such a thing. It must have been such a dreadful shock. Have you got anyone with you?'

The sincerity of her sympathy is like a small sharp stab under my ribcage. Tears prick at the corners of my eyes. I look down to blink them away and shake my head, but I can still feel the pressure of her hand. The Review section is open in front of me and I watch a tear fall, as if in slow motion, and spread, darkening the paper.

'So, what's going on here then, Sue?'

Murphy has popped up behind Mrs Samuels, his arms around her stomach, his chin resting on the top of her head. I wipe my eyes quickly with the back of my hand and try to smile.

'Now remind me. Have we met?' He is shorter in real life than on television, but also more handsome. Success has given him a physical confidence Zach said he didn't have before.

'Oh, Alan.' Sue tries to push him off.

He rocks her sideways in a little dance. 'You definitely look familiar.'

I clear my throat. 'We've met once, or twice. I'm Lizzie Carter. Zach Hopkins' wife?'

'Zach Hopkins. Of course.' He releases Sue and hurls himself on to the adjacent stool. 'How is the old dog?'

Sue raises her hands as if to try and stop the words from coming. 'Alan—' she begins.

'I'm so sorry,' I say. 'I don't know why you should know. He died. In a car accident.'

37

'Dead? *Is* he? God, did I know that? Forgive me. When did that happen?'

'A year ago.'

'I'm so sorry. About the same time Jolyon went missing, then. Terrible month. God.'

'Miss Carter works at Ellie and Grace's school,' Sue adds. 'In the library.'

We've been joined by other members of Murphy's group – two men who stand slightly to the rear of his shoulder. Friends? Family? Security?

'Patrick,' Murphy says loudly to one of them. 'Did you know Zach Hopkins died?'

The man called Patrick quietly says, 'I did.'

I have a strong desire to get out into the fresh air. Normal social interaction is beyond me and I don't deserve their kindness. That casual social lassoing by the upper class – I can't be part of it. Not now. I need to get away. But whispered conversations are taking place, something is set in motion and I am suddenly powerless. Grace and Ellie have taken Howard's lead from me, and Sue has thrown her arm around my shoulder.

'Alan's right, I'm sure Victoria would love to see you,' Sue is saying. 'She'll be so sad to hear about your husband.'

'Lunch!' Murphy is bellowing. 'The girl needs feeding up.'

'It's fine, it's fine, it's fine,' I say, but Sue is clutching me close. The softness of her jumper brushes my face. 'Come on, come up to Sand Martin with us. Murphy loves a crowd. Have one drink and then you can go off and do your thing. Just a quick one. I can't bear to think of you on your own.'

And maybe it's because she is so kind, or maybe it's because, as Zach told me, I am weak and easily led, or maybe it's because this is what it is like to be bereaved, I allow myself to be steered into a car and away.

Zach

September 2009

I went to London today. I told Charlotte I needed to work up there and took my sketchbook and paints, slung over my shoulder in the 'art satchel' she just bought me. (I looked it up on the Ally Capellino website: £278. I don't know why she thinks spending money on me will bring us closer.)

I caught the train into Victoria and then out again – with a vague plan of heading west towards Cornwall. I was pretty aimless. I'm not sure what I was searching for. I hate being so rootless. Nell and Pete seem to feel at home wherever they land. It was one of the things that drew me to Charlotte, that sense she has of being grounded. She wouldn't leave Brighton, her hometown, if you paid her. Whereas I could live anywhere. That's the problem of growing up in a dead-end place. Cornwall could be the answer – my sanctuary – but not alone. I'd need a soulmate, and I'm sorry to say, after all the time and effort I have invested, I now know that's not Charlotte.

Richmond was my first thought. I like that it is west: you could get on the road to Cornwall easily from there. I felt a flicker of excitement when I cut across the Green to the river. It was like a scene from Disney – water twinkling under the bridge, heritage street lamps, rowing boats for hire. I could imagine myself settling down here, falling in love, leading a conventional sort of life. But then an aeroplane passed so low you could almost taste the in-flight meal. All those big posh houses and the people in them — every three minutes they have to stop talking and wait for the noise to pass over. Who knew?

I took the train back into London after that, alighting briefly at each stop. Barnes: too villagey, plus the flight path is just as disruptive to normal conversation, or *thought*. Putney, better, but what is Putney when it's at home (if anyone calls it home, which I doubt)? Basically the A3 with a load of closed-down shops. Wandsworth Town, a one-way system, and Clapham Junction, at first glance, just a dump.

Standing outside a depressing Marks & Spencer in a dreary high street smelling of McDonald's chips, I was downcast and hungry, so I walked around a bit to find something I could countenance eating. Deli counters were obviously out, as were pre-packaged sandwiches, and I walked a little way until I found a road with smaller cafés and shops, bit of a market, an Italian restaurant that sold clean food.

I ordered a steak. Spinach on the side in a separate bowl. When I emerged, blood warmed by a rather nice glass of Bardolino, I looked at the street with different eyes. A couple in their thirties were canoodling against a wall on the corner; he was pressing a leg between her thighs; her hands gripped the seat of his jeans. It piqued my curiosity. A wedding band glinted on her ring finger. Perhaps it was illicit, this clinch, but I allowed myself to imagine they were married. After that I went into the first estate agent I came across. A jumped-up little tosser in a pinstriped suit told me this part of London was called 'Between the Commons'.

'What's your budget, sir?' he said. 'We find it's very much a seller's market round here.'

It always is a seller's market.

Charlotte left three messages while I was sifting through house details. I listened to the need in her voice as I ambled back to the station. She was coming home early. What time would I be back? She'd bought chicken breasts and that fresh pasta I like. Should she cook it, or would I rather go out? She'd cleaned the flat, and bought me a present – that spotty Paul Smith shirt I'd seen in the window. 'Hurry home,' she said. 'Let's see if it fits.'

All this concern: she can feel me slipping away. I'm already half gone. I try to imagine kissing her against a wall up a side street and I can't. Our romance is dead. She's lost her chance. She should have realised earlier. She could have had me. Now it's too late. Few things are as unattractive as desperation. Anyway, how many Paul Smith shirts does she think I need?

Nell and Pete came for supper. I didn't eat much. Roast pork – I told her in advance that was fine, but she bought it from Waitrose and it had a funny taste. She hid the packaging before I could inspect it but I suspect it had a marinade or a stuffing. It had that pig smell. I didn't like it.

After they left, I ran myself a bath. I haven't been feeling as in control as I like and I'd taken a pill from Jim's stash to recalibrate. But then I heard her crying outside the bathroom, pretend-quietly so I would notice. When I opened the door, she'd darted to the sofa. By her feet were small curls of black mud that Pete had brought in on the bottom of his shoes. Nell's wine glass had left a ring like a slug trail on the coffee table. I tried to divert my attention, though it was making my skin crawl, and asked her what was wrong. She said something about how I hadn't eaten the food on purpose, how I had done it to hurt her. She said I was 'toying with her emotions', a phrase she'll have got from one of her friends. She didn't understand, she said, how I could go from being normal in front of Nell and Pete to 'being like this'.

'Being like what?'

'Weird. Cold. You haven't said a word to me since they left. You haven't even helped me wash up. They're your friends. I only invited them to please you. You used to be so loving, so kind. I thought you were the sweetest man I'd ever met.'

Why didn't she just say what was really bothering her? People's inability to be straight with each other drives me insane. All this pretence. We would have to have a discussion about whether I am still loving and kind, when she was actually pissed off because Nell mentioned Gulls and I haven't taken her there yet. She is one of those girls who measures romance in terms of mini-breaks. Watching her on the sofa, her eyes red, her bottom lip swollen, her fingers twisting the belt of the clingy silk top she had bought to attract me, I felt a surge of resentment. Why was she trying to make me feel bad? It's not my fault. Sometimes I don't know why I behave the way I do. It's as if my brain has the ability to subdivide, to split and separate memory from the present. If I could just give in, slow down . . . I don't know. It's just how I am.

'I thought you were cross with *me*,' I told her. 'I was just getting out of your way. I thought you couldn't bear the sight of me. You've been behaving so oddly recently.' I gazed into her eyes. 'I'm hopeless. I haven't sold a painting in weeks. I bring nothing to the household. You've had your nose in papers the last few nights . . . I don't know why you put up with me. I thought you wanted rid.'

It was almost too easy to soothe the situation. She hadn't realised I was in such a bad way, she said. I shouldn't worry about money; she earned enough for both of us. She loved me more than anyone she had ever met. Some day soon, perhaps I'd find 'a purpose in life' that would bring me self-worth.

I felt a flash of anger. Something a little too patronising in her tone. I let her kiss me a bit more and then I put on a little-boy voice: 'I might have my bath, now it's run.'

'OK,' she said, in a small voice of her own. 'And I'm sorry to have upset you.'

I can hear her Hoovering up Pete's mud.

Chapter Four

Lizzie

It's a short drive to Sand Martin, but a steep one – up the hill behind the village, left beyond the caravan site, over the brow of a wide field – and I regret coming more with every change of gear.

Murphy and his entourage are leading the way in a long black saloon car with tinted windows. I am driving with the Samuels in a dented people carrier. Tim Samuels has saggy pouches under his eyes, and a forced cheerfulness. On the way up, he tells me he is a chartered accountant – 'deadly dull I'm afraid' – who has been out of work for eighteen months. 'Still hopeful!' Sue trills from the back. Tim makes a face more expressive of doubt.

Through a pair of wrought-iron gates, the Murphys' house rises, square and white, with tall Georgian windows and a pitched grey slate roof. It looks like a house in a children's book, or a novel by Mary Wesley, very different from the tight suburban scrabble of the seaside resort below.

We slam shut the car doors and walk along the gravel path to the click-clocking of jackdaws. Rhododendrons line the drive, the large lawn is edged with box trees, and lavender grows in pots on the terrace. Leaves cover the surface of a large trampoline on a rough stretch of grass between the cars and trees. The black safety netting is bowed in places, full of holes. Two smallish bikes lie, felled, beside it.

A cluster of white doves flaps off the grass and alights on the roof. Howard pulls away from Grace and careens after them, and then, diverted, dives into the undergrowth. He'll have smelt a rabbit.

'He'll be OK,' Murphy shouts. 'Won't go far.'

The front door, through a porch on the side of the house, is on the latch and he pushes it open. The rest of us funnel into a wide hall with a sweeping carpeted staircase to one side. The walls are faded pink and dotted with small framed watercolours. A stuffed fox on hind legs holds out a wrought-iron umbrella stand filled with tennis racquets. Murphy ushers the Samuels through a door into a drawing room – 'Make yourselves comfortable' – but he grabs my hand and, throwing his coat over the curled arm of the bannister, yells: 'Darling! Chuck another spud in, will you? I've brought Lizzie Carter home for lunch.'

'WHO?' The voice comes from another room.

'You know, lovely Lizzie Carter from—'

'NO. I fucking don't.' The voice gets suddenly louder. 'Fucking HELL, Alan. There's a fucking DOG in the kitchen.'

'Oh God.' I'm on the move and almost collide with Victoria as she emerges, wiping her hands on a butcher's apron, from the door at the far end of the hall. 'Sorry. That's mine. I'm so sorry!'

Howard bounds from behind her, lead trailing, causing her to buckle slightly at the knees. I catch him, but she swings her arms with the exaggerated force of someone gaining her balance and wanting you to know it. She is tall and willowy, with long ash-blonde hair. She's wearing skinny jeans and a man's grey cashmere jumper, frosted pink lipstick. One front tooth slightly crosses the other. Her forehead is puckered from her frown.

'I'm so sorry,' I say again.

44

Murphy puts his hands on my shoulders. 'Vic – you remember Lizzie? Poor Zach Hopkins' wife? Terrible accident. Did you know?'

I glance back at Victoria, expecting, I don't know, a softening, but if anything her expression has hardened into one I can't read: curiosity or contempt. 'I did,' she says. 'I'm sorry for your loss.'

'Thank you,' I say.

'Zach and I had fallen out of touch, but I used to know him when we were younger.'

'Yes. On the Isle of the Wight, wasn't it?'

'I had friends at Benenden who spent summers there. We tended to hunt in packs. You know what boarding school's like.'

When I don't answer immediately, she turns to Murphy. 'Where are the others?'

'I'm about to get them a drink.'

'The beef,' she says, and goes back through the door into the kitchen.

Murphy shrugs. 'Bit of tension flying around this morning. Vicky's column for the *Sunday Times* has been edited to buggery.' He lets out a shout of laughter in the direction of the door. 'Bloody copy-editors,' he says more softly.

Taking my arm, he leads me into the drawing room where the Samuels are sitting on a stuffed floral sofa, their hands on their knees. There are more watercolours on the walls in here, and a lot of fringed armchairs. A complicated spiral arrangement of brass fire-tools sits by the hearth. I move to the window and stare out at a horizontal expanse of sea, stippled, gunmetal grey, framed with trees, the sky lowering above it. I feel so lonely, I want to cry.

Murphy is making a fuss of fetching a bottle of champagne and glasses, smacking open packets of peanuts. He wanders to the door and shouts. 'TOM! PATRICK! VIC! Come and get a drink!' Tom appears. He is dressed in brogues and a buttoned-up Fred Perry, the kind of ironic geeky style you see in the richer year thirteens. 'My son, down from Oxford,' Murphy says, unable to conceal his pride. 'He has brains.'

'At least someone in this house does,' Tom replies.

'Talking of which – or not as the case may be – where's Onnie?' Murphy moves to the door to shout again. 'ONNIE! PATRICK! What's the point of having a right-hand man if he's never at your right hand?'

There's a sense that the house is full of people I can't quite see. Movements I miss in the corner of my eye.

'I'm not staying,' I say quietly. 'It's so kind of you, but I've got so much to sort out . . . honestly, I've got to get going.'

Through the doorway, in the hall, I catch sight of Victoria talking to Patrick. His hands are clasped behind his back and he's bending forward, priest-like. Their heads are close together.

'At least have a drink,' Murphy says. 'We're on holiday. And someone make Onnie come down.'

'I've tried,' Victoria snaps, stalking in and throwing herself into an armchair. 'I can't do anything with her. It's your turn.'

'I'll go.' Patrick, who is wearing neatly pressed blue trousers and a pristine white shirt, disappears up the stairs. His shoes – smart leather trainers – squeak on each step.

Under her breath, Sue whispers, 'Poor Onnie. Going through a difficult patch. Just got back from a short stint at a school in Switzerland.' She winces. 'Bit of a black sheep.'

Murphy bellows, 'Your husband helped Onnie out with her art GCSE. One of the many tutors I appear to have paid for, on top of private-school fees. Not that it made much difference. Only thing she's ever breezed through is her driving test.

46

In my opinion—' he raises his arm in a gesture of surrender and looks around '—it's that namby-pamby school's fault. She'd have been much better off at a tougher school, doing more rigorous subjects.'

Tom, in the armchair closest to the fire, stretches out his legs, and puts his arms behind his head.

'Was that recent?' I ask. 'The tutoring?'

Victoria smiles tightly. 'Two years ago – summer before last, was it? She's had a number of stabs at GCSEs: the initial stint at Bedales, followed swiftly by Esher College, a sixth-form college at Bodmin, and lastly and most expensively La Retraite in Lausanne – an establishment that is not, it turns out, keen to continue the relationship. My daughter tends to leave chaos in her wake. Which is not ideal when your father might be the next leader of the Conservative Party.'

'Darling! Sssh.'

I stare at a small cigarette burn in the carpet. Two years ago. The summer before he died. He'd spent some time down here on his own then. He was optimistic, working hard. A gallery in Bristol had promised him wall space in a show, though it hadn't come off in the end. He always insisted we told each other everything, but he had said nothing to me about tutoring a teenage girl. I feel a small and ironic prickle of betrayal.

A split in the clouds allows the sun to slide into the room. A square of light flickers in the centre of the rug. Patrick is descending the stairs with a tall young girl with long dip-dyed blonde/brown hair. Her entire body is concealed in a pink and white fluffy onesie, but I think at once that it's the girl I saw hovering in the lane outside Gulls.

'What the hell are you wearing?' Victoria says. 'It's Sunday lunch.'

Onnie shoots her a look and sits down on the chair opposite me with a defiant thump that tells the room she is here under

47

duress. She begins to pick at her cuticles, carefully, with little nail-pecks, one and then another. No one introduces us.

Victoria and Murphy exchange glances.

'A onesie,' Sue says. 'The twins are obsessed with them.'

'I can think of nothing nicer,' I say, 'than spending a Sunday all cosy in a onesie. Tell me honestly – am I too old to get one?'

Onnie looks up. She considers me carefully, from my uncombed hair to my wellie boots, but doesn't answer. After a minute, she says clearly, 'I'm, like, amazed Mother let you bring a dog in here.'

Howard has been lying at my feet, but he knows the word 'dog' and he stands up and knocks at a round side table with his tail. It's covered with a chintz cloth, which I grab to secure before it slips. Tom, still sprawled at the fireplace, says, 'Onnie, you can be such a bitch when you want to be.'

Onnie flushes. It occurs to me she meant the comment as a joke, but no one here gives her the benefit of the doubt. The conversation in the room resumes noisily without her. She stops tearing at her cuticles and instead takes a single peanut on the end of her fingertips and dabs it on her tongue. After a bit, she lays the desalted peanut down on a copy of *The Economist* beside her, lining it up precisely inside the cross on the 'T'.

'Did I see you over the other side of the village this morning?' I say quietly.

She doesn't look at me but the skin on her neck mottles. She shakes her head.

'Are you sure? I was getting something from the car outside my house and I saw someone who looked just like you.'

'I might have gone for a walk down there earlier.'

'Oh, OK.' I pause. I don't want to push too hard. I know how teenagers hate being interrogated. It isn't that they are private, so much as painfully self-conscious. 'Did you get to know my husband quite well?'

She doesn't look up. 'A bit.'

Despite her height, her face is small, her features neat. Finally her eyes lift and she looks directly at me, her tongue probing the corner of her mouth. 'Do you miss him?'

I can feel the blush creeping up my neck. 'I do. Yes. Very much.' My voice catches. Trying to cover myself, I say, quickly, 'Is art what you're interested in? Is that your favourite subject?'

She is picking at her eyebrows. 'I'm not like my brother Tom, brilliant at everything. I haven't even done my A levels. I've got stuck on GCSEs. They've all given up on me.'

'I never did very well at exams,' I tell her. 'My sister was always the clever one. I ended up leaving education and getting a job, but it wasn't a bad thing.'

'I like fashion,' she says. She studies her nails – a self-consciously casual gesture that makes me feel even more sorry for her. 'A girl at La Retraite – her aunt works for Shelby Pink and she says I can do an internship. But they won't let me go because it's in London. My dad's got a flat in Kennington but it's only one bedroom.'

Leaning against the fireplace, Murphy is deep into an anecdote, or possibly a lecture.

'Could you stay with a friend?' I ask.

'They won't let me.'

'Perhaps you could live with a family,' I say. 'You could help out, do babysitting, in return for a room.'

Zach used to say I had a compulsion to solve other people's problems.

Onnie is looking straight at me. 'You live in London, don't you?'

'Yes. I could ask around. My sister, she has children. She might know someone.'

'Do you have a spare room?'

'I've got a sofa bed.'

'So maybe I could stay with you?'

'Me?' I say.

'I mean, you're all on your own now. You'd probably like the company.'

'Well, I suppose . . .' I'm so taken aback, I don't know what to say, but I am spared my confusion when Victoria chooses this moment to cut in loudly from across the room, flashing a cold smile: 'That's very kind, but Onnie needs to work out her priorities. She has a lot of thinking to do.'

Murphy has reached the end of his story and the others are all laughing. Onnie, driven back into herself, lowers her head and starts working at her nails again. I imagine myself standing up and saying thank you for the drink. I imagine it so clearly I wonder if I have actually done it, but I still seem to be sitting. Murphy, over by the fireplace, says 'Very good' to a comment Tim has made, as if marking it with a verbal pen.

'Is it awful being a widow?'

Onnie is looking at me. I am not sure if it is a statement or a question, but I say, 'Yes. It is. It's very sad. I went to the scene of his accident yesterday to leave flowers.'

'Did you?'

Her eyes are fixed intently on me, and I find it hard to look away. I feel a flush of yearning, an overpowering sense of loss, and at the same time, madly, an overpowering sense of Zach's presence. The combination of these impressions dizzies me and, in the outer edges of my vision, the walls of the room begin to bend in and I wonder if I might be about to pass out.

I stand up blindly and say, to no one in particular, 'Do you have a bathroom?'

Murphy leaps to his feet. 'We do have a bathroom,' he says. 'In fact, we have several bathrooms. And they are all at your disposal.'

Next thing, he's leading me into the hallway. 'Posh upstairs, or bog standard through there, first right.' He points to the door at the end of the hall, then brings his hands together in a single clap. 'Make yourself at home.'

Immediately beyond the hall isn't the kitchen, as I had supposed, but a scullery, full of coats and muddy shoes, cricket bats, a set of boules. An air rifle leans against one wall. It's warmer in here. I can hear frantic sizzling from the oven beyond. I tie Howard to the boot rack – how organised some people's lives are, how rich with contraptions it would never occur to me to need. Then I push open the door and sit on the loo with the seat down. I lean my head against the wall and breathe deeply. Eventually I realise I am staring at a framed cartoon of Murphy: a winking Fred Astaire tap-dancing on a table, with various members of the Cabinet in his top pocket. Above the basin is a matriculation photograph from Brasenose College, 1986. I expect if I look hard enough I'll find the prime minister.

I put my head between my legs and close my eyes. I can smell pine disinfectant and a lower tang of ammonia. I feel concussed, wrong for company, out of place in the world. I feel as if I have no perspective on anything. I have a sharp sense of panic, as if I'm supposed to be doing something important, that I've abandoned it halfway through, that I should be somewhere elsewhere.

Quiet footsteps approach the door, pause, and then move away. A door slams.

I force myself to stand up and open the door into the scullery. I lean against the wall for a moment and try to pull myself together. Howard is still sitting by the boot rack: a row of inverted wellingtons. The last pair of wellies on the rack, half hidden under a beige mac, are green Hunters. As I unhook Howard's lead, my heart gives a small lurch of recognition – absurdly. They're just boots. Not Zach's. Not here. Why would they be here?

Upside down, the soles of this pair are spotless, unlike the others in the row – the mud has been brushed off; the treads are clean and definite, the rubber size stamp unobscured by soil. Size 43.

I step forward. My hands are shaking. I move the coat. I unslot the left boot from its wooden stand, and turn it over. There, at the top, are some marks and a snaggling line of rubber glue. And on the side a splatter of paint.

I leave through the back door without saying goodbye and run down the hill, Howard bounding beside me, jumping up, tugging the lead to one side, like this is some kind of game. We follow the farm lane down to the caravan site, across the field to the road below.

The keys to Zach's studio, in the old garage next to Gulls, are under a terracotta pot at the bottom of the garden path, and I tip the pot on its side, spilling earth and knotted bulbs. My hands are shaking. I can hardly fit the key into the door.

I push the door and a bottle of methylated spirits rolls, skids into the middle of the floor. Zach, as in everything else, was meticulous as an artist. He needed silence and clarity, white spaces, no mess. His brushes would be laid out in size order, his tubes of paint lined in neat rows, the labels facing up. The floor had to be clean, nothing in his line of sight to distract. When he worked, he placed his easel in the centre of the room and turned any other paintings in the room to face the wall.

The scene inside takes a moment to process – tubes, brushes, rags, glue, newspaper. The cupboard is tipped on its side. The table where Zach laid his tools is bolted down, but his chair has been upended and the beechwood easel, the one he would rub and oil before starting, is missing. No, not missing – pulled apart, snapped into pieces like firewood. And the walls . . .

The walls are splattered with blood.

I freeze in the doorway, my hand at my mouth. There is a ringing in my ears and a rawness at the back of my throat. One canvas is propped on the table, facing me directly. I know this painting well. It's an oil of the sea – gunmetal grey, horizontal, the horizon black, clouds low – his favourite view, his screensaver. A dark shape in the foreground – an empty fishing boat, unpiloted, setting out into the unknown. It's a picture of loneliness. 'My life,' he once said, 'without you.'

But the picture has been vandalised. I hold on to the door frame to stop myself from falling. I can feel the truth burning on me. In a scrawl of charcoal, he's added a raw figure to the front of the boat, facing into the horizon: a man, with his back to us, in a hat and a heavy coat.

A knot of fear. I hear his voice in my ear: 'Don't ever leave me. If you leave me, you don't know what I'll do.'

I ring Jane from the service station. I am pacing up and down between the lorries and the Snack & Shop. I tell her I've worked it out. Zach got to the bungalow and read my letter. He knew I was leaving. He can't take rejection, Jane, from anyone. But from me? You should see his studio. It's been wrecked. And there's blood. I don't know whose. But he didn't kill himself, Jane. He didn't. He wouldn't. I know him. I know what you're going to say, but it wasn't suicide. I wouldn't . . . I can't have driven him to that. It's something far more complicated. I spoke to him on the phone and you wouldn't have known. He was in control of his emotions. He's so clever, Jane. He left a message for me in a painting. This is my punishment. That body . . . what was left of the driver of the car . . . I'm telling you, Jane, it wasn't him.

Jane asks me where I am. She says to stay there, to get warm, she'll come and get me. Her voice is calm and gentle. She thinks I've lost it.

I don't care. I just repeat it to her, over and over. 'Zach's alive. Zach's alive.'

Zach

September 2009

This evening, I followed a woman. It was a little bit sordid – no denying that – but the thrill I experienced was extraordinary.

It was possibly dangerous, but I posted a profile on an online website. I was an almost immediate hit – thirty enquiries within twenty-four hours. That black-and-white photo, taken 'unawares' with my iPhone, was a winner. Three dates so far. The first, a lawyer, was too old, even without the forehead-freezing Botox. She was wasting her time, as well as mine. I kissed her vein-wrinkled hand as we parted and said, 'Madam, if our paths cross again, then we will both be the richer,' or something similarly naff and confusing. I didn't want to hurt her feelings, but really, who did she think she was kidding, posting that picture?

Date number two was divorced, pretty, quite bright (a biology degree from York, had worked for GlaxoSmithKline), but she lied to me, too. She told me she lived alone, but I worked out pretty pronto that she had a child. She kept checking her phone and when I came back from the bar, she was whispering into it. I caught the words 'Bed. *Now*.' This sort of deception – well, it's nothing to build a new life on. Disappointing.

These first two, I could tell, couldn't work out why an attractive, normal guy like me had resorted to Internet dating. Tonight's hopeful, the best of the bunch, thought she had my number. We met in a bar at the bottom end of the King's Road in Chelsea, 'just across the river' from where she claimed to live. She was wearing a purple wrap-around dress that clung to her curves and fell low over her cleavage. Spiky blonde hair, heavy eyeliner, a gap between her front teeth. Not bad actually. Reminded me a bit of a young Vic Murphy. The other two had simpered a little bit, gazed into their wine as they rolled it around the glass. Cathy? (Not her real name, I suspect.) She crossed her legs provocatively, looked at me straight in the eye and said, her vowels flat South London: 'You don't have to pretend. Cards on table. I know what you're in this for.'

'Relocation?' I said. I was only half joking.

She gave me a funny look and shrugged. 'Sex. You're married. You're pretending to be looking for "Love? Life partner? Let's see what happens?" Or whatever lies you concocted for your profile.'

'They weren't lies,' I said, truthfully.

'But I've been in this game for a while. I've met plenty like you. If a man seems too good to be true, then generally he is.' She licked her finger and ran it around the rim of her glass. It made a small squeak. 'That shirt – no way you picked it out for yourself. It's the kind of shirt a woman chooses for a husband.'

I pretended to gulp and stutter and deny all charges. I talked about shyness, and a long-term partner who had bought me the shirt shortly before running off with my best friend. 'A guilt purchase,' I said. 'Don't make any judgements on the grounds of a guilt purchase.' Oh I am good when I need to be. I am bloody good.

I can be brown, I can be blue, I can be vi-o-let sky . . . I can be anything you like.

'Look,' she said. 'I find you attractive. If you can remember my Encounters entry, I said, "long- or short-term commitment, I'm not fussy". I won't lie to you. I'm ideally after someone to share my life with, but I'm not going to turn down the opportunity for some fun if it throws itself in my path.'

I hate it when people say 'I won't lie to you'. It means nothing. It's just one of those phrases they use to make themselves sound more important. A verbal drum roll. And quite often they do lie, or tell a half-truth, or a truth they haven't properly thought through but quite like the sound of.

'What are you saying?' I stammered.

She studied me quizzically. 'Hmm. Not sure.'

I managed to change the subject to give myself time to consider my options. She was offering to have sex with me – tonight if I wasn't mistaken. I was tempted. But she was a little too sharp for my liking; well off beam, of course, but uneasily upfront, confrontational. And anyway, she was wrong. I was in it not for the short but the long game.

I asked her what she did for a living. A psychologist, administering cognitive behavioural therapy to patients in emotional distress. I pretended to be impressed. 'A doctor!' I said, though I knew she damn well wasn't – all that time lodging with medical undergraduates at Edinburgh taught me the difference between a simple psychology degree and ten years' hard medical training, even with a bit of postgrad thrown in. All talk, no drugs. Interesting, though, that she didn't deny it.

The evening went fast enough. She was good company, simultaneously indiscreet and flirtatious. I particularly enjoyed her description of how CBT is currently helping a couple who have ceased marital relations. 'On the second day, they can touch or stroke each other anywhere, chest and arms and upper thighs, though not breasts, or vagina, or penis.' She drew out the sibilants for my delectation. I watched her mouth as she spoke, the space between her tongue and the gap between her teeth. Sex: it has often been my downfall. Almost went home with her then and there.

She made a big play of paying for the drinks, flamboyantly slapping a pile of notes on the table before I could object. If I had been wearing a tie, I expect she'd have taken hold of it and yanked me out on to the pavement. I managed to wrestle control once we were standing there, told her I needed to head off as I had an early start the next day.

'Home to wifey?' she said, a little deflated.

'No.' I tapped her warningly on the nose. She tried to catch my finger with her mouth. 'But I am a gentleman and I will walk you wherever it is you're going.'

'I've read the small print,' she said, doing up the buttons of her coat. 'No personal details on the first date.'

'What do you think's going to happen? I'm going to strangle you?'

She laughed. 'I'm a big girl.'

But I insisted. I was intrigued enough to want to know a little more. 'Can't be too careful,' I said. 'It's late. There are a lot of nutters out there.'

She relented and let me walk her to the Tube – a bit of a hike, which put me in a bad mood. Still, I stooped to kiss her at Sloane Square, once slowly on each cheek, letting my lips open, feeling her flesh. I let my hand graze her breast. If she wasn't interested before, she would be now. She tried to keep it cool, waved, a coquettish trill of her hand as she disappeared down the escalator, called, 'Ring me. Let's do this again.'

It wasn't hard to keep her in sight. You need to stay two or three people behind, that's all. She didn't even look round. She stood on the eastbound platform – Circle line – staring straight at the ad for mouthwash on the other side of the track, fiddling with a piece of hair at the back of her head. She undid her coat to retie the belt on her dress, wriggled her shoulders as if to unstick the skin from under her bra.

When the tube came, I got into the carriage behind and watched her through the window. She sat down and took a magazine out of her shoulder bag. *The Economist* – well, that was a surprise. Useful, however, because although she got out at Victoria, the next stop, she kept reading all the way up the escalator and didn't put it back in her bag until she was on the main concourse. More intellectual, or more pretentious, than I thought.

Same deal on the train, though my view through the connecting doors was less direct, heads and bodies in the way. I stayed on my feet, close to the doors, checking at each station. When she finally got out, a long twenty-five minutes later, I found myself in a depressing low-level station, miles out in the suburbs. Had it been the Midwest, tumbleweed would have been bowling along the platform, but we only had crisp packets and Aldi plastic bags. I wish I had written down its name. It's a sign of its tedious anonymity that I can't bring it to mind. Of course I could look it up, but at this stage I don't care. Boxland? Moxton Eastfield? Gone.

Two boys in their early twenties and cheap suits, breathing beer fumes, alighted with me and I walked just behind them. She left the station, a flimsy construction made of cheap bricks and pretend pillars, and crossed the road towards a row of prefab houses. At the end – the boys still ahead of me, shirt tails dangling under their jackets – she took a left into an identical street. The boys went right, laughing, one of them leaping up to try and hit a street light. She glanced over her shoulder at that, her face lit by an orange glow, and I slunk back into the shadows and waited.

She kept walking for a bit, and I stayed behind my privet hedge. I wasn't sure what to do. I'd seen enough, but curiosity, the thrill of the chase I suppose, still flickered in my limbs. She stopped halfway along, rummaged in her bag for her keys, and went into a house. I gave her time to take her coat off, clean her teeth, make a cup of tea, and then I slipped along the road on the other side to see where she lived.

Deal-breaker, I'm afraid. Even if Boxland or Moxton Eastfield had revealed untold delights – a Michelin-starred restaurant, say – I could never be happy with someone who had chosen a house like that. Ugly aluminium windows blocked by grubby net curtains, an elaborate front porch that wouldn't have looked out of place at Versailles, an area for off-street parking that seemed to have been paved in shiny square bathroom tiles. Disappointing. But probably just as well. Not worth breaking in to check the interior. Sufficient danger signs – the job, *The Economist*, the clothes. If the property and its location had been tempting, I might have slipped up. I'm going to tinker with my profile. Probably best to find someone *without* a degree, narrow the field. I yearn for sweetness, I realise, not sassiness. I don't need to be patronised. People with university degrees – medical or otherwise – think they know everything. Often they don't have a clue.

I didn't feel guilty following 'Cathy'. If you agree to meet a stranger, what do you expect? It probably would have given her a thrill if she'd known I was out there.

I would never have imagined her living in a house like that. But of course the thing with people is, you never can tell.

Chapter Five

Lizzie

'I'd take a dead body over vomit any day. I'm not being funny. Last night, I was called to an incident at the Taj Mahal – some clever clogs had bitten off his mate's ear – and I was taking down statements when this young lad leaned forward and puked over my shoes. I was almost sick myself. You know that thing? That other-people's-vomit gag reflex? My mum said I had it bad even as a child.'

PC Hannah Morrow, my Family Liaison Officer, is sitting at my kitchen table. There's a cup of tea next to her, but she hasn't had a chance to drink it yet. She hunches her shoulders and tightens her grip on her stomach to illustrate the horror of the experience.

Jane, stilettoed feet on the bars of my chair, says, 'I think I'd be better with puke than a corpse.'

'Honestly? I'd rather have neither.'

They've been here for at least an hour, talking away like this. I'm like a ghost. I'm hardly here.

It was past eight when I got back, already dark. Jane was waiting outside the house, pacing up and down to keep warm. Hannah arrived shortly after. I wanted her here because she might be an unofficial social worker (we have that in common), but as a policewoman she has resources. I figured she would help.

But now she is talking. This chatter – it's been her way from the beginning, from that night she knocked on the door. She was only twenty-five then. I can't imagine what it must have been like for her. The inanities about what she had eaten that day, what her mum had said or thought, made me want to scream at first. I thought it was stupidity. Now, a year on, a year in which she has bought her own flat and lost five pounds and bobbed her hair, I understand what she's doing. It's a coping strategy. She is letting the mood in the room settle.

Her boss, DI Perivale, gave a talk on Internet safety at school last month and I told him how brilliant I thought Morrow was, how calm and constant even when other people were falling apart. He said something sniffy about how young officers are often better at 'doing an agony' than officers with more experience. 'Doing an agony': the phrase stayed with me.

Tonight she was off duty, but she still came. 'Are you kidding?' she said. 'I was bored out of my skull. Nothing on but *Antiques Roadshow*. It was either you or a phone call to my nan.'

'Was the ear salvageable?' Jane has leaned across to rest her hand on my knee. She is wearing a 1950s prom dress and fishnet tights. I expect she's supposed to be somewhere else. She gives my knee a squeeze to show I'm not forgotten.

'The waiter wrapped it in a packet of Birds Eye peas. It never occurred to me you'd find Birds Eye peas in an Indian. Matar paneer I suppose. Anyway, off to A & E and Bob's your uncle.' Hannah unwraps her arms and takes a long gulp of her tea. She slaps the mug back on the table. 'Surprising amount of blood actually. Not as much as the head injury inflicted by a frozen turkey I was called out to witness on Christmas Eve. But more than you'd imagine. Real blood, I should add. Not red paint.'

She gives me a conspiratorial smile and my gaze reverts to my lap. I am suddenly overwhelmed by tiredness, and it's as if the compressed afternoon has suddenly expanded beyond reason, so that it could be days, rather than mere hours, since I told Jane, to her audible alarm, that I was coming straight back, placating her by promising to pull over and call her every thirty minutes; days, rather than just an hour, since I first sat shaking in this kitchen while Hannah, who had the police in Cornwall check over the studio, attempted to calm me with their verdict. Paint, not blood, on the walls. Possibly a break-in, although in the absence of anything that could be reported as stolen . . .

I look down wearily. I'm still wearing my mother's skirt. It's filthy, covered in grass stains and muddy paw marks. I try to think when I got them. Was it from laying the flowers at the tree, or from charging down the hill earlier today? I unpick a shred of bramble tangled in the jersey at my shoulder. Under it is Zach's shirt. The one with the stain. I should try again to get it out. I'm wearing wellies, too. Did I drive back in them? How did I change gears? Or brake? It's the sort of thing Hannah might pick me up on. I don't want her to get cross. Not now.

Jane says, 'I wish you had let me come and get you.'

I shake my head.

She leans over and, with a small, contrite smile, rubs the side of my face with two of her fingers. It must be red lipstick from her earlier kiss. I take a deep breath and look around the kitchen. My breakfast things from yesterday are still in the sink. Crumbs litter the worktop. I haven't been looking after any of this – this room, this house – since Zach died. The woodwork is grubby and peeling. Brown splatters next to the bin show where a teabag has hit the wall. I'll have to clear up.

'You both think I'm mad.'

'No,' Hannah says. She is watching me carefully.

'But I do think Zach's still alive.' I try to talk calmly. Howard is at my feet, idly scratching. The MacBook is on the table. 'Why would his laptop be at Gulls? And other things were missing. His Hunter boots. I found them at Sand Martin. They were in the rack.'

'Sand Martin?' Hannah says.

'I don't know how they got there. The last time we were in Cornwall together, they were at Gulls, so it means something. I'll work it out. But that's not the important thing. Other stuff too. Things had gone. Clothes, a bag, a torch, money that was kept tucked away for emergencies, a picture, I think. I can't be sure about that.'

'And you searched the house properly?' Hannah asks. Leaning back in her chair, she rests her knees on the edge of the table. 'It's a long time since you were down there.'

'The police thought the studio had been broken into,' Jane adds. 'Gulls has been empty for a year—'

'No, but wait. There were flowers already at the tree, lilies. Someone else had left them there. This SUV, a silver one; I kept seeing it everywhere.' I shake my head, try and clear it. 'Maybe that's irrelevant.'

I'm not doing this right. I have to go carefully or they'll get it wrong. They won't understand.

To give myself time, I get up, take my boot out of Howard's mouth, and open the door. The garden is thick with shadows and windy. I watch Howard disappear into the complicated gloom of the bushes. When I find my chair again, I sit up straighter than before. A muscle in my leg starts shaking. 'I wrote him a letter,' I say. 'And when I got there, it was opened. He'd read it.'

'What letter?' Jane says.

'What did you write?' Hannah asks.

64

'We'd been going through a tricky patch, you know, with me not getting pregnant, and Zach ... I had been finding Zach a bit ... possessive. I wrote things perhaps I shouldn't have. I said I wanted to separate.'

Each word creates a new catch in my throat. I cough and then I try to laugh. I rub at an old mug ring on the table, and when I am doing that, Jane puts her hand on mine and holds it. Her nail polish is pale grey, like a nun's habit.

'Have you got the letter with you?' Hannah asks lightly.

'No. I burned it.' I don't look at her. 'The one thing I was grateful for was that he hadn't read it before he died. But he had, you see. He must have reached Gulls earlier than he said. He must have been there. You see? He reached the bungalow – that's how his laptop got there – and he read the letter. He was so angry, he broke up the studio.' I turn to Jane. 'It was in pieces, Jane. And OK, not blood – but paint on the walls. Like someone had gone wild in there. But then he must have pulled himself together. He lied to me on the phone. He left me a private message on a painting.'

'On a painting?'

'A "private" message?' Hannah adds. 'You mean in code?'

'In charcoal. He'd drawn himself setting off on a new life without me. He knew I'd see it. He knew I'd understand what it meant. And then he locked up the house ... And then he ...'

There is an expression on Jane's face, like it's being tugged. Her eyes are full and her cheeks have flushed. I look across at Hannah and her lips look funny, twisted. Jane's taken her hand away from mine and is holding it across her mouth. Her eyes are full of alarm. Neither of them says anything.

'So you see,' I say again.

Hannah nods very slightly. 'He read the letter and was devastated. He drank too much to drown his sorrows. And then he set off towards London. It explains the direction of travel. He hadn't doubled back. He was driving home to confront you, a bit angry, a bit too fast. Maybe . . .'

Jane takes her hand away. 'Oh, poor Zach. He—'

'NO,' I shriek. 'I know what you are about to say. He didn't kill himself. It wasn't suicide. He wasn't in the car. It wasn't *him*.'

Jane pushes her chair back and crouches next to where I am sitting. She puts her arms around me. I've started crying properly now.

'No body,' I say. 'There wasn't a body.'

'But there was,' Jane says. 'Sweetie, there was.'

'No. No.'

Hannah stands up too. I'm aware of her moving around the kitchen. She opens the back door. She must have let Howard in, because he noses around at my feet, rests his face on my knee. His beard is wet and grainy. I hear the kettle being filled. Eventually, Hannah sits back at the table, and puts the teapot down.

'We didn't need to do a DNA test, did we? Listen, Lizzie. That's because we were sure, weren't we? His mobile phone was in the car. There was CCTV footage of him getting petrol earlier in the afternoon. You told us he was in the car that night. We only authorise a test when there is doubt. And there was no room for doubt.'

I think about her coming to the door. The questions she said she had to ask, standing there with her neat ponytail, her clean uniform. Who did the car belong to? Did I know who was driving? Was I sure? I know now she was seeking proof, confirmation. But her words died in the air. I put my hands out to stop them from coming. She held out a CCTV picture of Zach taken at a service station. 'Is this him?' I crumpled it up, tried to push her out of the door.

I blow my nose. Jane dips her head to check I am all right. She pushes her chair a bit closer to mine.

The funeral was at Putney Vale crematorium. The car crawled along the grid of roads between the graves. It poured with rain. We were late – the next lot were already there, milling in black outside the chapel. Flowers heaped. Half-empty pews. Peggy and Rob, a few artists from the studio where Zach worked. The smell of sandalwood, the swish of a polyester curtain. The coffin seemed so lightly borne. His pitiful remains were so easily shouldered. It was a willow casket, but it might have been a child in there.

'Who was in the car, Lizzie? If it wasn't Zach, who was it?' Jane is talking very quietly.

'Teeth and bones,' I say brutally. 'Not even bones. Fragments.'

'Somebody,' Hannah says, 'was in that car, Lizzie.'

'I think he faked the accident. I don't know how. It was thick fog. A fireball. He was clever, so much cleverer than me. He would work it out.'

Jane moves away from me very slightly. 'Are you saying he killed someone?'

'No. Of course not.' My mind is racing now. 'He might have lent the car to someone and when they had that terrible crash, he grasped the opportunity. He was like that. He was always taking risks. He had this thing about being different, about breaking the mould. There are precedents, aren't there? Those people who used the Twin Towers as an opportunity to start new lives?'

'So where do you think Zach is now?' Jane asks.

'He could be anywhere, living rough or . . . He spent his childhood camping. By the sea probably. He had a thing about the sea. He took things he'd need if he was going cross-country. A torch, his boots.'

'Not in the bungalow, though?' she says. 'He hadn't been living there?'

I think for a moment. Gulls had smelled stale, uninhabited. A thread of spider's web had run from the kettle to the window. 'No. I think he's closer to me than that. Hannah, Jane – it fits, doesn't it, with all those things that have happened, the sense I've had that he's watching me? It hasn't been my imagination, has it? That break-in, Hannah – when the burglar just came in through the front door as if he lived here. That could have been Zach.'

'Didn't we decide perhaps you hadn't locked the door when you went to bed? That you'd left it on the latch, or even open?' Hannah says.

'That was the only explanation I could come up with at the time – but if Zach had his key . . .'

'I don't understand,' Jane says gently. 'Lizzie. This is Zach we're talking about. How can you possibly think that your husband who adored you would put you through the agony of the past year? *Watch* you?'

'The message on the painting. He might have been telling me he was all right. It might not be a taunt, it might be a reassurance. Or both.'

'Even so. To abandon you. What sort of person would do that? Torture you like this . . . ?'

'He . . .' I can't even begin to explain. 'He was complicated . . .'

'I know.' She gets up and gives me another hug.

Hannah has been busy with the remainder of her biscuit, snapping it into pieces. She nibbles one and leaves the rest a distance away from her on the table. She says in a matter-of-fact tone, 'He wouldn't be able to get a new identity. You used to be able to quite easily – send off for the replica birth certificate of someone who was born in the same year as you and subsequently died. Undercover coppers used to do it all the time.' She swallows. 'But that loophole's closed – all the information is computerised now. It's not easy, Lizzie.' She shakes her head, wiping her mouth with the tips of her fingers.

'He used to talk about it, living off grid,' I say.

Jane gets to her feet. She pats my shoulder as she passes the back of my chair. She starts filling the dishwasher with our tea mugs and my breakfast things from yesterday. She finds a cloth and wipes the crumbs off the surfaces, has a go at the table.

Her gestures are careful. She is one of those energetic, fast-witted people who usually does everything in a hurry, but there's no urgency to any of these movements. It's as if she is slowing them down on purpose. Hannah, meanwhile, is smiling gently.

I think back to all those early sessions we had. She used to record everything in a notebook, every word, each tiny detail. She hasn't written anything today. I know that neither of them believes a word of this. They think I'm making it all up. It's my state of mind they're concerned about, not Zach's whereabouts. *My* doubt. They need to be extra careful *for me*. And for a moment I feel bereft. I sit here and let the realisation seep in. Of course they don't get it. They don't know him like I do. He isn't in their bones, or under their skin. He isn't between their lips or on the lids of their eyes. I am alone in this. I was wrong to expect their help. I'll never be able to convince them. This is between me and Zach.

A silence falls in the kitchen. When the key rattles in the front door at the end of the passage, all three of us start.

Peggy has brought two of her three children – Alfie, who is five, and Gussie, three. 'You're home!' she says, ushering them into the kitchen. 'I've been so worried about you since Jane rang. It's such a long drive.' She throws her arms around me. I exchange a quick, panicked glance with Jane. I didn't tell her to ring Peggy. I don't know how much she has told her. She shakes her head slightly.

Gussie has climbed on to my knee, and is cupping my face with damp hands. She is giving me little bird pecks on the lips. Her hair – her mother's thick curls, not my frizz – flutters against my cheek. Alfie, dressed in a Batman outfit, is playing with Howard. I love them all, but I want to lay my head on the kitchen table and close my eyes.

'Hello, Jane,' Peggy says, hugging her, too. 'And *dear* Hannah. How sweet of you to come by. Loving the bob. *Très* chic.' The slightly mannered gush shows Peggy is put out by the presence of both Jane and Hannah.

She hoists herself up on to the kitchen worktop. Her hair is bunched into two Heidi plaits. 'I'm so, so glad you're back, Liz. I hated to think of you down there, missing Zach, all by yourself. You need your *family* around you.' Another small dig.

Gussie is demanding 'horsey-horsey' and I jolt my knee up and down, clasping her tight, resting my cheek on her back. Missing Zach: how simple that sounds. She squeals with pleasure. 'More. More.'

'Gussie is quite keen for a sleepover,' Peggy says. 'With her favourite auntie.'

'*Only* auntie,' I add.

'Not tonight,' Jane says.

'Maybe . . .' I say.

'No,' Jane says firmly. 'Lizzie has had a tiring day.'

'My bad,' Peggy says, smiling sweetly. 'Another time, poppet.'

Alfie, who has been upstairs, comes back into the kitchen clutching Zach's clear plastic box of Rotring pens. He pulls

70

off the lid, holds the box upside down and scatters them on the table.

Peggy says, 'Oh, well done. Felt tips. Ask Auntie Lizzie if she has any paper.'

'Where did you find those?' I say. Each pen has a different-sized nib. Zach took such special care not to blunt them. He was obsessive about them. The box has a compartment for each pen. 'They're not really for playing with.'

'Lizzie,' Peggy says. 'He's only a child.'

'Can I have them?' Alfie asks, flicking off the lids.

'Maybe . . . when you're older,' I say, not looking at Peggy. I think I hear her tut and maybe she's right to.

'Right, I must go.' Hannah gets to her feet. 'I still haven't rung my nan. It's her birthday in a week or two and we're organising a bash.'

I tip Gussie off my lap and follow Hannah out of the house. It's a relief to be in the street. I can feel the cold air on my neck, penetrating my jersey, flicking against my bare legs. Hannah has parked her moped in the car park at the bottom of my road by the pub. It's a cul-de-sac, at the junction by the main road, where the traffic is a constant roar. The street lamp trembles in the vibration. Hannah, unlocking her helmet from the pannier, has her back to me and my eyes scan the scrubby stretch of common ahead – grass and trees and brambles. Beyond it Wandsworth Prison looms. One thousand six hundred inmates – all those crimes, bad instincts, mistakes – living next door. It's the building, though, that seems evil. It's at its most malignant now, lit up, shadowy and weird, full of dark hollows, like a torch held up to a face on Halloween.

Hannah fiddles and grimaces, attaching the clasp of her motorbike helmet under her chin. Then she looks me in the eye and says, 'You eating? You look like you've lost weight.'

I tell her I am eating, although actually I can't quite remember when I last did.

'All right then. So that letter you wrote?'

'We had our ups and downs, like most people.'

She's still looking at me. I think about divulging some of his idiosyncrasies – how he didn't like me reading, would flick for attention at the outside of my newspaper, or hide my book so I couldn't find it, how such simple gestures – the closing of the dishwasher – were sometimes thick with anger. How careful I would have to be about what I wore, or how I acted, how I began to dread certain situations, like parties, where I would get it wrong, where he would find my behaviour insensitive. 'Trivial things,' I say. 'Nothing important.'

'This notion you have—'

I cut her off, make a gesture with my hands to indicate my own foolishness. 'I know. Madness.'

'Good.' She gives me a meaningful look. 'Stay strong.'

She waves as she pulls out. I watch her drive, with that comically upright posture of a person on a scooter, to the end of the road, indicate right to pass the prison and disappear. If she's not going to help me, I'll do it alone.

I stand for a minute, sensing Zach in the darkness of the trees beyond the railings, watching me from the shadows, from the clump of undergrowth behind the sycamore. I feel a quiver in the air, like electricity, or the brandishing of a sheet of paper-thin metal. I strain my ears above the whistle of an accelerating car for the sound of his breath. I close my eyes and open my arms. 'Come to me,' I whisper. 'If you're coming. Go on. Do it.'

After a few moments, I turn and go back into the house.

Zach

Initially I assumed Carefree201, date number four, was a saucy little puss. She gave me her phone number the first time I asked. None of the others had obliged. The moment I heard her voice I realised it wasn't self-assertion but naivety. She was diffident, bit of a stammer actually. Lower middle class made good. A librarian of all things. I asked her where she lived and she said Wandsworth, near the prison. Flat share or . . .? A pause. 'On my own,' she said. I got the area up on screen while we were talking. A little further west from where I witnessed that public demonstration from the amatory couple, but in the same general area.

I suggested that, rather than the conventional drink, we meet for a nice long walk. A silence while she processed the idea, and then a note of coy delight. 'That's so much better,' she said. 'How clever of you to have thought of that.'

It was. I had heard a dog bark a few minutes before, her voice more distant, as if it had been wedged under her chin, the sound of a door opening.

First appearances, not propitious. Funny colourless little thing, bird-like, wearing baggy jeans and a fleece, tugging on a huge animal she could hardly control. She may have described herself as 'a world traveller'; she didn't look as if she had ever been further

73

than Orpington. She blushed to her roots when she saw me. I'd dressed carefully – no Paul Smith this time, some random items that I'd picked up in Age Concern and thought might appeal to a bookish person. Slightly overwarm. Annoying, too, to have to carry that bag of art materials – bloody heavy for a 'nice long walk'.

As we set off for Wandsworth Common, I worked hard to put her at her ease. I kept looking at her out of the corner of my eye, and then realised she was doing the same to me. I was oddly touched. When I was able to look at her more closely, I saw she had quite a sweet face, nice little figure too, all the more appealing for the fact she seemed totally unaware of it. She was biting her nails and in the end I took her hand to stop her doing it.

She asked about my life and I kept it vague. I told her, staring ahead to indicate how difficult the subject was, that my father had been a violent alcoholic, that I'd moved around a lot as an adult, worked abroad, found it hard to settle. 'I'm sorry,' she said. Her own childhood had been easy, she told me, golden, though she later mentioned that her father had died of a heart attack when she was five. Cup half full then: interesting.

Finally, after we had trudged up and down and around the railway line, past a pond and a kids' playground, I asked whether we could go back to her house for a drink. I could see she was torn – Encounters gives you a good old talking-to about things like that. I let her fret as I steered her in the direction of the prison. I had seen its grey turreted roof, its huge barricaded doorway, a mouth with teeth, across the cricket pitch earlier. She looked at her watch a couple of times. We left the common, had walked the length of a street lined with Victorian mansions and were standing on the pavement of a noisy road that widened just to the right of us into a dual carriageway. 'It's over there,' she said, pointing to a small road opposite, 'but I'd rather we went to the pub if you don't mind. They do coffee.' She gestured to an establishment across the road.

74

I said I did mind, trying to be flirtatious, but no dice. Also, excuse me: *coffee*? Is that what she thought I meant by a drink? Christ. Some of us have self-medication to attend to. She wasn't to be budged. She went pink to her ears and said we could go next time, 'if there is a next time'.

It didn't matter. I'd had a chance to scout the location. She lives in a pretty row of flat-fronted Victorian cottages, probably built to house prison officers or market gardeners. Attractive brickwork, nicely planted, heritage lamps. A cul-de-sac, too, blocked off this end, so, although the noise from the main road might be invasive, at least there's no through traffic. Expensive area, hard to break into. A *seller's* market, as we know.

Saying goodbye, I leaned forward and kissed her. I rested my hand on the small of her back and she released a small moan from deep in her throat. I got the impression she hadn't been touched in a long time. I thought she might die of pleasure.

As we parted, I realised I was smiling. She had tasted of sugar mice, the ones they used to sell in the village shop, pink and sweet. Addictive. I had bitten her lip gently as I pulled away, felt the soft tug of it between my teeth. Delicious.

I can't stop thinking about it, that kiss.

Chapter Six

Lizzie

It's raining when I wake up in the morning, drops rattling against the window, the howl of wind in the joints. I was aware in the night of Howard padding into the bedroom, but he's not here now. The clock reads 10.30 a.m. In the early days, I could hardly sleep at all. Even as I longed for obliteration, for anaesthesia, my brain churned and sifted. My guilt-soaked grief became indecipherable from exhaustion. Now I often sleep the sleep of the dead.

The house feels strained, suspended, as if holding its breath to listen. I put on Zach's dressing gown, which no longer smells of him, and walk from room to room. When my mother was living here, the house was full of plants and knick-knacks. All the walls were papered in different colours – apple green and citrus yellow, flowers and vines. Zach stripped it all out, painted it this cool grey, Borrowed Light, monastically simple. I used to love the starkness of it. But now I'm not so sure. I almost miss how it was before. I wander down into the sitting room and perch on the sofa. I've moved it back to the bay window, which Zach wouldn't like. I bought a rug, too, the other day. Red and blue stripes. Another mistake. It looks ugly, garish; the room has rejected it.

The rug has a tread mark, I notice – the pattern of a large trainer. Jane was wearing stilettos and Peggy was wearing boots. I can't remember what Hannah was wearing but her feet are smaller than this.

I stare at it for a little bit. Then I kneel down and rub my fingers across it. The nap of the carpet moves, becomes lighter when I do that. When I sit back up, the pattern has gone.

In the kitchen, a chilly blast whips across my legs. The back door is open. The catch is faulty and it must have blown free in the wind. I stand and call for Howard with that familiar rush of panic. The relief when he barrels back in, shaking the rain from his coat, is heavy and unsatisfying. I put some food in his bowl and he eats it hungrily. I am more alert to his appetite since he was so ill last year.

I go back up into the bedroom and open my cupboard door. I put Zach's laptop in here last night and it stares up at me. The wardrobe is jam-packed and untidy. I haven't thrown away any of Zach's things and they are muddled up with mine. The clothes he gave me are in there somewhere – the expensively distressed jeans, the delicate tops. I was always snagging the fabric, or washing them too hot. It was a stressful business, pleasing Zach. Since he left, I have stopped caring. I have worn garments like a shroud. Tracksuit bottoms, a baggy T-shirt, a hoody, and underneath, an old grey bra and pants. The undergarments he picked out – transparent slithers of lace and silk and satin – lie curled at the base of the drawer.

Was it about control, his desire to take me in hand? It didn't feel that simple. It made me feel desired. He would study my face with an expert's eye, sometimes touching my cheeks, or my mouth, with his thumbs, an artist working out their proportions. He took me into a department store on one of our first dates and steered me to a stool at the counter. 'Do with her what you will,' he said, but his eyes followed every flick and dab of the assistant's fingers. We kissed afterwards, in the shop doorway, his tongue dabbing at my slick lips, licking the colour away.

I don't wear make-up any more. My face stays naked. It's a penance. The last time I saw my mascara, dried up like a chimney brush, it was on my desk in a pot of pens. That red lipstick he bought me then, the one he said made my teeth look like pearls, the one he liked to taste . . . I don't know where that is.

I loosen a red G-string from the pile of underwear and slide into it. I put on a clingy black dress, with tights. In the bathroom cabinet, I find the remnants of an old grey eyeshadow and I smudge it over my lids. Then I pinch my cheeks and bite my lips to bring some colour into them. If he is watching, I hope he'll take it as a signal. A white flag.

We leave the house, the dog and I, for a wet, blustery walk, head down into the wind, my vision limited by the hood of my anorak to a few feet of path. The area has changed a lot over the last ten years. The students and actors have moved out and the bankers have moved in. We don't know our neighbours: they change too often. My mother, who, before she was ill, liked to lend out sugar and water other people's plants, who noticed when milk bottles stayed out on the porch, hated that.

I cross the main road to the large stretch of Wandsworth Common on the other side – to where expanses of grass are interspersed with trees and paths. It's less busy than usual, only a few hardy walkers and fitness fiends. It's stopped raining, but the tennis courts are slick and empty under the writhing limbs of the sycamores. No one outside the café, though on the cricket pitch an exercise class battles on. I turn right when I hit the main track. I used to take in the wilder sweep beyond the bowling green, but I've avoided that area ever since a woman was murdered there last year. Instead, I take the 'trim trail', sticking to the path to avoid the muddy grass. I cross at the lights and walk up Bellevue Road to the Sainsbury's Local, where I tie Howard to the railings and go in to buy milk and a newspaper.

Inside, it's cold and smells of tomato sauce combined with the vanilla whiff of hot supermarket bread. A teenage boy from Wandle Academy, whose name I wish I could remember, is in the bakery aisle trying to pick up a croissant with the awkward tied-up tongs. I smile at him but he goes red, so then I wish I hadn't. Only one self-checkout is working and a queue has built. By the time I come out, a delivery van has pulled into the loading bay. Two large metal trolleys loaded with cartons of Walkers crisps are blocking my view of Howard. I can't see him at all. My heart stops for a minute. When I run down the ramp and have passed the final trolley, there he is, sitting quietly, watching the traffic, where I left him.

I read the paper as we walk back along the path. Minutes from a secret governmental meeting have been leaked. Alan Murphy has outraged the Opposition by his pursuit of 'back-door privatisation'. The article is illustrated with a photo of the MP outside a new, corporately funded library in Manchester, wearing a bright yellow hard hat, thumbs up.

As soon as I put the key in the lock and push, I get an odd feeling, like a through draught. I hear a sound, like the ruffle of a curtain, and there's a smell a bit like dirty washing, a bit like a neighbour's cooking seeping through the walls. I put the shopping down at my feet and rest the newspaper on top of it. The edges of the pages rustle slightly. The corners are moving by themselves. I stand still and listen.

Noises from the street seem unusually loud. A motorbike throttling into life sends vibrations up my legs.

The sitting-room door is closed. I don't remember closing it.

I push open the door, and stare in. I hear myself gasp.

The window is broken and a horrible object is lying on the sofa. It's a bird, head on one side, the poor wing flared out at an angle. It is dark grey, with a petrol gleam to its splayed feathers, eyes glazed, beak half open. Its feet are pink and horribly curled.

Surrounding the body lie thick splinters of glass. The edges of the broken pane behind are jagged, like teeth.

I don't want to go too close, but I edge into the room and sit down on the edge of the armchair. The sofa and floor glimmer with tiny shards. I can hear the hum from the fridge and the roar of the traffic. An unsettled loneliness comes over me. Pity merges with self-pity. Poor bird, I think again. Did it see the reflection of the trees behind and fly into the window? It would have had to be flying with force. I lean forward to peer more closely.

A pigeon.

My little London pigeon, he used to call me.

I stand up quickly. I've been so stupid. I've been looking for the wrong things, thinking about this in the wrong way. Zach isn't going to leap out at me from the shadows. After all this time, he wouldn't just appear. It would be too obvious. That's not what he is like. The back door – wide open this morning. The tread mark in the rug. The broken window. The pigeon. He would toy with me. That's what he would do.

I walk slowly into the kitchen.

My eyes are drawn to the kitchen table. The box of Rotring pens that was there this morning is gone. And in its place is a gold blunt object shaped like a bullet. My missing red lipstick.

I pick it up, and feel the weight of it in the palm of my hand. The metal is warm. I unscrew the lid and wipe it across my mouth, dab it on my bottom lip, smear the corners. I can taste it on my tongue, feel its stickiness on the back of my hand.

In the sitting room, I stare at my face in the mirror over the fireplace. My mouth is a gash. My eyes glitter. A flicker of anger, and fear – a fever, a hot thrill.

Zach can read me. He knows what I'm thinking. He's one step ahead.

Zach

December 2009

Things I now know about Miss Lizzie Carter:

1) She is better with children than adults.
2) She is trustworthy and sees the best in people.
3) She has never watched a reality TV show.
4) She likes to have a book 'on the go'.
5) She wears M & S bras and pants. White. (Or I think they are supposed to be white.) Her bra is 34C, which isn't the right size.
6) Her house is shit inside.
7) She lives with her fucking mother.

Three lunches, twenty-two phone conversations, one movie, one visit to the house. To get close to her, I have had to be surprisingly resourceful. I've found myself putting in more effort than I am used to. A better man would have given up long ago, but I find myself drawn. The fact is I've found it hard to get her out of my mind.

Our lunch dates didn't flourish. I met her at Marco's, close to her school. I was going out of my way for her. Conversation didn't flow. Every time the door to the restaurant opened, she flinched. 'Are Wandle Academy parents *really* going to be lunching at

Marco's?' I asked (35 per cent of students are on free school dinners). But it turned out it wasn't being seen by teachers or parents that she was worried about. It was leaving the kids. Some bleeding-heart nonsense about lunchtime being when the more vulnerable make their way to the library. *Really*? Aren't they too busy having their heads flushed down the loo? Didn't say that of course. I touched her hand and gazed into her grey eyes and told her she was a saint. Weirdly, while I was forming the words, I meant them. Her love could save me. I felt a stirring inside that was almost sexual.

Our phone calls were more successful. I walked down to the front while Charlotte was cooking my supper and sat on a bench. I watched the sea, all the way to the end of the horizon. Maybe because she couldn't see me, Lizzie opened up – about the kids at school, the other teachers, her sister, the funny things her tiny nephew has done, her dog, what she's reading, what she wants the children to read. She asked me quite a few questions along the way. What do I think of this? Have I ever that? It's peculiar. I'm not used to it. Most of the women I meet tend to talk about themselves. I have to be careful because it lowers my guard.

Charlotte was at a hen do in a spa hotel outside Winchester yesterday so I had the whole day. I had arranged to take Lizzie to the cinema. Jim had 'lent' me his bike – well, left it unlocked out the back of the studio – and I had brought it up on the train to Clapham Junction, cycled straight to the Picturehouse from there. Lizzie laughed when she saw me, said she hadn't imagined me on a bicycle. I had to wear a helmet, she said. 'Unless you're planning on killing yourself.'

I shrugged – don't mind if I do, don't mind if I don't.

'I'll have to buy you one,' she said, and blushed.

I was gunning for *2012* (a nice bit of global annihilation for a Saturday afternoon), but she wanted to see some quirky French job, set in the Paris suburbs, in which a truculent *jeune fille* 'comes of age' (i.e. has a lot of sex with older men). Some of her year thir-teens had told her it was good. I gave in – which is out of charac-ter for me. Afterwards, I treated her to a late lunch at a French restaurant, having spent most of the movie planning how to persuade her against the 'delicious cheap Moroccan' she had mentioned. (I can't eat tagine. I just can't.) We talked about the film, and about the pressures of growing up. She told me how clos-eted she was as a young girl, how her sister, her mother's favour-ite, had been wilder and had broken free. 'I think,' she said, 'after our father died, Mother assumed one of us would take on his role, and although I wasn't her first choice, that person became me.'

'No major love interest?' I said.

'There was one man . . .' she said. 'In my twenties. An electri-cian, but he turned out not to be a strong proponent of monog-amy. Old-fashioned of me to care, but . . .'

I felt a tug of sympathy. The restaurant was cramped and cosy, the darkness of a damp afternoon closing in outside. The wine warmed my veins and I told her how my childhood sweetheart, Polly, had cheated on me with my best friend. I must have got carried away, because in the course of unravelling that terrible story (though I edited out its ending), I let slip where I grew up. It might not have mattered. People can't generally locate the Isle of Wight, let alone my specific village. But her eyes widened. Did I know her great friend Fred Laws? I almost choked on my *escalope de volaille*. That lisping, stuck-up twerp. The last time I saw him must have been – what? 1987 – on the top of Tennyson Down. Mad Paul and I persuaded him to come for a drive one night. He couldn't believe his popularity. We raced him up to the monument at the top of the cliff and then we left him up there on his own, in the dark, twenty miles from home, for a laugh. God, but if she were to ring him to check up on me, I'd be done for.

I put it out of my mind – steps could be taken, I was sure. I was more concerned with getting back to her house. It had been my plan all along. I had held her hand in the film (when our wrists brushed her upper thigh, I heard her slightly gasp), cajoled her into sharing a carafe of Merlot over lunch. Outside the restaurant, I hugged her, registered the dotted stain of tannin on the inner rim of her lower lip, plum against the rose, felt the narrowness of her ribcage. She pressed against me, breathing in sharply – but then no, she drew away, said she had to go, had 'things to do'.

The frustration was extreme, but I couldn't push. It's a fine line. She was getting the bus home, so I had plenty of time. The route was downhill most of the way, the wind spitting in my face, funnelling across my hatless head. I got there before her, hid the bike behind the bins down the side of the County Arms, leaped over the railings, and crouched in a copse of trees on the small patch of common right by where she lived. I could at least find out her house number. It would be a small bonus.

It gets dark early these days. No one had pulled their curtains. People are weird, the way they don't care who's looking in. A young couple watching TV in number 32, pictures flashing across their faces, a baby on the floor, wriggling upside down like a beetle; in number 28, an elderly man playing patience, an overhead lampshade throwing shadows on the walls like the arms of a giant spider. At a top window of a house further down, a girl in a white towel, arms opened wide to close the curtains, in the shape of a crucifix. I studied these images hard. You never know when they might come in useful.

It was chilly crouching there, ears full of noise from the main road. As each car passed, the orange glow of its headlamps raked the underside of the branch nearest to me; what I had thought was moss was a fur of pollution. The ground was too wet, too dirty, to sit down and the muscles in my thighs twitched. None of it bothered me. I was fired by the plan, by the excitement of what might happen, but also by the execution itself. Like that time, most recently, I followed the psychologist home, it was as if my whole being had been subject to an electrical charge. I throbbed with it. What am I trying to say? I just felt alive.

When she turned the corner, she was chewing a nail, her teeth pulling at the cuticle, her brow gently furrowed. Even though I'd been waiting, her actual appearance came as an agreeable surprise. My heart actually stopped for a second. But then the pleasure soured. Here she was, walking down her own street, having made the decision to do it *without me*. She looked contemplative, too. What was going through her mind? I hate not knowing. If I could have drilled into her head and rummaged in her brains with my hands I would have done so.

She walked a little way down the street and turned into number 30. Neatly trimmed evergreens in the front garden, tatty paint-work, an enormous rubber plant taking up the entire front bay window. She let herself in. The hall light went on – one of those cheap paper balloons – and then she closed the front door behind her.

I stood up. My thighs were about to give out. I hadn't quite decided what to do – whether to head off back to Brighton or kill an hour or two in a local bar – when the door opened and she re-emerged, this time with the dog tugging at her from the end of a lead. She set off back towards the pub, her chin up now, spare hand thrust in pocket, her expression more cheerful than before. I waited until I heard the beep of the pedestrian crossing and watched her heading down the road that leads to the main part of the common.

Perhaps if she hadn't looked so optimistic, so *unbereft* of my company, I might have gone on my way, as planned. But I felt a need, I don't know, to wrest something back, to possess her in a way I couldn't put my finger on.

The front door was firm. The window solid, too, jammed with paint. Quick look under the mat. You never know. Some people have shit for brains. Nothing. A jog round the block, though, and interesting possibilities began to open out. Lizzie's row of houses backed on to a small 1980s estate — all gables, exposed brickwork and twee arches — and I found a high wall that provided indirect access to the fence along the bottom of Lizzie's garden. With the help of some bins, a little ingenuity and a considerable amount of upper-body strength, it wasn't long before I was standing in a worn hollow behind some shrubs at the bottom of her garden.

A narrow strip of grass, edged with beds, led to the house about sixty feet away. What I believe estate agents describe as a 'mature' plot. Not a bad size for London. South-facing, too. The kitchen light glowed on to a small garden table, two chairs and a raggedy collection of pots — tomatoes or herbs or what the fuck ever.

Rustling behind my head. A black-and-white cat hovering at the top of the fence, staring. It opened its mouth, pink tongue, sharp teeth. A miaow so quiet it was like a silent scream. I gestured with my arm and it scarpered, claws scraping, a thud. Adrenalin pumped as I ran across the lawn. I didn't have long.

Back door shut. Damn. A flickering of pique. I'd been so sure. How dare she?

I scanned the rear of the house. A first-floor window was open a few inches at the top. By standing on the garden table, I could reach the sill with my hands and swing my legs up to a small ridge above the kitchen door. With that as leverage I could free a hand to push up at the window and it gave.

I wriggled through on my stomach, collapsing on to the floor head first and tearing my shirt, thankfully not a Paul Smith. I used the facilities, then washed my hands — a nasty rust stain running from the tap to the plughole. Decided against drying them. None of the towels slung across the radiator was sufficiently clean. A weird contraption rested over the blue plastic bath, the sort of thing you might use for sit-ups, and a non-slip mat lay along the bottom. On the floor sat a large brown box, too big for the cupboard, containing what looked like packets of cotton wool. The smell, too, wasn't nice: sweet and cloying, the tang of acid. No lock on the door.

Two rooms opened out at the top of a small flight of stairs. The walls were covered in pink-and-yellow wallpaper depicting garlands of miniature flowers, and on the floor was an old-fashioned green carpet, like moss. Doubts began to grow. She had said she lived alone, hadn't she? The first room I went into was obviously Lizzie's – the trousers she had worn to the cinema had been thrown, inside out, onto the floor. Her best trousers. Too good for a dog walk. She must have put them on specially for me. I felt a stir of tenderness at the sight. The room itself was small and messy with clothes hanging untidily on an open metal rail. Worn shoes in tragic heaps. A Victorian fireplace housed a trailing spider plant, and books were piled on either side. A small desk with a diary and an address book neatly piled. I found details for Fred Laws, tore out the page and stuffed it in my pocket.

By her bed, bookmarked with a kid's drawing, *The White Tiger* by Aravind Adiga. In one alcove, a cheap white plywood chest of drawers splattered with photographs in mismatched frames. Several of the same infant – in a paddling pool, on a swing, in a highchair – her beloved nephew, I assumed. One photo of Lizzie as a teenager with another girl – her sister, by the physical resemblance. They had their rangy arms around each other, close enough for their cheeks to touch. Such ease, such love. It fascinated me. I couldn't draw my eyes away. I almost slipped it out of its frame and stole it.

I switched the socket off at the wall. A small trespass, but I couldn't restrain myself.

Her underwear was in the top drawer. Plain knickers probably bought in multipacks and a spare bra – only one – that seemed far too large for her slight frame. This was underwear that had never seen active combat. Home Guard undies.

I was easing the drawer closed when I sensed a shift in the air. I froze – a click, the shuffle of footsteps. Downstairs. The noises were indefinite, indecisive. I hadn't heard the door. Was Lizzie back? Or had she just let the dog in, while she did something outside? I thought about that cat on the fence, though these noises had too much weight behind them for that.

The bedroom window was stuck fast; the drop, looking down, alarming. I moved back to the doorway and stood, listening, my eye on the bathroom door, calculating how many paces I needed to reach it, whether I could jump the short flight of stairs in one, get through the window and back across the garden without being seen.

A creak and then another. The person, or whatever it was, was just below. If I took a step forward and looked over the bannister, I would be able to see who or what it was.

I was aware that my teeth were gritted. I was breathing more slowly. Quiet anger. A psychiatrist, or even that CBT psychologist the other night, would have a field day. I felt a current through my veins, as if this were my house, and this interruption was trespassing on my time. Before I knew it, I had walked out on to the landing and I was taking those three, four steps down to the bathroom in large strides.

I turned when I reached the door. A figure was in the hall, looking up at me. A blank expression in her eyes, her mouth half open. Old. Stark naked.

She said, 'Where's Elizabeth?'

'She's out,' I said conversationally. So much flesh.

'Is it time for my tea now?'

I thought for a moment and said, 'I expect Elizabeth will make it for you when she gets back.'

'What am I going to have? I want something hot.'

'Well, hot is what you shall have.'

'I might go down for the OAP menu at the Fox and Hounds. I can get a bus.'

'What? You're going to go out dressed like that?' I said. 'As my mother used to say.'

'She was a decent woman, your mother. Don't you go giving her lip.'

I stared down at her and she stared up at me. I swallowed a laugh and said, 'Well, cheerio,' and opened the door to the bathroom. I closed it behind me and leaned against it. It all fell into place. The box of cotton wool: incontinence pads. The contraption over the bath: a disability aid. The smell: urine, old age, decaying skin. I clambered out on to the sill, easing the window closed behind me. I didn't bother with the table – leaped out into the middle of the lawn. I took my time walking to the end of the garden, ambling as if the whole place belonged to me.

The poignancy of Lizzie's abandoned best trousers keeps coming into my head. I found Fred Laws' details scrunched into a ball in my pocket earlier today and felt a sense of loss.

Her number has just come up on my phone. She's never rung me before. She's always waited timidly for me. I wondered for a minute if she'd found me out. But I don't see how – there's no way of connecting me to the intruder. Not unless I return to the house and meet the mother legitimately, which I can't do now. I've blown it.

I forced myself to switch my phone to silent.

I should let it lie, chalk it up to experience. What's the matter with me? My mind keeps turning. I keep remembering the look on her face when she talked about the damaged children at school, how hard she tries to save them.

I must be getting soft in my old age.

She rang again today, and I couldn't stop myself. I answered.

She came straight out with it. 'Have I done something to offend you?'

I was taken aback, spluttered about having been busy. I felt like closing my eyes and lying down, letting her voice slip into my ears, over my body, giving myself up to it.

'It's just that until last weekend you were ringing every evening. We seemed to be getting on so well. But since the day we went to the cinema, you haven't rung at all. And then . . . my friend Jane said she saw your profile was back up on Encounters and . . .' She paused and then the rest came out in a rush. 'I've been thinking about it and wondered if you were cross about what happened.'

'What did happen?'

'Me not inviting you to mine.'

She didn't do that thing women do when they are upset, which is pretend to be upset about something completely different, so your subsequent row is surreal and pointless. Disarmed, I said, 'Yes, maybe I was. Hurt perhaps. I'd been longing to, I don't know, get to know you better.'

'Longing?' There was laughter in her voice, and something sexy too.

'Longing,' I repeated. I couldn't stop myself from smiling. 'I got the impression you didn't want to take it any further and, being the gentleman I am, I thought I'd give you an out.'

A short silence and then she cried: 'I do want to take it further. I don't want an out. I want an in . . . I just . . .'

I tried to detach myself. 'What?'

'I've kept something from you.'

And then an outpouring: how she lived with her mother, who had advanced dementia, and how she hadn't told me because she thought it would put me off, and that was why she was often distracted and didn't invite me back. Her mother had been confused and incontinent for a while now, but she had also started hallucinating. She claimed there were men wandering around the house. She had abused the neighbours, shouted obscenities at them over the fence, accused the carer of destroying garden pots and spat in her face. The other day, the police had found her up at the bus stop on Trinity Road with no clothes on, fixated on the OAP menu at the Fox and Hounds. Lizzie wasn't sure if she could carry on.

'Meeting you . . .' she said. 'It's just . . .'

'What?' I said again.

A silence and then, 'I was always the stupid one, and the not very attractive one. I never . . . I never imagined something like this might happen to me.'

'Like what?'

'A life of my own,' she cried. 'You're everything that . . . and that you're interested in me . . . I mean, bloody hell.' She laughed again; this time I wondered if it might not be through tears.

'What?' I repeated.

'What I'm trying to say is that the thought of "taking it further" makes me weak at the knees.'

I listened to the silence that followed. For a long time, I listened.

And then I managed to control myself. 'Poor Lizzie.'

I could hear her breathing hard.

'I'm not surprised you aren't coping.'

A small gulp her end.

I felt an enormous welling of relief. A new life could be opening, a rescue, for both of us: an end to her humdrum existence and for me, perhaps, a safe haven, a chance to start again. I was so stirred I could hardly speak. I managed to croak out the necessary. 'Have you . . .' I moved from tender to tentative. 'Have you thought about a home?'

Chapter Seven

Lizzie

I wrap the dead bird in newspaper and sweep up the broken glass. In the *Yellow Pages* I find a glazier, who is at the house within the hour. The broken pane was the original Victorian, he says, as he replaces it; rolled plate, you could tell from the imperfections. It was thin and unreinforced, would have smashed easily.

As soon as he leaves, I sit at the kitchen table and think hard. What does Zach expect me to do now? I need to second-guess him. He had this thing about how 'nice' I was to other people, how passive. Does he assume I will sit back and wait? Maybe he expects me to fall apart, maybe he *wants* me to. Is he waiting for me to prove my love for him that way? Surely I have done enough for him over this past year. He must have seen me, out in the street, eyes red-rimmed, hair unwashed. He could have put his ear to the walls of the house and heard me wailing late at night. No, this is something different. This feels more like one of his tests.

In the early stages of our marriage, he would ring me at work with small entreaties – a tube of particular oil paint he wanted, could I go to the art-supply shop and buy it for him? Or there was a cheque on the kitchen table that urgently needed to be banked. He'd do it himself but he was down at the studio and for once he was inspired, he didn't want to lose his flow. Usually, these requests would come in the morning so I would sort them out in my lunch hour. But then, early one afternoon, he rang in a state. He was locked out. He'd lost his key. A painting had gone wrong. He was a useless human being. He didn't know what to do, where to go.

A group of students was waiting outside my door. My extra literacy class was due to start. It was pouring with rain. I told him to meet me halfway, on the bridge. I ran all the way, unnerved by the desperation in his tone, and when he wasn't there, I ran all the way home. He had filled the house with flowers. He'd made a cake. The table was laden with treats – biscuits, chocolate. 'Surprise!' he said. He pulled me on to his lap and kissed the rain off my face. A long time before, I had told him about visiting a school friend when I was little and how her mother had prepared the kind of tea we never had at home, and how it had been a glimpse of a different kind of family life. He'd remembered. He always remembered things like that. I was touched. I left my students at the library door.

What does he want from me now?

His laptop. He must have known it was at Gulls. Why didn't he go back and fetch it? Is there something on it he wants me to see? Is there something on it I *shouldn't* see?

I fetch the MacBook from the bedroom cupboard and plug it in at the kitchen table. Again, the screen lights up; again Zach's name appears across the cliff scene and the cursor blinks expectantly on the password window. My finger hovers above the keys. Guilt creeps down my arms and stops me. I close the keyboard. If I came up behind him when he was writing, he would push his chair back into my knees and snap his laptop shut. He accused me of spying on him, which wasn't true. I trusted him. I always assumed he was writing down ideas for his painting. I understood. He was sensitive to criticism; he was like a child who covers his work with his arm.

I stare at it. He *must* have intended me to find it. I need to prove to him that I am looking for him. On here there could be answers, solutions. I could find out where he is, forgive and be forgiven, bring him home.

I open it again. The box for the password flickers. What would Zach use? Something impossibly obscure? Or something achingly obvious – a double bluff?

I move a trembling forefinger to the keyboard and, one by one, peck at the letters of his name.

Z A C H

Then I press 'Enter'.

The screen darkens and then illuminates. *INCORRECT PASSWORD*.

I peck again, a little more boldly this time – both his names. *ZACH HOPKINS*.

Again the screen flashes and the message comes: *INCORRECT PASSWORD*.

I try his birthdate, and then a combination of his birthdate and his name. I try the name of the village where he grew up, then *Cornwall, Stepper Point, Gulls*. Nothing. With a flicker of emotion, I try *Xenia*.

INCORRECT PASSWORD.

Frustrated, I take my own laptop out of my bag.

I Google 'Xenia'. The screen fills with a series of websites.

'*Welcome to Xenia, Ohio: the home of hospitality*.' Also Xenia: an online fashion company in Australia, currently selling an 'Ullawatu Playsuit' for A$58. Also Xenia: an American singer who came second in the first season of *The Voice*.

Google Images throws up a page of blonde women in a state of undress, which I close quickly.

After that, for inspiration, I Google 'pseudocide'. I find the word deep in an article about John Darwin, the 'canoe conman' who, after faking his own death, lived in a mocked-up bedsit in the family home, spending his own life insurance. The site lists 'how-to' books on the subject, including *Get Lost! How to*

Disappear Completely and Never Be Found. Notable faked deaths include John Stonehouse, 'Lord' Timothy Dexter, Dorothy Johnson. '*According to an unnamed study, as many as a quarter of suicides from San Francisco's Golden Gate Bridge in which no body could be found, could be faked.*'

I stand up and pace the kitchen. How absurd the word sounds. Pseudocide. It's a *pun*. The idea is so callous and empty. When the canoe man was in the news, after he had been discovered hidden behind his plywood walls, the talk at school was how heartless he was. What sort of person would put his loved ones, his own children, through that?

I sit down again and try to focus. If I try hard enough, perhaps I will visualise Zach in my head – work out where he is. The answer is out there. He must be somewhere. I close my eyes tight and nothing comes. There are no leads. The sea. The clifftop. The horizon.

Where would he go? John Darwin hid in his own house, with the collusion of his wife. For a dizzying moment, before I discount it, I wonder if Zach has been here all along, slipping into the house when I am out, sleeping in my bed in the day.

Where would he expect me to look? His parents are dead, and he swore he would never go back to the Isle of Wight. He had no friends from his childhood. There were only those, like Victoria Murphy, from whom he had drifted apart. Edinburgh? He studied there. Brighton? Or living rough out on Dartmoor?

I don't know. I've just got this sense that he is close to me. Now.

What do I know about his past? Less than I imagined. Both parents dead, no family to speak of. He had so few friends too. It was one of the things that concerned me over those last few months. At first, it was so new, so enticing, the feeling that I was enough for him. Once, early on, I said something about seeing more people, going out more, and he squeezed my cheeks between his hands, held my face close to his. 'It's what makes us special,' he said with a ferocity that made my heart beat faster. 'It's you and me.'

I told myself it was normal to cast off your friends, that it was what you did when you fell in love. Fell in love: am I allowed to say that? It's not the sort of language of which Zach approved. He would have said it was pat. And yet – *falling*, the lack of control, the bodily tumble, the sense of an abyss, it's what it felt like.

It was only in the last few months that it began to concern me. I went for a drink after school on Jane's birthday and he was waiting in the kitchen, in the dark, when I got home. 'Are you bored of me?' he said. 'Do you want me to fuck off?'

I told him he was being stupid. Of course I didn't. We argued. Later, we went to bed, as we always did.

Where would he have gone if I had then told him that I did want him to fuck off, that yes, that *was* what I wanted?

Pete and Nell: they are the only people I can think of. They were his best friends at art school. He and Pete were close – the only two mature students in their year. Zach stayed with them when he first moved to Brighton.

I met them once. Once only. Pete rang one Sunday morning when Zach was in the bath. They were up in London for the weekend – they'd been at a party in Battersea – and I invited them for lunch. It led to one of our first rows. Zach said it was thoughtless of me to arrange it without checking with him first, but I think he was just embarrassed about the house. My mother had only recently gone to the Beeches and, although he had redecorated downstairs, the first floor was tatty.

In the end, we met them in an Italian café on Northcote Road, close to the school. Zach recovered his temper and we chatted happily, the four of us, about Brighton, their plans to start a family. They had shown interest in my job. I had talked about my mother, how painful it had been caring for her (the slipping away of the person I knew, the distance, the loss of her love) and also how funny (her nudist period). Nell, who was wearing a green top that exactly matched the colour of her eyes, gave me a hug. I imagined them becoming my friends too. But a crack formed without me noticing. When I invited them back for coffee, they made an excuse. At the time, I wondered whether something had happened when I went to the loo, whether they had argued.

I mentioned them once or twice over the next few weeks. Zach always changed the subject. We never saw them again.

Pete was a graphic designer, and Nell was in film production. I rack my brain for their surnames. In one of our first meetings, Zach had mentioned a gallery in Brighton. He was friends with the owner, though the relationship had soured. Somebody owed somebody money. Zach felt betrayed. Pete and Nell had mentioned him, that time we had lunch – they knew him too. Jim. That was his name. Jim.

It doesn't take me long. Blank Canvas, a 'creative and innovative exhibition space' in the 'vibrant North Laine area of Brighton', run by Jim Ibsen, 'artist, sculptor and free-thinker'. There's a number and I call it. When it goes to answerphone, I leave a message, explaining who I am and asking him to ring.

Zach loathed Facebook. He said only the lonely and the disconnected needed social media, that it brought out the worst (smugness, insecurity) in people. I used to look at it in secret. Not that I have many friends – thirty-three actually, most of them people I haven't seen in years, contemporaries from my primary school or the occasional former pupil.

One drunken evening in Jane's flat, before I met Zach, we looked up her old boyfriends, to see what they looked like, to laugh at their photos, to pretend to be young. It was surprisingly easy to track most of them down.

No point searching for Nell and Pete: I don't have their surnames. But my mind dredges up someone else. Fred Laws: my old boss at Westminster Library. It turned out Zach had been to school with him. Fred and I were good friends; he was a sweet, serious man. We used to eat our sandwiches together in Parliament Square. In fact, it was Fred who encouraged me to do my day-release course. I was so childishly excited when we discovered the connection, but an expression came over Zach's face, scared, almost trapped. He covered it quickly – did an impression, not entirely kind, of Fred holding his index finger in the air when he spoke. I understood. I think he had spent all that time trying to put the violence and trauma of his childhood behind him; he didn't need reminders. So we never got together. Our wedding at Wandsworth Town Hall was tiny – just the six of us, me and Zach, Peggy and Rob, Jane and Sanjay. (Nell and Pete didn't come in the end.) But the cremation at Putney Vale . . . I've lost Fred Laws' contact details, but I should have tried to track him down.

Fred is not the Facebook type, but then a lot of people on Facebook are not the Facebook type. Lots of Fred Lawrences, plenty of Fred Lawsons. Only one Fred Laws. No photograph, or details, just a silhouette. I send a message anyway. I write: *Sorry if this is the wrong Fred Laws, but if it is the right one, please get in touch.*

How bold I have been, sitting here in my lipstick. Ruby red, the colour of cochineal, the colour of blood. But once I have done this, I snap the laptop shut, the lid cold and hard against my fingers.

After lunch – a tin of tomato soup I eat from the saucepan – I force myself into the world outside. I lay Zach down in the back of my mind and drive to Colliers Wood to the Beeches, the care home where my mother lives.

I find her today, after I have signed in, sitting in the lounge in front of *Judge Judy*. My heart clenches with love and guilt, as it always does. She is sitting next to a man with Parkinson's whom the staff refer to as her 'boyfriend'. He is fast asleep, his mouth open. My mother's head is cupped by the headrest of the chair, her eyes watering, the skin on her cheekbones thin and taut. She has lost a lot of weight, though I notice with concern that her legs are more swollen than they were before the weekend.

I've brought her the chocolate eclair toffees she likes and I lay them down in her lap.

'How are you, Mum?' I say, kissing the top of her head.

'That man,' she says, nudging the toffees on to the floor with the back of her hand, 'took all my money.'

I pick up the toffees and place them carefully next to her on the chair. 'On *Judge Judy*?'

'Here,' she said. 'The one who lived in the bathroom. He came into my room, pretending to be nice.'

'When?' I ask. 'What man? When was he in the bathroom?'

She puts on a different voice, almost sing-song. 'They're all the same. Cunts.'

I stare at her.

'Now, now,' says Angie, one of the nurses, who has been sorting Phil's medication in the corner. 'Language, Lyn.'

The caregivers here think my mother is rude and difficult, but it isn't what she's really like at all. She would never have sworn before the Alzheimer's. She was strong and capable. Widowed at twenty-eight, with two children under six, she got a job as a school dinner lady and then as a receptionist at the GP. She taught herself to type and in the evenings she took in secretarial work for a former colleague of my father. She wanted the best for us. She was so proud of Peggy, with her university degree and her rich husband. My poor mum. I always let her down. I'm still doing it now.

I gaze out into the atrium garden. The statue in the middle, an abstract form made out of concrete, is surrounded by swathes of dry ornamental grass. Nowhere to hide. I can hear voices in the reception area. A woman in a wheelchair is being pushed down a ramp to a waiting car. A male nurse is holding open the door. There's always someone on the front desk. It would be impossible just to wander in.

I persuade her to stand up and take her through to her bathroom to wash her hair. I run the water for a while to let her get used to the sound – it can startle her otherwise. I bring up a chair to the basin and she leans her head back and closes her eyes. I wash it carefully, dabbing the water from her eyes and face, blotting it with a towel so as not to irritate the skin. Her scalp is so dry it is like parchment. She doesn't say anything, but she also doesn't object.

Back in her room, I settle her on the edge of the bed and smooth her wet hair with a comb. I ask her about her childhood in Kent. She likes that. It seems to make her feel safe. She is telling me about the apple trees at the end of her garden while I fill her water jug, water her plants and tidy up. I try to work out if anything's been touched. I check again in the bathroom, searching under the basin and behind the bath. Nothing seems out of place. In her bedroom, the photographs are dusty, but show no fingerprints. I wipe them with a cloth – the picture of my father first, taken on a beach in Devon. I think I remember that holiday, the salt and ice cream on my lips, his smile, the scrape of his beard, but I am cheating. It's a memory of the photograph. Peggy and Rob's formal wedding portrait next, and then one of Peggy and me as small girls in matching dresses. Tucked into the corner of that is a small photo of Zach. I put it there once. It slips out of the frame as I polish and I study it for a moment. It was taken on holiday in Cornwall, on a rock, the water behind. He looks brown and windswept; he's laughing.

We'd just raced each other down to the cove. He'd let me win. After the picture was taken, we skimmed stones and threw sticks for the dog. We rolled up our jeans and paddled. He took off his top and rubbed my feet with it.

'Zach was always happy by the sea,' I say.

My mother is humming, plucking at the bedspread with the tips of her fingers.

When Zach first moved in with me, he couldn't believe how many knick-knacks my mother owned – the decorative wooden cockerels from Portugal, the dolls wearing Greek national costume, the pottery jugs and brass bells, the copious spider plants. It all got packed up in boxes, but there wasn't space in her room at the Beeches. We brought only her favourite items – the plants and photos and a collection of Coalport porcelain houses, which Zach thought hideous but we always loved, growing up. My father had given one to my mother on each birthday during their married life.

They're lined up on the shelf. I count them. Then I count them again. There are five and there should be six. One is missing. Which one? I check them off in my head. The yellow mansion is here, and the house shaped like an umbrella, the red villa and the twin cottages, encircled with roses; they're all on the shelf. But the blue-and-white Swiss chalet, Peggy's favourite when we were little: it's gone. I search under the bed, in case it has fallen down, and on the shelf by the television in case it has been moved there.

'You didn't come for ages,' my mother says suddenly. 'You never visit me.'

She is watching me, chewing her lip. I sit down next to her and take her hand. I remind her that I came on Friday. I couldn't come at the weekend, I say, because I had to go away. I start telling her about the last couple of days, or at least certain aspects: how I had been to the seaside and met a grand

MP called Alan Murphy. I tell her about the house at the top of the hill, the umbrella stand made out of a poor dead fox. I try and think of as many details as I can remember. It's the sort of story she used to enjoy.

'I like the other girl better,' she says when I pause for breath. 'The pretty one.'

'I know.'

'I wish you would leave me alone.'

'OK.' I kiss the top of her head. 'I'm going.'

'And tell that man I don't want him to come again either.'

'What man?' I say, my heart jerking, but she has set her mouth and turned to the window.

Flo, a different nurse, is on reception when I leave. She tells me my mother had 'a little problem with regurgitation' at breakfast and we talk about why that might be. I ask her casually if she knows anything about the missing ornament – whether it might have got broken. I don't want to make a big deal of it. My mother's wedding ring disappeared just before Christmas. Peggy, who was upset about it, made a fuss. The staff here felt accused – they blamed the hospital where Mum had been for a blood test – and I don't want to dredge that up.

'Not that I know of,' Flo says. 'Are you sure there were six?'

'Maybe I got it wrong,' I say. 'By the way, has anyone been to visit her?'

'Don't think so,' Flo says. 'But you can check the book.'

I flick through the pages but no one has been to see her at all, except me.

I take a detour on the way home, into the web of streets behind Clapham High Street, known as the Old Town. It's a mixed area – lovely big family houses opposite blocks of council flats, long Victorian terraces that were carved up and sold off in sections during the property boom of the 1980s, the odd row of 1950s infill semis. I park outside the big red-brick house where Zach and I discovered we must have once been neighbours. I rented a studio on the top floor, he lived in the basement, the tenant of a banker from Antwerp. We talked about passing each other unwittingly in the street. 'How could I have kept my hands off you?' Zach said.

From the car, I stare up at the house. Is this the sort of place he would be living now? A basement flat in an anonymous building? How would he be feeding himself? Odd jobs, maybe, here and there. Theft? I wouldn't put it past him.

As I gaze at the brickwork, a throb sets up in my forehead. My vision swims. Black spots bloom on the insides of my eyelids. I see Zach walking across the pavement towards the car, his hand on the door, hear the clunk as it opens, sense the cold draught of air on my face. I feel the yank of his arms pulling me, his weight against my chest, his mouth moist on the crook of my neck. I can hear myself gasp. I imagine it so vividly, it's like a crack of the heart when I open my eyes and remember I'm sitting here alone.

This is absurd, I tell myself. I get out of the car, lock the door and descend the short flight of steps to the basement. Rubbish has blown in – a dirty paper bag, a takeaway container smeared with curry sauce. I am not sure the bell will be heard above the blare of the television. *Deal or No Deal*. Noel Edmonds asking the questions. Music. Applause. An elderly man comes to the door, clutching a large, limp black-and-white cat. He looks vaguely familiar and so does the cat – though black-and-white cats often do. 'What do you want?' he says.

I explain that my husband once lived here, in 2001 or 2002, that he was the lodger of a Belgian banker. He had been working for a builder at the time. I am on a pilgrimage to places that had meant something to him. Would it be very rude to ask if I could spend two minutes looking around?

He fixes me with his eyes, this old man. They are a vague colour, the whites yellow with age. He juts his jaw over the cat's head and makes a chewing movement with his gums. 'That's a new one,' he says eventually. 'I give you marks for ingenuity, but I wasn't born yesterday.'

'Sorry. I—'

He begins to close the door. 'I've lived here since 1970,' he says. 'And my mum and dad lived here before that. So go and find someone else to con.'

Zach had claimed only to have lodged at this address for a few months, between working as a tour guide abroad and studying in Edinburgh. It was more than ten years ago. He could have misremembered the house number. He could have realised his mistake but seen how much pleasure the coincidence gave me and found himself unable to backtrack.

Excuses are there. Reasons. Explanations. And yet how uneasy this makes me feel. I feel unstrung, as if a thread in my past has been snipped. Small untruths – I did occasionally catch him out. Nell and Pete, for example: he told me he had invited them to the wedding, that they couldn't come due to a family commitment. When we met for lunch, it was clear they didn't even know we were married. I didn't bother to worry at the time. I knew he was private. It was a small puzzle I skipped over. It was the same when I heard him tell Peggy his mother came from a family of landed gentry in Somerset. He had told me Dorset. A tiny detail – and the counties are next door to each other. I passed over it. Now I'm not sure I should have done.

On the way home, my head thick and churning, I take the wrong road and end up heading into town, snarled in traffic, unable to turn round. I get lost in the backstreet one-way system of Kennington, trying to get out. When a road takes me round to where I started, I pull into a parking space and rest my head on the steering wheel to clear it. He was concealing things, I realise, ducking and diving, even when our relationship was fresh and apparently untainted. The thought gives me the impetus I need. I'm going to catch him out. I'm going to find him, whether he wants me to or not.

When I finally let myself into the house, the phone is ringing. It is dead when I pick it up. I dial 1571, but 'the caller withheld their number'. I clank the receiver down. I have had a lot of silent calls over the last few months. Peggy says it's just someone in India with an urgent message regarding a non-existent insurance claim, that the wires often don't connect. But now I don't know. Is he checking I am in?

Without taking off my coat, I leave the house and take Howard around the block – along the road past the prison where a large white Serco van is pulling in. The car park at the garden centre a little further on is almost empty. It's cold again, the sky heavy. The world looks bleak. I should have gone the other way – it might have contained more distractions. I walk fast and turn right on Earlsfield Road at the lights, up to the dual carriageway and down into the underpass. Four teenage boys are kicking a ball about down there, knocking it back and forth against the concrete walls. Out the other side, on the patch of common where the steam fair comes at Easter, two women with prams are drinking cups of Starbucks on a bench under a tree.

The phone in the kitchen rings again when I step through the front door, as if it has been waiting for me.

'Lizzie Carter?' The voice is deep and a little dissolute. You can hear red wine and late nights in the corners of it.

'Yes.' A nerve has started pulsing at the back of my neck.

'Jim Ibsen.' I catch the sharp inhalation of a cigarette.

'Oh gosh, yes.' I gabble nervously for a bit, thanking him for getting back to me. He says, 'You're all right' several times. I know I need to get to the point, to be listening to *him*, but I am walking back and forwards across the kitchen, trying to work out what to say, what to ask.

Finally, Jim Ibsen interrupts and says, 'I'm sorry for your loss. I heard about Zach . . .'

'You weren't at the funeral. I should have thought. It wasn't much of one. You know, because of the circumstances. I never got to meet you, or many of Zach's friends.'

'Were you married long?'

'Two years. Almost. Not long really, is it? There's so much I never got to find out about him and . . .'

'Yeah. Me and Zach, we'd kind of drifted apart.'

'Right.' My ears have been tuned to pick up clues of knowledge or collusion but his voice is flat and uninterested. This is a dead end. Jim Ibsen knows nothing. 'I see.'

Another inhalation of nicotine. 'Good to you, was he?'

'Yes,' I say. I sit down at the kitchen table. 'In his own way. Yes. Yes, he was.'

'Well, I am glad about that. Zach Hopkins. A forgotten talent. Did he carry on showing?'

I don't like his tone – it has a mocking edge – and I feel a tug of allegiance. 'Yes. In fact, he was doing well. In fact, I really think, at the time of his accident, he was on the cusp of something big.'

He laughs. 'He was always on the cusp of something big. No disrespect. He had talent. But you have to compromise, and he never would. We had a nifty little business going, the two of us, casting children's feet and hands – lot of young families in the Brighton and Hove area. It brought in some money, but he thought himself above it. He put clients off with his attitude. If he believed he could make a living with those tiny dark canvases, fair play to him. But some of us have to live in the real world.'

'A dealer in Exeter had just taken a lot of his work,' I say, defensively. 'They were planning a solo exhibition at his gallery.'

'Did it ever come off?'

'Well . . . well no.' After Zach's accident, I tried unsuccessfully to track the gallery down. I never retrieved the paintings he had left there. Someone is sitting on them. Unless – of course – unless *Zach* is.

'There you go. Same old story.'

'OK.' I want to get off the phone from him now, this chippy Jim Ibsen with his jaded assumptions. 'Look. I'm trying to get in touch with an old friend of Zach's . . . Xenia. Does the name Xenia mean anything to you?'

'Anya?'

'Xenia.'

'Doesn't ring a bell.'

'What about Nell and Pete: do you know them?'

'Nell and Pete. Course I do.'

'Perhaps I could have their number?'

A silence at the other end. For a moment I think he is about to be evasive, but he's only taking time to look them up on his phone. He reels off their contact details. I scribble them down on a corner of the newspaper, on the grey patch of brickwork behind Murphy's yellow hat.

I decide to ring the home number. It's only 5 p.m. They'll still be at work. They talked a lot about their jobs, that day we met for lunch. Long hours. Creative pressure. Demanding bosses. For Pete at least, a commute. I am brave enough to ring, but cowardly enough to want to leave a message.

My plan backfires. Nell isn't at work. She answers the home phone breathlessly, as if she had to run upstairs when she heard it ring.

I force myself not to hang up. I remember the stickiness of our goodbyes that Sunday. Pete, his eyes narrowed, gazed over Zach's shoulder as if something fascinating in the distance had snagged his attention.

'It's Lizzie Carter,' I say. 'I'm sorry to bother you.'

'Lizzie Carter?' My name means nothing to her. Or she's pretending that it doesn't.

'Zach's wife?'

A heartbeat and then: 'Oh my God, Lizzie Carter.'

'Do you remember?'

'Yes.' A slight delay – recognition, but other emotions too. I can't gauge her tone. I wish I could see her face. An eerie dizzying thought: she *does* know where he is.

She recovers quickly. 'Of course I remember. How are you? I heard about Zach. Jim read it somewhere, and I meant to write . . .'

'Did my sister Peggy get in touch? She was going to try to.'

'Maybe, yes. I think perhaps she did. Pete said something . . . But we've been busy, what with the new house, and juggling—'

In the background, a small hiccup rising to a proper cry.

'You've got a baby!'

'Yes.' She laughs. The crying gets louder and then stops. 'There we go. I'm on maternity until September. It's my second actually. Do you remember, when we met I thought I might be pregnant, well I was! But that was the first. How time flies. But anyway, Lizzie Carter, *how are you*?'

She says it a little too enthusiastically. A forced laugh, my name repeated like code, as if she is alerting someone in the room. I close my eyes. Have I struck lucky? Was my very first guess right? Is she shielding him? If so, she's on his side. I can't trust her.

Or am I running away with myself? Is she just embarrassed, wondering why on earth I've rung?

I try to talk normally. 'I'm sorry to ring you out of the blue. You're probably thinking, "Aghh. What does she want?" I'm on half-term from school and I'm going to be in Brighton this week. I just hoped I might be able to buy you a cup of coffee. I just . . .' *Stop saying, 'I just'.* 'I've got a few questions about Zach, and I ju— I thought you might be able to answer them for me.'

'Oh, right.' She sounds bright. 'I'm not sure I've got anything to say.'

'It would mean a lot to me.'

A pause – slightly too long. 'What day?'

'Thursday, though I could probably do Friday instead if that's better. If you had time . . . I expect you're pretty busy with the kids.'

'Hang on. Let me get the diary.'

A clatter as the phone is put down on a surface, muffled voices in the distance, footsteps getting softer. And then: 'Hello.'

It is the voice of a small child. 'Hello,' I say. 'Are you a boy or a girl?'

'I'm an alligator.'

'Ah. I thought you might be. I was just saying to myself: that, if I'm not mistaken, is an alligator.'

'Sorry.' Nell is back on a different extension. 'Put the phone down, Pidge.'

'Goodbye,' says the alligator.

'Goodbye,' I say. 'It was very nice talking to you.'

'Right. I could do Thursday morning. Sort of 11.30ish? If you don't mind coming here, to the house, it would be easier.'

To the house. Would she invite me to the house if she were hiding Zach? Thursday is three days away – gives them time to conceal the traces. I should have said earlier in the week, or tracked down her address and turned up uninvited. I haven't been thinking clearly. I should have been sharper.

'You still there?' she says.

'Yes, sorry.' I pull myself together. 'Thank you so much,' I say, 'you're very kind.' I take down her address, on another corner of the newspaper, and we hang up.

Zach

January 2010

Two major developments today.

First off, I met the sister. Peggy. A piece of work, though Lizzie won't have any of it. Or not much. Or only a tiny little bit, on the condition that it comes from me.

I was charming, of course. She didn't much like the Internet aspect of our relationship, but we got over that quite quickly. Jokes and smiles and washing-up, tossed the toddler until it squealed, caught it carefully, plenty of flirtation (the kind of woman who expects it). Pretty enough; not my type. One of those spoilt thirty-somethings who think they're seventeen, long blonde hair, boob-clinging top, skinny jeans. A social climber, smugly proud of nabbing her City-boy husband and the lifestyle that goes with him: 'Have you not been to Dubai? Oh we love Dubai.' A few irritatingly self-conscious verbal habits, too. 'Oh *man*.' Every other anecdote, involving a string of 'what have yous', was about other people's stupidity and ended with a self-congratulatory 'No shit, Sherlock.' Always moaning too. Anyone would think, the way she talked, she was an impoverished drudge rather than a privileged little madam.

The house, not far from Lizzie's, was decorated in the bland off-the-peg greige that those with money and no imagination consider the height of sophistication. I complimented her on her outfit

– 'Has anyone ever told you you dress like Alexa Chung?' – and she gave her sister a patronising tip of the head: 'Oh *man*. Tell that to Ms Fleece.' A little later, I found myself holding Lizzie's hand under the table, which was odd. I didn't remember reaching for it.

Peggy had 'news' and we were all privy to a self-conscious moment of confusion in which the desire to boast fought against a distant concern for her sister's feelings. The former won, natch. She took Lizzie to the other side of the kitchen to help her pour the tea. The flourish of a small black-and-white photograph – a twelve-week scan. 'We didn't want to tell you this time until we were *sure*. I know how fantastically boring other people's pregnancies can be.'

She made a good fist of it, Lizzie, I'll give her that. Kissing and hugging and hullabalooing. When we left, I asked if she minded and she said, 'No. Not at all. She told me when she was ready.' And I realised she had misunderstood. I had meant her younger sister having a second child and her having none. But it was the nonchalant 'other people's pregnancies' that had stung, the casual dismissal of the sibling bond.

As we walked home across the common, she told me Peggy's husband Rob wasn't a 'financier' at all. His whole life was funded by his parents. I laughed a lot and she seemed to enjoy my amusement. I said 'Oh *man*,' and she laughed again, more guiltily. She let me kiss her, there, up against a tree, in the middle of the common. We kissed for a long time. One hand against the trunk, the other cupping the back of her head. A train passed by and the earth shuddered. We broke off. I could come back with her, she said, if I wanted . . . Cue second development.

It was risky, but nothing I couldn't handle. I'd done some research. If Lizzie's mother screamed at the sight of me, pointed arthritic fingers, accused me of being her intruder, it would easily be discounted – the muddle of her poor mind, the blocking of her carotid arteries, the reduced synthesis of her neurotransmitters.

The timing was right, too. Sundowning, they call it, the increased confusion and agitation that often occurs in the early evening.

I needn't have worried. The old woman hardly registered my presence. She was sitting in the overheated front room, on an ugly bed-sofa contraption with the television on, twisting her fingers, yanking at her wedding ring. Lizzie made her supper and brought it to her on a tray. The dog and I both sat there watching while Lizzie spooned food into her gaping mouth. I was beginning to think the evening would never end when she finally nodded off. I took Lizzie by the hand and led her upstairs.

If she thought it odd I knew which door to push open with my knee, she didn't say. It was neater than on my last visit – no tangle of clothes and books. She had tidied it specially. She knew I was coming. *She had planned it*.

She was much more eager than I'd imagined, hungry, giving and, despite the fleeces and the practical underwear, surprisingly uninhibited. She would do anything I asked. It wasn't what I'd expected. Better. She brought out the best in me. Afterwards, a most unusual thing happened. I fell asleep, which I never, ever do.

When I opened my eyes, she wasn't gazing down at me as if trying to absorb my features, like Charlotte does. I couldn't even tell she was still there at first. It was dark outside. She was sitting against the headboard with her legs up, reading the newspaper. She was tilting it to hold it into the light from the lamp.

I said, 'Will you be lonely when your mother goes?'

She didn't look up from the page. 'I don't know,' she said after a while.

'I could always move in to keep you company.'

She put the paper down with a crackle and looked across at me. 'Don't be daft,' she said.

I pulled the duvet over my shoulder. 'Why is that daft?'

'We hardly know each other.'

'That's not true.' She had put on a dark grey T-shirt that brought out the slate in her eyes. There were golden flecks in the iris I hadn't noticed before. She thinks she is plain, but in certain lights she is actually quite beautiful. 'I know you now,' I said.

'You live in Brighton.'

'I could live in London.'

The door to her room eased open and the dog padded in. Lizzie bent over to stroke him, the newspaper crumpling under her outstretched arm. 'You are very nice and you are very silly,' she said.

I'm not very nice. I'm not built that way. And I wasn't being very silly. I was being very serious. I didn't like her tone. I don't know if she was talking to me or to the dog. The last time Charlotte patronised me like that it didn't end well. I opened my mouth to speak. Lizzie turned, as if she sensed it. She put her hand on my head. A piece of my hair twirled between her fingers. 'It's too soon,' she said softly.

Inside, I was panicking. I could feel it all going wrong, spiralling out of control. What was the matter with her? This felt right. It was perfect. Didn't she realise? Was she just going to waste what we had? I could hear my phone, in the pocket of my cast-off jeans, vibrating against the carpet. It would be Charlotte checking up, wondering where I was. The thought of getting dressed, leaving, catching a train to Brighton – the hassle – seemed jagged and ugly, and hopeless. I turned my head so Lizzie wouldn't see my face.

I couldn't stop myself. 'You shouldn't let the dog in the bedroom,' I said. 'It's unhygienic.'

Chapter Eight

Lizzie

I set my alarm to go off early on Tuesday morning. I don't want to sleep too long – the house awake, the streets busy, the road churning. I need to keep alert.

It's dark in the bedroom. I thought I'd pulled the blinds, but now they're tightly scrolled against the ceiling. The sky through my window, beyond the tree, is like an old bruise.

I dreamed of Zach, I know I did, but hard as I try, my eyes squeezed shut, I can't bring the dream back. I'm left just with a mood, a breath, a pulsing in my veins. I lie there, listening to the noises of waking London – the reversing of a delivery van, a bus rattling, a helicopter circling. Any fear I had of Zach has dissipated. I feel blank and bereft. I've remembered the lost look I saw in his face sometimes, if I caught him unawares: that time the gallery turned down his work, or when I said I would be late back. He would cover it quickly, replace it with resentment or irritation, but I saw the vulnerability before it went.

What does he want from me? Is it to make me sorry enough to deserve his return? Or does he not know himself?

I think of him out there, desperate, confused, bedraggled.

The dog's lying at the bottom of the bed, across my feet.

If Zach had crept into the room in the night, he would have barked. Wouldn't he?

★　　★　　★

With Howard in the back of the car, I drive down to Colliers Wood. I am at the Beeches by eight. My mother is still asleep. For a while I sit by her bed and watch, willing her to stir. I wash her hairbrush for something to do, and talk about her medication with a nurse. When she wakes up, I get her dressed and help with breakfast. I get to the bottom of the regurgitation – they've been giving her milk with her tea, which she doesn't like. Afterwards, I ask if that man has been to visit her again and she says, 'What man?' I bring up the safe subject of Kent and she talks again about the apple orchards. She seems more settled. As I leave, she asks when 'the other girl' is coming, and I have a little cry in the car. I used to do that every time.

I am meeting Jane at ten thirty in Wimbledon for a dog walk and, on the way, I find myself diverting into a grid of terraced backstreets, and then by a strip of wasteland along the River Wandle. My eyes scan every alley, every building site. Where would he be? Where would he hide? The task of looking seems insurmountable. A million sheds with broken doors. A million unofficial corrugated shelters. He could be anywhere, everywhere, in a crack between buildings, bunkered underground.

When I finally pull into the car park on Wimbledon Common, where Jane and I have arranged to meet, my senses feel impaired. I don't feel alert, but sluggish and heavy – disarmed. Who *was* he? Where is he? I close my eyes, but I can't picture his face. The backs of my eyelids are yellow and flickery, like the last spool at the end of a film. I can't conjure up his features, or his limbs, his chest, his back. I can't see him.

The windmill perches in a huddle of buildings a short drive from the main road. Today is flat and grey and the car park is quiet, an empty expanse of gravel pitted with puddles.

Jane's red Volvo estate is the only car on the far side. She is waiting inside, listening to Radio 4. *Woman's Hour.* I can hear Jenni Murray's voice vibrating through the bonnet. Jane waves when she sees me coming, starts wrestling on her boots. I smile at her as I approach and experience a strange, untethered feeling. Jane – my greatest friend. Zach has come between us again. I don't want to keep it from her, but I have to. She won't believe me and she'd worry. She'd get Morrow involved. She'd ring Peggy, like she did at the weekend. And they'd make it worse.

She opens the door and stands up. 'Hello,' she says. 'Are you all right?'

'Yes.' I speak too quickly because she is looking at me probingly. 'I'm so sorry about Sunday,' I add, as lightly as I can. 'I'm sure you were supposed to be somewhere else.'

'No,' she says, wrinkling her nose, though I know she's lying.

She rests her hand on my shoulder while she pulls her sock free from under her heel. She's pretending to be casual, but she's touching me to make sure I'm OK, that I'm not about to crumple.

I try out a joke to convince her. 'I can't believe I got on to bone fragments,' I say.

'Don't,' she says.

'I did, though, didn't I?' I bend down to let Howard off the lead. 'I started talking about teeth.'

She brings her hand to her mouth.

'What was I thinking? Morrow looked appalled.'

'I think she was taken aback.'

'I wonder if they prepared her for bone fragments when she was on her FLO course.'

'Poor Hannah,' Jane says. 'Poor you.' We've started walking down the path that leads to the woods. She puts out her hand to push back a branch. 'I wish you had told me about the letter.'

'Oh . . .'

'For you to find out that he read it before getting in the car . . . I can't imagine how that must have made you feel. But I've been thinking . . . I have to say this.' She stops in her tracks. 'Zach knew you loved him, Lizzie, that you didn't mean what you wrote. It was just a blip. It wouldn't have made any difference. You do know that, don't you? You were soulmates. It doesn't change anything.'

I feel a lump at the back of my throat. She thinks Zach killed himself and that I have persuaded myself he's still alive to free myself from the responsibility of that. For a moment her words open underneath me like a gaping hole. I make a small noise like a creak, and then I clear my throat. I wish I could convince her, but nothing I say will make any difference. She has no idea of the truth because I kept it from her. Soulmates – how simple that sounds. My fairy-tale prince, she once said. She had no idea. *She didn't know him.*

'Thank you,' I say eventually.

'I hadn't realised things were bad between you. I know he was a bit upset when you danced with Angus at the staff party . . .'

I look at her and away quickly. Angus, one of the NQTs, had grabbed my hand before I could stop him. It meant nothing. I knew Zach was watching, his eyes hot, in the corner. When I disentangled myself from the dance, Zach twisted my arm behind my back and said things in my ear that no one else should have heard. Jane didn't see. Someone must have told her.

'He could be a bit jealous,' I say. 'It was just a blip.'

'Really?' She bends to peer into my eyes. 'And the person who left the flowers? Did you work out who that was?'

117

'Xenia? No.'

'I was thinking, perhaps it was someone who witnessed the accident? No one he knew at all.'

'It could have been.' I have to be careful. She knows me so well. 'Maybe it was a good thing I went off the rails a bit at the weekend,' I add cautiously. 'Perhaps I needed it, one last maelstrom of madness before I could move on.'

'"One maelstrom of madness"?' she says, raking an eyebrow. I'm relieved to see she is smiling. 'Poor Lizzie. It will get better.'

She starts walking again and I know I've got away with it. It's back to being Zach and me now, like it always was.

We take our usual walk, down the hill, through the trees to the lake, silver and still in its deep hollow, like something from a fairy story, and then up through the woods to skirt around the rim of the golf course. Howard chases squirrels and rabbits and rooks. Patches of wildness, swathes of manicured grass, twisted trees, overhanging branches, thick hedgerows. Wimbledon Common changes all the time. When the roar of the A3 is cancelled by a dip in the landscape or a particularly thick thatch of undergrowth, you can imagine yourself in wooded depths far out of London. It does me good to pace. I wish I hadn't remembered the staff party. I ran out after the Angus incident. Zach caught up with me on the common. He was drunk – alcohol didn't mix well with the pills he took for his anxiety. He begged my forgiveness. He didn't know what had come over him, he said. He needed me so much. I try to concentrate on the weight and tug of Jane's arm linked in mine, not think about him, out there alone.

On the last stretch of bridle path, when we can see the tip of the windmill hoving into view above the canopy of trees, we start chatting about school. Jane slips Sam Welham into the conversation. She bumped into him buying okra and coriander in Tooting Market the day before, shopping for ingredients for a curry.

'Nice,' I say.

'He asked after you. He knew it had been the anniversary. He was concerned.'

'Kind of him.'

Jane, who worked with Sam at a previous school, has told me several times what an idiot his wife was for leaving him. She tells me this again. She also informs me that he asked if she could recommend a dentist.

'And did you?' I say.

'Yes. I did.'

'Excellent.'

'He's nice, Lizzie,' she says.

'I know he is.'

'Zach would want you to be happy.'

I catch my breath. The simplicity of her words makes me want to weep. Her arm has unlinked from mine. 'I know he would.'

'I'm just saying.'

'I know you are.'

I drive home a different route – through Wimbledon Village and down Plough Road, past the greyhound stadium. Zach rented a unit in an industrial estate behind this, an old warehouse that had been converted into a rabbit warren of studios.

I pull into the huge stadium car park and switch off the engine. Metal racks for the Sunday market are scattered, upended. A pile of cardboard boxes, crushed flat and sodden, lies by the entrance.

I've been here once before – shortly after his accident, to clear his studio. I was still in a state then. Jane came with me. The caretaker, a young man with long sideburns, used a skeleton key to open his door. I couldn't bear to look – all his work in progress, the piles of paintings and brown paper, the paints, all that evidence of his interrupted life – and I hung back to let Jane go ahead of me. She just stood in the doorway, not moving. After a bit, I stepped forward. There was nothing there. A bare easel. Bare walls. Scrubbed floor. Three bottles of white spirit lined up, labels parallel. We'd bought Jane's estate to fit it all in. I could have carried the residue of his working life on the back of a bike.

Jane said some horrible person must have taken it, heard he was dead and broken in to steal what remained of his stuff.

Now I'm not sure. It's playing on my mind: did he come back to retrieve it himself?

I get out of the car into a puddle. The warehouse is around the corner, in a run-down street pitted with potholes. It's a low-slung Victorian building, all wrought iron and fire escapes, small windows. The door this end is open and I walk straight in. An entrance hall, painted neon pink. An archway leads to the main corridor. The air smells of turpentine and heat, chemicals and wet earth. The buzz of a saw, a hammer banging, tinny pop music from a distant radio.

Most of the doors are open. An old man is crouching in the first unit, taking pliers to an eviscerated armchair; in the next, an aproned woman is bent over a mud-splattered kiln. I pass a watercolourist, a screen-printer, a scrap-metal artist, a young girl making sculptures out of bandages and pins. They all look too busy to interrupt.

The music is coming from the kitchen, a double unit halfway along, where a woman with spiky black hair and a ring through her eyebrow is warming up lunch in the microwave. She looks vaguely familiar. I've met her before. She came to Zach's funeral. She might know something.

I say hello and tell her who I am. She nods. Yes. Her name is Maria and she is a knitter. It is true, she was at my husband's funeral. Someone had rung the caretaker to tell them about it and she and her friend Suzie, who is a sculptress, had decided to go. 'It was not so far.'

I smile, but her words sting. She makes it sound like a trip to the cinema.

'Such a shame,' she adds. 'Such a lovely, handsome man.'

The microwave pings and she takes out a tray of ready-made teriyaki chicken with rice. I sit down opposite her. I've got to be careful. We talk about how it is a year since it happened, and I explain that I am trying to piece together a few facts. His empty studio, for example: did she think anyone here might have taken his stuff?

Maria looks uneasy. 'We are a close community,' she says. 'Artists, not thieves.'

'OK. Of course. I'm just surprised how little he had.'

She shakes her head. 'Zach, his door was always closed,' she says. 'We have open days twice a year to show our work, to give wine, to sell. But Zach, he locked his door. He never joined in. He told me that his work was no good. I don't know what his studio was like.'

'How odd of him.'

'Some people here it is chat chat chat, but Zach he talked with his eyes. Such beautiful blue eyes.'

'They were very arresting,' I say. 'His eyes. Did anyone ever come here? Did he have visitors?'

She shakes her head. Her mouth is full of chicken. 'No.'

'Do you know of anyone here called Xenia?'

'No. No Xenia. Not that I know.'

'And he really kept himself to himself?'

She puts her finger in the air while she swallows. 'He used to tap-tap on his laptop. Long emails. Once, he was upset. I can't remember when. His face was red. I saw him later as he was leaving and asked if he was all right. I don't like people to be unhappy. I am a kind soul.'

'I am sure you are.'

I watch her eating for a little longer. She smiles at me a couple of times.

'His studio,' she says. 'A photographer is in there now. Very nice man.'

'Good.'

I can't wait to leave after this, think about this image of Zach and his closed door, his private anguish. I hurry out of the building and back to the car. I see a hole in the chain fence I hadn't noticed before and crawl through, standing up too quickly and snagging my anorak on a loose wire.

My car is the other side of the lot, over by the café. I begin to walk towards it, but then I stop.

A figure is standing between the bonnet and the fence, leaning in. Floppy hair, a thick overcoat, one shoulder slightly hunched. I feel a rush of triumph – and, at the same time, of terror. I begin to run, stumbling over the potholes. Muddy rainwater splashes up my jeans. My vision blurs. The car park spins. I miss my footing, trip, stagger and fall. Hands in the gravel, knees sodden, face inches from the ground. I sit up and get to my feet.

An item of clothing – a dangling black sweatshirt, hanging limply – is poked into a hole in the fence above the bonnet.

Zach has gone.

Zach

March 2010

I am in Cornwall for a few days. It's cold and bleak, miserable without a car. I was going to drive down in Charlotte's Golf, but a bottle of milk had spilled on the passenger seat and, although she says she scrubbed it clean, I can still taste it at the back of my throat, sour and curdled like the skin of an old person.

The wind on the clifftop walk to the village is icy. I managed to lug a bag of logs up from the farm shop to make a fire. It lasted an hour, but I couldn't keep the logs straight. As they burned, one of them kept slipping out of place. I tried not to look, but it was no good. My eye was constantly drawn. I couldn't sit still. I felt as if my skin were crawling. In the end, I stamped out the flames with my foot. I'm waiting for the ashes to cool so I can sweep out the grate. I'll feel better when it's clean. If I had a car, I could drive to the Shell garage for rectangular eco briquettes. You can line those up.

This agitation, it's much worse than usual, even with the pills. I'm not in control.

The double life is killing me. It's the frustration, the sense that everything could be settled, lined up, but it isn't. I'm like one of those businessmen who keep it up for years. One week in Maidstone, the next in Maida Vale. Charlotte is at work too much to notice my absences, busy with what she has begun to refer to as her 'proper job' — a dig. And Lizzie's demands are mild in comparison to other women I've known. Content to see me when I make myself available, she never nags at me to meet her friends, or hang out with her family, or attend dinner parties or christenings of babies I've never set eyes on belonging to people I wish I never had.

The lack of pressure makes me want to see her more. I feel as if I'm going out of my mind.

Can't sleep. Can't paint. Somewhere along the way, I've lost my day job. Jim, the bastard, found a student from the uni to do the metal casting, says I didn't show enough 'commitment'. He owes me money from that last commission, says he's keeping a couple of pictures as collateral. What a stupid fuss. Just because I didn't get round to paying for that last stash, and missed a couple of appointments. I knew he was tight, that he wouldn't reach into his pocket unless he had to. But unscrupulous? I didn't expect that. Luckily I've still got his bike. He thinks it was nicked by the homeless guy who used to doss outside the studio. People are so narrow-minded. I keep it in London now, securely locked, along with my new white helmet, to the railings at the station. It isn't theft. It's payment in kind.

Time is hanging ludicrously heavy. It's ridiculous we're still where we are, that nothing has changed. Lizzie has agreed that a home is what her mother needs. The Beeches in Colliers Wood has a vacancy. It's perfectly adequate. But Lizzie keeps going on about her 'head' and her 'heart' — as if they are separate items. She cried the other night. She said she'd always felt so worthless, that Peggy was her mother's favourite, and she — Lizzie — had hoped that by looking after her through her final illness, she would have a chance to prove her worth. But she'd failed at that, too. Her mother was right. She was a waste of space.

I felt a surge of fury — that stuck-up old woman and that uptight snobby sister of hers. Lizzie is worth more than both of them put together. How toxic families are. And of course Peggy herself isn't helping matters. She's not at all happy about Mommy Dearest being 'looked after by strangers'. What she wants is for Lizzie to carry on sacrificing her life so Peggy can happily carry on living hers guilt-free.

I persuaded Lizzie to go round for a 'family meeting'. While we were there, I said: 'I suppose you could take it in turns. Even when the baby comes, the lovely thing about this house is that you have so much *space*.' After that Peggy changed her tune pretty sharpish.

The wind dropped today. I passed Alan Murphy, Victoria's tosspot husband, running on the beach early this morning, shoulder to shoulder with a younger man – an aide, or a personal assistant, or a bodyguard. He was out of breath and when he put out an arm to wave, he stumbled briefly. I doubt he recognised me, probably just saw 'Voter' plastered across my head. He's a crony of the new Tory leader. Getting fit for office, no doubt. Well, I tell you what he can't count on. My vote, that's what. He was never the sort of man Vic used to go for when we were young. She used to be such a laugh. She's changed, become conscious of her own standing, lost her spirit.

I was heading towards St Enodoc Church, just to clear my head, and I'd reached the point where the rocks end and the beach suddenly stretches out, stippled and striped, when I saw a figure dressed in black crouched on the sand. Mist was still licking at the cliffs, curling off the golf course. No one else in sight.

When I got a bit closer, I could see it was a girl, about fourteen or fifteen, and she was crying. She looked up at me and there was something about her eyes, swollen as they were, that stopped me; very blue, piercing. They seemed to drill straight through you.

I said, 'You OK?'

'What's it to you?'

'Nothing.'

'Well . . .' a jut of her chin. 'I'm not then. No.'

I asked what her name was and she said Onnie. Vic and Murphy's child. That's why she looked familiar, though she was skinnier and spottier than the last time I'd seen her.

'Well, you can't sit out on that wet sand,' I said. 'You'll get worms.'

'That's not how you get them,' she said. 'You get them from chewing your nails.'

'Well, you clearly know more about it than I do. I bow to your superior knowledge and no doubt experience.'

She stuck out her tongue, which made me laugh.

I was about to walk on but she called after me. 'I'm running away.'

'Oh yes?' I stopped to listen.

She told me she was at boarding school and she hated it. Some girl was bullying her, excluding her from conversations, telling her she couldn't sit on her table at lunch.

I told her to stay put, wait it out, to pay the little bitch back in her own time. 'You know the saying?' I said. 'Revenge is a dish best served cold.'

She made a face as if to say, 'Whatever.'

I blew her a kiss and walked on.

Back in Brighton. I can't believe it. I've got to get out. London and Lizzie – I can't stop thinking about both.

It's all going wrong.

We were in the pub last night and Charlotte started flirting with the barman, leaning forward so he could look down her cleavage. She was trying to get my attention, make herself desirable, and I wouldn't have cared except she did it in front of Pete and Nell. It was disrespectful. She made me look like an idiot.

We were climbing the stairs to the flat at the end of the evening and she started on again about Cornwall. She should have known when to stop. She was fumbling for her keys and the sight of her tarty leopard-skin coat falling off her shoulder, the smear of lipstick on her teeth, was too much for me. I told her to shut up and at the same time my hand impacted with her face. She wobbled and almost slipped. If I hadn't grabbed her, she would have tumbled all the way to the bottom. It's lethal, that seagrass.

She screamed at me and I begged forgiveness, told her how much she meant to me, how if anything happened to her, I wouldn't know what to do with myself. I promised I'd get out my toolbox at the weekend, and nail the loose seagrass down.

Chapter Nine

Lizzie

I have promised to look after Peggy's kids during half-term, to give her a break, and on Wednesday she brings them round.

She hovers in the hall, eager to get away. She and Rob, she tells me, are so desperate for some 'us time' they are 'literally on the verge of divorce'. They are planning a lunch and a movie and dinner and what have you, and then home for a shag, 'if that's not TMI'. I never used to notice the way Peggy talks. She was just Peggy. Zach drew my attention to it, how she repeats certain words, or picks up phrases she has heard. I see her more clearly now, but I sometimes wish I didn't. The older two have each packed a suitcase, though Gussie's consists mainly of jewellery from the dressing-up box.

I take them swimming at the Latchmere, where there's a wave machine, and then for chicken and chips and unlimited refills at Nando's, and then a stomp over the common with the dog and the buggy to the big playground. Back home, we empty out the cupboards to create magic potions – fizzing up our gruesome concoctions with a teaspoon of bicarbonate of soda. We play snap until Gussie gets cross, then decorate pizzas until, finally, we throw ourselves on to my bed and watch the DVD of *Stuart Little* I bought last week.

I have made up the sofa bed in the study but we end up sleeping where we are, with Gussie starfished across the mattress, Alfie hogging the duvet, Chloe curled in my arms. I sleep fitfully. Foxes in the garden disturb the dog and he barks intermittently. I lie there, wondering if Zach watched me out with the kids. He used to tell me Peggy took advantage, that I should stand up to her. But I love them. I love my sister too. He never seemed to understand that.

In the early hours, I hear music, plangent and slow, eerily reaching across the gardens from the cul-de-sac behind. The words are just out of reach, reverberating, bouncing against garage doors.

I get out of bed, extricating myself from small limbs, and cross to the window to listen. 'I Wanna Be Loved'. Elvis Costello and the Attractions. Zach's favourite song. Here it is again. Light pollution has turned the sky apricot. A white moon slips behind an orange cloud. I push up the sash and lean out, straining to catch every note, but the music stops.

They are awake, all three of them, at five but I find things to do – TV and colouring – before it's ten, a decent enough time to drop them home. I'm in a hurry. I don't want to put Peggy out, but my train to Brighton leaves at ten thirty.

'Oh,' Peggy says when she sees us at the door. 'You're early. Rob and I were about to go and have breakfast.'

'I'm so sorry. I could look after them again at the weekend? It's just I have a busy day.'

'A busy day?' She frowns, uncomprehending. 'Doing what?'

I flush, swing back from the door frame to hide my annoyance. 'Meeting a friend,' I say.

'Oooh.' She purses her mouth suggestively. 'That new teacher Jane was telling me about?'

I laugh. 'No.'

'Who then?'

A car toots, idling in the street, and Peggy waves. 'How was Quiz Night?' she shouts to the passenger, who has rolled down their window. I escape before she can ask me anything else.

I drive home, park in the nearest space at the end of the road and let Howard into the garden. I should have asked Nell if she minded me bringing a dog, but I didn't have the courage. The house is a mess – stuff everywhere. The sofa bed's still pulled out in the study. No time now. I'll tidy it when I come home.

As I leave the house, I notice a young woman out of the corner of my eye. She is sitting on the ground, against the railings, her legs out across the pavement. She is wearing shorts over ripped black tights, those long, thin plimsolls with no heels the girls at school wear, a leatherette jacket slung over her shoulder. Prison visitors often hang around in the street, or on the edge of the common, having a last fag, waiting for the welcome centre to open.

I walk briskly to the end of the road and am waiting for the lights to change at the pedestrian crossing when I hear footsteps and a cry: 'Oi! Don't ignore me!'

I turn. The girl is standing right by me. Close to, I see she has long limbs, a precise oval face and an upturned nose with a scattering of small spots. I catch an expensive scent, shampoo or body lotion of basil and lemongrass. And not leatherette, a real leather jacket.

And with a rush, I realise who she is. Not a grumpy girlfriend or teenage mum, but Alan and Victoria Murphy's daughter.

'Onnie!' I say. 'Hello!'

She flicks a sheet of dip-dyed hair forward over one shoulder as if to hide her face. 'I was waiting for you to come home,' she says, 'and you, like, walked past me. Twice.'

'You've come to see me?'

'Yes,' she says, widening her eyes slightly as if I'm being dim.

I almost smile, despite feeling so disconcerted, but manage not to. Her tone is off, but you often find that with shy kids. What comes across as rudeness is often acute embarrassment. They find it hard to open their own mouths. 'I'm sorry. I didn't see you. I wasn't expecting . . .' I shake my head. 'How did you know where I live?'

'Zach gave me the address.'

'When? Recently?'

She frowns. 'Not *recently*. Ages ago.'

'And you . . . kept it? All this time?'

She shrugs. 'Yes.'

I stare at her, baffled. Zach would never have given out our address. He was too protective of his privacy.

'Didn't you think I would come?'

I grasp to make sense of her words. Is there a detail from last weekend I'm not remembering? It seems so long ago. Something about a work placement. Did I tell her to get in touch? Also, why did she wait for me outside the house? Why didn't she knock?

'Gosh, I've been so busy. I'm not sure.' I look at my watch. 'I've got a train to catch. Could we chat on the way to the station?'

She shrugs.

The green man is flashing and I begin to cross. 'Are you in London for a while?' I ask.

She doesn't answer. A horn sounds behind me. I reach the other side and turn to see Onnie stranded in the middle of the road, cars accelerating on either side of her.

'Onnie!' I reach out, my hands clutching at the empty air. An engine roars, a motorbike swerves.

She waits for a gap, neck craning – a bus looms and passes – and then takes three quick strides, landing on the pavement with a small leap.

'Oh,' I say in pantomime relief. My fingers, finding her sleeve, clutch at the slippery leather. 'What happened? Did you drop something?'

'No. I just – I don't know.'

Her expression is closed, but she has gone red.

'It's a quickie, isn't it, that traffic light?'

'I wasn't concentrating.' She looks away and I realise she might be about to cry.

I let a beat pass before looking at my watch. Not long until my train. I try to talk calmly. 'I really do have to go,' I say, moving my hand to her shoulder. I can feel her collarbone through her jacket. 'Can you come back later?'

'It's OK.' She pulls away. 'I shouldn't have come anyway.'

'Of course you should have come.' I smile at her. 'If it was any other day, I'd drop everything, but I've got an appointment. You do understand, don't you?' I feel a bit worried about her suddenly. 'I'm really pleased to see you,' I add, 'and if there is something I can help you with, I will.'

'Really?'

'Yes. Are you going to be in London for the day? Could we meet for a coffee this afternoon?'

She blinks slowly. Her eyes, an arresting dark blue, are bloodshot. 'I don't drink coffee. I'm not allowed. Apparently, I get too—' she shrugs to express contempt with whoever it is who has opinions on this matter '—agitated.'

'Tea then,' I say cheerfully.

Onnie nods, twisting her lip.

'Walk with me for a bit,' I say. 'I'm heading towards the station, which is probably the way you've just come.'

'I took the tube. It's literally miles from here.'

'Sorry about that.' I laugh again. 'The train is better, or buses.'

We are approaching the common now, passing the last row of Victorian houses. Onnie is carrying a small khaki rucksack and it bashes my shoulder with each step. She doesn't say anything and there is a set to her mouth. Her eyes look sullen. I think how alienating teenagers can seem. Didn't someone say she was eighteen? She seems younger than that. The important thing is not to be put off, to talk normally.

'So what's new?' I say, cheerily.

'Nothing.'

'What happened about that work placement? Did you persuade your mother to let you do it?'

'That's what I wanted to talk to you about.'

We have reached the main path and have turned towards the café and the tennis courts.

'Oh yes?'

'The thing is she'd let me do it if I had someone sensible to stay with, so I thought I might take you up on your offer.'

'My offer?'

On the bowling green, two crows are stalking a squirrel.

'You said . . . I could, like, rent a room?'

I am fiddling with the gate that leads on to the football pitch. Rent a room? Did I offer to do that? I wouldn't have done, surely? I don't want someone in the house. Not in normal circumstances, and certainly not now.

I'm trying to think how to let her down gently when I realise Onnie has stopped and is hanging back against the fence. Her arms are thin, the wrists narrow. She pulls the sleeves of her top down over her fingers, one after the other, hunches her shoulders. I check my watch again. Ten minutes until the train leaves.

'It's only two weeks,' she says.

'When does it start?' I'm still holding the gate open for her. She doesn't move. For a fraction of a second I wonder wildly

133

if she has been sent to distract me, to delay me from Brighton, to make me miss my train.

She shrugs nonchalantly, but she is flushed around the eyes. 'Monday, but I was thinking I could come, like, today?'

'I'm not sure . . .'

'I could come on Sunday? Or even Monday. I could take the train in for the first day and come when I finish work.'

I push my hands into my pockets, let the gate clang. 'I don't think it will work really. But listen – I might be able to find a solution. Can we talk about it later?'

She looks up at the sky. A few drops are falling. 'When will you be back?'

'Early afternoon. That café we just passed: we could meet there at two?'

She gazes out across the grass as if it were the frozen wastes of Antarctica. 'What shall I do until then?'

I want to say; 'Go to the library – there's a good one on Northcote Road, or read a book, or buy a newspaper.' The expression in her eyes stops me. It isn't belligerent or sulky, but lost. She looks so hopeless. All that money and privilege, all that pretence and posturing, she is no different from some of the young people at school – the ones who, for whatever reason, don't know where to put themselves.

I think about the house, and Howard alone in the kitchen. I think about Zach giving her our address. Did he feel sorry for her, too? I find myself rummaging in my bag for my keys. 'Listen, let yourself in now. I used to have a spare key hidden, but I've lost it. Take these. You can keep the dog company. There is bread, cheese, a few slices of left-over pizza in the fridge. It's a bit messy, I didn't have time to clean up, but make yourself at home. I'll see you when I get back. If you need to go out at all, hide the keys under the plant pot.'

She takes the key ring and dangles it so casually on her middle finger, I want to snatch it straight back. Oh God. What have I just done?

She shrugs as if she might do what I suggest, or she might not. 'Cool,' she says.

Sunlight flickers through the high arched roof of Brighton Station and outside, on the forecourt, patches of blue sky are poking between the clouds. A family is consulting a map. Teenagers of different sizes hover by the entrance to Fitness First, sharing a cigarette.

Pete and Nell's house is only a short walk behind the station, up the hill, in the middle of a pretty terrace. The front door is sea-green and opens directly on to the pavement. I feel nervous, off kilter, waiting for Nell to answer. I was stupid to come. It's a fool's errand. Ozone sparkles in the air. Seagulls, white and shrill, are lined up on the roof. Someone somewhere is practising the recorder. I can't imagine Zach here. It is all sharpness and radiance. No dark corners to slide into.

'Live in the moment,' he used to say. 'Never go back.'

I am about to turn and run away when Nell opens the door, breathless. On her shoulder lies a tiny baby, a shock of dark hair, purple cheek against white muslin.

'Oh,' I say before I can stop myself. Small babies sometimes catch me out.

She smiles and opens the door to let me in, making a gesture to indicate the baby is asleep. She is plumper in the face than I remember and her thick brown hair is longer. She is wearing red woolly tights and a knitted green dress. We greet each other, as quietly as we can, and I follow her along a narrow passage, straining my ears, and down a few stairs into the kitchen.

I look around for clues. It is an untidy room – washing-up

in the sink, piles of paper on the work surfaces. Parrot tulips, in different colours, spill from a jug on the table. The kitchen units are pale grey; one wall is peacock blue. A huge cork-board is pinned with household detritus: letters and phone numbers, a child's drawings. No sign of Zach – no oil paints or rolls of paper. I check the backs of the pine chairs at the table for a messenger bag, casually slung. But there are just kids' clothes and tea towels, and a man's zip-up fleece. Not his. Zach would never countenance fleece.

On the floor, a small, cross-legged boy in dungarees is building a tower with blocks of Lego. 'And another one down,' he chirrups as the tower collapses.

Nell lays the baby carefully in a Moses basket in the window. Outside, up some steps, is a small garden.

Would you conceal a man from his wife if you had children in the house?

'Lizzie,' Nell says, turning. 'I'm so sorry about Zach. It's just awful. But it is lovely to see you again.'

She stretches out her arms. I move towards her for the statutory hug – the bereaved are embraced a lot – but she turns, just as I reach her, to throw the muslin over the back of a chair.

'Such a lovely baby,' I say, to cover my confusion. 'Boy or girl?'

We both peer in. 'Girl,' Nell says. 'Gladys.'

'Gladys. I love those old-fashioned names. Clever of you to find one that hasn't been used up.'

Nell doesn't respond. 'She's six weeks,' she says, and adjusts the baby's blanket. Above it a tiny fist furls. I stroke the baby's head, touch her hand, which grips my finger.

'You and Zach – you didn't have children?' Nell asks.

'No.' A tug of discomfort, a stirring.

'Coffee,' Nell says, straightening up. 'And then a good old catch-up.'

She rattles around with the kettle, fetching the mugs down from a cupboard, asking about my journey, apologising because she meant to make a cake but didn't have time, instructing Pidge instead to dig out those 'yummy' biscuits from the treat jar. 'Right, right, right,' she keeps saying, ticking off the sequence of small actions that are required. I watch her, checking her eyes and the muscles at the corner of her mouth, for any indication. I don't think she would have asked whether we had children if Zach was here. But still – her manner is odd, a strain runs beneath the surface. She knows something.

Finally, clearing the table with her elbow to make space for two mugs of coffee and a plate of oat crunchies, she sits down. 'Jolly good,' she says, half sighing. 'So.' She looks at me and then quickly away. 'How utterly sweet of you to come and visit me.' I hadn't noticed how posh she was last time – she'd seemed more Estuary than Bloomsbury. Parenthood, I've noticed, often brings out people's true origins.

'I wish we had seen more of you,' I say, taking a sip. 'We had that nice lunch, and then . . . I don't know. Life took over.'

'God. Yes. It's so close, Brighton from London, but psychologically . . . weekends we just seem to *flop*. And then having kids – bloody hell, you never have any time for anything.'

'Zach wasn't great at communication,' I say, still testing the waters. 'Some people have a knack with friendship. He didn't. I think he longed to see more of the people he loved. I don't know what stopped him. Pride, perhaps. Shyness.'

Nell laughs, but there's a brittle edge to it. I look at her carefully. 'OK, well, not shyness,' I say.

'Maybe not shyness,' she repeats.

Is she trying to tell me something? 'He did compartmentalise his life, though, didn't he?' I say, still scrutinising her features. 'Work, Cornwall, childhood, the Isle of Wight . . .'

137

'The Isle of Wight?' She removes her hand from her chin, tucks a hank of hair behind her ear.

'Where he grew up,' I say.

'I thought it was Wales.'

'Isle of Wight. I think.' Is she being purposefully vague? 'Did he not talk to you about it?'

'Not really.' She shakes her head.

How well, then, did she really know him? I think about his head in my lap, my hands in his hair. The well of unhappiness he would decant, cup by cup. The terrible underlying reasons for his behaviour – how his father would fixate on some aspect of his mother's appearance, or cooking, how he tortured her physically and mentally. And Zach, poor Zach, an only child, desperate for his father's approval, watching, powerless to intervene, carrying those images into his life as an adult, caught up but desperate to break free. How could I blame him for how he sometimes treated me?

'It wasn't a great childhood,' I say.

'Oh, really? I know they died a long time ago, but I thought they were loaded?'

'Big house – Marchington Manor. Nannies. Posh school. Yacht club. All worth nothing if, behind closed doors, your father is a violent alcoholic and your mother is too weak to stand up to him.'

'I didn't know.' She brings her knees up to lean against the table: 'He must have loved you very much, Lizzie, to have been able to open up to you. I'm so sorry,' she says awkwardly, 'you know . . . a terrible loss, it's such a shame.'

'Thank you.' I sigh, rub my face with the tips of my fingers. She's just embarrassed, I realise, that's why she has seemed odd. I forget how bereavement can make people uncomfortable.

I sigh again. I have such a sense of deflation, I want to cry. 'You and Pete meant a lot to him, too,' I manage to say.

'Did we?' Her eye has been caught by a rogue tulip, a pink one. She takes it out and cocks her head to study the arrangement.

'You were the only people he still saw from Edinburgh. I didn't go to uni. I studied librarianship on a day-release course. But I know the friends you make at university are important and—'

'Well, it wasn't really from university that we knew each other,' she says, putting the pink tulip back in a different position, next to an orange one.

'Wasn't it?' I lean forward. 'I thought you studied fine art together? I thought Zach and Pete were the only two mature students on your course.'

'Pete was a mature student. He and I both studied fine art. But Zach didn't.'

'What did he study then?' Blood infuses my cheeks. 'Wasn't it fine art? A different sort of art?'

She laughs. 'No. Nothing. He wasn't at the art school, or the university. He didn't study anything.' She laughs again dismissively, an edge of contempt. 'Not as far as I know.'

I take a gulp of coffee. 'I don't understand. He said he met you at Edinburgh.'

'We met *in* Edinburgh, not *at* Edinburgh. If you see the difference. Zach was a shop assistant. He worked in the art-supply shop on Princes Street. DaVinci's, it was called. We were in all the time before our finals, getting new charcoal, string, endless blocks of paper – displacement activities probably. We used to hang out in the pub.'

Heat in my neck. A coldness in my legs. Another lie. I picture the biographical notes I saw him write for 'Light on Water', the show in Bristol that never came off. He had written *Edinburgh College of Art*. 'So where did he study?'

She gazes at me. 'He was a good artist, Zach. He had a certain rough talent. No one can ever take that away from him. But he was self-taught. He just had this ability, this sense . . . He didn't always paint what people wanted to see.'

My voice sounds high-pitched and strained. 'I thought you all moved to Brighton together the summer after graduation?'

'Pete and I – *we* did. Pete had a job lined up. He'd been interning at Bull Trout Media in the holidays. I came down with him and found work quite quickly. Zach? It was a bit of a surprise, actually. I mean, obviously we knew him to chat to. He was very helpful in the shop. I also suspected he hooked up briefly with our flatmate Margot. He certainly had an eye for her. And then he just turned up. Here. In Brighton. He hitched down in the September. He found out where we lived—' She breaks off, frowns. Her nose concertinas. 'I don't know how, actually, but anyway he was waiting for us when we got back from work. He loved the sea, didn't he?' She rocks her chair back to check the baby in the basket.

'Yes,' I say, firmly. I look at my hands splayed on the table, feeling the solidity of the wood. 'He did love the sea.'

'And then,' Nell says, rocking forward, 'he moved in. We'd rented a flat down in Hove, but it was pricey and we'd been looking for a third person . . . the timing seemed too good to be true. We had a laugh while it lasted. He was such a big character.'

She puts her hand out to cover mine. 'I *was* fond of him.'

'*Was?*' She seems to be emphasising something that was in doubt. Such a 'charmer', a 'big character': there's a code in judgements like that. Teachers use them at parents' evenings all the time.

Her reply makes it sound as if I'd simply drawn attention to the use of past tense. 'I'm so sorry,' she says. 'I didn't know him very well really. But I'm glad he was happy. I'm glad he met you.' She half smiles.

Pidge climbs down from the table and says he wants to go into the garden. Nell unlocks the back door but tells him not to get too dirty because a friend is coming to play. I watch as he climbs the steps and sits on the small square of muddy grass with a trowel in his hand. He appears to be digging for worms. Safe, normal activities. Did she just say she hadn't known him very well? That doesn't make sense. They were best friends. I know they were.

I take a deep breath. 'On the phone I said I had some questions and you might think they're odd. Zach's accident has left things a little . . . open-ended.'

'Oh yes?'

'In Brighton, for example, he didn't live with you the whole time, did he? He rented a flat on his own or—?'

'No, he only lived with us for about four months. He moved in with his girlfriend. She had a flat in the centre of Brighton, just up from Churchill Square shopping centre.'

A twist in my chest. He told me I was the first woman he had ever lived with, ever been close enough to even to consider it. But he lied. His body in her bed. Limbs curved. His face in her neck. I dig my teeth into my lip. 'I didn't know that.'

She gives a quick, reassuring smile. 'He wasn't there for a huge amount of time, either. Hardly even a year. He met you and—'

A sudden, swirling thought. 'I don't suppose she was called Xenia?'

'She was called Charlotte. Charlotte Reid.'

Nell turns to watch Pidge in the garden, but I catch something dart across her face, confusion or guilt. I'm not sure. Her body language is telling me to drop it.

'What was she like?'

'She was sweet. Younger, quite a lot younger, than him. She had a high-powered job in the City, one of those smartly dressed girls in trainers who carry high heels in her handbag. When they were going out, we saw quite a bit of them—' She breaks off, swivels her eyes to mine and then bites her lip as if stopping herself from saying more. 'She doted on him. I liked her. She was lovely. He could have done a lot worse.' She brushes some invisible crumbs from the table.

I take another gulp of coffee, harsh at the back of my throat, and cradle the mug. 'So what happened?'

Nell sighs. 'She wanted to marry him, and he didn't want to marry her. The same old same old.'

She stares out of the window again. She's probably wondering how Zach, who could have had lovely, sweet, high-powered Charlotte Reid, ended up with the odd little person sitting here. And I am feeling guilty that I did, and grateful and heartbroken, and also muddled because neither of us is really saying what we want to. Zach isn't here and I shouldn't have come. Amid the ordinary cheerfulness of this house, this life, I feel like an oddity, a splinter in a smooth surface.

The room seems unnaturally quiet. I can see Pidge's arms moving, but I can't hear him. And then, I catch a sound – a noise above our heads – two separate creaks, a beat apart.

A shower of dirt hits the glass doors. Pidge has dug his trowel in a little too enthusiastically and sent turf flying.

Nell leaps to her feet, throwing back her chair. 'Careful,' she shouts, through the glass.

'What was that?' I say.

'Little tyke,' she says, misunderstanding or choosing to.

She begins to clear away the coffee cups and I help. As I rinse them under the tap, I strain my ears for more sounds, glancing up at the ceiling. They were footsteps. Someone is up there. Nell has started talking again. She asks after my mother and I explain briefly how quickly, after diagnosis, her condition deteriorated.

'And your dog?' she says, with the jaunty enthusiasm I remember from last time. 'Didn't you have a dog?'

A twist of anxiety: I haven't thought about Howard since I got here. Onnie and the key dangling from her finger. I should get back.

'Yes. He's been a great comfort to me,' I say. 'Does that sound stupid? Zach loved him too.'

'Not at all,' she says sympathetically.

I make movements to leave. She takes me to the front door and we hug and she tells me to keep in touch.

'I will,' I say in a cheerful sing-song.

The door closes and I walk a little way down the road before I stop. I lean against the wall of a house and stare at a strip of sea pencilled above the rooftops. Is that it? Am I going to travel meekly back to London? She was hurrying me out of the house, I know she was, and of course there could be a million reasons. But those footsteps: I need to know for sure.

Pidge comes to the door this time – I can tell because of the fumbling and the time it takes to open. 'Oh,' he says, disappointed at the sight of me. 'I thought you were my friend.'

I look past him into the kitchen. Nell is standing in the doorway, staring down the passage at me, and behind her, at the table, is a man.

My heart stops.

'Did you forget something?'

Nell walks towards me, blocking my view, dusting her hands on her dress. Behind her, the man gets to his feet. I wonder if he's going to move out of sight, but he comes as far as the kitchen door. I lean against the wall for support. The light is behind him, and I can't see his face. I hold my breath until I hear his voice.

The words fall like ashes. 'Hello. Sorry to have missed you earlier. I was working upstairs, not feeling too hot, and . . .'

Nell, looking both resentful and abashed, says, 'You remember Pete?'

'Yes,' I reply. My legs seem to be disintegrating. How stupid I've been. 'Nice to see you again.'

Nell is making excuses. She is talking about how Pete had been feeling a bit woozy, how he would have loved to have popped his head round the door to say hello, but he was full of germs and had nodded off. 'Bit woozy'. 'Popped'. 'Nodded'. Nursery terms to cover her discomfort.

'Back up to the old grindstone, actually,' Pete says, stepping quickly behind her to the foot of the stairs. He is much shorter than Zach; his hair isn't chestnut brown, but dirty blond, his face is round, plump-cheeked. It doesn't have Zach's hollows, or tight lines around the mouth. 'So sorry for your loss, Lizzie.'

He can't wait to get away now he's been rumbled. I can just imagine the conversation they had before I came.

'Do I really have to talk to her? Can't I just stay out of sight?'
'Oh, all right. But you owe me.'

God. I don't blame either of them. I wouldn't want to have to make polite conversation with the widow of an old friend. No, not even friend – 'I didn't know him very well really.' The truth of it hits me. Zach wasn't their great mate. He was just someone they used to know and probably didn't even much like. He's not here. He never has been.

Pete disappears up the stairs, taking them two at a time. 'It's fine,' I call weakly after him. 'Don't worry.'

I turn back to Nell. 'I'm glad you came back,' she says. 'I felt awful after you left. It's obvious you didn't know about Charlotte and I clearly put my foot in it.'

'It took me by surprise, that's all.'

'I'm sorry.' She pulls herself together, looking over her shoulder. 'Anyway, did you forget something?'

'Um. Yes. No. But . . .' I flail momentarily and then I realise. Charlotte. I should talk to her. She might know something, or at the very least, understand. 'Yes, actually. I couldn't have Charlotte's phone number, could I? If you've got it. Odd request I know, but it would be helpful.'

Nell screws up her face. 'Sorry. But no,' she says. 'No.'

I begin to back away. 'Of course not. Tactless. I don't know what I was thinking. Insensitive of me. The last thing she would want to do is talk to me.'

Nell is just staring. 'It's not that,' she says.

I'm suddenly cold. Her tone has made me shiver. 'Oh you just haven't *got* the number. It was a long time ago. Why would you?'

Nell is shaking her head. 'You don't understand,' she says. 'I can't.' She lowers her voice and glances over her shoulder. Her words when they come, spoken so softly, are like falling snow, small glances of ice. 'I can't give you Charlotte's number,' she says, shaking her head, 'because she's dead.'

Zach

July 2010

A small wedding. Luckily it's all Lizzie wanted. Wandsworth Town Hall on a Wednesday morning. Her and me and a small collection of her close friends and relations. Sorry, Alfie — you can't be a pageboy (only tricky moment). None of my chums could make it, sadly. (Probably as a result of not being invited.) Lizzie understood. 'You're all I need anyway,' I told her, and she smiled at me in that way that makes my insides clench.

After the ceremony, we partook of champagne and sandwiches at the County Arms, and then, as soon as we could get rid of every-one, we went to bed — Lizzie naked at last in my arms. A delicious consummation, all the more so for being legal. Surprised me, that. The happiest day of my life, I told her. It wasn't a complete lie. In fact, now I think of it, it wasn't a lie at all.

The old woman is at the Beeches now, packed off with her boxes of hideous possessions. I've begun on the house, but only slowly. I've pulled up the horrible carpet and stripped the wallpa-per. The walls I've painted a cool blue-grey called Borrowed Light — the colour of Nell and Pete's walls in Edinburgh. It's a work in progress. I've still got to decorate the bathroom and the kitchen. Lizzie says we have to wait for her next pay cheque, but I persuaded her to buy a new mattress for the bed, pretended the old one was too soft. It was a germ thing really, but I didn't tell her that.

Work is going better than it has for months. I've found a small studio space in an old converted warehouse near the greyhound track in Wimbledon. My room, tucked away on the ground floor, is the size of a shoebox and has no natural light. The rent is cheap, but the landlord reduced it further on condition that I assist the caretaker with the odd repair about the place. Most of the windows in the building need replacing, but he says I can take my time.

I like the darkness. I've rigged up an extra bulb in the ceiling, and I can direct both on to the canvas when I'm painting. I'm in the middle of a series. It's called 'Broken Days'. Is that shit? Now I write it down, I think that's shit.

The studio is full of busybodies, people wanting to poke their noses in – a punky young Slovakian girl who knits at the end of the corridor; a guy about my age who Photoshops hideous horses running through surf; a couple of screen-printers; a sculptress. Lunchtime they congregate in the little kitchen over their Pot Noodles. They all wanted a bit of me when I arrived, but there's a lock on the door and I keep it shut and bolted, even when I'm in. I set my iPod to white noise. Most of the time, no one knows I'm there.

Lizzie can't cook. I'm teaching her how to do it my way, step by step, protein by protein. The state of her fridge made me feel physically sick – all the veg muddled up in the drawers, soiled carrots, out-of-date food. I found a jar of Branston Pickle that must have celebrated the Coronation. She is untidy too, sluttish in that regard. I'm trying hard to teach her.

None of it seems to matter as much as I thought. Sometimes when I'm with her, I close my eyes and feel an approximation of happiness. It's so near I can almost touch it. I feel less restless than I have for years. You could almost call me relaxed. I've cut right down on the medication, only half a pill here and there, when my knees begin to shake.

I never thought I'd end up with someone like Lizzie, but here I am. Is this what being normal feels like? It'll do me, if so. She doesn't bore me: that's the thing. I feel safe with her, and appreciated, a better person for it. She'll never let me down. Ever. 'Me and you (against the world),' I said the other day. I was quoting from that Joe Jackson song. But she held my chin and gazed into my eyes. 'Me and you against the world,' she said.

Summer in the city. Swifts screaming high in a blue sky. Bees stabbing at the open faces of roses. You really can't complain. I'm in a deckchair on the grass, glass of your finest Glengoyne malt at my side. (Damn dog better not knock it over.) Lizzie makes an effort in the garden. I like that. It reminds me of my mother. She was always pottering, too. She's 'planting out' the flowers we bought yesterday at the local nursery. I was expecting tedium, but I was touched by her industry, the way she picked up each plant and studied it before making her selection. She chose candy-pink geraniums to fill the pots, and blooming white bedding plants for the gaps in the borders. I kissed her, among the wallflowers, told her she was the only white bedding plant I needed. We came home and had sex. 'You can't get enough of me, can you?' I told her. She wasn't even offended. 'No, I can't,' she said and lay her soft naked body down on top of mine.

She's plumper than she was, her breasts and hips are fuller, a small roll around her stomach. Married life has brought out the best in her, too. The tension has eased around her mouth, now she's no longer dealing on a daily basis with her mother. I've taught her to say no to her sister, too, not to drop everything the moment the new baby wants bathing or Peggy needs a lie-down. Lizzie's new haircut suits her, if I say so myself. More of a bob, too short for her to chew the ends. 'You could take it up professionally,' she said. 'If ever you wanted a prop— I mean new job.' (I decided not to rise to that.) She's terrible with make-up, even after all the money we shelled out at Bobbi Brown. She's made an effort today – she's wearing that red lipstick I chose. It makes me want to suck it off her.

I yelled across to remind her to wear gloves. She'll be ruining her fingernails. She sat back on her haunches. 'I told you it was a waste of time paying for me to have a manicure,' she said. 'Not that I didn't appreciate it. You're very kind. A very kind man.' She came over to try and kiss me, but I pulled away. I told her I didn't like dirty hands, and she laughed again and said I'd have to wait until she'd finished as there was no point washing them now.

Christ. She's impossible to affront. I know she sees the best in people, but I didn't expect her to see the best in me. Lizzie does me good. See, I've said it. It turns out I only needed to find the right person for everything to be all right.

Oh, I could almost go to sleep, lazing here.

London is doing me the world of good.

Lizzie is doing me the world of good.

If it weren't for the fact that Charlotte keeps phoning, I'd be in pig's heaven.

I suppose I shouldn't have slept with her the night before I moved out, but hey – one for the road.

Chapter Ten

Lizzie

On the train, I stare out of the window, through Hassocks and Burgess Hill, Gatwick Airport, East Croydon, my mind churning. I can't get warm. I keep thinking about that poor girl's parents. A different sort of grief to mine. I can't even touch it.

A terrible accident, Nell said, when I asked. 'No one's fault. Just one of those awful things.' She'd told Zach, she said, that day we had lunch.

'I wonder why he didn't tell me,' I said. 'I don't understand.'

She shrugged: 'I'm not sure it affected him hugely.'

I know she's wrong. He would have been affected. It would have gone deep. I wish I knew the full story. Half of one is more disturbing. I can't put a finger on how I'm feeling. I feel responsible and implicated. I keep thinking how easy it is to *die*.

At Clapham Junction, I take the underpass by mistake. It's a shorter walk if you take the bridge exit, and it's brighter up there. But I'm not thinking straight. I feel as if things are falling off me. I stop in the middle of the dank tunnel, commuters jostling past, to check I've got my wallet and my phone. What else am I supposed to have? Keys. A moment of blind panic before I remember. Onnie. The dog.

I'm in a hurry then to get home.

Leaving the station at the lower exit, between the super-market and the flower stall, I become convinced I'm being followed. Up St John's Hill, past the kebab shop and Admiral Carpets, and left to the South Circular, edging round the big houses at Spencer Park, an electrical current at the back of my neck, a tingling. I look over my shoulder every few paces. On the second turn, a red-headed man in a shiny black puffer stops abruptly and stares through the window of a shop selling modern furniture. Not Zach. Has he set some-one else on my trail? Have I found out more than I should have? I'm shaky from not having eaten. My eyes aren't to be trusted.

I run the last stretch of Trinity Road, over at the pedestrian crossing and down into my turning. Adrenalin is pumping as I ring the bell – an eerie feeling, ringing the bell to your own house. I wait. Silence, no footsteps. I look through the front window – the sitting room is empty. I ring again and then I bang on the door. No answer. The flowerpot: I told her to leave the key there if she went out. I shift the base of it to one side. A wad of root clings to the bottom. Woodlice seethe. No key.

I stand up and peer through the letter box. I can see through into the kitchen. The back door is shut. No dog comes trotting to lick my nose. No welcoming bark. In the distance, above the steady squeal of traffic, the beeping of a vehicle in reverse, a police siren.

I try to stay calm, but my thoughts are racing. What had I been doing, giving my house key to a girl I barely knew? Why on earth did I think I could trust her? I have no judgement, that's the problem. She might have just gone, disappeared, taken off with my keys, my dog. The car key was on the ring too. I scan the street. The Micra is still there in its spot. At least she hasn't taken that.

I walk to the other end of the road and stand on the corner. No footsteps behind. If the man in the shiny puffer was following, he's waiting now, hanging back to see what I'm doing. I listen. The prison is quiet today. An elderly man is reversing out of the prison-warder car park. An official in uniform, key chain hanging from his trouser pocket, is talking on a mobile phone at the gate. Overhead, the clouds are darker, shifting, thickening. Big drops of rain begin to patter.

I turn left so that I am on the road that runs at a perpendicular angle to the gardens of my street. My house is halfway down, but I strain my ears harder here in case I can hear Howard barking, sniffing in the undergrowth. I call his name. Nothing.

I keep going and cross Magdalen Road, on to Lyford Road, past the scout hut where Peggy and I went to Brownies, and the big posh houses belonging to pop stars and TV presenters. I've just crossed the next road when I notice the car following me, driving slowly, clinging to the kerb. I look over my shoulder. A red Ford. It jerks to a halt, and then, as I continue to walk, begins to accelerate. Two figures inside. I pick up my pace and then I start to run.

The pavement is empty. No one in sight. I run as fast as I can, out of breath almost immediately. I reach the small patch of common on this side of the main road, and dart to hide under a tree. There is a dead end, just beyond. I see the red Ka approach. When it reaches the no-entry side, it idles. A man is behind the wheel; an older woman in the passenger seat. He seems to be looking around, but he doesn't spot me. The car pulls out into the middle of the road, and then stalls. It fires to life and then lurches, jumps, eventually completes a three-point turn, and drives off.

A learner, a young lad out practising with his mother. Leaning back against the tree, I let my breath out.

I turn then on to the narrow path that leads through the trees to the main road. It's a little spare handkerchief of common, this bit, an island cast adrift, overgrown, a nest of trees and brambles and litter bins, holes to burrow in, an umbrella of branches. It is quiet, though – only the rustle of small birds in the undergrowth. No sign of anyone.

When I get back to the house this time, I'm convinced Onnie will be there. It's a replay. I will ring on the bell and she will open the door. I'll have to hold on to the door frame in case Howard tries to bowl me over. The kettle will be on. Onnie will have nipped out to get milk. She will be eating toast. (Teenagers eat a lot of toast.) I have time to run a little fantasy through my head – of a meal on a stove, and a warm kitchen, of a welcome, of how it used to be, a year or two ago, when Zach lived here.

Nothing has moved. The flowerpot is still felled. Poor flowerpot. I haven't done any gardening this year. Normally, I would have planted it out with winter pansies, or pink cyclamen. Now it's just dead, spilled earth. The letter box, rusty in its hinges, is stuck open an inch from when I pushed it earlier. No one comes to the door when I knock.

I ring directory enquiries for the Office of Economic Thought and Development. I am put through to a voicemail for Victoria Murphy and I leave a message, explaining who I am, and asking her to call.

I sit on the kerb opposite my house after that, in the semi-shelter of dripping ivy, knees up to my chin, and wait.

Later, I will look back and realise it was only fifty minutes, not even an hour from start to finish. When I do see her, walking down the road, Howard padding along behind on the lead, her expression is blank. She has zipped up her leather jacket and her hair is half tucked in at the back, artfully arranged.

She doesn't seem aware of the rain. I want to shout. I want to punch her.

But I don't.

'Hello there,' I say, standing up. 'Where have you two been?'

Howard pulls free and bounds over, trailing his lead, jumping up and licking my face.

Onnie has stopped in the middle of the road. High spots of pink in her cheeks. Her mascara has smudged, a violet streak blooming high across her cheekbone. 'I came to meet you,' she says. 'I literally walked all the way to Clapham Junction. You said two o'clock. You weren't there. You must have walked straight past me.'

I'm checking Howard over, running my hands over him. Wet. A matted patch on his back where he's rolled in something. A dank smell of pond, a tang of unfamiliar perfume. 'I'm sorry,' I say. 'I came a different way back.'

'Didn't you think I might come and meet you?'

'No,' I say. 'I'm sorry. I didn't think that.' Sometimes the more disturbed kids are rude to me at school – I don't have the authority of a teacher. I think again how Onnie isn't in control of her own tone – too spoilt, or too unloved, or both. She's just echoing how people have spoken to her. I have to force myself to be patient. I feel less understanding and more irritated this afternoon.

I extricate myself from Howard. 'Have you got my keys?'

'Yeah.'

She hands them over and I open the front door. Howard darts from behind my legs into the kitchen. I hear him slurping water from his bowl. Onnie hovers behind me in the doorway. I don't look at her. Throwing my waterproof over the bannister and joining Howard in the kitchen, I decide that I will ask her to leave. I bury my head in a clean tea towel, rubbing my wet hair to give myself time. I do feel sorry for her. She's clearly troubled, but in my current state I don't know how to deal with it. I don't have the resources or the strength. I need to think through what I've discovered today.

'So? Are you pleased?' she says behind me. 'Do you, like, like it?'

'What?' I take my head out of the tea towel. She makes a gesture with her hands, encompassing the room. I look around me. The mess I left behind this morning – the pools of spilled milk, the piles of cereal bowls, the half-finished drawings, the furled-up nappy – has been cleared. The surfaces are scrubbed clean, the draining board empty. Bucket and mop lean against the wall. The air is tight with a sharp chemical smell of antiseptic and lemon. The kitchen table, which was covered in papers, is clear.

'Gosh. How kind,' I say, touched and dismayed, turning to smile at her. 'You've cleaned up.'

She is holding my waterproof across her arm, smoothing it, shaking it out, looking around for a proper place to hang it. 'It was really dirty in here,' she says.

'How lovely . . . I'm quite taken aback.'

Her eyes catch mine and she juts out her chin as if she is trying to narrow the space between us. 'Zach hates mess,' she says. In the light from the back door, the smudge of her mascara looks like a bruise. 'He says you're a slut. He asked me to do it. I did it for him.'

I'm upstairs, on the landing, with my back against the wall. My mouth feels full of chalk; my head thuds. I can hear her below me in the kitchen, cupboards opening and closing. I don't know what she's looking for. I have been thinking of her as a distraction, but now I don't know. Is she the link I've been waiting for?

I can't get her to tell me the truth. I asked her what she meant, but she clammed up. 'When did he say that? What do you mean? What are you talking about? Why are you here?'

She slunk back from me, slipped into a chair as if trying to make herself small. She said she was sorry. 'I shouldn't have said it. I was on my own here. I started imagining things. I'm talking rubbish. I always do. Don't be angry.'

I wanted to push her, to squeeze the truth out of her. She's only a teenager, young for her age – not much more than a schoolgirl, I had to force myself to remember. 'I'm not angry,' I said. 'Just tell me. When did he tell you to clear up the kitchen?'

'Ages ago,' she said.

'What did you "imagine" today?'

'Nothing.'

'But you just said you were imagining things. Did you see him?'

'Who?'

I fixed her with my eyes. 'It's just you said . . . You said you imagined . . .'

'I was on my own for ages,' she mumbled.

She drew her head into her neck and started fiddling with the skin around her fingernails.

I told her I needed a minute and came up here, to pull myself together.

She might have meant nothing by it. It might have been a clumsy attempt to show how well she knew him, to justify having turned up on my doorstep. But 'slut'? He called me that before – the night of the staff party. She used the present tense. I think about the Hunter wellies in the rack at Sand Martin. And her presence outside Gulls, loitering. She'd been watching me. She knows something.

The back door opens and closes. I go into the bathroom and peer out of the window. She is standing down there, in the rain. She's not wearing her jacket. She's found a tennis ball and she's throwing it for Howard. He is barrelling in and out of bushes, scattering earth.

She looks up, her pale face glistening. She's seen me. I push open the window. 'You'll catch your death,' I call.

She doesn't answer, but her body gives a shudder. Oh God, I've made her cry.

'I'll run a bath.'

I close the window and turn on the taps. When the water is nearly at the top, I hear her footsteps on the stairs. I'm kneeling down to adjust the temperature and I try to think of something normal to say. 'There you go,' I say. 'That feels hot enough.' She doesn't answer, but I can hear her taking off her clothes. One plimsoll, muddy and sodden, hits the side of the bath. I can hear her breathing heavily.

'Towels on the back of the door,' I say, standing up. 'I'll be downstairs if you need me.'

Closing the door, I lean against it. Not much more than a child, I think to myself again. I mustn't forget that.

My phone is ringing in the kitchen. I get to it just in time.

'Victoria Murphy,' says the voice on the other end.

I begin to say, 'Hel—' but she interrupts.

'You called? I'm not sure what I can do to help you.' Her voice is strained. It's as though the words are being pushed out from behind closed teeth. I don't think she even remembers who I am.

I remind her – I'm her teenage friend Zach Hopkins' wife, the annoying woman who delayed their lunch. And then I launch into an explanation. Onnie has come to visit me. She's safe now, but she wandered off for a bit; I stupidly panicked and I'm sorry to have disturbed or worried her.

Victoria is silent during my rambling speech and then she asks me to repeat things. Yes, Zach had given Onnie the address and she travelled to London to find me. Yes, she left for an hour or so and came back. 'Can you be clearer: you've lost her or you've got her?' Her manner is similar to that of a science teacher at school, Joyce Poplin – sharp in the playground, but kind in the classroom. Her brain works too fast for niceties.

'I've got her.'

'So she's with you?' she barks. 'Now. In your house?'

I explain that she got wet and is now having a bath to warm up. I'm about to suggest Victoria comes to collect her when she interrupts. Her voice gets louder, more rhythmic – how *inconsiderate* Onnie is, how *hopeless*, how she *throws* their money back in her face, how she *never* listens to a word, the *trouble* they have gone to sort her out, all those fucking schools, she probably hasn't even brought her medication, she is just so *contemptuous* of all the doctors who have tried to help . . .

'She's a sweet girl,' I hear myself say, with a spurt of defiance on behalf of all eighteen-year-old girls who have messed up their exams and are a disappointment to their mothers.

'I need to speak to her,' she says crisply. 'Please put her on.'

The bathroom door is closed and I knock quietly, holding the phone against my shoulder to mask the sound. 'Onnie,' I hiss.

'Come in,' she calls.

The window is wide open. A small squall is blowing through. Rain has pearled on the window sill and lies in puddles on the lino floor. The tree outside seems to lean in.

I'm expecting Onnie to be in a towel by now or even dressed. But her clothes are in a pile on the floor. Zach used to fold his clothes like that. She's still lying in the bath, her thin body distorted beneath the ruffled surface, pale and white. Perhaps it's to keep warm that she's keeping her limbs under the water, her arms close by her side, her hands tucked under her mottled legs.

'Your mother,' I say, holding out the phone.

The water ripples. Onnie shakes her head at me. 'Make her go away.'

'I can't,' I mouth. She stares into my face, scrunching her nose in hostile fury, and then reaches for the receiver. The bath erupts. Drops scatter. I turn away quickly, but not before I have seen the livid red scars on the inside of each wrist.

Zach

September 2010

Term has started and I want her to give up work. It was so perfect in the summer. I liked the way we passed our days. Food. Garden centres. Sex. It's the secret of happiness. Someone should write it down in a self-help book.

She says she loves her job because it allows her to meet so many different people: students, parents, teachers. I don't think that's healthy. I should be enough for her. I'm trying to make that obvious. She goes on about the new kids: how adorable they are in their overlarge uniforms, how proud they are of their diaries and pencil cases. They don't see her as I do. They don't understand. Soon they'll be sneaking into the library to use their phones and stuff their faces with sweets. They know she won't tell. They just use her, take advantage of her kindness.

Yesterday, she told me she was worried about one of the NQTs on the Fast Track programme. She'd found him weeping in the stacks.

'Him?' I said.

'Him. Yes. Angus. He's never taught a class before.'

I said: 'You're not paid enough to be a psychiatrist. In fact, he's probably being paid more than you.' I expected her to flinch, but she just laughed. 'Too true, chum,' she said. 'Lucky I don't do it for the money.'

'"Too true, chum"?' I said. 'Is that really what we say?'

This Angus lurked in my head for the rest of the evening, stewing up there. I started thinking about Polly Milton – her infidelity didn't end well. I had to bite my lip not to warn Lizzie. What did the French call an orgasm in medieval times? *A little death*. In bed, just as she was about to come, I pulled away. I sat on the edge of the bed until I felt her hand on my shoulder. I shrugged it off and retreated to the bathroom. I heard her outside the door softly calling my name, but I ignored her. Jerking myself off, I tried to think of other women – the sexy knitter along the corridor at the studios – but it was Lizzie's face I kept seeing, the way her eyes crinkle shut when she kisses me, her hair frizzing damp against her flushed cheek.

When I came back to bed later, she was asleep.

She didn't wake either. I was the one who tossed and turned, unsatisfied. Charlotte rang in the middle of the night; I'd left my phone on silent. At breakfast, Lizzie was humming behind her newspaper as if nothing had happened. Angus's cissy-boy snivelling, Lizzie's nonchalance: it all rose inside, melding into a seething red three-headed beast. It came into my mind to tell her I was going to go to Gulls for a while – I've hardly been there this summer – and instead of complaining, or crying, she said, 'Good idea.' She didn't even put down her newspaper.

I flicked it with my finger. It crackled. She lowered it just enough to look over the top. I said something about how she could come with me, if she gave up her job, and she said, 'And what would pay the bills?'

'We could sell the house.'

'It doesn't belong to me. It still belongs to my mother. And when she dies, it'll belong to Peggy too.'

I pushed down a twinge of anger. I said: 'We could grow our own food. A simple life. We could have a baby.'

I meant it, too, in that moment.

'We could,' she said. Her eyes lit up. And then she laughed, to cover. 'You said you wanted a new car. I thought we were saving up. You can't buy a soft top with home-grown veg.'

'I could sell a picture.'

She folded the paper and stood up to leave. 'But for now, until we make our millions, why don't you go alone? It will probably do you good.'

We've only been married a couple of months. She shouldn't want to let me out of her sight. I could feel her, treading around me – watchful of my moods. What's happened? Is it Angus who's made her change?

I thought I'd test her. 'Bunk off for a few days,' I said, 'tell them you're sick.'

She was halfway out the door, but again she just smiled. She said something about being late home – she had a meeting after school and she'd go straight from there to visit her mother.

The dog yelped. 'Sorry, Howard,' I said. 'Did I tread on your paw?'

Back she came, checking he was OK. I pretended to be contrite – got down on my knees and gave him a good tummy rub. When I stood up, she wrapped her slender arms around my neck. 'You know I adore you,' she said.

My fingers were tight on the waistband of her jeans. 'I adore you too,' I said.

'I couldn't live without you.'

I buried my face in her hair, pushed the dog away with my knee. My fingers were digging in so tightly I could feel the warmth of her flesh beneath my knuckles, her blood pulse. She would have to tug hard to free herself. 'I couldn't live without you, either.'

I've got as far as the studio. White noise. Bolted door. Tubes of paint lined up in the right order, lids tight. The square of kitchen paper they rest on kept wrinkling, but I changed it for a drier piece and it's straight now. Flat.

One of the electrical sockets isn't parallel to the skirting – an inch out. Shoddy. I'm trying not to look, but I can't stop myself.

The Slovakian knitter heard me come in. Her eyes met mine and she looked surprised. I don't normally show emotion.

I shouldn't have answered the phone. I was angry with Lizzie, scratchy-eyed with exhaustion. My guard was down. Is it insurmountable? Does it ruin everything? Just when it was all going so well. I WAS FUCKING HAPPY.

No. Nothing is insurmountable. It's a question of thinking it through, finding a plan, a strategy.

Charlotte has had a scan. 'You can see its little hands and feet,' she said. 'Are you there? Zach, are you still there? I've been trying to get hold of you. Is it a shock? I'm sorry. A chance in a million. I didn't even realise. Will you come and see me? I've taken the week off work. I know you need your space, but if you want to be part of the baby's life . . .'

Part of the baby's life? Who is she fucking kidding?

I asked if she used my sperm the moment I could get a word in and she said, 'It must have been when we made love that last time.'

Made love: fuck off.

I told her she had to get rid of it, and she started crying. 'It's too late for that. We need to talk. When can you be here?' She thinks I've got a job working for an arts collective in Cardiff ('too good an opportunity to turn down'). I was going to wait for the calls to dry up and then write to her. That would have been the end of it. Job done. I hadn't banked on this.

'Perhaps at the weekend,' I said. 'Rest up.'

Improvisation, I'm good at that. Adapting to circumstances. I just need to use my brain.

Lizzie will be back late tonight. She is visiting her mother after work and then 'nipping in' to bathe Peggy's kids. The fact that the

Slovakian knitter noticed me come in is good after all. At 1 p.m. she'll join the others in the kitchen for their communal Pot Noodle. I'll leave then. The window in the corridor is rotting. I can be there and back without anyone noticing that I've even downed tools.

It was so much easier than I thought it would be. I try not to feel depressed about that.

I don't know what I was thinking. I've seen sense now.

A no-scalpel vasectomy is carried out under local anaesthetic. The doctor feels each vas deferens beneath the skin of your scrotum and holds them in place using a small clamp. A special instrument is then used to make a tiny puncture hole in the skin of the scrotum. A small pair of forceps is used to open up the hole, allowing the surgeon to tie the tubes without the need to cut the skin with a scalpel.

I read about it first on the NHS website. Little bleeding and no stitches. Less painful and less likely to lead to complications than a conventional vasectomy.

Whether Dr Harris performed the operation exactly as they said, I don't know. I had my eyes closed throughout the entire procedure.

I am actually quite squeamish.

Chapter Eleven

Lizzie

Onnie descends the stairs with heavy thumps – more noise than you'd expect a slim person to make. Zach, who was a bulky man, stepped so softly around the house I often wouldn't know he was there. He would creep up on me when I was texting and if I jumped, he would take it as a sign of guilt. I had to show him – 'Look, it's to Peggy, she's asking if I can babysit.' It was all part of the same insecurity. His quietness was a skill, he told me, that he learned growing up. You're less likely to get hit that way.

Onnie's footsteps are belligerent. She is making a point.

'There you are,' I say with determined cheerfulness when she arrives in the kitchen, fully dressed. 'You've washed your hair! You should have called me. There's a trick to the shower attachment. You wouldn't have been able to rinse it.'

'I did rinse it.'

'Really?'

'Yes. You get out of the bath and switch on the tap in the basin to get the pump working through the shower.'

'Oh.' I gaze at her, surprised. 'That was clever of you.'

She shrugs, pulling her wet hair back into a loop at her neck.

'Did you just guess? Or is yours like that at home?'

'I'm not stupid. OK?'

'It's just a peculiar plumbing quirk. I wouldn't have thought . . . You'd expect you'd have to be shown first.'

She raises her eyebrows very slightly and I have to force myself not to interrogate her further. I turn back to the stove. 'I've made some food. A delicious bowl of pasta. Well, I don't know if it's delicious.' I'm talking too much to cover my disquiet. 'But that's what my mother always used to say. Pasta was always "a delicious bowl", just as a walk was always a lovely long walk and a bath was always a nice hot bath. You could never have a horrible warm bath, even if you were in a hurry.'

'Whatever,' she says. Her wrists are covered by her jumper. She gazes down at the floor. 'My mother's coming to get me. I'm supposed to be taking antidepressants. I left them at home.'

I read an article recently about the death of rebellion in young people – how teenagers used to rise up against the status quo (politics, parents), but now that anger has turned inward. It explains the surge in psychological problems: depression, self-harming, suicide. I don't want to think about the scars.

'Maybe food will do you good.'

'I'm not hungry.'

'Well, do your best.'

I plonk the bowls down on the table. It's spaghetti carbonara – a new addition to my limited cooking repertoire. Zach would never have countenanced cream mixed with bacon.

We both pick at it. After a moment, I say, 'Look, I'm sorry if I upset you earlier. It's lovely of you to have cleaned the kitchen. I'm sorry if I was a bit aggressive. But those comments you made about Zach – they put the wind up me. When you said you'd seen him, I thought you meant—' I laugh to indicate my own foolishness, but I watch her carefully nonetheless '—today!'

She glances up at me. 'You mean like a ghost?'

'Maybe.' A sinking feeling. She hasn't seen him. She didn't falter. It didn't even occur to her that I meant it literally.

She bites her lip. 'Everyone thinks I'm mad. It's why I have to see doctors all the time.'

'I'm sure they don't.'

She makes a face like who cares anyway?

'Everyone thinks I'm mad too,' I say. 'It happens to all the best people.'

She studies me for a moment. I can see her thinking hard. 'I shouldn't have said "slut",' she says eventually. 'It might not have been what Zach said anyway. He might have said "sluttish".'

I half smile. 'That's a bit better.'

She looks away, twirling spaghetti around her fork. She doesn't smile.

'I don't want to labour the point,' I say. 'Forgive me for being an annoying old bat, but could you just explain when Zach asked you to clean up the kitchen?'

'He didn't.'

'But you said he did.'

Her eyes have a glazed, hooded look. 'It was ages ago.'

'Here or at Gulls?'

She looks at me and then quickly away. 'Gulls, probably.'

'OK,' I sigh. It begins to make sense. He tutored her, probably she came to the bungalow, maybe he was cross with me – that time I missed my train, perhaps – and ranted to her about how untidy I was. Quite a thing to say to a kid who would have been – what, sixteen? – but he wasn't always in control of his temper.

'Did you spend much time with him?' I ask. 'Those tutoring sessions, I mean. How many of them were there?'

She shrugs. 'Three times. Four? Still didn't get an A.'

'Was he helpful?'

'He said I had an eye and that I should use it.'

I nod. 'Well, he was a hard judge, so I hope you took that as a compliment.'

'I did.' She moves her uneaten bowl of pasta to one side and looks up. Our eyes meet and something passes between us. I see the emotion she's holding back and feel a small connection, a stirring of fellow feeling. She cared about Zach's opinion. She saw the greatness in him. I think that's all it is. I just need to be sure of a few things first.

'Did he tutor you at Sand Martin or at Gulls?'

She answers without pausing. 'At Gulls.'

'It's just . . . when I came for a drink last Sunday, I saw some Hunter wellies on the rack that looked just like Zach's. I'm trying to think how his might have got there.'

A faint flush blooms at the top of her cheeks. She pouts, eyes widened, an almost comic face of incomprehension. 'Why do you think they were his?'

'One of them was mended at the top. I did it myself. You don't know anything about them?'

'No.'

'And when I saw you that morning, hanging around outside Gulls, you were just out for a walk?'

'Yup.'

'And turning up here today . . . ?'

'I just wanted somewhere to stay.'

'OK.'

I push my own bowl away, lean my elbows on the table and rest my face in my hands. It's all riddles with silly answers. I was right. She *is* a distraction. It's all an irrelevance. 'So many questions,' I say lightly. 'So little time.'

She laughs.

'I don't suppose you know anyone down in Cornwall called Xenia, do you?' I add idly.

'Xenia?'

'Another little mystery I'm trying to clear up. At the roadside, where Zach had his accident, someone had left flowers. Lilies. The note said Xenia.'

Onnie stares at me for a moment and then quickly stands up and runs herself a glass of water at the sink. She drinks it down and when she turns, she says, in so polite a tone I can only imagine she's been practising in her head: 'So, would it be an inconvenience if I came to stay, as arranged, next week?'

I start clearing the plates, not looking at her. 'Oh, Onnie. I don't think it's a good idea. The timing is bad for me. Sorry, but I'm going to have to say no.'

'I thought you said I could.'

'I don't think I did.'

She moves out of the way for me so that I can reach the sink. I sense something heavy in her body, reluctant. She pushes away into the room, almost spins back to her chair. 'What if I told you that I knew who Xenia was?' She is breathless, I realise.

'Xenia? You know Xenia?'

'I might do.'

I sit down, too. '*Might?*'

'Yeah. No. I do. I just haven't seen her for a while.'

'Is she one of your friends?'

'Not really. I wish I hadn't said anything now.'

'For God's sake, Onnie. Please.'

I've raised my voice. She stands up. 'I'll need to check with her first.'

'Can you at least tell me who she is?'

The doorbell rings. I stare at Onnie but she looks away. The bell goes again.

Victoria Murphy is standing on the front step in a black jacket and black jeans, a large black leather handbag in the crook of her elbow. 'I don't know what possessed her,' she says. Her tone makes it sound as if it's my fault.

'I'm so sorry,' I say. 'I should never have . . .' What? I can't think what I should never have done. 'Sorry,' I say again.

'Is she inside?' she asks wearily. She peers over my shoulder into the house. Her hair is in a ponytail and she puts both hands back to tighten it. A muscle in her cheek is clenching and unclenching. She is tense, like a tennis player about to serve. Her shoes – trainers with high built-in wedges – make her look as if she is on tiptoe, on the edge of flight.

A dustbin lid flops past on the pavement. Rain spatters the step.

'Would you like to come in?'

'No, thank you,' she says. 'If I could just have my daughter.'

I go back into the kitchen where Onnie is putting on her leather jacket. 'Thanks for supper,' she says.

'You didn't eat anything.'

'I don't really like egg.'

'Nor did Zach. Also it was dry, wasn't it? Sorry about that.'

She looks up from her zip. 'You say sorry a lot.'

'Yes. Zach used to tell me off for doing that.'

'He used to have a go at me for saying "like". He said I used it for punctuation and that it made me sound dim.'

Our eyes meet again. 'He could be harsh,' I say.

'He thought people's words were a reflection of their minds.'

'It's not always the case.'

'Are you coming?' Victoria's voice sounds shrill.

'Onnie,' I say. 'I need to know who Xenia is. Please tell me.'

'I'll ring you.'

I scribble my mobile number on a piece of newspaper and she tucks it in the back pocket of her jeans.

'What the fuck?' Victoria suddenly shouts.

We both leave the room. The front door is open, rain splashing into the hall. Victoria is standing halfway down the garden path.

A red Mini with black arrows down its bonnet is revving in the street, horn blaring. Victoria makes an irritated upward swipe with one arm. 'Get a fucking life.' The man in the Mini rolls down his window and begins to yell, his words swept up in the wind and rain. Victoria has left her 4 x 4 blocking the road.

She doesn't even register my presence. 'Onnie, hurry up,' she shouts and turns on her heel.

It's too late to visit my mother. Now I'm alone, I am both bored and agitated. The street is full of stray howls and rattles, the sense of inanimate objects coming alive, on the move. In the garden, shrubs thrash.

I tell myself to relax, that nothing I do tonight will make any difference.

I go upstairs to the study to fold up the sofa bed which I pulled out for Peggy's children, but I stand in the doorway when I get there. It's already put away. The sofa sits squat and neat, its matching cushions in an orderly line, the sheets and blankets in a tidy pile.

The bookshelves along the main wall look different, too. I take a step into the room. I've been disorganised in here this year. I've just been shoving books back wherever I want, a small relaxing of Zach's ordered code. But the spines have been levelled. When I look closely, I see they have been returned to alphabetical order.

I sit down abruptly on the chair. The desk has been cleared, too – the pens are laid, parallel to each other, down one side, the pieces of paper piled. And in the middle of the surface rests Zach's laptop.

Is this Onnie's work, or was I right? Has he been here? Did she see him? Or hear him? Something alerted her – I know it did.

Why hasn't he taken the laptop if he was here? Did he plug it in to remind me? What does he want me to find on it? I yank it open. The demand for the password blinks. *What do you want from me?* I write.

INCORRECT PASSWORD.

I slam the laptop shut, shove it away from me.

Under the desk is a box of photographs. Zach didn't like being photographed. It made him self-conscious, he said, too many memories of his father knocking him about if he didn't smile. But I caught him a handful of times: on a headland in Cornwall, hair blowing around his face, laughing, reaching for the camera. Another on the common, kneeling down, his arms tight around the dog's neck. My favourite, though, was taken on our wedding day, on the steps of Wandsworth Town Hall. Zach is in that suit he wore the first time we met. He is trying to bend down to rest his head on my shoulder. I am laughing, almost tipped backwards under the weight of him, and he is grinning – his grin so broad and honest, a pure sort of happiness seems to shine from his eyes. It was the happiest day of his life, he told me.

I kneel down and begin searching. If I can find it, it will be proof of something – that he loved me, that we were happy, that the torture he is putting me through has a *reason*.

I tip the contents of the box on to the floor, and sift through them, but the photograph has gone.

Zach

Wrong to relax. People like me can't relax. We may roam outside the boundaries that restrict the behaviour of other people, but we're never free. Occasionally, the people inside reach out and grab at us, squash our faces against the wire.

I was in the bath when I heard Lizzie talking on the phone. Her voice had an eager lilt to it. Angus, I thought, sickened. That cunting NQT. But no – a different problem altogether. Not her mobile. *Mine*. I'd left it on the kitchen table and she'd picked it up. I've been letting her get away with too much.

It was Pete, she told me. He and Nell were about to get a train from Victoria – they'd been up for a party the night before – and, knowing I was in London, were ringing me 'on the off chance'. Lizzie had invited them over. She'd given them the address.

'Here?'

'For lunch,' she said. 'I thought you'd be pleased. It was so sad they couldn't make our wedding. I can't wait to meet them. I said I'd pick them up.'

She was wearing the designer jeans and a slim-fitting Breton T-shirt I bought her, from the new boutique on Northcote Road. She's only had them a few weeks but the jeans were stained at the knees and the top already had holes in it – a rash, a cluster of

173

pinpricks. She followed the direction of my gaze. 'I know,' she said, glancing down. 'I don't know how it happened. Aren't I stupid?'

'Yes,' I said, watching her face. 'Do you know how much time I took choosing that top, working out what would suit you?'

'I'm sorry,' she said.

'Do you know how expensive it was?'

But she didn't crawl away, as I thought. She looked up at me with a defiant jut to her chin. 'Of course I know how expensive it was,' she said. 'I paid for it. If you don't want Pete and Nell coming here to the house, that's fine. I understand. We can go to the Italian instead. But just say it. Don't pick a fight about something else.'

Wrong-footed, I said: 'I don't like my phone being answered. I need—'

'It's fine,' she said firmly. 'I understand. Now pull yourself together and ring them back.'

Weird thing is, as soon we were in the restaurant, I stopped worrying. I seem to be able to get out of any situation if I need to. People have so much less curiosity than you expect. Half the time they can't even be bothered to dredge their own memories. Lizzie cottoned on pretty quickly that I hadn't actually invited them to the wedding. 'Hitched already?' Pete said, slapping me on the back. 'You're a dark horse, mate!' But she gave me a small wink as if it didn't matter.

I could see Nell, a little Roedean snob beneath the hip clothes and the dropped 'h's, looking her up and down. But Lizzie won her over. She can be funny, that's the thing you don't realise when you first meet her. She told good stories about training as a librarian – the employee who had a nervous breakdown and stuffed all the reservation slips down the loo; the secret place in the bowels of one of Wandsworth's libraries where you can only borrow books by 'special permission'. She talked about her mother, and how improved her health is since she's been receiving proper care at the Beeches. 'I have Zach to thank for that,' she said, smiling at me. Ironic really – it was never her mother's well-being I was concerned about – but I'm glad it has made her happy.

174

Nell couldn't keep her curiosity in any longer and said: 'When did you meet?'

'A year—' Lizzie began to say, but I interrupted: 'We were just friends at first, weren't we? It was a long time unravelling.'

Lizzie smiled – she thought I was being doubly gallant, referring to her early modesty and protecting her from the Internet stigma.

Nell said, 'But, Zach, when did you actually leave Brighton?'

'You disappeared, mate!' Pete added.

I apologised and took Lizzie's hand. I told them I'd left in May, which was a lie. It was actually the end of June, but Lizzie thought I had been at Gulls and it covered me for . . . well, whatever else was coming. I said I'd had things on my mind, that I'd . . . I gave them a loaded look, hoping they'd realise not to mention Charlotte.

Nell nodded as if she were relieved, as if I'd cleared something up.

She turned to Lizzie and asked, with a directness some women seem to feel they can deploy on matters of other people's fertility, if we were thinking of starting a family. Interesting moment: Lizzie went bright red. She's desperate now. I've noticed she's buying special ovulation kits. Nell ploughed on, regardless. 'I'm hoping I might be pregnant myself. We timed it right and I've been feeling a low ache, not really period pain, but . . . anyway, I haven't done a test yet.'

Pete caught my eye and we exchanged a blokeish look.

They were trying to behave normally. Beneath the surface I began to sense snakes seething – a shake to Pete's hands, a feverish light in Nell's eyes. They hadn't simply tracked down their old mucker Zach Hopkins to find out what he was up to. They had a purpose. They had a mission.

I found out the moment Lizzie went to the loo ('toilet', she called it; I watched them to see how they reacted; Nell gave a patronising smile).

'We're so sorry,' Nell said. 'I didn't know if you had heard. We wanted to tell you ourselves. I didn't want to say in front of your lovely new wife – she's *sweet* by the way – but . . .'

I just kept repeating 'Dead? Charlotte. Dead?' It seemed better to pretend I didn't know. In fact, Jim had already rung. He was keyed up about the drugs – the diazepam and the Xanax – worried they might be traced to him. Had I left any in the flat?

'I'm sorry, mate.' Pete was looking increasingly uncomfortable.

'How? Was it suicide? I know she was unstable.' (I'd asked Jim the same question. 'Headfuck, that's what it was,' he said.)

'A terrible accident,' Nell replied, enjoying every minute. 'She slipped down those stairs of hers. You know how steep they were. And seagrass carpet is so slippery – I told her, when you were redecorating last year, it's unsafe for stairs. She'd been drinking. The police say she had taken some pills. It wasn't suicide. No note. But they found a lot of balled-up tissues in her flat, as if she'd had a bad cold . . . or been crying.'

I kept saying, 'I can't believe it. I can't believe it. When?'

'Last month, I think,' Nell said. 'I wanted to ring, but we thought it would be better to tell you in person.' Of course she did: the delicious pleasure of passing on bad news.

'Thank you.'

Interesting that they didn't mention her pregnancy. Did they not know?

'When did you last see her?' I added.

'Not for a while.' Nell shook her head. 'I feel bad. She was so upset when you left, and I went out for drinks with her a couple of times after that, but there was only so much I could say and . . .'

You see? No one cares. You're on your own in this life. Nell didn't stand by Charlotte when she needed her. She became a drain and she dropped her like a used tissue.

'I can't believe it,' I said again.

'Can't believe what?'

Lizzie had come back from the loo without us noticing.

I pulled her on to my knee. 'I can't believe how long it's been since I've seen these guys. Mustn't let it happen again.' She put her arms around my neck and rested her chin on the top of my head. Quietly, into my ear, she said: 'What do you think? Are we brave enough to invite them back to our hovel for coffee?'

'I doubt they've got time,' I said loudly.

'Oh—' Lizzie had remembered something. 'Our new walls!' She turned back to the table. 'Borrowed Light. We've painted the downstairs this gorgeous cool grey and apparently we have you to thank for it. Zach said it was the colour of your flat in Edinburgh.'

They creep up, these moments, tie your ankles to a chair, set your pulse racing. How could I have let that detail slip out?

Pete frowned. 'Borrowed Light. That's right. We did. Farrow & Ball. Me and my expensive art-student tastes.' He thought. 'But Zach, you never came to the flat in Edinburgh, did you? I don't think we even knew you back then, not when we were decorating.'

'Must have told me about it, mate,' I said.

'He's such an anorak when it comes to his colours,' Nell informed Lizzie. 'It's the graphic designer in him.'

'It's not snobbery, Nell. It's the quality of the paint, the opacity, I like.'

The moment passed. I got away with it. Just as I got away with my unofficial visit to their apartment in Leith. It was their flatmate I was interested in. What was her name? Margot, was it? I had hardly even registered Nell and Pete at that stage. Strange feeling of power, thinking back. After I broke in, I dipped a wet finger in the breakfast crumbs on the kitchen table, buried my face in their crumpled sheets, inspected Nell's contraceptive cap in the drawer. The tins of paint were in the half-finished hallway. I slapped a bit on the door frame just to see, let it dribble on the floor.

Tombstoning, we used to call it – that feeling when you leaped into the Solent from a high harbour wall. The adrenalin, the rush of air, the surge as you hit the water, the release as you surface: there's nothing else like it. It was the risk that made it worthwhile. Hidden rocks, unexpected shallows – mistime it and you could break your neck.

Chapter Twelve

Lizzie

The storm on Thursday night has battered the garden. I stand and look out on Friday morning at the lawn strewn with broken twigs and stray debris. A branch of the apple tree beyond the shed is hanging half off, like a fractured limb. I should spend the day out there, tidying and nurturing. A year ago that would have been my first instinct. But my instincts have changed, and I turn away from the window and leave it as it is.

I spend the last three days of half-term largely alone. Weekends are hardest when you're a widow. People tend to fill them with families and loved ones. I try not to intrude. I can't help wondering, sitting at the kitchen table on Saturday morning, how different it would have been if Zach and I had had a child together.

I visit my mother and babysit Peggy's kids. I buy food at the supermarket and force myself to eat it. Normal activities. But my brain turns constantly, searching for places to look, ways to draw him out. On Saturday morning, I hover in the hall with the front door open and speak loudly to estate agents based in North Cornwall. It's a depressed market, I am told. Can I wait until spring?

I move to the doorway. 'Not really,' I say. 'I'd like Gulls sold as soon as possible. Perhaps by auction? I'm not that fussed about price.'

A local estate agent visits, on my invitation, to value my mother's house, too. The mortgage I raised to pay for the Beeches was never a long-term solution. The capital is running out. I know all that. Peggy has been giving me time to grieve before a summit meeting on the subject.

I stand in the street with this freshly shaved man in a suit and discuss side returns and square-footage. He takes photographs with his phone.

'Do you need to buy?' he asks.

'No,' I say. 'I'm looking to rent. A short lease. I don't know when I might be moving on.'

At night, I paint my face carefully with blusher and lipstick and slip into his favourite clothes: the tight jeans, the silky top I've mended with a fine thread. I think about the first night I wore them – our sixth-month anniversary. We ate at a restaurant high above the river, on the South Bank, the lights of London twinkling at our feet. We laughed at the poshness of the menu – the food that came in toppled layers, how many of the ingredients listed ('crispy leek', 'blanquette sauce') hardly figured (a fragment! a dribble!). Zach ordered champagne. In the taxi home, my head on his shoulder, feeling his breath in my hair, I was as happy as I'd ever been.

Now I stand on tiptoe at the bedroom window and stare out across the ravaged garden.

I try not to feel anything too clearly; my body has its own ideas. No single person inhabits my skin, no simple emotion sets up home in my head. I swerve almost hourly. At times, I am crippled, bent over with a sense of self-protection. I want to clutch my arms, curl into a ball, close up. At others, I feel like breaking through brickwork, striding out into the world, screaming to the sky, my arms outstretched, my heart exposed.

I veer between dread at something happening, and disappointment that it hasn't.

I can't decide if he wants to love me, or to kill me.

On Sunday, I take the dog for a long walk around Wandsworth Common and through a knot of backstreets all the way to Tooting Common, its wilder sister further south. Both commons are still battered by Thursday night's storm – many of the paths unpassable. It's a good five-mile round trip. We're soaking wet when we get back, footsore. Howard curls up in his basket and I sit at the kitchen table. The room is untidy. Newspapers are piled by the sink. My sewing basket is open on the floor. I left the milk out.

I check my mobile phone.

Onnie hasn't rung.

I fetch my laptop from underneath my bed and open Facebook. I search 'Onnie Murphy'. In her photograph, her mouth is pouting, her hair a blurred curtain – any one of a million teenage girls. Her privacy settings won't let me access her timeline, or her list of friends. My fingers flex. I probably shouldn't do this. I shouldn't be encouraging her. I don't need Onnie in my life. Xenia may well be irrelevant. But I just want to *know*. I press 'Add Friend'.

Friend request sent.

In the corner of my screen, I have one notification. I click on it.

It's from Fred Laws. He has written, *Hello stranger*. And left a number for me to ring.

I lean back in the chair.

Fred Laws. My old boss. Zach's old school friend. It's years since we last met up. It was an easy progression, letting him slip out of my life. I got my job at the school, and he moved to Durham to take up a post in the university library. Zach had no interest in seeing Fred again and I knew he didn't want me to either. He was possessive. Stupidly so. He was threatened by the least likely people. Rob, Peggy's husband, who I know used to refer to me before I got married as 'Peggy's spinster librarian sister' – he only had to compliment me on my new haircut to convince Zach he was trying to get me into bed. 'That slimy bastard, his eyes were all over you,' he said on the way back from their house. I laughed and told him he was silly; it took me a night of kisses to persuade him. Perhaps I should have minded more, made a stand then.

The phone is answered by a very small child. There is a clatter as the small child drops the phone. 'Dada!' the small child pipes. '*Dadaa*.'

Listening to the muffled clumps of his house, I walk into the garden. The wind feels as if it is holding its breath out here, though in the tops of the trees it is going berserk.

'Hello. Sorry about that. Fred Laws.' He was always on the formal side.

'Hello Fred Laws,' I say. My voice doesn't travel as far as I'd hoped it would.

'Lizzie!'

We each ask how the other one is three times while we are dealing with the embarrassment of speaking to each other after all this time, and finally I say, 'You've got a child!' and he tells me, his stammer much less noticeable than it used to be, about Penny and how they met in the library three years ago. She was a postgrad, 'little bit younger', he says, 'not that that matters. All good.' I can just see him poking the air with his finger. Zach's impression made it seem pompous, but I thought it was sweet. I'd forgotten how he made me feel, too: young and hopeful and on the brink of possibility.

'God, it's nice to hear your voice,' I say.

'I was so hoping you'd come to the wedding. We sent you an invitation, but I quite understand why you didn't make it. It's a long way to lug yourself . . .'

An invitation? 'Did you? How brilliant, but I never got it!'

'Buggering Royal Mail. I knew I should have rung to follow it up. Although, actually, didn't I ring? Didn't I leave a message?'

'Gosh, Fred. No.' A rustle in the viburnum. I can make out Howard's dark form chewing on the grass. He raises his head, alert. A flurry of wind begins to build. My arms are suddenly very cold. 'I didn't get it.'

'Bugger.'

'If I had, I would definitely have come. I'm so sad I didn't.'

'Bummer.'

I laugh. I'd forgotten how funny I found it when he swore; it was sort of unexpected. 'You still say bummer and bugger – even though you're a parent?'

'Only very quietly.'

I laugh again. Howard darts into the viburnum to investigate.

'Any kids, Lizzie?' he adds.

'No.' And then, because that sounds too gaping, 'Not at the moment.'

'Dare I ask? Any nice man?'

'Oh Fred . . .' I lean over the garden table, dip my finger in the raindrops that have collected in inky patterns on the metal top, and explain that, yes, I did meet somebody, and I did get married – just a small wedding – but that sadly, there had been a car accident and . . . Fred is trying to say things, 'How sor—' and 'Oh poor Li—' and he wishes he had . . . but I keep talking because I want to get to the end. I shiver a bit. I finish with, 'The thing is, I think you knew him when you were a child.'

'Oh Lizzie. I'm so sorry. I wish I'd known. What was his name?'

'Zach. Zach Hopkins.'

A short pause. 'Jack?'

'Zach.'

'Yes.Yes, yes, yes. Of course, I know who you're talking about.'

I'd been holding my breath, and I let it out in relief. 'Oh, good.'

'He lived in the village. Small place.' I'm waiting for Fred to echo his initial enquiry, to say 'nice man' in a confirming tone, but he doesn't. His voice is strained.

'Tough childhood, I think,' I say. 'His father was impossibly cruel to his mother.'

'Was he?' Fred sounds vague. 'Didn't know him well. Just from being around, you know.'

'This is an odd question, but does the name Xenia ring a bell?'

'Xenia?' He is quiet for a moment. 'I didn't know many of his friends.'

'Are you in touch with anyone else from your school,' I say. 'Who might . . . or who I should tell . . . I don't know.'

'No. No, I don't think so.'

There is something final in his voice, something cold. I shiver. Mottled clouds chase across the sky. I wipe the heel of my palm across the table, scooping the rainwater on to the ground. Then I go back into the house. I tidy up the kitchen while Fred and I put some distance between us and the awkwardness, chat a bit more, agree not to let so much time go by, promise to be in touch, then I hang up.

Later, remorseful and timid, I tidy the house. I put the newspapers into a bag for recycling and close up my sewing basket. I wash the plates and empty out the fridge. I clean it carefully, right into the corners, checking for spilled milk. Zach hates the smell of sour milk – he used to say it infected the' air, seeped into his pores. I replace the carrots in neat piles.

Zach

March 2011

She's back late again tonight. I started drinking early.

Most days I follow her to school. I wait outside – on the common, under the trees. I watch her pulling up the blinds at the library window, taking kids on to the grass at break. I like to know exactly where she is, to keep her face, caught in a half-smile, printed on my memory.

I've got that feeling I used to get with Polly. I think she's lying to me. I still don't trust her relationship with NQT Angus. I've seen her, through the doorway, laughing with him, the silly fucker with his tufts of red hair, his clashing pink cheeks. 'He's just a kid,' she says. She thinks she's cleverer than me, that that will put me off. All those rooms in that school, all those closed doors. I can't stop it – the thought of him pushing her up against the wall, her legs wrapped around his waist. I'll kill him if I catch him. In the mean-time, I stay alert. So far her stories have checked out. She did drive that boy home to Earlsfield yesterday, the one who wears slippers to school, and she did have a meeting in Waterloo with that pretty rep from Puffin. But one slip and she knows I won't be responsible for the consequences. It's a game we play. I think she likes it.

Tonight, she's at Peggy's helping with bedtime. Why would anyone need help with that? Don't you just chuck them in their cots and throw a bottle at them? I stood behind their poncey ornamental bay trees, looked down into their basement kitchen. Peggy was sitting at the kitchen table, flicking through a magazine. Lizzie was reading to the infants on the sofa, an arm around each one. Her expression, eager, loving, when it caught the light almost stopped my breath. What she sees in the grubby little tykes I don't know. As for Peggy, she's really let herself go. Of course I tell her every time I see her she looks gorgeous, 'a real yummy mummy', giving her waist a squeeze (if I can find it).

At the weekend, I went for a drink with Rob at the Nightingale (or 'the Gale' as he so chummily calls it), 'leaving the girls to it'. He's such a creep. He wants Lizzie, I can tell. He's working hard to win me over so I won't notice his roving eye. Monogamy is beyond him. Over a pint of John Smith's, he told me he'd found himself enjoying 'a bit of slap and tickle' at a class party with one of the other school mums. I congratulated him, 'You dirty dog, you', and he preened. Literally. Caught his own eye in the mirror above the bar and smoothed his eyebrows. He has no idea the contempt I hold him in. I'd feel sorry for Peggy if I didn't know she'd married him for his money. Infidelity — it's so naff. People's lack of imagination never fails to amaze me, their crashing mediocrity.

I wonder how to share the news with Lizzie, when to hurl *that* bomb. Of course, she'd be straight on the phone to her sister. They tell each other everything, as Peggy is always saying. It's a power game. Every private joke, every concerned hug, informs me that Lizzie would choose Peggy over me, just as each flirtatious comment, each casual-fingered brush of my body is a covert message — we all know I'd rather be with her if I could. She came first with their mother, has come first with every man since. It would never occur to Peggy that I'd rather stick pins in my eyes than trade Lizzie in. It amuses me to watch. She thinks she's in control. How far from the truth, how very far, that is.

This thing from Rob — it's a useful piece of information. No denying that. A million patronising little cuts; this would salve the tiny stings. It would destroy Peggy. Destroy Lizzie, too, of course. I shall store it up. Use it when I need it. Biding your time, patience: it's what it's about. Light the fuse too quickly and you're too close to appreciate the glory of the firework.

The house is in order – I've just checked. Upstairs and downstairs, all done. Surfaces are clear, sockets aligned. I've alphabetised all her books. A catastrophe a few months ago, when she arranged for the front door to be painted without telling me. Red. It's changed now. She cried with disappointment. 'I give up,' she said. 'I can't do it. You choose. I have crappy taste.'

It's not her taste that's the problem. It's red. I've started a thing about the colour red. It's burning inside me, shifting and setting my nerves on edge. The battle with the kettle is ongoing. She likes it closer to the sink, but the steam crinkles the new paintwork. I move it. She moves it back. It's a joke. I think. She couldn't be that stupid. As long as I win in the end.

She'll be home soon. We wait, the dog and I, his head on my foot. He knows I hate him. It's creepy the affection I instil. He's like a battered hound, his life weighed daily in my hands. I've done some research. Chicken bones seem the simplest solution. A splinter may become lodged in the animal's throat, oesophagus or internal organs. A puncture of the intestine could lead to peritonitis and almost certain death. Otherwise drugs. Drugs, if I can personally spare them, are still an option.

I stroke the back of his neck. She loves him, and – loath as I am to admit it – at the moment that keeps him safe.

I've upped the Xanax, tried cutting it with a small dose of tramadol I bought online. I'm just looking for something to stop my nerves from jangling, my heart from racing. I'm not there yet.

I was first up this morning. I like to get to the post before Lizzie. Today: a thick white envelope, addressed to her. I ripped it open in the bathroom with the door locked. A wedding invitation. Mr Frederick Percival Laws and Miss Penelope Olivia de Beauvoir. Well, well, well. Who'd have thought he'd have found someone to share his bed? I put it in my bag and brought it with me to work. The very stiffness of the card and the self-importance of the raised Perpetua Italics set my teeth on edge. I poured boiling water over it in the studio kitchen and ground out the etched text with a scourer.

Chapter Thirteen

Lizzie

Wandle Academy hoves into view the other side of the railway bridge, a converted candle factory, large and flaxen-bricked and covered in scaffolding (a new sixth-form block is under construction). If the black edifice of Wandsworth Prison embodies villainy and corruption, the school's facade, windows gleaming, seems like a physical manifestation of hope.

Howard and I pick our way towards it on Monday morning, overtaken by a steady stream of kids in Wandle uniform on bikes and scooters. I'm in my own school uniform – boots and tights and a sensible skirt – but it was an effort to get ready in time, a struggle to leave the house. I feel distracted, reluctant to steer my mind back to the trivial necessities of work. I should have phoned in sick. If I hadn't missed so much time over the last year I would have done.

The school doesn't have a formal staffroom – it's part of the ethos of its foundation, no barriers between 'learners and educators' – but there is a small kitchen downstairs, a corridor between the art room and the office, where the teachers tend to congregate. I am slipping past it, hoping to reach the stairs unnoticed, when Jane calls my name.

I pause briefly.

'Quick coffee?' she says.

'I'm not sure . . .'

'Come on.' She pulls me into the kitchen where Sam Welham is leaning against the counter. We greet each other slightly awkwardly and he makes a fuss of Howard. Jane clicks on the kettle and washes out some mugs.

I ask after her weekend – she has been to Salford to visit her in-laws – and she recounts in some detail a film she went to see, a thriller about a corrupt airline pilot that was so good she can't stop thinking about it. Sam stretches, drumming his fingers high up on his chest and says, 'Sounds interesting.' He yawns, or rather half yawns, and then says: 'Do you fancy seeing it sometime?'

Jane is widening her eyes behind his back, silently ordering me to agree. It's just a movie, for God's sake, her eyes say, I'm not asking you to marry him. And yet I'm so full of panic I don't know where to put myself. I can feel my face grow hot. The fridge gives an alarmed rattle.

'I'm not sure,' I mumble. 'I'm not really one for the cinema.'

'Don't worry.' Sam grins. 'Another time.' He is a nice man, I know. With his crumpled face, closely cropped hair and crinkled hazel eyes, there is an overall carelessness to his appearance that makes you think of men in 1970s sitcoms. There is nothing threatening or dangerous about him. If he'd asked me two weeks ago, I might have agreed. But now, the idea is inconceivable.

I have abandoned my coffee and am halfway up the stairs when I meet Sandra, the head teacher, click-clacking in high heels on her way down. 'Lizzie! I was about to email, but as I've seen you . . . Ofsted are sending the inspectors in any day, so—' she gestures to Howard '—keep the dog at home for a week or so, is that OK?'

'Of course.'

Howard is wagging his tail and it has left a mark on the newly painted white wall.

'Today is OK,' she adds over her shoulder on her way down. 'They won't come before tomorrow. They have to give us a day's notice.'

I carry on up the stairs, trying not to feel panicked. I could leave Howard at home, but it's a long day. I know I'm lucky to have been able to bring him at all. It began with the occasional day, but I owe the blanket dispensation to a special needs assistant who noticed what a calming effect Howard had on kids with concentration or sensory-adjustment issues. I rack my brain. I could ask Peggy, I suppose. I'll ring her as soon as I can.

Upstairs, the school feels quiet and clean without the students, though they'll be here any minute, thronging the corridors, shouting across heads, the taller boys jumping up and thwacking the ceiling with their palms as they pretend not to run. I unlock the library door and walk into a dark room – it takes a moment to switch on the lights and flick up the blinds. Out of the window, the common stretches grey and empty – a blanket of churned mud fringed with large trees. I scan the dark hollows, the shadows under the bushes. There is no one there.

A large box of books is waiting by the desk to be stamped, sealed, security-labelled and catalogued. I sit down and gaze at them – work to be done, routine, a sequence of activities I can do with my mind half shut. Howard curls up in his basket in the corner. He has been a bit off colour this weekend, but he'd lie there quietly, even if he wasn't.

I have time to ring Peggy and leave a message before the bell peals and students start arriving. I am swept up in my duties. I open the packages and sort through the new books. I'm in the middle of trying to introduce a pared-down catalogue system.

(The Dewey classification used in most British libraries is complicated, particularly for children who might not have got to grips with decimal places yet.) I sort out the new books and then I work my way through my emails. A mother has complained because I recommended a picture book to her daughter, '*who may be 12 but has a reading age of 16.8*'. It was Patrick Ness's *A Monster Calls*, a novel about illness and grief and loss; Jim Kay's illustrations are a beautiful part of that. She's probably too *young* for it. I begin to write a reply along those lines, but in the end I just say sorry and tell her to send her daughter in to choose something else. It's always the middle-class parents who have issues and they usually just need to be appeased.

My reading group charges in for the lesson before break. We're doing *The Book Thief* by Markus Zusak. Conor isn't wearing socks, I notice, and the pockets of his blazer have come unstitched again. I'll try and get it off him later, take it home and mend it.

At lunchtime it begins to drizzle, a flat, dreary rain that keeps the students under arches and in doorways. A little gang of year sevens, all girls, arrives to see if there is anything they can do to help. Next year, it'll be chewing gum stuck to the backs of books and secret texting in the Social Science section but for now they are willing helpers. Ellie and Grace Samuels, who are part of the gaggle, hover by the desk and Ellie holds out a square parcel wrapped in paper decorated with blue birds. 'From my mum,' she says.

I open it carefully. It's a book, *The Flowering of Your Passing*, with a note paper-clipped to the front: *I saw this and I hoped it might be of some help. With very best wishes, Sue.*

I thank the girls and tell them I'll write a letter to their mother that evening. 'How kind you are,' I say, thinking how often the job of the bereaved is to shore up the self-worth of the comforter.

I flick through the pages when I am alone and realise what a distance I have come since Peggy gave the same book to me last year. Every chapter filled me with rage when I first read it – how could the writer even begin to know how I felt? The very typeface seemed pious.

Now I feel disengaged from its contents, as if it were a travel guide to a country that someone has made up, that doesn't exist, that lives inside their head.

'You've got time to come to the pub, haven't you?'

Jane is waiting at the front door and catches me as I am leaving.

'Not really.' I open the carrier bag and show her. 'I've got Conor Baker's coat to mend.'

'You can do that later,' she says, taking Howard's lead and slipping her arm through mine.

'No. Actually, honestly, I don't have time.'

'You do. I'm sure you do. Come on. Pat's been left by her husband. She needs cheering up. Staff solidarity.'

She looks at me expectantly and when I begin to protest, interrupts. 'And you should have said yes to Sam. Really, Lizzie. It's a year now – you can't hide away for ever.'

I feel something inside shift and harden. She has no idea what I have discovered this week, or what I'm hiding, or *not* hiding, from. I haven't told her about my trip to Brighton, or Onnie's visit. It's wrong of her to set me up with Sam. It's an action from another world.

'Ten minutes,' she says, pulling at me. 'What harm can it do?'

She's my friend. My oldest friend. She loved Zach. I feel a tug of nostalgia for that time, for when things were simple, for when I knew who I was.

'Ten minutes,' I say.

*   *   *

The Bird and Bush, at the end of the road, is another unofficial staffroom – an old-fashioned pub the gentrification of the area has left behind, with wooden chairs and swirly carpets, the treacly smell of cooking oil and spilled beer. A crowd of Wandle teachers is to be found here most evenings, though it's a long time since I've joined them.

Pat, a pint of beer jolting in her hands, is holding court at a large table in the back. She half stands. 'Lizzie,' she yells. 'You think *you* had it bad? At least your husband didn't leave you. At least he didn't run off with a woman half your age.'

'That's true, Pat,' I say. 'At least he didn't do that.'

I sit down unthinkingly in the first empty chair. The person next to me clears his throat, and I turn to see Sam. 'Death or divorce,' he says under his breath. 'Tricky choice. Apparently you got the better deal.'

'So it appears,' I say.

Jane is fetching drinks and I rack my brain for things to say. Now I am here, I must make a fist of it. I remember that he lives the other side of Tooting Common and I mention my walk the day before. We talk with a determined friendliness, neither of us letting a silence settle, about Thursday night's storm. A tree came down in Streatham High Road and all the buses were diverted. Tiles came off the roof of Sam's building, but the new tenant in the building is, luckily, handy with a ladder. My garden, I tell him, is in quite a state.

Jane joins us with a handful of glasses and a bottle of wine and sits down on the other side of me. While Pat is being comforted at the other end of the table, we start comparing half-terms. Jane leans forward to tell Sam and Penny, the English teacher, that I came across their bête noire Alan Murphy, and details are demanded. I tell them about Sand Martin and his creepily soft-shoed 'right-hand man', the pantomime friendliness of Murphy himself. Jane remembers a speech Murphy once gave on the importance in education of the 'three Fs: facts, facts and facts' and everybody splutters in indignation. 'And Victoria Murphy, his wife!' Penny adds. 'Did you see her column in the *Spectator*? She was extolling the sanctity of marriage, unless you happen to be gay, in which case it's an abomination. Children should be brought up in a safe environment with a role model of each sex. She's a fascist.'

'Just because I'm a mature woman with opinions he finds challenging.' Pat's voice cuts across our conversation. 'He can't cope with that, oh no.'

Sam's arm is lying along the back of my chair, and Jane has refilled my glass. I can feel the wine warming my veins, slipping into the knots in my neck. The conversation swims and swells around me. I hear myself laugh; my voice joining theirs. We are at the back of the room, several feet from the window, at the furthest point from the door. The pub is filling up – people are waiting at the bar, standing. You wouldn't be able to see me sitting here, tucked away, unless you were properly looking. You would have to push people aside to find me.

I lower my head. What harm will it do, just to slip out of life for a bit, not to have to think?

My phone rings in my back pocket. It's Peggy. I rock back my chair to hear her. She has been frantic all day and, what a shame, but she can't take Howard tomorrow. She's got friends coming to lunch and is '110 per cent sure' their little girl is allergic to dogs.

'That's fine, don't worry,' I say. 'It doesn't matter at all. Thanks for ringing back.'

'Your selfish sister. You'd think she would be able to put herself out for once.' My chair is tipped and I can hear Zach so loudly it's as if he is crouching next to me. *'After everything you do for her.'* He stood up for me, he always did. He had, *has*, my best

interests at heart. What am I doing, allowing myself to feel relief in his absence, allowing myself to forget that?

I down my drink and grab Howard and my stuff.

I think about Zach waiting outside this pub the last time I came here. 'I thought I'd surprise you,' he said. 'You've been ages. What have you been doing?'

'Just drinking.'

'How much?'

His voice was full of concern, edged with panic. He couldn't bear other people drinking. I knew that. The memory of what it did to his father tortured him.

'Not much. You should have come in. Joined us.'

'I didn't want to ruin your evening.'

I kissed his face. 'You wouldn't have done. Next time we go to the pub, come!'

'Or next time,' he said, when he had kissed me back, 'don't go.'

I say goodbye to everyone at the table. When I kiss Pat, she throws her arms around me, tries to make me stay; I wriggle to disentangle. I'm in a hurry now, desperate to get outside. I have an ache in my stomach, like flu or the first quiver of food poisoning. I've been sitting here as if nothing is happening and the disloyalty is unbearable. He might think I've forgotten, that I don't care.

Outside, it's still raining – that steady flat stream of wetness that seems peculiar to London suburbs. The pub awning drips. Once, on a different night like this, Zach came up behind me on Bolingbroke Grove and forced me against a lamp post. He thrust his hands under my jumper, tore at my bra. I tried to push him away, his fingers twisting my nipples, his mouth biting my neck. But the shock I had felt, the fury, darkened and twisted, plummeted and turned to something else. I kissed him back, yanked my own hands into his hair, felt the rain on my exposed skin.

That's the thing I find hard to admit. I liked his obsession. I thrilled to his need for possession. I willed it on. His jealousy – it made me feel loved and needed.

'Nasty night,' says a voice at my shoulder. 'You're going to get soaked.'

I turn. It's Sam. I feel a flood of fury. He must have followed me out. He lets out a small laugh that has embarrassment built in. I breathe in sharply. He's standing so close, I catch soap and pencil shavings and hops.

'I'll be fine,' I say crisply. 'I don't mind getting wet.'

'Come on. Share my umbrella. Let me help you – you've got a lot of clobber.'

'Yes.'

'What is it? Dry-cleaning?'

'Oh . . .' I'm flustered. 'It's Conor Baker's blazer – needs a mend.'

'Come on. I'm going your way.'

For the second time this evening, someone takes my arm against my wishes. It's not my fault. I am not in control of this. I don't want to be here, but I don't know how to get out of it. I hide my head under his umbrella so that my face is hidden. All these people – Sam, Jane, Pat – they are holding him back. I have the horrible, uncomfortable feeling of having to extricate myself from a situation I didn't engineer in the first place. This is what I'm like, what Zach told me to fight against. I go along with others. I do what they say, not what I want. 'Stand up for yourself,' he used to insist. Is he waiting for me to do that now?

'Poor Pat,' Sam says, stepping out of the way of a puddle. 'She's at the inappropriate-disclosure stage of separation, isn't she?'

'Yes,' I say shortly. 'She is.'

'It's as if she's lost her social and emotional bearings. I remember feeling a bit the same when my wife and I split.

Kept finding myself offloading on people I hardly knew. You feel so raw, it's all you can think about, and you forget that even your close friends aren't that interested in the fine details, not really.'

I ask him, keeping my voice low, if he has been divorced long and he says, 'Four years – actually, five.'

'That's a good sign,' I say. I look over my shoulder. The pavement behind glimmers. No one is following.

'What is?'

'That you can't remember.'

'That's a positive way of looking at it.'

We have reached Bolingbroke Grove. The path crossing the common glistens under its low lights. Streatham, where Sam lives, is in the opposite direction, and I think I will be able to get away from him now, but he has still got hold of my arm, his fingers gripping above my elbow. He pulls me over the road to the common. I tell him he doesn't have to come any further, that it is no distance from here, but he says he will see me 'safely back to civilisation'.

It's dark and blustery. I don't know how long we have been in the pub. I look at my watch. It's eight. Ages. It's hard to tell if it's raining or whether it's water shaken by the wind from the trees. My eyes dart all over the place. On the bare stretch of empty common the football posts stand like sentries. A woman with a black Labrador walks towards us and passes. Two kids on bikes cycle ahead. Sam is filling the silence, trying to make me laugh. He has begun a story about a boy in year seven who sticks his chewing gum behind his ear at the beginning of each lesson 'for laters, sir'. He leaves the shelter of the umbrella to execute an impression of the head teacher's rather queenly walk.

'You're getting wet,' I say.

He rubs his hand across the top of his head. 'One advantage of having very little hair. You dry off quickly, a bit like a duck.'

'Though it's trying to keep her hairdo in position that makes her walk like that, so I'm not sure your impression really does her justice.'

He laughs.

On the other side of the railway, we hit the commuters heading home from the station, a drip-drip feed of men in suits and women in clippety heels. They come in waves, like cars through the traffic lights. I watch each face as it passes. The rain has eased – you have to look into the orange glare of the street lamps to tell it's raining at all.

On the corner of Dorlcote Road, we wait for the lights to change. I let Howard off the lead earlier, but he is still at my side and now he lies down and rests his head on my feet.

'You all right, boy?' Sam says, bending to scratch the back of his neck. 'Not quite himself, is he?'

'No. He must have eaten something that disagreed with him. I'll get him home.'

'Listen.' Sam touches my arm. He leaves his hand there for a moment. 'I'm really sorry if I embarrassed you earlier. Jane put me up to it. I quite understand if you're not really "one for the cinema" . . .'

I look away, wanting to tug my arm free. Zach used to tease me about being a 'world traveller'. If I went to the supermarket the other side of the river, he would say, 'Oh, not further today? Is our world traveller not venturing into Hammersmith?'

'I don't want you to think I'm hassling you. If you fancy going out for a drink sometime, great. But if you don't, well, that's great too. I like you, but I'm not desperate. Well, I am . . .'

I can't help myself. His expression is genuinely funny, both hopeful and self-deprecating, and I laugh.

'Take the brolly.'

'No. I'm fine.'

We tussle for a minute. He doesn't put up much resistance and I manage to leave without it. At the corner of the road, in case I've been rude, I turn round to wave, but he's already gone.

The house is in darkness.

I let myself in and switch on the hall light. A design classic, Zach said when he brought it home. It's shaped like an artichoke and throws hand-shaped patterns against the walls. I put down my bag and pick up the post – a Bose catalogue for Zach.

And then, from upstairs, I hear the toilet flush.

A creak, the bathroom door opening. A square of light on the landing.

Howard barks. Once. Twice. His hackles have risen.

A figure. A person. Their shadow ripples across the bannisters. The body moves, is coming closer. I feel the house crack. The top stair shudders.

I hardly breathe. My head is spinning.

'You're home,' says Onnie.

My vision clears. She is halfway down the stairs now, running her hand along the bannister. 'I didn't think you'd be this late.'

I stare at her. She is in ripped jeans and a long-sleeved T-shirt. Her feet are bare. 'Onnie,' I manage to say. 'How did you get in?'

'I got a copy cut when you lent me the key last week.'

'You got a copy cut of my key?'

'That's all right, isn't it?' She smiles, biting her lip.

'You got a copy cut of my key?' I am so shocked, so disturbed, I can only repeat it. I feel cold inside.

'I thought it might be sensible, just in case.' She is helping me off with my coat, smoothing it over her arms. 'And it turns out it's a good thing I did as you're so late back. I thought you'd be much earlier than this.'

'I didn't know you were coming,' I say, pulling away from her. 'I was waiting for you to ring. We didn't make a plan. And . . . and yes, I do mind about the key. It's not really the sort of thing you should do without asking. It's presumptuous.'

'Is it?' She steps back, flushing. 'Shit, I'm sorry. My mum's always having extra sets of keys cut for builders, and cleaners, and people who come to do the garden. I should have mentioned it last week, but she came to get me and it went out of my mind. You said you'd lost your spare key and I meant to give it to you. I thought I was being helpful.'

'I see.'

She hangs my coat over the bannisters. 'Is that all right, then, or are you still cross?'

I smile weakly and move carefully past her into the kitchen. I put water and food down for Howard, but he sniffs at it and curls up, with a small noise, in his bed. I'm trying to remember the last conversation I had with Onnie about staying here. I'm sure I didn't say she could come, but it's hazy. Maybe I wasn't clear. This is what Zach was always on about. I'm no good at saying what I mean. I let people walk all over me.

'Listen,' I say. 'You can't stay. I'm sorry if I gave you the wrong idea. It's not a good time for me.'

'What?' She is standing next to me now. She is wearing heavy eyeliner, smudged along her lower lids, and it makes the whites of her eyes stand out. They look magnified, or as if they are filling slowly with tears. 'But you said.'

'I don't think I did.'

'You friended me on Facebook!'

'That was—' I break off. 'Sorry.'

201

She wrinkles her nose, makes a hopeless gesture with her hands. 'But I told my mother I was staying here. It's the only reason she let me do the Shelby Pink thing.'

She is looking at her own outstretched palms, and I wonder if she won't meet my eyes because she's lying. It is all too complicated for me. I'd send her packing right now if I didn't want to find out about Xenia. I run my hands through my hair, give myself a mental shake. 'Let's have a cup of tea,' I say. 'Now you're here.'

I turn to put on the kettle. It's not where it should be. It's been moved – away from under the shelf to the socket by the fridge, where Zach used to like it. The sight sets a small chill up my arms. 'You've moved the kettle.'

'No. I haven't.'

'Well, you have.' I point to it.

She slides into a chair at the table. 'Wasn't it there before?'

'No.'

She frowns slightly. 'Well, maybe I did then, without thinking. It's better by the fridge, isn't it?'

'You're the one with the eye,' I say tartly and then regret it. I laugh quickly. 'Unlike me. Zach used to say I put furniture and things in all the wrong places. He said I had no innate sense of style.'

She is sitting with her hands folded in front of her. She seems to be waiting for me to make a decision.

'Did you alphabetise my books the other day?' I say suddenly.

'Yes, I did,' she says, looking up at me. 'Was that all right? Or was that presumptuous too?'

She is sharper than I realised, or more sensitive to slight. Zach was like that. I once told him he was imagining things. He fixated on the phrase. He forgot my apparent transgression – that I'd been flirting with a teacher at school – in face of this affront.

'Am I imagining *this*?' he said, when I turned away from him. 'Am I imagining *these*?' he said, flicking away my tears.

I bite my lip. It must be the kettle that's brought that back. 'No, it was kind of you,' I say.

I make a pot of tea and open the fridge to see what food there is, moving around the kitchen as slowly as I can to give myself time. I find a loaf of bread and some cheese, which I put on a plate, and place both on the table. I pour two cups of tea.

'How old are you?' Onnie says suddenly.

'Forty-one.'

'Are you older than Zach?'

'No.'

'He seemed younger.' I am aware of her eyes moving across my features. 'Did he seem younger to you?'

'No.' I bend to stroke the dog.

'Were you too old to have kids when you met?'

'No,' I say again, and then straighten up. I hope she can't see how red I am. 'Would you like some food?'

'Not really.'

'A girl's got to eat,' I say lightly and sit down opposite her. I don't think she means to be rude. She is tactless and clumsy, but perhaps she's just trying to make conversation. I cut two slices of bread and put one on a plate in front of her. 'So tell me about Shelby Pink.'

She shakes her hair back from her face. 'Loads of people wanted to be an intern. They chose me out of, like, hundreds. It's the only good thing that's happened to me since . . .'

'Since?'

She looks away. 'Since I got kicked out of that stupid Swiss finishing school.'

'That's great.' I push the cheese towards her. 'You should be proud of yourself.'

She ignores it. She hasn't touched her tea. 'Tell that to my parents. I'm like this great big fucking disappointment. They're only interested in Tom, my brother. He's at Oxford. I didn't even get into Cheltenham Ladies' College. And I was never in any teams at school. I was in a play once, but neither of them could be bothered to come and watch.'

Outburst over, she breathes in deeply and then rubs the point between her eyebrows with her forefinger, a small, clumsy gesture like a child rubbing out messy work.

'They're both very busy,' I say. 'With their jobs and everything. It doesn't mean they're not proud of you.'

Onnie rolls her eyes. 'They think I'm dim. It's because I'm dyslexic, that's why I'm rubbish at exams. But I passed my driving test first time, theory and practice. I'm not stupid.'

'And you got picked for this internship!'

She presses her hands together and looks at me pleadingly. 'Can I stay here? Tonight at least? Please?'

I tear off a small piece of bread and stab it with cheese. I eat it. I'm going to have to let her stay; I feel the possibility of anything else diminishing. It's late and raining and I haven't managed to find out anything about Xenia. Also she seems so pathetic, sitting here, so ill-equipped for life, the way she swings from aggressive defiance to a sort of pitiful dependency. I can't just reject her like everybody else has.

'You can stay tonight,' I say.

I think she might jump up, or say hurrah, express delight of some kind. But she considers me quite carefully. 'OK,' she says, nodding. 'That's good.'

I let a beat pass. 'Did you manage to get in touch with Xenia?' I say. 'I wondered if you'd had a chance to ask her if she would talk to me?'

Her eyes slant away. 'No. I will, though.' She raises her chin. 'I've got to track down her number. Tomorrow – is that OK?'

I consider her as carefully as she has been considering me. 'How did she know Zach?'

Onnie stretches. 'From Cornwall.'

'And how do you know her?'

'Just from around.'

'Were they friends? Is she your age, or older?'

'About my age.'

I try and smile. 'Are you going to tell me any more?'

She closes her eyes slowly and then opens them. I think about the heart on Xenia's flowers, the possibility he was having an affair. Onnie cracks her knuckles – one hand and then the other.

'Sorry if I'm making you feel awkward,' I say.

'Were you faithful to Zach?' she says quietly.

I feel something clench and plummet inside. 'Yes. I was.'

'Because you loved him?'

'Yes.' Is this her gauche way of telling me he wasn't?

She tilts her head. 'So who was the guy this evening?'

I stare at her in incomprehension. 'What guy?'

'The guy you were with on the common? I saw you.'

I laugh, shocked. 'Someone from school. We'd all been out for a drink.'

'So he's not your new boyfriend?'

'Sam Welham? No! He's not my new boyfriend! He walked me home. He lives . . . round the corner.'

I stand up and start clearing away the plates. I place mine in the dishwasher and scrape the uneaten contents of hers into the bin. I collect the mugs and tip her cold tea into the sink. My hands are shaking slightly, though – the hints about Xenia and her questions about Sam have set my nerves on edge. I spill a bit of tea on the floor.

I hear Onnie stand up and open the cupboard where the kitchen roll is kept. She unravels one, two sheets and then puts her hands on my shoulders to move me to one side. She bends down to mop up the spillage and then she returns the kitchen roll to the cupboard. 'He wouldn't like you seeing other men.'

'He would want me to be happy,' I say.

She opens the bin and throws in the wet paper towel. The bin is full and she takes a moment to pull out the old bag and twist it shut. She places it by the back door and then she opens the drawer where the spare bags are kept – how capable she seems suddenly and how quickly she's got to know my house – and unfolds another and slots it in. Her face is hidden behind her hair. When she flicks it back, her mouth is a thin line.

'He wouldn't want you to be happy,' she says. 'Not without him. You know that. You know what he's like.'

Zach

May 2011

I am in Cornwall. Lizzie says she'll join me on Friday. She said: 'It will do you good to have some time alone.' What does she mean? I can't get her words out of my head. Why do I need time alone? Does she mean it will do *her* good to be away from me? I keep picking it apart, trying to make sense of it.

She's always going on about Gulls being my place, how great it is I have somewhere on my own to work. How ironic. Finally I find a woman I don't mind bringing down here, and she doesn't want to come.

The weather is warm. A misty haze over the sea. I've been painting in the garage with the door bolted and the venetian blinds folded down. Strips of light trickled in at first, but I bought some masking tape in the village and closed up the cracks. Five small pictures completed. Abstracts. Phthalo Blue. Lamp Black. Zinc White. 'It's a series,' as Lizzie said when I rang. 'You'll have to sell them together.'

Kulon introduced me to an old school friend, John Harvey, who runs a gallery in Bristol. He took my card. He is putting on a big exhibition in September – 'Light on Water' – and he came in to take a look at my work on his way out of the village. We shared a joint and he said if I 'go a bit easier on the black tones, slap on a bit more colour' he'd be seriously interested in what I had to show him. 'More than seriously interested,' he said, which is either sloppy language or a commitment.

I've been down in the Blue Lagoon most evenings. Kulon has been on holiday to Cambodia and has brought back a suitcase full of prescription drugs. 'Chemists are like sweet shops over there.' I won a few tabs of oxycodone off him, playing poker, which he traded for diazepam. He says he can buy Adderall from some American college kids he met in Newquay, which would be good. I can work all night on Adderall. He says I'm looking more relaxed than he's seen me in a long time. 'Married life suits you,' he said.

A girl came in last night, a bit unsteady on her feet, and sat herself down at our table. She said, 'I know you,' and it took a moment to place her. Onnie, Victoria and Murphy's daughter, the sad case from the beach. She's changed a lot over the last year. Then it was spots and black sackcloth. Now it's all flicked eyeliner, intense eyes, white girl's dreadlocks. She looks twenty-five, though she can't be much more than sixteen. I felt sorry for her. She told me she was kicked out of Bedales for cyber bullying and drinking, and Mummy and Daddy have banished her to Cornwall in disgrace. You have to love the hypocrisy. I could tell her a thing or two about Tarty Tory, as the yacht club boys used to call her, what happens to her after a glass or two of cava. Poor little cow. Up there in that isolated house, with just some Middle European au pair as jailor – no wonder she's hitting the wine cellar big time.

She was in no state to walk so I drove her home. I was way over the limit myself, but I put down the soft top and gave myself up to the exhilaration of country lanes at speed. Drive it like an Italian, the dealer said. Throttle and clutch, pieces of hedgerow flying, nasty moment on a tight bend – all part of the fun. Onnie: a familiarisation of Aine, she tells me. Irish, pronounced 'Onya'. The pagan goddess of wealth and summer. For fuck's sake. 'Aine' is allowed back into school to sit her GCSEs, 'which I'll fail so it's basically just a waste of time'.

When we pulled up outside, the au pair was tapping at a laptop in the window, oblivious to the predicament of her charge, drunk in the possession of a stranger. I leaned across her to open her door. 'Aine' didn't budge, carried on sitting there, banging on about her exams with the tedious self-preoccupation of the young ('I'm doing Double Science not Triple which is literally a joke'). The only subject she cared a toss about was art. I told her the harder she worked, the better she'd get. 'That bilge about natural talent,' I said, biting back my own bitterness, 'it's all bullshit.'

'Do you think I'll pass then?' she said. 'My dad says I won't.'

'Course.'

She threw herself across me. Straddled, I think the word is. Nuzzled my neck.

I managed to extricate myself by volunteering to help with her portfolio – it was the only way I could think to get her out of the car.

I stayed up late finishing that sketch of Lizzie, rubbing her eyes out over and over, trying to get them right.

Lizzie rang. She asked if she could come on Saturday instead. Gives her time to babysit for Peggy and to visit her mother. Is that OK?

I left a silence, long enough for her to drown in. 'Are you still there?' she said.

These last few days, I've been waiting to see her, to touch her. I've been counting off the minutes until she's in my arms. A delay makes me want to smash my fist against the wall.

'I'd rather you came sooner,' I managed to say.

'Are you lonely?' she said.

Lonely? With Kulon's company and the Adderall, not to mention the hours with 'Aine'. *In-aine*. It's not loneliness that's the problem, but this low dull feeling that I'm not enough. She's poised to let me down, just like all the others. I thought she was different. I still hope.

I remembered her cycle in the nick of time. 'But it's day eleven,' I said. 'You're at your most fertile. Let's not miss ovulation.'

She sighed, and agreed to come on Friday. 'We're happy, aren't we,' she said. It was more of a question than a statement. I've told her I don't want to muck about with doctors, endless tests, that what will be will be. She's trying to accept it.

'We don't know how happy we could be,' I said, 'unless we try.'

Onnie spent the day here again, just turned up with her little box of paints and her sketchbook. Her project is on 'Force' so I gave her some ideas, told her to concentrate on images of physical strength, brute force, muscles, to make a collage to give an idea of texture. She gave me her mother's phone number, told me she wanted me to ring, to discuss her progress, so I left her to it and took the phone into the garden.

Vic's not happy, I can tell – doesn't want her little darling mixing with the likes of yours truly. 'I'll pay for a couple of hours' tuition,' she said. 'But that's it. Please send her on her way when that's finished. She has other work to be getting on with.'

Onnie wouldn't leave when the two hours were up. I tried to get on with my work, but she kept wandering around the studio, picking things up. 'Can't we go in the house?' she said. 'Can't you show me what it's like inside?'

I told her I couldn't. I was working on the seascape – horizontal line above horizontal line – when I felt her chin on my neck, her small damp lips in the crease, her breasts pressed against my back.

My phone was ringing in my pocket: Victoria checking up on her precious daughter. 'Come on, now,' I said, using my elbows to steer Onnie away. 'I'm a happily married man.'

Unusual restraint. If I say so myself. Lizzie should realise what kind of sacrifices I make.

*　　*　　*

She missed her train. She was held up. Angus? Anyone else I should know about? It's a *joke*. The thought of another man touching her sets up a rhythmic pain in my stomach.

She caught the later train. It arrived just before midnight. I paced until it got there. She ran towards me down the platform, dragging that mutt behind her, and threw her arms around me. I'm learning to conceal my emotions. I kept smiling and talking on the long drive from the station to Gulls. 'Tired, darling?' I said. 'Busy week?' I wanted to put my hands around her neck. *Think of Polly*.

She fell asleep on the last hill, like a child late for bed. I sat for a long time, parked outside the bungalow, gazing at her. Bobbles on her tights on the insides of her knees. A faint down of hair above her upper lip. Her lashes dark below the blue of her lids.

Above us, a barn owl shrieked. From nowhere I remembered some random piece of poetry from school. Onnie's ramblings must have prompted it. My English GCSE. Othello: 'If it were now to die, 'Twere now to be most happy.'

Party up at the big house tomorrow night – 'just drinks', Victoria said, not like the parties she used to throw. Silly In-aine would be all over me. But I won't let Lizzie go.

I want to keep her separate from all that. I won't tell her about Onnie, and I won't tell her about the party. I need to keep her to myself, or everything I've worked so hard for will be spoiled.

Chapter Fourteen

Lizzie

I make up the sofa bed in the study and then tell Onnie I'm tired and am going to have an early night. I sit on the edge of my bed and mend Conor's blazer, poking the needle into the fabric and out again, trying to calm myself. I listen to her move around the house. She spends a long time in the bathroom. I hear the groaning of the pipes, the running of taps, the murmuring of her voice in the kitchen, talking to Howard. There are small creaks and rattles from the study, but finally she is quiet. I can tell from the darkening around my bedroom door that she's switched off the light.

He wouldn't want me to be happy – not without him. She's right. I do know. I learned not to laugh on the phone if he was in earshot. If Peggy talked about our childhood, trips to the seaside or the fairground, he would become silent. I'd change the subject quickly, or divert it – away from the dark-haired boys who spun us on the waltzer to the dodgy hot dog we ate on the way home. Usually it was too late. He would interrogate me when we were alone. 'So it came every year, the steam fair? Always the same boys? Did they fancy you? Did you let them kiss you?' I'd try to joke it off, to soothe him. His own upbringing had been devoid of joy. He was insecure. It was my fault he was like this. I should have made him feel loved and safe. I was failing.

He's not coming back to pick up where we left off. I've got to remember that. He's not going to put what happened behind us. But I need to know what he is planning. I need the waiting to be over.

Out of the window, clouds race and gather.

My mobile phone rings twice in the night – 'private number' – but the caller hangs up when I answer.

It's 8 a.m. when I look at the clock. I was awake until the early hours and then overslept despite myself. I throw back the covers. It's quiet in the house. I wonder if Onnie has got up and slipped out without waking me, but the study is in darkness, and the sofa bed has a person on it. I cross the room to shake her, tripping over a pile of her clothes. She grunts, waves her arm ineffectually. 'Go away,' she says.

I pull open the blinds and a dull light creeps into the room. An empty mug is resting on the desk, and next to it Zach's laptop is open.

I tap the keyboard. The screen brightens – Stepper Point and the request for a password. She hasn't stirred again. She is turned towards me, but her eyes are shut. My fingers tap lightly, skating across the keys. I try two things in quick succession.

SAND MARTIN.

ONNIE.

INCORRECT PASSWORD.

Onnie moves, yawns. I snap the laptop shut.

'Time to get up,' I say, retrieving the mug.

'I'm not going in,' she says, half asleep. 'You can't make me.'

I laugh. 'It's not school. It's Shelby Pink! Come on. Up you get.'

I leave her and get dressed. I haven't time for breakfast, but I make a quick cup of tea and let the dog out while it's brewing. He sways into the garden, cocks his leg against a pot by the door and comes back in. He bumps clumsily into the table before collapsing into his bed. His food is still uneaten.

I kneel down and stroke him. Poor old boy. I haven't been paying attention. I've been too distracted. I lift his head and study his eyes. It's the same symptoms as before – listlessness, a wobbly gait, loss of appetite. Last time, blood tests came up clear. I tell myself it's nothing this time, too. As the vet says, dogs are the worst hypochondriacs. But still, I start making calculations. I'll make an appointment as soon as I can.

Onnie walks into the kitchen in knickers and the same long-sleeved T-shirt as last night. Her hair is unbrushed, her face creased.

'Not dressed?' I say.

She lays her phone on the table. 'I don't think I'll go in today,' she says.

'What? I thought you were loving it?'

'It was all right.'

'But you told me what an opportunity it was, that they'd turned down all those other people.'

'It's just, like, really awkward. No one even talks to me.'

'I know.' I stand up and smile with as much sympathy as I can muster. 'I remember being new. You feel so self-conscious, don't you? You don't know where anything is and you have to ask about everything. You feel like everyone's looking at you and you try and look busy even when you're not. You start rearranging things on your desk.'

'I didn't even know what I was supposed to be doing.' She puts her hands out. 'I had to, like, ring all these suppliers to find a lace swatch to match some Pantone reference. For a paillette or something. I didn't even know what I was asking for. I had to write it down and just read it out.'

I laugh.

'Plus I'm not being paid.'

'It's experience.' I start putting on my coat, then check my bag for my wallet and keys. 'Work can be boring, unless you're lucky and happen to do what you love, and even then you're answerable to other people.'

'Unless you're self-employed like Zach. He wasn't answerable to anyone. He was free.'

'Yes, but he also didn't earn any money.'

'Does that matter?'

'It does if you want to live in the real world. He had all these big ideas about being self-sufficient. But it's one thing to talk about it, another to put it into practice. All I am saying is, if you have the opportunity, the *privilege*, of getting experience, then you shouldn't let it pass you by.'

She rubs the back of one hand with the tips of her fingers, concentrating as if it were important, ignoring me.

'Anyway,' I say, half out of the room, 'I've got to go to work now, or I'll be late.' I run upstairs for Conor's mended blazer, and then back down. She hasn't moved from the kitchen. I want her to leave the house at the same time as me, but that doesn't seem likely. 'Could you lock the front door when you go and stick the key through the letter box? And Onnie?'

She looks up from her hand.

'Please ring me when you've spoken to Xenia.'

'OK.'

I am halfway along the passage when I hear her say: 'I might just walk out of here, disappear and never come back. No one will notice.'

I hesitate. Irritation runs through me. I'm tempted to call, 'Go on then, Onnie, I dare you.' But I don't. I lay my bag and Conor's blazer down in a heap in the hall and walk back into the room. Her head is bowed. She is kicking the legs of the table rhythmically with her feet – a toddler in teenage form. I crouch down and put my arms around her from the side. 'Don't be silly. Think how upset your parents would be, and all your friends, if they didn't know where you'd gone.'

'I haven't got any friends.' She tries to pull away from me. 'They wouldn't even notice. I told you, no one at home cares what I do.'

'I'm sure they do,' I say, as kindly as I can manage. 'I'm sure they worry about you.'

She laughs bitterly. 'Has anyone rung me while I've been here?' She picks up her phone and then throws it down again. 'They don't care about me.' She turns her face towards me, her eyes small, her mouth twisted with misery. 'All they worry about is that I might embarrass them during a photo opportunity. That's the only time my dad ever wants anything to do with me, when the press are around.'

I say, 'I'm sure that's not true.'

'How do you know? You don't know anything about me. You don't even want me here, and why should you? I don't blame you for hating me.'

'I don't hate you. Why on earth would I hate you? You're being silly now. Come on.' I rub her shoulder and smooth her hair, picking a small feather out of it. 'There we go.'

'Why are you being nice to me?'

'I'm not. I'm just . . . I think—' I bend so I can see her face '—that you should pull yourself together and go to Shelby Pink. You'll feel better today, more confident.'

'I can't.' She rubs her eyes. 'I've got myself too upset now.'

I feel a seeping boredom. 'Go home then, watch TV, see a friend.'

The dog in his basket gives a small shudder. I reach back and stroke his nose. It feels dry. 'You're not feeling great either,' I say under my breath. I stand up. 'Onnie, I'm really sorry, but I've got to go. I'm going to be late. I've got a lot to do today and I'll have to take the dog to the vet at lunchtime so . . .' I make a cheerful face. 'So, I'll see you.'

'I know!' she says.

I'm at the door. 'What?'

'I'll look after Howard today. I'll keep an eye on him. I'll take him to the vet for you, if you like.'

'No, honestly. It's fine.'

Howard is lying in a strange position, head down, his sides moving fast. I look from him to Onnie. She's stopped crying. 'Go on. Let me,' she says eagerly. 'I'll go to Shelby Pink once he's better. But let me look after him.'

'He's only eaten something dodgy,' I say. 'That's all it is.'

'But what if he hasn't? What if it's more serious than that? Leave me the vet's number. I'll sort it.'

I don't know if it's because I'm worried about Howard or sorry for Onnie, but against my better judgement, I hear myself agree.

Something has happened at school. I can tell the moment I walk in. The head's door is closed and Michele, the school secretary, who's talking to a young man in the foyer, doesn't smile at me when I walk past. Hushed voices in the kitchen. Jane and Pat are hovering by the fridge. Pat's holding her hand over her mouth. Jane's eyes look red and swollen.

'Have you heard?' Jane says, seeing me.

'No. What?'

'Sam.'

A twinge of unease. 'What about Sam?'

Pat leans forward. 'He's in hospital. He's had an accident.'

'What kind of accident?'

'He's been mugged,' Jane says. 'Badly. Head injury. He's unconscious.'

217

'He's at St George's,' Pat adds. 'His ex-wife is with him and rang to tell Sandra last night.'

'Is it serious?'

'Yes, I think it is.' Jane nods, and then nods again, as if to calm herself. 'He hadn't gained consciousness when Michele rang this morning.'

Something dark pulses in my chest. 'When?'

'Shortly after he left the pub,' Pat says. 'He was found just after nine by some teenagers on the common, the other side of the bridge, near the pond. He told us he was going straight home when he left us, but—'

'He walked me home,' I say. 'He had an umbrella. It was raining. I told him I was fine.'

Jane is staring at me.

'You should tell the police,' Pat says. 'It's possible you were the last person to see him.'

Zach

June 2011

She swam this evening, down in that cove that only appears at low tide.

We'd been walking back along the cliff from Daymer Bay and bumped into Victoria and Murphy coming the other way. I panicked for a moment in case they mentioned Onnie's 'sessions'. I needn't have worried. Victoria, who even as a teenager used to refer to people as 'common' and call tourists 'grockles', was too busy looking down her nose at Lizzie to expand the conversation beyond casual niceties. 'Sorry you couldn't come the other night,' she said.

'We had a laugh,' Murphy agreed, though he pronounced it 'laff' because he thinks he's one of the lads.

'Nice people,' Lizzie said when they'd gone, and then, as if to release the tension their company had induced, dragged me along the path to the sea.

The air was quiet down there, tucked out of the wind, and she threw off her clothes and ran, squealing, into the gathering foam. Trails of seaweed clung to her thighs. She dipped, like a porpoise, into the water and came up spluttering. Her white skin, pale limbs, the flash of her wet hair. How ordinary she is, I thought, how plain, and yet she holds my heart in her hand. I realised if she ever slept with someone else, I would kill her.

And him.

Chapter Fifteen

Lizzie

I am up in the library, staring out of the side window across the grey streak of common and the red rooftops of South London. I press my forehead against the cold glass. The conviction is back, unfurling inside, spreading out its fingers – the clenching of dread and fear, and something else, lower down, a stirring so shaming I want to crush my head against the glass, bite my lip until it bleeds.

I am luring him into the open, forcing him to action. It's working, even if it's at Sam's expense.

I hear Hannah Morrow's voice in the corridor. 'Goodness me, those stairs,' she is saying. 'You wouldn't need a gym membership if you worked here.'

'Murders your knees,' Michele replies.

Hannah strolls straight into the room. She's in her uniform today – dog-tooth tie, chevroned hat, walkie-talkie under her chin. It's only when the students stand up and begin to file out that I see someone else is with her, a tall, dour man in jeans and a grubby waxed jacket. DI Perivale, her boss. He's leaning against the far wall of the corridor, his arms folded. When he walks in, he nods but doesn't sit down. Instead, he stands by Fiction, A–H, pretending to study the shelves, his head to one side, cupping his chin with his hand, stroking it back and forth as if deep in thought.

Michele asks if they want a tea or coffee or a glass of water and Hannah, whose new bob is pulled back into a tiny pony-tail with the aid of a blue fabric scrunchie and several kirby grips, says, 'Oh go on then. Cup of coffee. Lovely.'

Perivale, his back still turned, doesn't say anything and Michele waits, grimacing – she's forgotten his name and doesn't know how to get his attention – before scurrying out.

Hannah came up here once before, the morning after my break-in, but she hovers by the window and makes small talk about the view. 'Is that Crystal Place? God, you'd think it was the Eiffel Tower.' Her chatter is more bullish today, as if she needs to prove Perivale's presence is not intimidating. We're waiting for Michele to come back, to be clear of interruption, but I want to get on with it. Zach needs to be stopped before he does anything else. Before I do, or think, or feel anything else.

Michele pushes the door open with the tray and I pile up books to make room on the desk for her to put it down. 'Biscuits,' she says.

Hannah sits down at the desk and helps herself. 'Ooh, rude not to,' she says.

Perivale closes the door quietly behind Michele and joins us at my desk, spinning the free chair round and sitting on it backwards, resting his chin on the bar. It's the gesture, I think, of someone who likes to be in control, or who is so bored he will do anything to shake up his environment. The hems of his trousers are coming undone. The heels of his brown leather shoes, which he is tapping, are worn on one side.

'Right then,' he says on a sigh. It's a routine visit. He wants to get this over with. He runs his hands through his lank locks. 'PC Morrow says you were the last to see Sam Welham yesterday evening.'

I explain what happened. He writes notes. He has unkempt eyebrows, a tiny flicker of dandruff in his hair. I try to be as factual as I can. I run through the relevant details, the weather, the flow of commuters from the train station, the few minutes we spent on the corner of Dorlcote Road. 'We talked about my dog, who's ill,' I say. 'We argued over the umbrella. He wanted me to take it.'

'And did you?' Hannah asks.

'No. It was his. I told him he needed it more than I did. I was nearly home.'

Perivale scans the pages of his notebook, listing his questions in a mechanical monotone. 'Did you see anyone at any stage? Was anyone behaving suspiciously? Did anyone appear to be following?'

'Only the commuters. No one stood out.'

'And did Mr Welham say where he was going after he left you?'

'Home, I assumed.'

'Was he carrying anything valuable as far as you are aware?'

'No. His phone. His wallet, I suppose. Is that what they took? The muggers?'

'No,' he says. 'They didn't take his phone or his wallet. It appears, unless we're missing something, to have been a random act of violence.'

'Random?' I say.

Perivale doesn't look as if he is going to answer for a moment. He narrows his eyes and then says, almost conversationally, 'Did you know Mr Welham well?'

'No. No, not really,' I stammer. 'He only started this year.'

Perivale grips the back of the chair, his elbows jutting out at an angle, like a driver bracing himself at the wheel. 'Do you know of any reason why anyone might want to do him harm?'

I glance across at Hannah. I wish she had come alone. This is my moment. This is when I could be telling her everything. My heart begins to race. I look back at Perivale, so sure of himself, so brusque.

'No,' I say falteringly.

'OK, then.' He stands up, swirls the chair quickly in the air and replaces it on the ground. 'I think we're done,' he says to Morrow.

She too stands up, brushing biscuit crumbs from the corners of her mouth. Perivale, arms at his side, heels together, gives me another nod, more formal this time, like a courtier taking his leave, and strides out of the room. He stands in the passage, talking loudly into his mobile.

One more chance. I haven't got much time. If I tell her now, she can catch Zach before he does anything else.

'He's a funny one,' Morrow says quietly. 'I'd love to meet his wife some day, find out how she puts up with it. Anyway,' she adds, 'you all right?'

'Actually. No. I'm not,' I say. I'm breathless, my voice is tight. I am close to tears. Saying this out loud is almost unbearable. 'I need to talk to you about Zach. I think Zach is responsible. I . . .'

An expression fleets across her face. It's gone as quickly as it came, but I caught it. It wasn't concern, her usual expression, but boredom, tempered by slight irritation.

Perivale is still talking on his phone. I hear a door shut loudly – Joyce Poplin in the lesson opposite expressing her disapproval. Any minute the bell for the next lesson will go.

'Responsible for what?' Morrow asks, her freckled nose wrinkled in sympathy now, her head tilted.

I let a beat pass. My hands are clenched, out of view, in my pockets. 'I found out that his last girlfriend died,' I say. 'Shortly after they split up. She was in an accident.'

223

'What kind of accident?'

'I don't know. I wish I did.'

'What was her name?' She sits back down at the edge of the desk.

'Reid. Charlotte Reid. She lived in Brighton.'

'Right. PC Morrow.' Perivale looms in the doorway. 'If I could *drag* you away, we're needed at the hospital.'

'What is it? What's happened?'

Perivale darts me a look, heavy with impatience. Ignoring me, he says to Morrow, 'Sometime today, this week. Unless you have other plans?'

'All yours,' she says, getting to her feet. 'Developments?'

'That was the doctor. We can take a statement.'

It takes a moment for his words to sink in.

'He's conscious?' I ask.

'Apparently so,' Perivale says.

Relief makes my legs feel weak. I sit down on my chair. Better to say nothing. It needs to play out, this game. It's the only way.

Perivale is looking at me. He rubs his cheeks with one hand, thumb and finger splayed. 'KISS,' he says suddenly.

'What?'

'KISS. K: Keep your bag and mobile close. I: If you suspect you are being followed, cross the road once, then again, and if your suspicions are confirmed, enter a public place. S: Stick to busy, well-lit streets. Final S: Shout "fire" not "help" if accosted. It's more effective.'

'Oh. Thank you.'

'Just in case you're thinking of wandering around any other dark commons any time soon.'

'I'll bear the advice in mind. Thanks.'

Morrow has joined him and they walk together towards the stairs.

Zach

August 2011

What a tosser. Waste of space. All that effort for nothing.

It wasn't even a gallery so much as a poster shop, tucked down a side street in Bristol, between a shoe shop and a patisserie. John Harvey, Kulon's friend, had forgotten we'd even made an appointment. He flicked through the canvases slowly, massaging his chin, nodding wisely. Interesting, brave, original, he said. 'I can see you have a lot to say, but . . .'

There's always a 'but' with people like him. No imagination. Can't take the leap. Not the sort of thing his customers are looking for, he said. Too much darkness. He'd love to take a punt, 'but . . .' If he had the cash himself, 'but . . .' But. But. But. But.

I stood in silence, watching him as he wriggled. A spider on a pin. Narrow-hipped, slight build, wispy beard. Jeans and Jesus sandals. I weighed it all up. He couldn't even afford me. He'd been mucking about from the start, keeping in with Kulon. My fist impacted with his jaw; it had happened before I could do anything about it. He lay on the floor, clutching his mouth, blood spilling through his fingers. I bent down. 'If,' I said in his ear. 'If I ever see your face again, I'll hit you so hard you'll know the meaning of "too much darkness".'

I drove straight back to London. All I wanted was Lizzie, to see her, to hold her, but the house was empty. Just the dog – I kicked him until he whimpered and hid under the table. Then I rang her over and over, ten times in total, until she answered. She was in school, she said, she'd told me, didn't I remember? She'd gone in to help a group of sixth-formers who wanted to defer their university applications. I drove straight round there. The door to the school was locked and I banged and banged – but no one answered. In the end, I sat on the pavement to wait.

When she finally clipped down the steps in her sensible shoes and saw me, she flushed red to her roots. She covered it well, I'll give her that. She ran over and put her little arms around me, kissed my bruised hand. (I told her I'd caught it in the car door.) I explained what had happened – the first part anyway – and she said I shouldn't blame myself, that I was brilliant, 'exceptionally talented', the guy was a philistine. She stroked me with words. She wasn't clever enough to hide what she really thought. I could see it in her eyes.

It's more than I can stand, the disappointment, the leaching of faith. She was supposed to save me. She's the one I chose. She's everything to me. Yet she wasn't even in the house when I got home. She couldn't let her students down, but she lets me down over and over again. She needs to learn how much she needs me. It's the only way forward. I am the one. She'll know it in the end. I just have to work out how to prove it.

I shouldn't have given Onnie my address. It was a weak moment. Still, even if I hadn't, the dirty minx would have tracked me down.

Two things played into her hands. 1) Lizzie was out for the morning – some health crisis with her mother – and 2) I was in when she knocked. I haven't been able to work this week, not since my trip to Bristol. In fact, I've thrown away a load of paintings – dumped most of them in a wheelie bin around the back of the greyhound stadium. I was just hanging around the house, avoiding the dog, and there she was at the door. She was crying, too snotty to speak for a while.

'Results,' she managed to sob out eventually. Took a moment to work out what she meant. Her exams. The GCSEs. Three Es, two Ds, a C, and a B. 'Which one was art?' I said.

She wiped her nose on my shoulder. By this stage, she had wrapped herself all over me.

'The C,' she said. 'Sorry. The B was for Religious Studies. God knows how I got that.'

I pushed her off. 'Perhaps you could train to be a vicar.' Honestly. Fuck, I worked hard for that exam. All that work I put into her sketchbook. All the thought I put into 'Force'. *C*. What does that say about my talent?

She begged to come in. I was sick to the back teeth of my own company, and God knows when Lizzie would deign to return, so I made a sweeping gesture with my arm. 'Enter,' I said.

I made her a coffee in the kitchen. It was clean – I had cleared away Lizzie's mess. I told Onnie how untidy my wife was – 'She's actually quite slutty. It's the cross I bear.'

'I hate mess,' she said.

'Yeah, me too.'

The dog was sniffing about and I pushed him into the garden and shut the door on him. 'Filthy animal,' I said, under my breath.

'I hate dogs,' Onnie said.

'Yeah, me too.'

'I don't get what people see in them.'

'Me neither.'

We both laughed.

My phone rang – Lizzie. She'd taken her mother to hospital. They were still in A & E, waiting for tests. She had no idea what time she'd be back. It's just one betrayal after another. If she'd picked up on my tone, had the sensitivity to know when I needed her and come straight home, then everything would have been all right. 'Will you be OK?' she said. 'Will you make yourself something to eat?' All week she has been talking to me as if I were a child. I don't need her pity.

So – if I succumbed to Onnie, mea culpa. She was gagging for it; girls her age always are. I only had to look at her – that lingering glance, that skew of the lips – and she was peeling off her clothes, opening herself like a present. We did the deed there, on the floor in the sitting room, and later upstairs, in the marital bed. Fresh skin, new breasts. Brazilianed. Up close, she has spots around her nose. Her hair, dyed, feels coarse. Passive, too, on her back, waiting for me to show her what to do: so young of course.

Did it make me feel better? This small victory? I thought about Lizzie the whole time, imagined her face, the soft feel of her limbs. So, no, it didn't. I felt sickened with myself, with the fear of what she had made me do. That's the thing about revenge. People get it wrong. It isn't always sweet.

Chapter Sixteen

Lizzie

I open the front door to silence and the smell of furniture polish. Tiny motes of dust twirl in the hall light. No music, no TV. No click-clack of Howard's nails.

He raises his head when he sees me enter the kitchen but doesn't get up.

I crouch on the floor and feel him all over. When I spoke to Onnie at lunchtime she told me he was better. She'd walked him to the vet and they could find nothing wrong – 'Something he'd eaten probably, you were right.' But now he's breathing fast and his eyes look milky. He lifts his front paw, suspends it in the air, so I can rub his stomach. 'Poor old chap,' I say. 'Are you not feeling yourself?' The whiskers of hair below his mouth are tinged with white. He is what – nine, ten? It's no age. 'Is it?' I say. 'No age.' He puts his head down on the edge of the basket. 'We'll make you better,' I say, stroking along the side of his head. 'Won't we?'

'What would you do without your dog?'

Onnie is standing above me. Her voice is flat, and odd.

'God, you gave me a shock,' I say.

'I was in the front room. I dozed off. I heard you talking.'

She's wearing a jumper above bare legs and she pulls the sleeves down over her hands, rubbing her face with the wool

229

at her shoulder. It's pale blue, baby soft, and bears the small embroidered symbol of a pheasant.

'You're wearing Zach's jumper,' I say.

If you hold it to your face, it still smells of Acqua di Parma Intensa. Close your eyes and you can imagine the warmth of his skin. I can smell him now.

'Do you mind?' she says, in a little girl's voice. 'I hope you don't. I was cold.'

I want to snatch it off her, wrestle it over her head. 'Of course, that's fine,' I say, hoping to sound bright. 'I'm sorry. The heating is timed to come on twice a day. It must have been freezing. Poor you.'

'I turned the heating to constant,' she says.

'Oh. You found the timer then?'

'Yes – in your wardrobe.'

I take a moment to register this – the control panel is concealed at the back of a shelf, behind some clothes. She would have had to search the house to find it. I turn my attention again to Howard. 'Did the vet really say he was OK? He doesn't seem it now.'

'God . . . he's fine. The vet said it was nothing. We went for a literally massive walk when we got back. I think he's just tired.'

'Which vet did you see?'

She shrugs. 'I didn't catch their name.'

'The man or the woman?'

'The man.'

I study her carefully, and then look down again at Howard. 'And they really didn't want my credit card number?'

'No. I told you. We were in and out in seconds.'

'OK. Thank you.' I look at Howard again. He is licking a patch of skin on his side, the same patch, worrying at it. She's lying, I'm almost sure. I could confront her, but if she *is* telling

230

the truth and I'm over-reacting, then I am the one who will seem unhinged. I have to check first. I'll ring the vet without her knowing. I stand up and stretch to give myself time.

Onnie doesn't seem to have noticed that anything is up. She is sitting on the counter, swinging her bare legs. 'People are funny about pets. I don't get it,' she says conversationally. 'A man died in Cornwall last November. He went into the river to rescue his dog. The dog lived, the man drowned.'

'It happens a lot. I'd probably do the same. Climb down a cliff, jump into a river. At the time, I don't expect you give yourself time to think.'

'Pity you don't have a baby,' she says. Zach's jumper is stretched over her knees. 'You'd make a good mum. It's a shame, isn't it, that you won't be one?'

I turn away – try to rise above the casual callousness, put my hand out for the kettle. The kettle isn't where it's supposed to be. She's moved it again, back over to the fridge. I click it on.

She leaps to her feet. 'I've done more tidying today,' she says, throwing open the cutlery drawer with such force the knives and forks jangle. 'Tra-la!'

I feel a fresh wave of resentment. If she's done all this and not taken the dog to the vet, she isn't just hopeless, but insane.

'And there's more. Follow me!'

She slips off the counter and heads out into the hallway with a dramatic flourish of her arms. I follow, and she throws open the sitting-room door. 'I've feng shuied,' she says.

My eyes scan the room. She's moved the furniture. The sofa is no longer in the window but along the wall facing the fireplace. The table is in the bay again, with the lamp on it.

'Where's the rug?'

'I'm sorry. I spilled a cup of coffee and tried to get it out, but it just spread. I basically just kept making it worse. I've rolled it up behind the sofa. The polished boards are so nice, though, aren't they? Do you like what I've done, or have I been presumptuous? I think it's better this way, don't you?'

Zach's jumper has slipped off one of her shoulders. I'm transfixed by the smooth ball of fresh skin, the sinew and the bone beneath it.

I am aware of a strange tingling at the back of my calves.

Onnie calls my name as I reach the landing. 'Wait!' she says. 'It's a surprise.'

'Just a minute.'

The bedroom door is shut but I push it open and close it behind me. I lean back against the wood. The old familiar scent is here – Acqua di Parma. Intensa, not Assoluta. It's not lingering, but strong and astringent, freshly sprayed. Zach hasn't been in the bedroom today, not necessarily. But Onnie has. She came in to search for the thermostat, and she put on Zach's jumper, and anointed herself with Zach's aftershave. I think about her questions, the way she wants to pry me open, her knowledge of Zach's ways. A jangling has been set off in the deepest unlit depths of my heart, a dark suspicion I don't want to examine.

I cross the room quickly and open the cupboard. My side is in its usual chaos, but Zach's portion has been gone through. His shirts are lined on their hangers, in colour order, his jeans separate from his suits. On the shelves his sweaters and T-shirts and underwear are in neat piles, the socks coiled in pairs. The rack underneath has been swept and his shoes – a pair of brown suede lace-ups, washed-out Converse, old trainers, still bearing the imprint of his feet – are lined up, dusted and polished.

Her hands have touched all this, these clothes that have hung on his body. She has sorted and caressed them. I slide a pair of jeans off their hanger and drop them to the floor. I tug

232

at the pearly buttons of a Paul Smith shirt, scrunch the fabric to my face. I think about the things Onnie said about Zach, the knowledge of his character. He kept the tutoring secret from me. Why would he have done that unless there was something to hide?

I sit down on the bed until my head has stopped swimming, and then I go back downstairs into the kitchen. She's sitting motionless at the table, her knees hunched up to her chin. She turns her face when she sees me. Do I see hope, vulnerability? I don't know.

'Thanks for all the tidying,' I say. 'Though I'm sorry, I have to say it, but I'd rather you didn't touch my things, or Zach's.'

She glances away. 'I was just trying to be helpful.'

'It just feels invasive.'

She scratches her palm, head bent. 'Sorry,' she says finally, but not as if she means it.

In a minute, I'm going to ask her to leave. Nothing she says will sway me. In a few minutes, she will be out of my house and I'll be alone. I won't have to deal with her oddness. I won't have to feel inadequate any more, or suspicious, or angry. I feel better now I know that, and more bullish.

'Could you just tell me,' I say, 'where Xenia fits in? Is she one of your friends? Or are you lying when you say you know her?'

Her face suffuses with colour. Her mouth hardly opens. 'No,' she whispers.

'No to which bit of that?' I am not bullying. I am just speaking firmly and clearly. I'm very aware of the way I'm standing, my legs apart, arms crossed.

'No. I'm not lying.' She still isn't looking at me, but she makes an abrupt movement with her fingers, brushing something away from under her eyes. 'Anyway.' Her voice is cracking. 'I meant it for the best.'

'What?'

She gazes up at me. Her dark blue eyes have filled. It was a tear she brushed away. 'The tidying. I wanted to make it up to you, to make amends.'

'For what?'

She throws her arms out towards me, and then, seeing something in my expression, lifts them to her head. 'I miss him so much.' Her voice trembles. 'I can't believe he's not here.'

I don't move.

'Was Zach more than a tutor to you?' I ask. The words feel bulky in my mouth.

She doesn't answer.

'More than friends?' I'm still trying to hold it at bay. It was a crush, that's all. She was fixated on him, obsessed – he did that to people. He did it to me. And he wouldn't have taken advantage, even Zach in his darkest moods wouldn't have done that. No. She is young for her age now. She would have been a *child* when he died.

She sinks her head into her shoulders and looks at me with a different expression, from under her lashes. A grown-up expression I want to wipe off her face.

'He could be such a charmer,' I add after a beat. 'Much older than you, of course.'

'That didn't matter.'

She answers too quickly. Her head is bowed so I can't read her face, but I don't need to. My insides have turned to red. I have a sharp pain across my shoulders as if someone is leaning on me from behind. I feel as if I might pass out. Zach and Onnie. He thought he could do anything he liked. *How could he?*

'We had a connection,' she says.

'You had a connection? You mean you had sex?'

234

She lets out a small, alarmed laugh, as if I have shocked her. How dare she force her way into my kitchen, with her callous self-obsessions, her petty concerns about whether her parents love her or not, knowing that all the time she slept with my husband? *Slept with my husband*. It is almost unbearable.

'OK.' I'm so calm on the surface. She has no idea. 'I thought you had. When did it start?'

She begins to speak in a high little girl's voice. If she's doing it to make me feel sorry for her, it doesn't work. 'The day I got my GCSE results. August 2011.'

'And where did you do it?'

'What do you mean?'

'Where did you fuck?'

She makes a face, jutting out her lower lip.

'Here then? In my house?'

She nods. I think, in a detached way, that explains how well she knows her way around it, the workings of its plumbing system, the location of the heating controls, the whereabouts of the kitchen towels.

'OK. And how long did it last?'

'We only did it a few times. He ended it because of you. He told me he loved you. I promise.'

'And how many times have you seen him since?' I'm unable to keep the bitterness out of my voice.

'What do you mean, how many times? Of course I haven't seen him since.' She's frowning, shaking her head at me.

I stand. I shouldn't have let that out. I've slipped up.

'What do you mean?' she says again. 'Why are all his things in your wardrobe? You keep talking about him in the present tense. It's like he's still living here.'

Howard gets to his feet, turns a circle in his bed and collapses down again with a groan.

'Did you take Howard to the vet?' I say. 'Or were you lying about that?'

She covers her face and peers out at me from behind spread fingers.

'Oh, fucking hell, Onnie.'

She is weeping again, but more quietly this time, into her hands. 'I make a mess of everything,' she says. 'That's why no one loves me.'

I don't want to prolong this. I don't want to start feeling sorry for her. I am too angry, too upset. There is no room in my head for anything else. How dare she? How dare he? All those accusations he levelled at me, his suspicions, and all the time he was the one who was unfaithful. Not me. Him.

I realise I am twisting my hands, screwing up my mouth, and that Onnie is watching. She looks scared, suddenly diminished, as if she doesn't know what I am going to do next. Her shoulders are trembling. Goosebumps pucker her slim young legs. And I do feel sorry for her. I can't stop myself. None of it's really her fault. She wasn't in control. He was. It's what he did, *does*. He draws you in until there is nowhere to go. He is all you can think about. She knew him and she loved him. She is as obsessed as I am. She's the only other person except for me who knows what that feels like. It's only a couple of steps and I give her an awkward hug.

She says something into her hand that I don't hear.

'What did you say?'

She lifts her face, thrusting her arms at me. 'I cut myself sometimes. I get these feelings that rise and rise, and it's the only way to break the tension. It's been much worse since Zach died.'

I take her wrists and inspect the red ridges. 'You should get help,' I say.

'I've already got help. The latest doctor has given me those antidepressants, but they don't work. It's all my parents ever do – pay for help.'

'Well, you should start helping yourself. Work out what you want from life and do it. You're young and talented, picked for an internship at Shelby Pink above hundreds of others.'

She rests her head on the table. 'You're very kind.'

'I'm not really very kind.'

'I suppose I can't stay, now you know?'

I could shout, No, of course you can't. But I don't. I shake my head.

Onnie nods.

She gets up and collects her things from upstairs. I'm waiting for her at the front door when she comes down, clasping her rucksack in both arms.

'OK,' I say. 'You know the way to the station?'

'Yup.'

'You'll be OK?'

'Yup.'

As she turns to go, she does that gesture I've seen before: she rubs the skin between her eyebrows with her left forefinger several times quickly. I put my hand on her sleeve. 'I'm sorry,' I say.

'What for?'

'For Zach, for the damage he's done.'

She tilts her small, perfect face towards me. 'I wanted to find out what he saw in you,' she says. 'That's why I came.'

'And did you?' I ask, but she has already turned into the street, and if she has an answer for me, I don't hear it.

In bed that night, my mind slides into places it shouldn't. Her hair in his face, his hands on her body. Did she like what he did to her? His deep, hard kisses? Did he bring her to the edge where desire tipped over into fear?

237

I knew, didn't I, in my bones? The week before Christmas, when I came home from school, there were two whisky glasses, unwashed, in the sink. I remember staring at them. I felt a creeping under my skin. The tap dripped, and the water pinged, like a tiny liquid firework. He'd been odd all month, washing his hands even more than usual. He'd upped the drinking. I'd found more pills under his pillow. He had stopped answering his phone in the day when I rang.

He was sitting at the table, tapping manically on his laptop – notes for a painting, he'd told me. 'Are you seeing someone else?' I said.

He threw the accusation back at me, said I was paranoid, that it was evidence of my guilt. 'Who are *you* fucking?' he said.

I felt ashamed to have asked.

He should have told me then. It wasn't too late. The slightest remorse and I'd have forgiven him. I would have acknowledged my own guilt – my failure to look after him. I'd have gone to bed with him right then. I was helpless, powerless in his hands. He only had to touch me and I would lose control.

Well, now I know. Has he been waiting for me to find out? He ended it with Onnie, she said, because of me. And then I told him I was leaving – for no one. He wasn't enough, or he wasn't right. I feel a twist of resentment and guilt. He's certainly had his revenge now. We need to have this out.

One of the curtain pins has come away from its ring and a slice of window gapes at the top. I get out of bed and stand on a chair to refix it, arms outstretched, exposed to the garden, the houses beyond.

Zach

October 2011

Onnie says I'm 'the best thing that's ever happened to her'. She's supposed to be doing retakes at Esher College, but no one notices if she's there or not. She has been coming to the studio almost daily. I can't say she's much of an interruption. I haven't worked in weeks. Vanilla sex – not bad. It's just the clichés I can't take.

I'm 'the man of her dreams'.

I've been trying to break it off. Lizzie suspects. I lurch between panic and fury. If only she understood. If she was only ready to give up her own flirtations. I know what she gets up to at that school of hers, seething as it is with sexual tension. We'd be happy if we moved to Cornwall. I wouldn't need Onnie if I felt safe with her. I'd be the best person I could possibly be – the man who, at the best of times, I see reflected in her eyes – handsome, kind, sexy. Other people ruin it. We have to get away. Lizzie doesn't – or won't – understand. My lunchtime trysts with Onnie – well, they're all Lizzie's fault. She won't give up her job. Or leave her mother – which is absurd. She's so far gone, after that bout of pneumonia, she doesn't even recognise her own daughters. And Peggy needs her, she says – pregnant again, *poor little love*. How many children do they fucking need?

Lizzie wants a baby. We're 'trying'. I've forced myself to ape concern, to pore over ovulation sticks when what I really want is to grip her by the shoulders and shake her. 'Why aren't I enough for you?' I should ask her. 'What would a baby add to what we've got?' I don't, though. She needs to reach that conclusion for herself – that's the pure test of her love. I've told her we'll let nature take its course. I'm waiting for her to realise the mistakes she's made, how her happiness is in her hands. Things will be better then. If she gets pregnant – that'll be a different sort of proof. Someone else will pay. And if she won't drop it, won't accept our life as it is, then it will be proof of her disengagement.

The dog's got to go. She doesn't realise what a commitment he is, how much of her attention he takes up. A cocktail of temazepam and valium is lethal in the long term. (I Googled it.) The mutt's so stupid, he scoffs his daily sausage as if his life depends on it. So far, he's just sleepy, a bit wobbly on his feet, but I'm assured that it's cumulative, and also undetectable. Better this than an outright accident. She'll learn to live without him so slowly she'll hardly notice when he's gone.

Onnie just rang.

'I'd do anything for you,' she says. 'You only have to ask.'

240

Chapter Seventeen

Lizzie

The following day, I put Howard into the car and drive him to the vet. It's almost obscenely cheerful in the waiting room. Dogs yapping and cats in baskets under displays of 'Mini Bone' dog treats and 'Jolly Moggy' catmint-stuffed toy mice. After my tortured night it feels like a cartoon version of the real world.

The vet doesn't know what's wrong with him. He takes some blood tests, gives him a vitamin shot and tells me to keep his fluids up. It's probably a bug, he says, or something he's eaten. He gives Howard's ears a breezy rub. 'What us veterinary professionals call trash-can gastroenteritis.'

I take the dog home and arrive late for school, though no one seems to notice. The inspectors still haven't been and there is a feeling of waiting in the building. Less chatter in the kitchen than usual. Most of the teachers seem to be preoccupied with tidying up their classrooms and fine-tuning their lesson plans. Michele organises a whip-round for Sam, who is out of intensive care. Flowers are ordered, a card circulates.

At lunchtime, I buy a sandwich in the canteen and pull a chair to the window in the library. It's an old habit. Zach used to wait for me out there, sometimes, under a tree. A kick-boxing class is in process – a row of women in Lycra, legs at angles. A line of small children in gingham pinafores from the local nursery are heading towards the playground in a straggling crocodile. In the distance, towards the row of sycamores in shadow, a couple strides holding hands. It still comes as a surprise to me to realise the world is going about its business.

I leave school as early as I can and visit my mother on the way home. She's in a fractious mood and is refusing food. It's an uphill struggle, trying to persuade her to try her cottage pie. She asks me who I am three times. 'I've got a daughter,' she says, shaking her head contemptuously. 'You're not her.'

Peggy was in on Monday, one of the carers tells me. 'She brought your lovely baby granddaughter with her, didn't she? What's she called again?'

Mum smiles coyly but doesn't answer.

'Chloe,' I say. 'She's called Chloe, isn't she? And the older two are Alfie and Gussie.'

It doesn't seem to register and it breaks my heart a little. She wants to watch television and I take her slowly through to the bedroom and put on the small set we bought her. *Pointless* is on and she sits in the chair, her eyes fixed eagerly. Before the dementia she hated quiz shows. I think about Iris Murdoch watching *Teletubbies*. I stroke her hair for a bit and then I make a cup of black tea and put it down gently next to her.

I walk around the room and stop by the shelves. How many Coalport china houses should there be? I count four. There were six. One was missing, I know that. But now there are only four. The little white hexagon house with its mossy garden and its umbrella-shaped roof is gone. I search the floor on my hands and knees, and pull the curtains away from the window sill in case it has been put there. No sign.

Zach hated these houses. He thought they were twee. I told him they reminded me of my childhood; he told me nostalgia was a weakness I needed to free myself from. What would he be trying to tell me if he were removing them one by one?

I check the shelf again in case it has fallen over, or slipped behind her books – the Georgette Heyers she used to love when she could still read.

But it has definitely gone.

Zach

November 2011

My head pounds constantly. I've stopped sleeping again. I've upped the dose. It makes no difference. I am still shaky, on edge. The mood swings are worse. I can't concentrate. I think it's the temazepam. Those pills from Kulon – I'm not sure about them. My hand trembles when I hold the brush. I have no energy. My eye twitches. I can imagine placing the paint on the canvas, but I'm paralysed by the anxiety of getting it wrong. So, I just sit, or pace, or shag Onnie when she turns up.

'How's your painting?' Lizzie said last night, in the tone in which you might say, 'How's that poor dying baby? Still on dialysis?' She put her head on one side. She used to plead to see my work, beg me to show her round the studio. She thought I was a genius, a giant. She's lost all faith in my ability. She has no idea what's happening in my life.

Is she seeing someone else? She talks about Angus and Pat. I've dealt with Angus. Who the fuck is Pat?

I go through her laptop when she's at work. Nothing in her Internet history yet. No revealing emails. I wonder if she has another account at school. I open all her post and regularly search her bag. No clues. She's too clever.

She was home late again last night. It rose inside, a hotness, a snake licking at the back of my throat. I pretended everything was OK, let her work out for herself what had upset me. At supper, she got up from the table, took her plate with her and left the room.

I counted to sixty before following.

She was at the table in the sitting room – in the bay window where I moved it. Her plate was empty. The dog was sitting under the table, gazing up at her.

I asked her what she was doing. She smiled and said she could tell she had been irritating me, that she saw me wince every time she chewed and as she couldn't chew any quieter she thought she would chew elsewhere.

I felt trapped, *managed*. Words streamed out of my mouth. I told her she was a disgrace, the way she made no effort with her appearance. Most wives don't floss in front of their husbands, I said. They shave their legs, wear make-up, wax. The women at the studios have artificial eyelashes. I told her she had a mole at the top of her cheek and she might think she was plucking out the hairs, but there were others that grew around it like weeds.

'Who's Pat?' I said. 'Tell me who he is.'

'You've been at the booze,' she said. 'When did you start? How much have you had?'

I ranted. Who would blame me for having the odd drink, putting up with what I have to put up with? Stronger men than me would have cracked. Is it any surprise, looking as she does, that I'm her first proper lover? What kind of a mother does she think she'd make? She sat there, not saying anything. A tear dropped on the table and she blotted it with the sleeve of her cardigan.

It was new, that cardigan, cashmere; I had bought it for her myself. A pale green to bring out the flecks in her eyes. All I could think was how little respect she had for me if she didn't mind wrecking it. I spent some time lining up the photographs on the mantelpiece, wiped some dust from the top of the television. Her knife and fork were placed carelessly at different angles to the plate. I corrected that. Then I looked at her. She was trying to stop crying. I leaned across to stroke her face, but tweaked her nose instead, twisted it hard.

She came to me later and perched on the edge of the mattress, not wanting to touch me, but in the end she lay down. She tried to talk but I didn't let her. Stopped her mouth with kisses, undressed her, promised never to do it again. My childhood. My past. We are made for each other. Just the two of us. A special bond. No one else has ever understood.

'Don't ever leave me,' I whisper in her ear. 'If you leave me, you don't know what I'll do.'

Downstairs, shut in the kitchen, the dog still barked.

Chapter Eighteen

Lizzie

An empty house – it's both a relief and a disappointment. If Onnie was a block to Zach's plan, I would expect him now to show himself. Or for there to be broken crockery on the doorstep. Another smashed window. Another dead bird. Another sign. Nothing.

The dog has come to the door. He is well enough to get up at least. He moves his tail when I stroke him and follows me around the house. I check the sitting room first. It's as Onnie left it. I do my best to mess it up. I rearrange the furniture, scattering the cushions on the floor. I knock over a chair and leave it on its side. And I lay back down the hideous red and blue rug. There is no coffee stain. She must simply have disliked it.

In the kitchen, I move the kettle back to under the shelf where I prefer it. I pour myself some wine and then I go upstairs to the study. I expect Onnie to have left it tidy, but she hasn't. The sheets and blankets are rumpled on the floor, the pillows piled on top. I collect it all up and put the linen in the washing machine, then fold the bed back up into a sofa. It's not until it's all done that I sit down at the desk, with my glass of wine, to have another go at Zach's password.

It takes a moment for my brain to catch up with my eyes. The desk is empty.

I look on the floor, on the shelves. I open every drawer.

Am I going mad? Imagining things? The china house and now the *laptop*. Have I started losing time again as I did at the beginning? I check the bedroom, under the bed, downstairs, back upstairs. I look under the desk again.

It was plugged into the socket at the wall.

Has he been here? Has he taken it?

The thought swells and changes colour, fills my head. But then I have an image of Onnie as she left – her loaded rucksack clasped to her chest.

I grab my phone and call her. Voicemail. I leave a message. 'I know you've taken Zach's laptop. Bring it back immediately.'

I hang up, my hands shaking.

A noise. I lift my head. The door. Not the bell, but a knock. The rattle of the letter box.

I run downstairs.

DI Perivale is standing a few feet back from the door, legs apart, his hands thrust into the pockets of his jeans.

'Ms Carter?' he says. 'Am I disturbing you?'

I hesitate. 'No. Not really.'

He tucks a lank of hair behind his ears. He has deep furrows on either side of his mouth. It's as if they've been gouged with a pen. They look like scars. 'Just wondered if I could have a quick chat.'

I pull the door open. He enters the hallway, stooping unnecessarily. I hold out my arms for his jacket, which he shrugs off. In my hands, it smells of cold air and damp and something chemical. I hang it over the bannister as calmly as I can. We go into the front room.

I pick up the cushions from the floor and lay them back on the sofa, then I return the chair I knocked over to its feet. I sit on it, gesturing for him to sit at the one facing me across the table.

248

Perivale sits down, looks around the room and then at me. 'Nice decor,' he says. 'Monastic.'

'Yes.'

'Interesting colour.' He strokes the wall. 'I'm thinking of redecorating. What is it? Off-white? Baby blue?'

'It's a pale grey called Borrowed Light.'

He pulls down the corners of his mouth, mock impressed. 'I'll have to remember that.'

'Do you live locally?' I say, thinking, *What are you here for?*

'Not far,' he says. 'Battersea. Other side of Clapham Junction. Winstanley Estate, to be precise.'

'We lived there when I was little,' I tell him.

'Really? I'm told the area is "on the up". Anyway . . .' he brings his hands together, as if in prayer '. . . I'm sorry to disturb you. It's not a big thing. Just a niggle, if you like.'

A niggle?

'Yesterday you asked Morrow to look into the death of a young woman. Charlotte Reid.'

'Yes. Do you know what happened? She was in an accident. Was it in a car?'

'I'll get to that.' He wipes the tips of his fingers along the table and then taps the wood three times. He looks up at the ceiling. 'Twenty-fifth of December, 2011. Christmas Day. A Sunday. The police were alerted to a disturbance at this address. A neighbour heard loud noises, barking, screams. When PC Evans arrived on the scene, the woman in question claimed to have fallen down the stairs.'

'Yes.'

After a moment, he says, 'OK.'

'OK,' I repeat.

His eyes roam the room, look everywhere except at me. I'm trying to keep my gaze level. I'm not going to be drawn on this. I promised Zach. This will only complicate matters. The night Perivale is referring to . . . it was between him and me then, and it's between him and me now.

'I've been sent on a lot of courses this year. My penance. I wasn't as efficient with a recent case as I should have been. My instincts turned out to be wrong.' His eyebrows twitch and his lower lip juts. 'These courses. Applied Criminology. Specialist Firearms. Advanced Database Usage. Waste of time. A brief secondment with Domestic Violence, on the other hand, part of my gender-equality training – that turned out to be fascinating. When I've heard about an abusive relationship, I've always thought, like most people I imagine, why doesn't she, or he, just leave? Do you?'

'What?'

'Think that?'

'Probably, yes.'

'I'll tell you why they don't. They're often under the illusion that the relationship is somehow "special". The partner may themselves have been the victim of abuse and the victim may make excuses and feel responsible.'

'I can understand that.'

'The victim may also not appreciate the inevitability of escalation. They're sucked in before they realise. They may even feel as if they deserve it, as if they're in collusion. For one thing, the threat posed by the abusive partner might not be physical from the beginning. It could be psychological, emotional, financial, sexual . . .'

'I can see the secondment was useful.'

'But it always ends up with good old-fashioned violence.'

I want him to be quiet now. I don't want to have to listen to any more. I smile. 'I don't know what this has to do with me.'

'No,' he says, blinking slowly. 'OK.'

'Is that it?' I shift to release my hands. Shouts of laughter from the street. A car horn sounds.

'No.' He studies me thoughtfully. 'So – Charlotte Reid. The coroner concluded she slipped. A piece of loose carpet, or, rather, not carpet. *Rush matting.* She lived in a top-floor flat. The stairs were steep and she fell head first to the bottom. Cause of death: craniocerebral trauma. Unfortunately for her, she was alone in the building. Had her neighbours not been on holiday, had she been found earlier . . .'

I shake my head.

'She was pregnant,' he adds casually.

I'm unable to speak. I'm gripping the table as if I might fall.

'Not Zach's,' I say eventually. 'It wasn't Zach's.'

'No. Maybe not. He's not listed as her partner at the time.'

'I'm not sure where you're going with all this.'

He throws his head back and wrinkles up his nose, squinting. Then his whole body contracts again, and he crouches across the table. 'Am I correct in thinking you told PC Morrow you think your husband faked his own death, that he's still alive?'

I keep my voice steady. 'At times, I have thought that, yes.'

'Were you afraid of him?'

Afraid. How simple that word is. 'I don't think it's any of your business.'

'OK.' He stands up, gives a fake stretch. I walk ahead of him to the hall and hand him his jacket. He takes it from me and shrugs it on, digging around at the hem to locate the zip. 'Lucky escape. Your fall down the stairs, I mean.'

'I suppose so. Yes.'

At the door, he turns. 'Forgive me.' He gives another of his mock courtly bows. 'I thought I might be able to lay some ghosts, that's all.'

Zach

December 2011

Am I a bad person? I've made mistakes in the past. I never meant to hurt Polly, or Charlotte. I had begun to think that was behind me, that I had a chance to be someone different. But perhaps it is too late. I think too much. Thoughts build until I'm not sure what's reality and what isn't. I wish I could escape from my own brain.

Last year, we spent Christmas at Gulls. I had to force her, now I think of it. All those excuses she came up with. It was 'my sanctuary'. I expect she was already seeing someone else. This year I agreed to be in London. See how nice I can be – how kind, how reasonable, for fuck's sake. I put my foot down about spending it with Peggy and Rob. It was to be just the two of us, I said. A special time. We've had a tricky year. The strains of trying for a baby, the pressures of my work, blah blah. We'd wear our pyjamas, make a fire, hunker down, block the rest of the world out. *Lock down*.

She agreed grudgingly. A long dog walk with Jane – an opportunity for a full-length bitch about me. A heart-rending phone call with Pregnant Peg. Promises of midnight Mass on Christmas Eve and mulled wine on Boxing Day. 'Would that be all right?' she said when she finally hung up. Oh, I'll play along. I'll go. I'll smile. Muck about with the kids ('It's Uncle Zach!'; 'Uncle Zach will play football'; 'Ask Uncle Zach!'). I'll put my arms around Peggy in the hallway, smile at her, enjoy a lingering look. Discuss the rugby with Rob. Pretend I give a flying fuck. But Lizzie will pay for it later. Silent treatment. A 'withholding of sexual favours' (you have to say that with pursed lips). She'll be on her knees. She'll learn to deserve me.

Christmas morning.

I opened my eyes, and she was already out of bed, getting dressed. She said she was going to take the dog out, did I want to come? No, I didn't want to come. I tried to pull her back under the covers, but she drew away.

I could easily have taken offence, but it was Christmas. I made a pot of coffee while she was out and laid the table. I layered smoked salmon on two plates and buttered toast. By the time she walked back in, breakfast was ready. She expressed delight, surprise. She was worrying about the dog. He'd been 'so quiet'. I told her she was imagining it. 'He's fine.' I unwrapped her scarves, took off her coat, steered her to a chair. I opened champagne. We pulled a cracker. We laughed ('A man walked into a bar . . . Ouch!'). We kissed.

I'd give Howard a day off, I decided. Seasonal good wishes.

We went back to bed. I closed the curtains and in the semi-darkness felt my way around her body, from her toes up. She came before I'd reached her thighs. I took my time. I lingered there, until I felt her move again beneath the tips of my fingers. I delayed as long as I could, played with her, stroked, toyed. Even the sound of her breaths, short or held, turned me on. When she touched my cock, I came at once.

We ate mid-afternoon. We didn't have turkey. (I don't like the texture.) Chicken, no gravy. Stuffing cooked in a separate tray, not inside the bird. Roast potatoes, peas. She put *Goodbye Cruel World* on the iPod and we danced to Elvis Costello there in the kitchen. I've never been able to dance. Mad Paul back home used to crease up laughing at the sight of me. He said I looked like a constipated donkey. But with Lizzie it doesn't matter. I can be what I am. No front. I told her I loved her, that I'd never felt anything for anyone as I felt for her.

253

It was dark before we remembered presents. I had taken trouble: a gold necklace with our initials entwined, an Orla Kiely multi-stem silk scarf, pretty underwear – God knows she needs it. I wanted her to open all hers first. I couldn't wait. I was excited in anticipation of her response. She put on the necklace, wrapped the scarf around her neck, twirled the bra set in the air, promising 'a fashion show for later'.

I was happy. I forgot.

She kissed me.

And then she said: 'You shouldn't have spent so much.'

Later she came upstairs to the study to say sorry. 'I didn't mean it. It was tactless. But you misunderstood. I just meant – three whole presents! It's a lot. I've only got you one.'

I was pretending to read. What with the champagne and the wine at lunch, the whisky I had knocked down when she was out dragging the dog, I had reached the stage where the world was blurred around the edges. I'm not defending myself. It wasn't my fault what happened next. I am just explaining my part in it. 'You have nothing but contempt for me,' I said, keeping my eye on the page. 'You don't have to be so obvious.'

'What I earn is yours. We share it. It's not an issue. It's Christmas Day. Come on. We've had such a lovely day. I've got your present here. Open it, you big grump.'

She had her arms around my neck. She was tickling under my chin, trying to make me laugh. It's what she does with Peggy's eldest when he is on the edge of a tantrum. But I am not a spoilt brat. I won't be spoken to like that. I didn't turn round.

I heard her leave the room, her steps down the small flight of stairs to the bathroom. She had left the present next to me, a small, heavy cylinder wrapped in flimsy red paper, cheap cartoon Santas climbing into chimneys. Twenty-two of them. I counted.

Inside: a yellow box. Aftershave. My favourite. My *signature* scent. Acqua di Parma. For a fleeting moment, I was gratified. The bottle in the bathroom was nearly empty. Lizzie must have seen me pressing and re-pressing to vaporise the dregs. But this was Colonia Assoluta. Wrong. Badly wrong. It is Colonia Intensa that I wear. It's the thought that counts. And the fact is she *hadn't* thought. She had just grabbed it off the shelf in a hurry. Even the wrapping was patronising, the kind of paper you would use for a gift to a child. *A fucking child*.

I was out of my chair and in two strides met her as she came out of the bathroom. I had time to note the fear on her face, to wish that I could wipe it off, and then I had my hand around her neck and was holding her up against the wall. I told her she didn't love me. She pushed back. Her knee met my groin. I twisted away. She screamed. Our legs became entangled, and somehow she was falling, tumbling, not head over heels, but sideways, arm over torso, hand clutching at thin air, down the flight of stairs.

When the police came, we were sitting together at the bottom. Neither of us had the strength to move. I was cradling her head, whispering how sorry I was. The dog lay at her feet, panting. The exertion had almost done him in.

A walkie-talkie emitted disembodied voices into the night. I could feel the vibrations of the vehicle they had left idling in the street. The throb of the blue and red lights discoed on the hall walls.

The doorbell rang.

She didn't move. She hadn't looked at me yet. 'You need help,' she said. 'I don't know if it's the booze, or those pills I keep finding, but you need to see someone.'

'I know.'

She stood up gingerly. 'I mean it, Zach.'

'I will.'

She had her hand on the latch. 'Do you promise?'

The bell rang again. A face pressed against the frosted glass.

I nodded. 'It's not me,' I said. 'I can't stop it coming.'

She stared at me, and a million silent words passed between us. An unspoken pact was made. And then she opened the door.

Chapter Nineteen

Lizzie

Pregnant. Charlotte was pregnant. Was it Zach's? *Could* it have been? It depends on the dates.

Christmas Day 2011.

He cooked me breakfast. We laughed and opened champagne. We spent half the morning in bed, tangled with each other. I was on my guard – a shift could take place at any time, like a plunge from heat into icy water. I never knew when his temper would flare – the muscles in his face twist, his pupils enlarge. They were like fits, mercurial flashes, but I knew what to do. I would stay calm, unconcerned, quietly do everything I could to prove he came first. It was my fault. I could handle it.

That day was different. It wasn't just the paranoia that exploded into violence. It was the dull look in his eyes, as if he'd forgotten who I was. I don't remember much – the world turning black and white, spinning, dizziness, the exploding pain deep in my head.

Afterwards, he was tormented, tortured by his own actions. It wasn't him, he said. It was a person inside that he didn't want to be – the abuse he had suffered as a child, the drugs. He said he would do anything to keep me. He'd see a doctor, give up the booze. Then things would be different, the demons kept at bay. He just needed to be sure of me.

'You can be sure of me,' I wept.

When term started, it still hurt to swallow. The bruises I covered with long-sleeved tops. Jane noticed the broken veins in my eye. 'Too many late nights,' I said.

He had begun to break me. I felt responsible for his happiness and sanity. I came home straight from school to be with him. I turned down invitations to see my sister or friends. I only walked the dog, who was under the weather, when Zach could come too. I visited my mother much less than I should have done. If I felt swipes of guilt, I batted them away. It was Zach who needed me now.

Shortly after term started, I caught a cold that turned into flu. Zach rang the school to tell them I was ill. He brought me lemon and honey in bed, and scrambled eggs on toast. He read to me, and played me songs on his iPod. He took care of the house and the dog, and he bought me vitamins in Boots. Redoxon Double Action Vitamin C and Zinc and Pregnacare Conception: 'specially formulated for when you're trying for a baby'.

'We need to get you fit,' he said. 'We need to get your body ready.'

A week off work stretched to two. Jane came to visit one afternoon. I heard them talking on the doorstep, but he came back up alone. He'd told her I was asleep. 'But I wasn't,' I said. 'It would have been nice to see her.'

He looked hurt, as if I were casting doubts on his capabilities. 'You need to rest,' he frowned.

I wanted to see the doctor; Zach persuaded me not to. It was just a virus, why waste their time, risk a waiting room full of bugs? He would nurse me. We would do it on our own.

I was dizzy. My limbs ached. But he still wanted to make love. He was gentle, though. And there were reasons.

We talked about the baby we would have – whether it would be a boy or a girl, have his looks or mine, whose brains. Zach wrote lists of names and looked up nurseries and primary schools in the South London area. And then he started talking about Cornwall, as he often did. I was dozing. My ear was resting in the crook of his neck. I could feel his words vibrate in his throat. The stories he told were of small children running in the surf, of log fires and village schools. He spun images of the perfect life we could live, and I heard myself agree.

When I went back to work at the end of January, I handed in my notice. Sandra asked me if I was sure. I told her I was, but that I hadn't told my friends or my sister so I would be grateful if she could keep it quiet for now. I was 'taking it step by step'. It's what Zach had told me to say.

I was late back a few evenings after this – not very late, just later than I had said I would be. It wasn't yet six. Zach was pacing the house in regular swirling patterns. He'd switched all the plugs off at the sockets, and his hands were red. He'd been washing them in boiling-hot water. He ignored me and started bashing away on his laptop, writing notes, emails, whatever it was he did, his strokes frenzied. The dog was lying under the table, still poorly. I saw Zach kick him.

I tried to explain. Jasmine, a girl in year eight who was on the at-risk register and was due to be fostered the following day, had come into the library, upset. She had started throwing books off the shelves and stamping on them, swearing and shouting. 'It took me a while to calm her. I just had to keep talking and telling her how everything was going to be OK, and after that I couldn't leave until the social worker came.'

I was standing at the sink while I was telling Zach this, talking too much, giving too much detail to cover my nerves. He pushed his chair back and stood up. He crossed the room and came so close his feet were on mine, crushing my toes. He stared into my face. His hands stretched out, as if he were going to caress it, and then he reached for my hair and yanked back my head. He put the tap on full force and cold water flushed on to my face, went up my nose, filled my mouth. I struggled and panicked – I thought I wouldn't be able to get away, that he might turn the tap to hot – but as suddenly as he grabbed me, he let me go, and I sank to the floor.

Would that have been enough to make me leave him? Probably not. He was repentant, of course he was. And I blamed myself. I should have rung him. I didn't because I kept thinking I would be able to get away, that I would be home before he noticed. And then, when I explained to him what had happened, I should have been more relaxed, less self-conscious. If he thought I was guilty, it was because I felt it.

The next thing that happened was in the second week of February. All this time we'd been trying to have a baby. Peggy had told me you needed to wait six months before you could begin to be concerned. I knew Zach wanted to let nature take its course, but what harm could it do, I thought, if I saw my GP? I could find out what our options were, just in case there was anything we could be doing to hurry it along. I made an appointment for one lunchtime.

Zach was in good spirits that week. A new dealer in Exeter, whom he'd met down at the Wimbledon studios, was seriously interested in his work – the landscapes – possibly wanted to commission more. It was a new beginning for him, a chance to put the failure in Bristol behind him. He was making plans to meet this new bloke and, after that, spend a couple of days at Gulls, getting it ready for our arrival. We'd be moving to Cornwall sooner rather than later, but that was all right, wasn't it? How soon would Sandra let me leave?

'She needs to find a replacement first,' I said.

He frowned, looked baffled. 'It's not like anyone depends on you,' he said.

I left the room after this conversation and lay on the bed. It was nothing, I told him, just a headache. He had no idea what he'd said. I lay there, feeling panicked. Did I want to move to Cornwall? How could I leave my mother and my sister and my friends? They depended on me, and some of the kids at school did too. I thought about Jasmine, who had started coming into the library at lunchtime, and Conor – he might not have known I kept an eye on him, but I did. Zach was wrong. People did depend on me. People other than him.

I tried to put it to the back of my mind. Zach could swing from one idea to another. It was all London, London, London when we first met. Perhaps if I just waited he would think differently. Or maybe if I got pregnant, *I* would.

I had blooked my appointment for the day before Zach was due to leave on his trip. The doctor I saw was new to the surgery. She didn't look much older than some of the sixth-formers at school – blonde and pretty with a cheerful smile. She met me at the door to her room. They used just to sit and wait for you to knock. It must be a new directive, I remember thinking.

I sat down in the chair and said it was probably stupid of me to come, but I was a bit sad that I hadn't got pregnant and wondered if it was worth talking to someone.

She had my notes up on her screen. She asked how long we had been trying and were we timing it at the right time of the month? Did my husband have any health problems that I knew about?

'Nope,' I said. 'He's pretty healthy. Takes a few anti-anxiety pills, but that's about it.'

'OK, and is your husband called Carter too?'

'No. Hopkins. Zach Hopkins.'

She nodded, and looked back at her screen, pressing a few keys. She looked confused for a moment. 'Does your husband feel the same as you?' she asked perkily.

'Yes,' I said. 'He's desperate to start a family. Growing up, he didn't have a proper one of his own.'

She nodded and clasped her hands together. 'OK,' she said. 'Well, it's not the end of the world. People often change their minds. It's usually reversible. Send him in and we'll get going on that.'

Nothing she said made sense. 'What's reversible?' I said.

'His vasectomy. It says here—' she swivelled back to the screen '—he was seen by us on the second of September 2010 and referred to the Lister, a private hospital. The operation took place seven days later on the ninth of September. Fast turnaround, but . . .' she smiled '. . . we often find that once men have decided to have the procedure, they're keen to get it over with.'

'A vasectomy?' I laughed. 'You must be looking at the wrong notes. Zach Hopkins.'

She glanced at me and then away again. 'Um,' she said. 'You should probably send him in. Make another appointment, a double one, and we'll all talk about it together.'

I don't know how I got out of the surgery. I felt as if I'd been hit in the stomach. She hadn't made a mistake. I remembered September – how he went off sex for a week. He had walked with a slight limp. He said he'd twisted his groin getting off his bike. He didn't want a baby. He wouldn't have been able to share me. He was jealous of my *dog*. He wanted me all to himself. He'd been toying with me, playing along to get his own way.

I didn't go back to school. I rang the office and said I was sick. I spent the afternoon walking the streets, trying to work out what to do. If I moved with him to Cornwall, he would crush me. I sat in a café and wrote him a letter. It was poised and distant. It said none of the things I felt.

That night, I cooked supper from a recipe Jane had given me. I was distracted, added mushrooms to the sauce. He refused to touch it. I tried to eat normally. Every scrape of my own knife and fork jarred. I chewed as quietly as I could. He watched every mouthful, winced with every swallow. We didn't speak until all evidence of the meal – my insurrection – had been removed. I still might have confronted him, given him the opportunity to explain. But he made some dismissive comment, his lip curled.

You run from a big wave or you dive into it. I decided to run.

He was in the bathroom, washing his hands, when I posted the letter. It wasn't a big thing, slipping the envelope into the mouth of the box at the end of the road. It wasn't monumental. Nothing crashed and burned. Not then.

Zach

January 2012

She's mine now. I can feel it. It's not so much an illness, as a stupor. She is intoxicated by love. I'm happy. Each day is a gift, one we share. It's calm in the house, and still. No one comes near. (Apart from Jane, whom I sent packing.) I keep her mobile phone about my person. No lover has tried to get in touch – unless he's being careful. I ran her a bath earlier and checked under the pillow but no second phone. I think she's telling the truth. After her bath, I wrapped her in towels and dried her and took her back to bed. She lay there, weak and grateful, as I stroked her hair, her face. I tucked her in tight, and tentatively laid out my plan – cutting all ties, moving to Cornwall, starting again.

'OK, my love,' she said drowsily. 'If it will make you happy. Yes.' YES.

Shame about Onnie. I've cut the connection. She was getting on my nerves. If I'm honest, I didn't even like her, let alone desire her. I broke it off by phone. Her parents have found out about the Esher no-shows. They've banished her to Cornwall to do retakes in some shitty sixth-form college under the auspices of some crap au pair – away from all distractions. (Not sure that suits me. I'll have to think my way out of that.) She sobbed down the line. Was it something that she'd done? Was she too fat?

'Of course you're not too fat.'

'What is it then?'

'It's nothing.'

'Is it *your wife*?' she said, disbelieving.

'Yes,' I said. I couldn't stop myself. 'Yes, it is.'

My wife. My Lizzie.

Chapter Twenty

Lizzie

Thursday is one of those days that doesn't get light. The sky is low, as if stage curtains have been strung across it. I snap at the year elevens for mucking about on the computer. I evict two of the year twelves for chewing gum. Every time the library door opens, I jump.

You can torture yourself with 'ifs'. I shouldn't have written that stupid fake letter. I should have confronted Zach. That would have been the grown-up thing to do. It would have meant a terrible scene. He might have denied it, or twisted it against me, but we might have got beyond it. And perhaps there were excuses I might have understood, to do with Charlotte? Had she been carrying his baby? Was the tragedy of her accident behind his decision? Or did his affair with Onnie have something to do with it? Or Xenia? Or was it simply the overbearing influence of his upbringing – his fear of what families do to each other? I don't know because I didn't ask. I hid. I behaved like the old Lizzie who, for an easy life, let people get away with murder.

When I see her standing outside the house, I stop in my tracks. I almost turn and go back the way I came.

She has seen me, though. She is holding flowers, a frail bunch of blue anemones – one colour.

'Please, please, please,' she says, thrusting them at me. 'I'm so sorry. I know it was wrong. Let me explain. Please.'

I walk past her, without saying anything, and put the key in the door. 'I don't need flowers,' I say. 'I'd just like the laptop.'

'Yes. I'm sorry. I know.' The rucksack is hanging on her shoulder and she pulls it off and puts it down on the ground. She starts rummaging through. Items of clothing – a scarf, a black vest top – fall on to the path.

The laptop is finally extracted and, still crouching, she holds it up to me.

'Thank you.' I take it and am poised to close the door on her. It would be easier if she stood up. Psychologically, I don't want to leave her prone at my feet.

She looks up at me. Her eyes wide, rimmed with black eyeliner, she looks like a strange woodland creature. 'Please,' she says again. She is stuffing her possessions back into her bag. The anemones are on the ground. 'I know more than you think. I can be helpful. We should do this together.'

'Do what?'

She stands up. 'Find Zach, of course.'

Ten minutes later Onnie is sitting again on my sofa in the front room. She has cried a little bit – snotty tears that seem genuine – and told me how sorry she is. It was a spur of the moment decision. She just saw it, sitting there on the desk, and she thought if she just had a bit of time, she might be able to crack his password. She hadn't, and now she knows I haven't either, we should do it together. 'Two brains are better than one,' she says. 'We're not enemies. We should be friends, do it together. Between us we must be able to work out what he would choose, what was important to him.'

I haven't said much. I am standing against the fireplace, holding the laptop to my chest.

'I heard you,' she says, 'when you left Sand Martin that time you came to lunch.'

'I didn't come to lunch.'

'OK, that time you didn't come to lunch. I'd left them all in the drawing room and I was on the stairs. I heard you muttering as you ran out of the house. I couldn't make much sense of it – something about having to find Zach. But now I know. All those things you said the other day, the way you talk about him.'

'What?'

'He's still alive, isn't he?'

I don't answer straight away.

'How could that be possible?' I say eventually.

'I've been thinking about it. All day yesterday, I just tried to work it out. He must have faked the accident.'

'It's very unlikely,' I say carefully, in a slow, schoolteacher-ish voice. 'Lots of people were involved in his crash. The farmer who called the fire brigade. The driver of the Asda delivery lorry who stood in the road to stop the traffic. The tow truck – three people involved with the removal of the wreckage. Witnesses, coroners, two different police forces. It was a big deal, Onnie.'

'Have you heard of Jolyon Harrison? Do you know who he is?'

'The name's familiar.'

'He disappeared. He went missing from Cornwall. The same week of Zach's accident. Don't you think that's weird?'

I feel a racing, a tightening in my chest. 'It's a coincidence.'

'The last sighting of him was in Bude. Kulon said he'd been in the bar before Zach came in.'

'Zach was in the bar that night?'

'Yes. It's where I found him.'

I look past her out of the window. The new pane of glass has a different glint. Less dimpled. Flatter. I thought he had been in Exeter that night. What does it mean if he was already in Cornwall? I study the glass, try to keep calm.

'Zach would be clever enough to have worked it out. He and Jolyon could have been in the car together. Zach got out in time – threw open the car door, rolled into the ditch and when the car went up in flames, he decided just to walk away. Or he was never in the car. Jolyon was driving. Jolyon died. Zach has kept under the radar ever since. He's waiting until it's safe and then he's coming back.'

I say, testing her, 'You can't pretend to die and then carry on as normal. You need documents, a driving licence, a passport and National Insurance number. Ordinary things, like renting somewhere to live or getting a job – none of it's possible without a legal identity. All those loopholes to do with babies who died the year you were born, applying for their birth certificates and pretending you're them – it doesn't work like that any more . . . It's impossible to just start a new life.'

I notice that I have raised my voice.

Onnie stands up and takes a step towards me. Her eyes are glittering. 'What if you don't want a new life?' she says. 'What if you just want to mess with the old one?'

Zach

February 2012

She's better. The fever broke. She says she's given in her notice, but I don't believe her. She's lying, as she always does. It's changed again. I can tell. I can feel the slippage, sand slinking under my feet like a tide on the turn. I don't know what she does there, all day, up in that school. She's like a fish. I can't hold her. I have to press so hard to keep her in one place. It was the flu that made her love me, I realise now, not her heart.

When she's late, I lose it. Shouldn't. Can't help myself. I start drinking too early, pacing the rooms, fiddling with plugs. Checking and double-checking. My hands are sore from washing. It all goes wrong. The pills, I think. She watches me. I feel judged. I love her so much I can feel emotion rise until I want to spit in her face.

I've invented a gallery in Exeter. The dealer is mad for me, I told her. Nothing like that waste of space in Bristol. This bloke's serious. There's a meeting in the diary. It's the abstract landscapes he likes – he wants more. We'll have to move down to Cornwall sooner. She thought I wouldn't see the horror that came into her eyes, but I did.

Howard, old chap: I'm afraid your time has come. I have finessed my slow poison campaign. I bought some marrowbone in Pets at Home, which I hacked into slivers, inserting a pill into each section. I've hidden them in a bin bag hung from a discreet nail under an unravelled tarpaulin in the garden shed. She never looks in there.

Chapter Twenty-one

Lizzie

On Friday, Jane appears in the doorway just before the final bell. She plans to pop down to St George's and wonders if I want to come too. I stare at her. I'm so tired, my mind so fractured, I don't know what she's talking about. 'See how he's doing,' she says. 'Show him a friendly face.'

'Who?' I say.

'Sam! Who else?'

I have left Onnie at home trying to crack Zach's password. I have reluctantly accepted her help. We are dubious accomplices. It seems bizarre – his wife and his schoolgirl mistress joining forces to work him out. We spent the evening brainstorming possible combinations. I would have given up. 'It could be anything,' I said. 'A random assortment of letters.' But Onnie is tenacious. She's convinced Zach would have been as careful with this as he was with everything he did. 'It will be something that is meaningful to him.'

She told me not to worry about Xenia. She is still trying to get in touch with her.

I think she is stalling but I don't know what else to say.

I wonder whether it would amuse Zach or annoy him, our complicity, or whether it has been his plan all along. I feel uneasy about it and slightly sick, but at the same time defiant. What is the worst he can do now? Kill me? Kill us both?

Onnie has promised to keep an eye on the dog, to ring me if he seems any worse.

'OK,' I tell Jane. 'Life goes on.'

She drives us there in her beaten-up estate. The back seat is laden high with boxing gloves and fold-up chairs, props for *Bugsy Malone*. I can't see out the back to see if we're being followed.

'You're quiet,' she says. 'Feeling a bit . . . ?'

'I'm fine.'

I text Onnie to tell her I'll be home a little late and then switch off my phone.

We find Sam in one of the men's surgical wards. He is lying, dressed but without shoes, on a bed at the far end. His head, bandaged, is propped on several pillows and he is reading a book entitled *Evil Genes*. He doesn't see us approach and I think two things as we walk towards him. The first is how nice it is to see him, how uncomplicated he is. And the second is how odd it is to see a colleague horizontal. And without footwear.

'Ah,' he says, putting his book down and smiling. 'A delegation from work.'

Jane says: 'Is that any way to greet your fellow workers, the providers of buns?' She kisses his brow, just below the rim of the bandage. It's tinged with greyish yellow, Magic Mustard, the iodine ointment they used to put on our scrapes at school. I had imagined a bump. I hadn't envisaged a cut. I don't kiss him, but it's not because of that.

He is looking at me as if he knows I'm embarrassed. 'Carter,' he says. 'Nice of you to drop by.'

He offers us chocolate muffins from a swan-shaped wicker basket and tells us what happened, or as much of it as he has pieced together. He left me at the edge of the common and walked along the diagonal path towards the railway bridge.

That's all he remembers. He assumes he must have crossed over, because an hour later he was found on the other side of the tracks, in the bushes, with a head injury and two broken ribs. 'Random attack,' the police think. 'Mistaken identity perhaps, or robbery gone wrong.' He is due to be released today when the relevant nurse brings the relevant paperwork for him to sign in the relevant places. Paula, his ex-wife, is driving down from Hackney to take him home. Jane asks if he will be all right, looking after himself, and he says Paula is going to stay the first night just to check he doesn't wake up foaming at the mouth.

'Oh?' she says knowingly.

'It's not like that,' he says and gives me a quick look.

I hardly speak. I'm no company for anyone. But as we are getting up to leave, he says, 'I'm sorry about this' sweetly, as if it is his fault. Our eyes meet. There is a dark fleck, like a comma, beneath one of his pupils, and deep smile lines around his mouth. He is wearing a checked Viyella shirt, open at the neck. His collarbone is pale, with a thumbprint of a bruise.

Jane persuades me back to her flat in Tooting after the hospital. Sanjay is working late and she could do with the company. I expect she's checking up on my state of mind, but I go anyway. I want to stay out of my house, and away from Onnie, for as long as I can. I don't mind her being there, I feel responsible for her, but I'm reluctant to spend too much time with her. She will ring, she promised, if she gets anywhere. In the meantime, I need to get a grip on something firm, calm my mind.

Jane and Sanjay live in a flat that takes up the top two floors of a large house behind the Broadway, decorated like a Victorian bordello, full of rich drapes and chaises longues and red velvet screens. We have a cup of tea in their little kitchen and then a glass of wine. Jane rustles up some microwaved baked potatoes and cheese. We talk about work – whether Michele's boyfriend will propose and whether Pat needs Prozac and whether Ofsted will come next week now instead. My mind has split into parallel lines. I'm disconnected from my friends. This is what happens when you keep things back. It becomes impossible to bridge the gap. I'm not going to mention Zach, but I do tell her a bit about Onnie – to try and explain how distant I have been. I don't go into details – just say the daughter of an old friend of Zach's has turned up and is behaving erratically. Jane says she sounds like she needs professional help. 'She's not really my problem,' I say casually and I wish I meant it.

Before I know it, it's past nine. I could get a bus, but I decide to walk – along Garratt Lane and up Magdalen Road. It's stopped raining for the first time in months. The wine has gone to my head. It's a forty-minute stomp and I stride past the shops, out in the open, under the street lights. I turn round and stop a lot. I wonder who he is watching: Onnie or me? Is he confused? Erotically stirred? I say, under my breath: 'I'm ready. Where are you?'

He's too clever for that.

Standing outside the house, I hear the strains of familiar music. A voice, half-sway, half-boom, over drums and an electric guitar. It's Elvis Costello: not *Goodbye Cruel World*, but a song from an earlier album, *My Aim is True*. 'Alison', a song about betrayal that's pretending to be about love. I fumble for my key and jump when I realise Onnie is next to me, in the bay window, the other side of the glass, staring at me. Her face is a pale moon, her hair drawn across her shoulders like curtains.

She comes out of the sitting room into the hall when I open

273

the door. 'You're so late,' she says, her head on one side. 'Where have you been? I've been so worried.'

'Oh, I'm sorry. I texted you. I went to visit a friend in hospital.'

'You didn't answer your phone.'

My mobile is in my pocket and I take it out. 'Damn. Sorry. I switched it off to go into the ward. I must have forgotten to switch it back on.' I press the top button and the screen illuminates. Five missed calls. Four texts. 'Sorry,' I say again.

She looks at me and slightly shakes her head. 'It's OK. It's not spoiled.'

The dog has pushed his way out of the kitchen and has come to greet me. The music is louder with the door open. Spoiled? I can smell cooking. I stroke Howard and say: 'I would have thought you were a bit young for Elvis Costello.'

'Just like it, that's all.'

'It was Zach's favourite.'

'I know.'

I push down the small wave of jealousy and follow her into the kitchen, where Elvis Costello is playing from an iPod dock. The table is laid. Onnie is opening the oven and pulling out a tray containing two chicken breasts. She lays them on separate plates and adds mashed potatoes and peas from saucepans on the hob. 'Tra-la,' she says. 'I bet you didn't know I could cook, did you?'

'How lovely,' I say. I should be able to tell her that I've eaten. It shouldn't feel so insurmountable. But I can't. It's how I used to feel with Zach, trapped in his expectations, controlled. I have the same loss of perspective, too. I don't know what I'm *allowed* to feel, whether I am in the right or in the wrong. I fetch a glass of water and drink it, leaning against the sink. I can sense Onnie watching my every move.

'Nice, isn't it?' she says, when I have put the glass down. 'To come home to a cooked meal?'

'Lovely.'

'Have you been drinking?'

'Hardly at all.'

She laughs and wags her finger at me.

'No, really, I haven't. One or two glasses.'

She passes my plate to me and we both sit down.

'So who were you visiting?' she asks as we start to eat.

'Just a colleague from school.' I swallow down some chicken. It feels like punishment.

'Sam Welham?'

'Yes! How do you know that?'

'I remembered, that's all. You told me about him, the other day.'

'Did I?' I put my fork down and stare at her. How odd that she would pick up on that.

She carries on eating, but, feeling my eyes, looks up and smiles at me. 'So you haven't asked how I got on today?'

'How did you get on?' I realise as I'm asking that this is a mistake. I don't want Onnie looking inside Zach's laptop without me being there. I don't actually want her looking inside his laptop at all. I hope she *hasn't* found anything.

'I didn't work it out, she answers quickly. 'But I have been thinking hard. One in five people apparently use their pet's name. I tried "Howard" but it didn't work. Did Zach have any pets when he was growing up that you know about?'

An image of Zach's cold childhood home comes into my head. A large house, with empty rooms, and a small unloved boy in a corner, ducking the blows. He longed for a dog – Zach told me that early on – but he would never have had the courage even to ask. 'I don't think so.'

275

'First girlfriend? The love of his life? He would have chosen something that meant the world to him. He was such a romantic man.'

'Was he?' I stand up and surreptitiously scrape the rest of my potato into the bin and wash my plate under the tap. Now she thinks I've accepted their affair, she's talking as if we're equals. 'Well, I suppose his first girlfriend would have been on the Isle of Wight, when he was growing up.'

'The Isle of Wight! We should go.'

I turn round and laugh in mock horror. 'We can't. I promised Zach I'd never set foot in the place. He didn't want me corrupted by it. He had sworn never to go back.'

'He made you promise never to go to the Isle of Wight?' Her expression, pinched around the cheeks, is baffled, and a bit pitying.

'It was no great hardship,' I said. 'Until I met Zach, I don't think I properly even thought about where it was. And, to be honest, it wasn't on my itinerary.' An idea is taking root, even as I'm talking. The Isle of Wight. *Of course.* I've been fixated on the thought of him nearby. He could be waiting at a distance. The Isle of Wight: yes. It's the last place he'd expect me to look. It would be the perfect place to hide.

'You're funny,' Onnie says. She's looking at me quite fondly. 'It wasn't on your itinerary!'

'It wasn't that funny.'

'Thanks for letting me stay. It's OK now, isn't it? I think when Zach finds out, he'll be so glad that we're friends.'

Zach

I'm off to Cornwall today. She thinks I'm seeing the new dealer in Exeter, spending the night there, but I'm going straight to Gulls. I'll make it nice for us to move into. I need to calm down a bit, too, get some more medication from Kulon. I want her to miss me, to miss my hands on her body, between her legs, the touch of my lips. She'd bloody better miss it. She'd bloody better miss me.

Valentine's day tomorrow and I'm not going to be here. Last year, it was roses and candlelight, cards and kisses. We spent the night entangled. This year, it hasn't been mentioned.

She was in a weird mood last night. She cooked chicken with mushrooms, actually *cooked* with them, touching, snarled up with garlic in their snappy little limbs. A pre-emptive stab at romance? I don't think so. It wasn't that I didn't speak to her. I *couldn't* speak to her. How could she pay so little attention to my needs? She rendered me literally speechless. When I left my entire plate, she took it away silently, scraped the lot into the bin. Later, she said in a peculiar tone, as if commenting on a subject that barely glanced off her life, like the weather in a distant part of the country: 'You could try mixing your food up a bit. You won't know if you like it unless you try.'

'I'm an adult,' I said. 'I don't need coaxing to eat my greens, thank you.'

'I'm just saying it might not kill you to try.'

I said: 'People always want to tell other people what to do.'

'People?' she said. 'You're always talking about "people", Zach. You make sweeping generalisations about "people", lumping them all together, as if the rest of the world behaves identically and you, alone, are different.'

She apologised this morning for upsetting me. I'd been angry, I think. I can't remember now. Did I push her? Bit of a blur. Still, it was too little, too late. We pretended to be normal. She'd hardly slept, I could tell – blue smudges under her eyes. The radio was on, broadcasting the results of another by-election in another town. She put her coat on and she was halfway out the door when I called her back.

'I love you,' I told her. 'You do know, don't you?'

'I do,' she said. She was lying through her teeth.

'More than anything,' I said. 'More than life itself.'

I kissed her as hard as I could, but I could still feel her pull away.

Chapter Twenty-two

Lizzie

On Saturday I am awake before it's properly light. Howard gets to his feet when I creep into the kitchen and eats the food I put down for him. His tail wags, knocking a spoon off the table. It clatters, and I freeze, waiting. No movement upstairs. I quickly write Onnie a note, thanking her for last night's meal and for her tidying – *I really appreciate it and the house definitely needed it*. I explain that I have a friend coming to stay and wouldn't mind having the sofa bed back if possible. I add a final line: *On reflection, I don't think us looking for Zach together is the best way to go about it! Sorry! If I don't see you before you leave, best of luck with everything!*

It's a nasty little passive-aggressive letter, but I don't care.

I hide Zach's laptop under my mattress and leave the house as quietly as I can.

Ryde esplanade in March: faded and bedraggled like a row of Victorian dolls left out in the rain. High tide crunching against the sea wall. At the top of the town, a church tower punctures a pillow of low cloud.

I feel as if I'm trespassing, entering forbidden territory. It was an evil place, Zach said, the repository of all his unhappiness. He swore the day he left he would never return. That day, he had stood up to his father for the first time and been

279

kicked out of the house. His mother was weak and took his father's side. When he died a few months later, his mother told Zach he wasn't welcome at the funeral. He didn't even go back to sell the manor – most of the proceeds went to pay his father's debts.

'Did the neighbours not know what was going on?' I asked him. 'Did no one step in to intervene?'

'They knew I was being beaten,' he said. 'Curtains twitched. They knew but they did nothing.'

I don't blame him for deciding to hate where he grew up, to blame it for everything that had happened. But it wasn't the island's fault. It was only the scene of the crime. He couldn't escape it just by moving somewhere else. He lived every day with the consequences of his father's brutality and his mother's collusion. It was behind all his problems. Maybe he has come to realise that. If he's hiding here now, how desperate he must be. And if he isn't, and he's followed me down, has seen me defy his wishes, how angry. Either way, this should draw him out. I want him to see me do it. I want him to *know*.

I take a train and a bus and a hovercraft. On the train, I scanned the faces of the other passengers, changed carriages and seats several times. There were only four of us on the hovercraft – two girls in their twenties and an old man who sat at the front, reading his newspaper.

I'm surprised how gentle and normal the Isle of Wight looks, a chunk of mainland set afloat, with its own pedestrian bridges and mini-roundabouts and fish and chip shops. Ryde has the melancholy air of any seaside town out of season – shuttered-up hotels, cut-price wetsuits, aimless teenagers.

I set off along the front, Howard pulling ahead, past a skating rink, a penny arcade, a mini Peter Pan amusement park. One of the rides is upended, its workings revealed like oily intestines. None of these landmarks are as tacky and awful as Zach claimed. At an artificial lake, next to a chained-up link of pedaloes in the shape of swans, a young woman and a small child are feeding bread to a few ducks. I remember a holiday in Bognor Regis, my mother upright and plucky in her darned summer frock with her two neat girls. She dressed us in matching swimsuits, marine blue with white skirts, from a shop called Cuff's. 'Suits your sister better,' I remember her telling me. 'She's got the figure for it. But there you are.'

I let Howard off the lead when I reach a wide arc of beach. To my relief, he seems much better today. I've picked up a map from a stand at the hoverport so I know roughly the direction I need to go in. I follow the sea path, past a shut-up café, a row of abandoned beach huts, and through a park to another main road. The path is quiet. No one follows me. Beyond a sweeping view of the grey Solent, the towers of Portsmouth are teeth marks on the horizon.

At the end of this raised walkway, where the huts dribble out, a path leads back down to the road. I put Howard back on the lead and have another look at the map. The next turning leaves the sea and climbs sharply up a hill. A few houses, mostly divided into flats, are set back from the road, interspersed with trees. It's so very different from Cornwall. Zach was right about that. It feels tamer here, more suburban. Most of the buildings look like holiday lets and are shut up.

At the top, past the entrance to a noisy Wildlife Encounter where Howard struggles to break free, I reach the main road and it's a fifteen-minute walk along this to the village where Zach grew up.

I'm not sure what I am expecting – a pretty green maybe, Miss Marple, some *thatching*. But this is more – well, it's a brow of hill, a curve of road, a junction. The village has a primary school – though I know Zach went to Tennyson Prep, the 'best education on the island' – an off-licence (heavily barred) and a Londis. A pub advertises Sky TV and a Sunday carvery.

I sit on a bench on a scratch of grass next to a dog-poo bin. Howard lies down at my feet. I'm glad he's with me. There's no one in sight. I hadn't imagined feeling so desolate. I thought the house Zach grew up in, Marchington Manor, would be obvious – a sweeping driveway, a walled garden, a tennis court. I haven't seen anything resembling that.

In Londis, the young girl with the nose-ring doesn't recognise Zach from the photograph I have brought – him on a deckchair in our garden, half asleep, his head tilted to the sun. It's my favourite. I took it one day without him noticing. She hasn't heard of anyone called Hopkins. The only big house she can think of is the Priory, but that's a luxury hotel. Zach once mentioned a nanny called Miss Caws. She wore a starched uniform and lived in one of the farm cottages. The girl with the nose-ring says there is a Caws Avenue, but she doesn't know of any old ladies who used to be nannies. As for farms, 'There's a petting farm over at St Helen's. The café's under new management, not sure they've got cottages – maybe holiday lets?'

Zach's father didn't drink in the pub. He imported his own booze into the house, preferring to drink alone. I ask behind the bar anyway. The landlady, who's from Thailand, knows nothing. She suggests I take the road back down to the coast, to the small seaside resort at the bottom of the hill. The man who owns the gift shop has been there for years – he might know something.

It is spitting with rain now. I zip up my fleece, pull the hood over my head, and set off in the direction the landlady sent me. As a teenager, he must have drunk in that pub, wheeled down this hill on his bike. He must be living a life, if he's hiding out here. He will have to be walking these pavements, using these shops. Have I got this wrong? I hear his voice in my ears. 'I thought you trusted me.'

The village is genteel in a higgledy-piggledy way, all blue and yellow curtains. It's hard to feel scared. I find the gift shop at the top of the high street. The door dings as I enter. It smells sweet and stale inside, of pencil shavings and second-hand books. Did my husband spend his pocket money here, on paper planes, water pistols or art materials – wax crayons and pads of sketching paper? I try to imagine him as a little boy, choosing carefully. When I can't, my heart lurches. I ask the owner, a fat man with rosy cheeks and new teeth, if he remembers him, or has seen him recently, but he doesn't, and he hasn't. He suggests I ask next door at the post office.

In here, three blond schoolchildren are choosing a crab net and a bald man in red trousers is extracting money from the cash machine. I'm beginning to feel frustrated. It's much bigger, this island, than I anticipated. The map says twenty-five miles by thirteen. He might not be here. He could be anywhere. The young woman at the till doesn't recognise the name Hopkins, either. Caws, though, oh yes, they're an old family in these parts, but no nannies as far as she knows. As for big houses, not so many round here, most of them were converted into flats way back.

'Sorry I can't be of any more help,' she says, reaching for a packet of Silk Cut to give the man in the red trousers. 'I'm sorry he's gone missing, love. It must be a heartache.'

I stand in the street outside the post office, where two dachshunds are tied up, yapping.

An elderly woman with swollen ankles is sitting in the pharmacy opposite, on a chair by the counter. The chemist is tall and thin with hollow cheeks and a prominent Adam's apple. I give my spiel – I'm looking for a friend, Zach Hopkins, who has gone missing, and I'm on a hunt to find him. I describe what I know about his childhood home. The chemist shakes his head, with only a glance at the photo, but a younger woman with long dark hair comes out of the back room with the old lady's medication and cranes her neck.

The old lady peers too. The younger woman says: 'Do you think that's Jilly Jones's son? It could be, couldn't it?'

The old lady takes it and holds it up to her nose. She nods and hands it back to me. 'That's Jilly Jones's boy.'

'Jones? No. I don't think so. I think you must be—'

The younger woman has turned away. She doesn't seem to want to talk any more. I feel awkward, as if I've said something wrong. When the old woman slowly gets to her feet, I hold out my arm to help her up, and she and I leave the shop together. She leans on me as we cross the road to the yapping dogs. As she unties them, she says: 'Do all right, did he, in the end?'

I nod. 'Yes. If we're talking about the right person, he did OK. He became an artist. A good one.'

'Mrs Bristock – you should talk to her. She was Jilly Jones's next-door neighbour. Still lives in the same house. She'll remember – she used to babysit for the lad. Go on. Take that picture and show her.'

She gives me the address, indicating the direction with her stick, and shuffles off with her dogs.

I cross the road again and take the turning she pointed at into a modern estate. The road bends and I follow it, take a left and a right, doubling back on myself at one point – it's confusing, the houses all look the same – until, after ten minutes of spiralling up the hill, I reach the right address. The house is small and square, with a patch of grass at the front and a large satellite dish attached to a mansard roof. Scalloped net curtains at the single window.

I expect it to be embarrassing and a waste of time. I imagine Mrs Bristock taking one look at the photograph and shaking her head. Part of me is hoping for that.

To the door comes a small woman with tight white curls and milky blue eyes behind enormous glasses. She is wearing bulbous pearl earrings, a floral dressing gown and gold lamé slippers on heavily veined feet. When I explain what I have come for – I am still using the name Zach Hopkins – she puts a bony hand on my arm and tells me to come in. 'Don't worry about the dog,' she says. 'He can run around in the garden.'

She takes a while unlocking the back door to let Howard out. He sees a cat and tears past her. The two of us go into her sitting room.

It's hot and crowded with knick-knacks. A gas fire is bubbling under a fake mantelpiece and the television is on, with the sound off. There's a dizzying, synthetic smell of rose petals.

'Right, dear,' she says, lowering herself into an armchair. 'Tell me again what you've come for.'

I perch on the edge of the sofa facing her; on the side table next to me is a bowl of potpourri and a tall black cat made of twisted glass. I take out the photograph and lay it carefully on the table.

'That's Jack Jones,' she says immediately. 'Poor Jilly's son.'

Jack Jones. I feel myself slipping back into the sofa, the cushions giving way beneath my head. 'Are you sure? When I met him he was called Zach Hopkins.'

'No, Jack Jones. She called herself Mrs Jones, for appearances' sake – but she was never married. It was her maiden name, though . . .' She waves one hand in the air. 'Now you mention it, I think the boy did take his father's name, when he got old enough. Changed it by deed poll.'

'His *father's* name? What do you mean?'

'It upset poor Jilly quite a bit. His father never had anything to do with him, you see – one of the fairground lads, or one of those boys over from the naval academy on a day trip. Came to visit once when the boy was about five. But I know he didn't pay maintenance.'

'I don't understand. The Zach I knew had two parents. Are you sure . . . ?'

I pass the photograph to her again and she brings it close to her face. 'Yup. That's Jack from next door all right.' She leans forward and pulls the lace curtain apart with her index finger. 'That house to the right, over there. Exactly the same as mine, only their garden is on a slant and I've got a bigger airing cupboard.'

I look where she's pointing. A house like this, with a satellite dish on the roof. A small blue trike lies on the front path. No manor. No tennis court. No staff. No abusive father. No father at all.

'I think you've got the wrong person,' I say.

Mrs Bristock heaves herself to her feet and opens the cupboard under the television. She brings out a photograph album and flicks through it. 'There,' she says, pointing. 'There he is. With Jilly at the village fete.' She brings it to her face again to read the writing under the photograph. 'In 1985. He must have been thirteen or so.'

She holds the album out and I look at it closely. The woman is thin, with a pinched face. She is in high heels and wearing a pink coat, cinched at the waist with a black patent belt. Next to her, unwillingly, half moving out of the picture, is a tall boy with brown hair and blue eyes and a distinctive mouth.

'Did she beat him?' I manage to say eventually.

'She *doted* on him, did Jilly,' Mrs Bristock says. 'She worked up at Tesco. When they opened the twenty-four-hour superstore she took on double shifts. She never learned to drive, but she used to cycle up there. Nothing was too good for her boy. Spoilt, of course. Overindulged. That was his problem.'

After a long pause, my voice cracking, I say: 'Where did he go to school?'

'Local primary, then the comprehensive over at Newport. Jilly wanted him to go to the grammar school in Portsmouth, but he didn't get in. He was mad keen for art college, I remember. He won the village art competition one Easter and he had a stall doing caricatures of people in the fair at Regatta Week. But it wasn't to be. He didn't get the grades.'

She stops talking and smiles at me. My expression must have stopped her. 'Can I get you anything, dear? A drink?'

I tell her I wouldn't mind a glass of water but I can fetch it myself. I ask her if she'd like anything and she quite fancies some tea – 'bit early but what the heck'. I tell her I'll bring it and I stand in the kitchen, waiting for the kettle to boil, staring out of the window. Howard is lying in the middle of her lawn, next to a low bird bath.

No abusive father, no beatings, no cold corridors and freezing cellars. An ordinary childhood in an ordinary village. A mother who doted on him, who gave him everything he wanted. A single parent – but no one died of that. Nothing he told me is true. It's all lies. How many times did I excuse his behaviour, his need for control because of what he went through? How much did I let him get away with?

He didn't go to art college. He never lived in Clapham. I think about the bare white walls of his Wimbledon studio: did he paint at all? The gallery in Exeter, how hard I tried to track it down after his death, to reclaim his work – was *that* an invention? This man I loved. I lay next to every night. I touched each part of his body. I let him inhabit me, possess me. *He slept with Onnie*. He is a stranger. Even his name is a fabrication.

When I finally make it back into the lounge, Mrs Bristock is gazing through the crack she has made in the lace curtains. She is 'ever so grateful for the cuppa: my goodness, waitress service', and starts to tell me about her husband, Mr Bristock, who had run a school-uniform shop in Southsea. He had been unlucky enough to suffer an early death from cancer in the 1960s.

'Jack Hopkins,' she says thoughtfully. 'I always wondered what happened to him. Remind me why you're after him?'

'He was a friend of mine. Is. I lost touch. You haven't seen him . . . in the last year or so?'

'Not since the day he upped and left. I believe he became a tourist guide. Coach trips. Over in Europe?'

'Probably. That's what he told me, but . . .'

'After everything – I thought we might see him when the house was sold, but the only person through the door was the estate agent. He probably didn't want to show his face after . . .' She loses her thread. 'Well, the new lot, they're nice enough. They've let the garden go to pot, though. Jilly loved her garden.'

'What was he like?' I ask. 'As a child.'

She glances at me. 'A gorgeous face. Butter wouldn't melt. Sweet as pie. Those big blue eyes: he could make you do anything. I used to sit for him, when Jilly was at work. When he was very little, of course. That stopped later.'

She pats gently at her fine white curls. Her eyes fix on a patch on the carpet. 'He was a complicated lad.' Her voice flattens. 'I'm not sure it's my place . . .'

'Go on.'

'Well, if you're sure.' She begins to tell stories, long anecdotes. At first, they sound like nothing, schoolboy pranks:

288

fireworks set off at odd times, tortured frogs, dissected mice, her missing pet cat. 'I always said he had something to do with it. She scratched him once when he was quite small and he hated her after that. He wouldn't go near her, said she was evil. He searched for her with all the other kids – I'd promised a reward – but I caught him giving me a look that was almost gleeful.'

She takes off her big glasses and rubs at the red mark on the bridge of her nose before putting them back on. 'There's not much to do around here for young people in winter. Summer's different. Once he got a bit older he used to spend time with the holiday lot. He got a job at the yacht club, in the bar. One girl in particular I remember him being doolally about, a boarding-school lassie – she was only here a month, on the way down to Cornwall where her family had a place.'

'Was she called Victoria?'

'No idea, dear. But that was typical Jack. He was on and on at Jilly to move to Cornwall. Nothing here was ever good enough for him.'

'Actually, he loved Cornwall. He bought a small bungalow down there – with the money . . .' I gesture through the net curtains at the house next door.

'Well, I hope it brought him happiness.'

I laugh quickly, then sigh. 'I don't know.'

She gives me a beady look. 'I didn't blame him. Despite what folk said. I like to think the best of people, and the coroner . . . well, he came down on his side.'

I feel myself smile oddly. 'What are you talking about?'

'The accident. The summer before he left.'

'The accident?' The sofa I'm sitting on is beige velour. I stroke it carefully. The colour darkens.

'Didn't he tell you?'

'No.'

'Well, someone else will if I don't. It was Polly Milton, his girlfriend, her father ran the yacht club.' She nods to herself. 'She was a beautiful thing, headstrong, like they all are at that age. Played all the boys off against each other. It almost killed her parents.'

'What did?'

A small boy has come out of the house next door and is riding up and down the street on the blue trike, ringing his bell.

'She drowned. She'd sailed out to the fort, over by Bembridge, on her father's Laser with Jack. Her body was washed up at Gosport a month later. She was the love of Jack's life at the time. He was devastated. Jack said she'd jumped in for a lark and that by the time he managed to turn the dinghy round, she'd disappeared. He tacked back and forth, trying to find her, but . . .'

All feeling has gone from my face. My tongue feels heavy in my mouth. 'And what did other people say?'

'Well, people thought he'd killed her. They'd been arguing – someone on a passing boat heard raised voices. No one believed she'd have jumped in, not there, not with the current as strong as it was, not so close to the shipping lane.'

'Was he arrested?' I say, louder than I mean to.

'Yes, though it never went to trial. Not enough evidence. But he wasn't welcome round here after that.'

Zach

13 February 2012

On the way out of town earlier, I parked up near the school. I stood on the common and watched her up in the school library. The lights were on and she passed by the window twice. The third time, she leaned her elbows on the sill and looked out. She seemed to stare straight at me, though I knew I was hidden, my back pressed against the tree, my face concealed behind a web of branches. I had it in mind to step forward when a man came into view behind her, and as she turned, I saw her laugh, a chink of white throat. I imagined his lips then in the dip of her neck, where the vein throbs, her eyes closing, his hands on the swell of her breasts.

If I know for sure that she has moved on, that she has forgotten what we had, I'll kill her.

She has no one to blame but herself.

Gulls isn't the same without her.

I rang her just now, pretended to have reached Exeter with my six months' worth of imaginary canvases. The gallery owner took them all and wants more! We're having dinner later to celebrate! At his local wine bar. I'll have a salad. Shower and a shave in the bathroom at the B & B. Nice woman runs it. Elderly. A widow.

It's almost comic, her willingness to suck up my lies. Her

imagination met me halfway. 'Was it the abstracts he liked best?' she said. 'Or the ones where you play with personification?' She wants me to do well so she can be free of me, fuck whoever she's fucking with impunity.

I felt tears at the corners of my eyes. The booze makes me maudlin.

I've hardly moved from this chair since I arrived. If the rain lets up, I'll collect my stuff from the boot. Might read a book. Might not. Peace, quiet: that's what I need.

I might drive down to the Blue Lagoon later, see if Kulon has had a chance to replenish his suitcase of goodies. I'm a bit short of cash. I'll take the emergency money. She'll never know, as long as I fill it up before I leave.

Chapter Twenty-three

Lizzie

I don't get a taxi. I need air.

When I reach the seafront, I stare out across the water where she drowned. Polly Milton. He told me about a Polly long ago, at a French restaurant opposite Clapham Picturehouse. Steak. Red wine. The warm glow of personal disclosure. She was the childhood sweetheart who slept with his best friend and broke his heart. He didn't tell me she was dead, or that he had been there when it happened.

I stagger along the sea wall. Polly's hair like seaweed trailing in the water. Her body bloated, her eyes unseeing, I think about Charlotte – her fall. Zach miles away. The clunk of her limbs against the bannisters, the thud of her head.

Two deaths. This man who lied and lied to me.

I make it back to Ryde, and onto the hovercraft and catch the bus and a train. I feel as if I'm walking underwater, pushing against the tide. The carriage is busy. A woman bounces a baby. A huddle of teenage boys listen to music on a mobile phone. Women with shopping bags. A man with the *Daily Star*.

Out of the window, I scrutinise the world as it flicks by – gardens, fields, shops, factories. He's out there. I know he is. He isn't going to come back and make happy families. He isn't traumatised. It's more twisted than that, more calculating. Zach isn't afraid of me. He doesn't love me. All those excuses I made for him. All the things – the *thing* – I forgave. This is revenge.

At a station, the doors open and a man gets on. I tense, dig my fingers into Howard's collar. The man has his back to me while he slots the handle down into a wheeled suitcase and lifts it up into the luggage rack. When he turns round, he is much older and shorter than Zach, in his sixties with a bulbous nose and ruddy cheeks. But I have bitten my lip so hard I taste blood.

What does it say that I loved him? Troubled as he was, I thought he needed me, that I could help him. I did believe he was my soulmate. I did feel a connection. Despite everything, I couldn't get enough of him. What does that say about me?

I fumble for my phone and try Jane and then Peggy. Neither of them answers. Saturday afternoon and normal people with normal lives, normal relationships, are at the cinema or out with friends.

The train has trundled past Guildford when I ring Sam. He's the only person I can think of. He is in his flat, recuperating. Yes, much better, thank you. Good to be home. No, that's right, impossible to sleep on a ward. Very nice to be back in his own bed.

He answers my questions politely until I run out. 'Are you all right?' he asks then. 'You sound terrible.'

I'm pressing my forehead against the glass, biting back tears.

'Come over,' he says.

I walk quickly from the station to take Howard home. I stick to the main roads, up St John's Hill, which is thronging with buses, across to Battersea Rise and on to the long drag of Spencer Park, which has the railway on one side, big houses on the other. For the first time I am properly scared walking. I know what he's capable of now. He's a violent man. He isn't troubled, ready to be saved. He is a liar and a murderer and he wants to kill me.

I've left the main bus route behind and I'm walking away from the shopping bustle of Clapham Junction. It's getting dark and, though there is a steady stream of traffic, no pedestrians are in sight. In the dip to the left of me is the railway cutting – trains pass, with a splattering judder of light and noise. I keep turning, just to check. I am halfway along when I notice the cyclist in the white helmet five hundred yards or so behind. It's a man. I can tell from the bent shape of him, and he is pedalling slowly – his knees at an angle, the bike wobbling to and away from the kerb.

Still looking, I start to run. I keep looking behind. The cyclist lowers his head and speeds up. The distance between us narrows. I run faster, Howard tugging at the lead. I turn round again. Two hundred yards now, cycling towards me with intent.

Zach's bike, the white helmet I bought him: they were in the shed. I stop, my breath hot in my chest. I should push this to a crisis, force him to act. A train lurches to a halt. I can see the carriage lights, the smudged faces of the passengers, through the railings.

The cyclist is overtaken by a taxi. It has its light on. I put my hand out and, as if in slow motion, the taxi pulls over and Howard and I get in.

Through the rear window I watch the cyclist, pedalling wildly, diminish in the distance.

The taxi driver waits for me while I take Howard into the house and feed him. There's no sign of Onnie. My note has gone from the table. She hasn't left one in return, though the flowers she bought me and which I had arranged in a vase are stuffed in the bin – a message of sorts. I wash my face as quickly as I can, settle Howard in his basket, and then I'm out of the house, the door locked behind me, and back in the taxi.

He isn't a talker, this taxi driver, which is good. My mind is racing. I haven't been looking for a cyclist. I've been looking for someone on foot, or in a car. I'd forgotten Zach's bike. The traffic is heavy. Could he have caught up with the taxi? I look behind me. A bus – the 319 I was planning to take – fills the rear-view. He could be idling behind, or have overtaken and be waiting at the next lights. That's the thing about a bike in London: you can duck and dive, get anywhere.

Streatham High Road has a fast-forward blur to it, people falling out of pubs and falling into McDonald's. Sam's road in contrast, second right after the police station, behind the cinema, is dark and quiet. The taxi stops halfway up, next to a disused church, and I get out to pay. A cat slinks out of an alley and darts across the road. A door slams behind, and metal clangs: a woman putting something in a dustbin. The taxi driver closes his window and purrs up the road. Silence, except for my footsteps on the tarmac.

I stand on the pavement for a few moments. No bike rounds the corner, no white helmet. But there are several alleys on this road, the empty church, several unlit places to wheel a bike and lurk. Have I been foolhardy? Is it wrong of me to put Sam in more danger? Or is this the only way to draw Zach out? All I know is I can't carry on now, knowing what I do. I need to force the moment to its crisis, to bring it to an end.

The top window of Sam's building, a Victorian red-brick converted into flats, is lit. A bare bulb dangles.

I wait, and then I push the gate open.

Sam's is the bottom bell. I try to arrange my face. I am a normal person going on a normal date. I have a thought and rummage in my bag for the lipstick. I haven't got a mirror but I rub it on my lips anyway. I can hear Sam's footsteps, but I turn quickly away from the house, tip my face to the light. In my imagination, a camera whirrs – click, click: evidence of my crime.

Sam opens the door in jeans and a fresh white T-shirt. I can see the shape of the bandages through the fabric. He grins when he sees me, his eyes crinkle. He is so normal-looking, I almost cry.

'I was going to shower,' he said. 'But I didn't have time. I'm in a bit of a mess. Sorry about that.'

The T-shirt looks new – I can see lines across it from where it was folded in the packaging. 'I don't mind a bit of mess,' I say.

His flat, the other side of a scratched white door on the ground floor, is small and untidy and full of books. There's a mishmash of furniture that suggests the post-divorce division of spoils – threadbare sofa, a Victorian desk, Ikea shelves. We go into the kitchen, where the sink is piled with washing-up. A cupboard is open, revealing cornflakes, Rose's lemon and lime marmalade, a small packet of Uncle Ben's rice. Piled on the table are newspapers and exercise books waiting to be marked.

A wooden door opens on to a small backyard, scratchy grass edged by humps of brambles. At the end, a rickety fence to the next garden. The door has two bolts, one across the top, the other across the bottom, but they're drawn back.

Sam has his back to me. He's busy opening a bottle, finding glasses. I jam the bolts home while he isn't looking.

'You're not much of a gardener then?' I say, still looking out. I'm wondering about the next-door plot: whether there is a side passage; how easy it would be to break into it from the street. But I sound like someone making idle chit-chat at a cocktail party.

'No.' Sam comes up behind me with a glass of wine. 'It's shared with the upstairs flat. The couple who rented it before used to have the occasional barbecue, but the new guy hardly ever uses it. Occasionally, in the summer, he sits out there and works.'

'What kind of work?'

'God knows. He works at home. Writer? IT? Basically he fiddles away on his laptop.'

'Have you got to know him well?'

'Nah. Not my type. Bit brooding. Keeps himself to himself.'

'What does he look like?'

Sam laughs. 'Why, do you think you know him?'

'Just curious.'

'Dark hair. Big beard.'

As I reach for my wine, I notice my hand shake.

Sam seems to notice too. He puts his hand over it. 'I don't know why I said that about not showering,' he says. 'I did shower. It was quite hard, keeping the bandages dry. I've put on a new T-shirt specially. I didn't want you to think I was making an effort just because you were coming.'

His tone is too matter-of-fact for flirtation. I begin to laugh, and then I realise I am crying.

I start with Zach's lies – everything I've discovered about his past from his childhood to his affair with Onnie – and move on to my life with him. I tell Sam the things I've kept from my sister and my best friend and which, over the last year, I have tried so hard to forget. Once I start, I can't stop. I say that I loved Zach, that he *was* the love of my life. It wasn't just sex – though a lot of it was about that. When I met him, he was sweet and kind. He looked after me. He thought I wasn't happy. He *wanted* me to be happy. I couldn't believe how lucky I was, that *he* would be interested in *me*.

I tell Sam how Zach changed so gradually I hardly noticed, that it began with small things – objects having to be in certain positions in the house – and then escalated. He opened my letters. He followed me. Another teacher at work – middle-aged, married – gave me a box of chocolates to thank me for ordering in some extra books and Zach flushed them down the toilet. Once, in Sainsbury's, I borrowed change for the pay-and-display machine from a man who was standing there, and when I got home Zach was beside himself. He interrogated me for hours. He'd been watching the whole time.

Sam clears the plates, balances them in the sink on top of the pans. 'Was he violent?' he asks.

'It was more the threat,' I say eventually. 'Mostly.'

He sits down again. 'Did you tell anyone?'

'At first, it all seemed trivial, as if it were in my imagination. By the time it felt serious, I had learned to think of it as my fault. I thought I was in the wrong. I was making him do these things.'

'And you didn't feel you could leave him for that reason?'

I feel my eyes fill with tears. I brush them away. 'I was going to,' I say eventually.

'And what gave you the strength to make that decision?'

I take a deep breath. 'I haven't told anyone this.'

Sam waits until I am ready.

'We'd been trying for a baby,' I say, in a high, stiff voice. 'Zach had agreed, but when it didn't work, he said it was a sign that we were better off as we were. He said he should be enough for me. But the fact is he wasn't.' I shake the hair out of my face. 'That's the truth. I wanted a baby, and I went to see the GP behind his back to find out why it wasn't working, and she thought I knew.'

'Knew what?'

'She looked a bit confused, but she said I wasn't to worry.

299

People often changed their minds. The procedure was usually reversible. I should send him in.'

'He'd had a vasectomy?'

'Yes.' I bite my lip. 'He hadn't told me. He lied. He let me think . . .'

'What a bastard.'

'I know. He was a bastard. It was a bastard thing to do. The fact that he had concealed it, let me think we were trying, when all the time . . . It's unimaginable that someone you loved would do that to you.'

'What did he say when you confronted him?'

I gaze at Sam. 'I didn't. I should have done, but I knew he would twist it, manipulate me into thinking that I was in the wrong. I just wanted to escape. I wrote him a letter. I didn't tell him why I wanted to separate. I . . . Oh—' I gulp. 'It was such an awful letter. It's such a relief to tell someone. I wrote, "*My beloved Zach, I will never forget what we had, but I think we could do with a little time apart. I need space of my own. Please don't contact me for a bit. All my love, Lizzie.*" Oh my God. I've just understood something. "*Please don't contact me for a bit.*" That's why he's waited.'

Sam's looking confused. 'When you were together, did you ever think about going to the police?'

'No. I thought I could cope. But I think I should go to them now.'

He nods, pushes a bowl of peanuts towards me. 'Not a bad idea. Why don't you? They could put you in touch with professionals, people who could talk you through what happened. I hate to use the cliché, but it might provide, you know, *closure.*'

'That's not what I mean.'

Sam looks up, surprised at my fierceness.

'It's not about *closure*,' I say. 'I think I should go to the police

300

because he's still alive. He's out there, now, Sam. He probably knows I'm here. And he's dangerous. The two women I told you about who died in terrible accidents: it's not a coincidence. I'm scared.'

Sam's expression doesn't change. He puts out his hand and cups mine. His fingers are blunt, the nails neatly rounded. He lowers his head slightly.

'Oh, I know you think I'm mad,' I say. 'Everybody does.'

He puts his hand on my elbow and steers me, so I am sitting close to him on the threadbare sofa, not in the armchair as I was before.

'I think you should tell me what's been going on.'

So I do. I tell him about being followed, about the things that have been placed in my house when I wasn't there – the dead bird and the lipstick – and the items that have been taken, the iPod, the Rotring pens, the china houses, all the possessions he collected from Gulls. I tell him about the music I keep hearing and the time I saw him in the stadium car park, the message in the painting. I tell Sam I think it was Zach who beat him up.

He doesn't say much and his expression hardly changes. Once or twice, he nods. I look up at him when I have finished. 'Do you believe me?'

'What do you want me to say?'

'I want you to say what you think.'

He stands up and crouches at my side, wobbling slightly. His words are careful. 'I think you've had a harrowing experience. It sounds to me like your marriage was intense, that Zach was, at the very least, an extremely troubled man. And then the ghastly event of Zach's death . . . I think it would be understandable if you were experiencing some sort of post-traumatic stress.'

'You're saying it's in my head?'

'I think you've had a lot to deal with.'

He is still crouching and he stretches, pushing his shoulders back. He winces. 'Ouch. Sorry. I better . . .'

It's a good thing he stands up then because I'm about to scream with frustration. One more person who won't believe me. I've told him *everything*. I thought he could save me. I wonder whether I should get up and leave. But then maybe I should stay a little longer. Two doors between this flat and the street; the bolts on those were strong, even if the back entrance is flimsy. I think about the police station I passed in the taxi. Sam has crossed over into the kitchen and is making coffee. I have another thought, too, soft and comforting, like cashmere. Post-traumatic stress. None of it is real. I've made it all up. I'm in no danger at all.

'Frothy milk?' Sam asks. 'I've got a gadget.'

'Yes please.'

There is a pile of books on the table in front of me. I pick up the one on top. It's a paperback, neon-pink, the kind of pop psychology self-help book that makes the best-seller list. I flick through it. One chapter is called 'Sociopathy', the next 'Narcissistic Disorder'. It goes on. There are checklists. My eyes scan quickly. '*Lacking empathy . . . superficial charm or charisma . . . a belief in their own superiority . . . a chronic dissatisfaction . . . a deep-seated desire to control those around them.*'

When Sam comes over, I thrust the book at him. 'Do you think Zach is in here?'

'Possibly. Four per cent of the population is supposed to fit the definition of "sociopath". That's one in twenty-five of us living without a conscience.'

Despite everything, my first instinct is loyalty. 'It's not as if the rest of us are so saintly,' I say. 'I'm always nice to people and agreeable. Like Joyce Poplin, who can be such a bitch. I'm always making her cups of tea, being *pleasant*. But quite often inside I'm furious. Zach used to have a go at me for "seeing the best in people", but it's a trick. I'm scared of not being liked.'

'I hear what you're saying.'

I suddenly hate Sam and everything he stands for, all this calm and reason. 'When people say they hear what someone's saying, they usually mean they aren't listening at all. Zach told me that.'

Sam smiles. He's leaning right back on the sofa and his face looks lopsided from this angle, his brow knotted. I imagine him repeating, 'I hear what you're saying,' but I don't think he actually does.

'It's partly genetic,' he says. 'It's not about being nice or not nice to Joyce Poplin. It's how your cerebral cortex functions.'

I watch his mouth as he forms the words. 'Is it?'

'Are you feeling any better?' he says softly. His eyes are not like Zach's eyes. His features seem to melt.

I breathe deeply, so deeply my heart hurts. My body feels light, the atoms in my face are tingling. The hatred I felt for Sam a second ago changes colour, deepens and becomes more complicated. Watch me do this, I think. See how I'm letting you go. See what you have made me do. Watch me. I lean across to press my lips against his.

In the morning, I wake up early. It's still dark. I can hear purposeful movements in the flat upstairs, creaks, the gush of water.

Sam is still asleep, scrunched to the side of the bed, one arm upraised, his head in the crook of the pillows. There's a red mark across his cheeks. I get out of bed and creep around the room, finding my shoes and coat, a pain in my head rocking with every move. In the kitchen, I splash water on my face. I think I hear him get up, the twang of the bed springs, but he doesn't emerge. It's just sighing in the joints of an old house.

The garden looks blank and unloved. A fold-up chair, the sort you get at petrol stations, is propped in the centre of the grass. I don't remember seeing it the night before. I think about this man upstairs writing out there on his laptop. Tapping, tapping.

At the door to the flat, my hand resting on the handle, I wait for a moment or two, braced. Heavy footsteps descend the communal stairs, seem to pause in the hallway, and then the front door slams, and I follow.

Zach

It was dead down there. Three couples eking out the romance, with Kulon and Jolyon, one of his white dreadlocked surfing mates, at the bar. *Le patron* fell upon me like a long-lost lover. 'Zachamundo, my man.' We played poker and knocked back a few. When Kulon had to serve some customers, Jolyon tried to get me to go with him to some happening, Love Face, in Bude. He was getting on my nerves, to be honest. I let him take my car just to get rid of him. He's promised to bring it back by tomorrow.

When Kulon rejoined me, I brought up 'the suitcase' as soon as I could. The bad news: Kulon spent January with his parents in Alicante – 'Needed to, man, they're bankrolling the joint'. The good news: he picked up some MDPV from some boarding-school kids at New Year. He'd let me have some, but he had to cover his costs – 'Sorry, man, not cheap, you know what I'm saying?' I gave him what was left of the forty quid from the box of muesli, promised to get him the rest later in the week.

It put me in a bad mood, that information about his parents. You think people are like you, and then you find out they're as privileged as all the other tossers. Just another hippy trustafarian. When he took over the Blue Lagoon a few years ago, I assumed he'd worked hard for what he'd achieved, saved up, was

305

putting everything he had into it. But no, turns out the café is a hobby, a lifestyle choice; his parents are putting everything *they* have into it.

I was about to go home, fed up with the lot of them, when who should burst in but Onnie. Eyes like saucers when she saw yours truly – all over me. I would have shrugged her off, if I hadn't noticed the fury on Kulon's face. Him and her, then: hmm, interesting. Didn't take her long. Another older man. Seems she can't get enough of us.

Anyway, it was enough to make me stay, just to piss him off. So much for Cornwall being short of distractions – doesn't sound as if Alan and Vic factored in the attractions of the Blue Lagoon and its owner. Not to mention his suitcase. She was shouty and silly and kept grabbing food off Kulon's fork. She wanted my attention. Her clothes were skimpy – miniscule skirt, Uggs, no tights – and her pupils were dilated. She'd changed her hair.

'I'm all alone,' she said every time Kulon had to serve a customer. 'The shitty au pair has abandoned me for a shag with a Young Farmer, left me to my own devices for the whole night. I'll be all on my own up there. You not with wifey?'

'No.'

'I thought she was so precious to you.'

I shrugged.

She said, 'Haven't you missed me? Can I come to Gulls? We don't have to do anything, just hang out.'

'No.'

'You're so weird. Mum says she's never been inside your house – even back in the Ice Age when you were friends. Have you got dead bodies in there? What are you hiding?'

'I'm not hiding anything.'

'So why can't I come?'

'You might bring in dirt.'

She laughed. She thought I was joking. Shortly after that, she sidled off upstairs with Kulon. Filthy little whore.

I'm back now. Had to walk. Forgot I'd lent out the car to that loser. He'd better bring it back in one piece. I keep thinking about that big house at the top of the hill. When Vic was newly married, I broke in once. I feel almost nostalgic, thinking back on that time. I was still learning. I thought the decor, all that Colefax and Fowler, those tables with skirts, was the height of sophistication. I wonder if they've updated their look.

It'll be empty now. The au pair's away. Onnie's hooked up with Kulon. I might take the torch and have a snoop. The windows in the drawing room, if I remember: pretty, but inefficient antique latches.

14 February 2012

I'm back at Gulls now, soaking, filthy. I have lost a night and most of a day. I've got to calm down. Are these normal reactions? I have a feeling I'm supposed to be responding in a certain way, that there's a manual I should know about. Am I drunk? Still? Really. I feel like laughing. I want to see Lizzie. I need her. I'll ring her – the moment Onnie's out of the shower. Lizzie will save me from this. All along that is what she's been doing, saving me from myself.

She's written to me. I found the letter on the mat just now when I got back. A Valentine's card maybe. Her lovely writing on the envelope. I'll open it in a minute. I'm expecting an apology and an outpouring of love. The angel. I already forgive her. I'm even beginning to forget why I was angry.

It's my art, or the wellies, that have given me away. That's funny too.

I got myself up to Sand Martin. I was sober then, wasn't I? Perhaps I had dipped my finger in the bag of white crystals I'd bought from Kulon. It's here now, in front of me, but you can't count crystals, of course, so I can't be sure. Maybe I had. I can't remember. Memory loss: it's one of the things I worry about. I'm mixing it up too much, losing control.

307

Lizzie will sort it. She'll know what to do.

The house looked deserted as I got close, looming out of the darkness like a rock in the fog. I scrambled over the flower beds to the front windows easily enough, and managed to fit the credit card in and under – the latch swung to one side. I was worried the joints might have been painted in since the first time I was here, but the window pushed up smoothly. My boots were thick with mud from hiking up the hill, so I sat on the window sill and winkled them off, chucked them on to the grass before climbing over.

Through the air they flew. There they lay. An abandoned pair of Hunter wellies.

It was just as I remembered it. Not a chintz apron or a carriage clock had shifted since I was last here. Insipid sea-scene watercolours. Mahogany drinks tray along one wall. Decanters and glasses, sherry, Dubonnet. A half-empty bottle of distillery-only ten-year-old Glengoyne, my whisky – though of course it isn't actually mine, it was Murphy's before it was mine. The first time I tasted it was in this room. I poured myself a finger and sat down in the wing chair. I put my feet up on the coffee table, dislodging a copy of *Country Life*. I knocked it back and felt the fire turn my throat amber. I closed my eyes for a second. What happened to Vic? I think idly. What a great girl she'd been. Those parties on the Isle of Wight, those naked midnight swims. When did she change? I felt the room spin.

'So you came.'

I opened my eyes. Onnie was standing in the doorway. I don't know how long she'd been watching me. She was wearing a fleece all-in-one catsuit-type garment and her hair was scraped back. For a second, I was confused. I'd seen her going into Kulon's flat at the Blue Lagoon. She wouldn't have had time to get here – unless it was later than I thought, unless I had lost a chunk of time. Luckily, I'm a good actor.

I got to my feet with a leisurely stretch. 'There you are. I've been waiting for you.'

She stared. 'Were you just pretending down at the bar?'

'Something like that.'

'Were you jealous?'

'I'm always jealous.'

I thought I might have to fight her off, but she started behaving like her mother in recent years, all Tory airs and graces – pouring me a drink and fetching nuts from the kitchen. Little upper-class madam at heart, of course, despite the rebellion. I was acting, too, playing up the role of ancient roué, gasping for some excitement in this *godforsaken hellhole*, and after a while she went to get her 'stash' – enough for a couple of joints. When I asked if she had anything else to make an old man happy, she produced benzpheta-mine, a diet pill. She said it would have us flying like the best E.

It's a bit of a blur after that. Music played loudly from an iPod in one of the rooms upstairs, and we cooked up food in the kitchen, though I can't remember eating it. She found me another bottle of Glengoyne (eighteen years old) in the larder. Those five or six times we met in London, we'd had mechanical sex. I wasn't going there again. Keep it cerebral, I remember thinking that. I told her my philosophy of design, the importance of simple lines, how a house should be a blank canvas for a busy mind. She told me I was brilliant, that she'd remember it for ever. She danced for a bit, careering off the sofas. I lay on the floor and watched. She played the piano. I sang: 'Alison' from *My Aim is True.* Elvis Costello, I told her: the greatest singer who ever walked this earth. I told her never to forget that either. At one point, we ran frantically from room to room, chasing a wild dog that got in. Or perhaps I imagined that. Perhaps it was the ghost of Howard, haunting my narcotic dreams.

At one point, exhausted, we collapsed in the sitting room. She began to dance again, more slowly. I tore a blank page out of a book on the coffee table and told her to stay still for me. She pushed her all-in-one outfit off her shoulder, let it slip and slide down until her breast was exposed, lay down on the floor with her neck thrown back. I drew her, half-naked, and when the drawing was finished, I put it aside and knelt next to her, pulled the catsuit off her, yanked it down over her knees.

It was light when I fell asleep. Or rather, I remember still being awake when it turned light.

The sound of screaming woke me. Opening my eyes, Onnie's hair was all I could see, spread across the pillow. It was like netting. I could distinguish the shaft of each individual criss-crossed strand. Her mouth was half open, the bottom lip slightly cracked. For a moment, I thought the screams had come from her, that she was dead. But then more screaming, deep downstairs, the slamming of an internal door. 'Onnie!' A screech. 'Where are you? What the hell has been going on?'

I leaped up, banging my shin. We were in her bedroom. I had no idea what time it was. Gloomy outside. Early morning? No, late afternoon. The thud of rain. A dressing table, strewn with make-up. Pink cherry wallpaper. Onnie's eyes opened. She lifted her head. She was lying across a white sleigh bed, next to the dip where I had just been, naked. 'My mother,' she said. A smile curled her lips and langorously she got to her feet. 'That's weird.'

I think I said I didn't think it was funny and it seemed to click her into action. The door was already wide open, and she peered out, listened. Victoria was just outside the front door, in the porch, talking on her mobile phone. Onnie was throwing on clothes and she grabbed me by the arm and we ran down the backstairs, through the scullery and out the kitchen door, across the sopping wet grass into the copse of trees. Neither of us was wearing shoes. My wellies were still on the front lawn. I was in socks. The 'feet' of Onnie's outfit were black and sodden.

We paused as soon as we were hidden in the semi-shelter of a tree. The wind took the branches and shook water down on us. She was laughing. I was angry. Cold and wet and furious. We argued. She said, 'It's, like, really raining.' I said it's not 'like' really raining. It is really raining. She'd never get anywhere in life if she didn't learn to speak. I told her to go home and she said she wouldn't go without me. I grabbed her by the shoulders and shook her until she began to cry. I walked off and she followed, stumbling behind, through the wood and out into the field on the other side. Heavy mud where the cows had trodden. We needed each other to get through the worst of it. We'd waded to the stile on the other side, and I was halfway across it when my phone rang. It was Lizzie. I remembered, like a knife in my chest, that I was supposed to have been in Exeter today. What had I been thinking, going down to the Blue Lagoon? I glared at Onnie. I shouldn't have slept with her. It was all her fault.

Lizzie asked where I was. I told her I was on Dartmoor, painting. The scenery, I said, was glorious — not a person as far as the eye could see. Onnie made a noise, as if she found it funny, or was so stupid she wanted to put me right. I almost put my hand over her mouth. Luckily, from my position astride the stile, I couldn't reach. I might have suffocated her. Lizzie was worried about it being dark. 'I'm fine,' I said. 'Just setting off back to the car now.'

It took a good forty minutes to reach the bungalow. My feet were scratched and sore, trousers filthy, socks stuck to the skin like black bandages. Onnie was limping. The rain continued to stream. We didn't talk. I was too busy trying to think through the thumping in my head.

I didn't want to let her into the house, but I didn't know what else to do. The lantern was glittering in the porch of the bungalow opposite; their car, a grey Hyundai, was parked outside. I pushed her up the path, opened the front door and shut it behind us. It was dark in here even then. Onnie stood on the mat, bedraggled, dripping on today's post. I found her a towel and we felt our way towards the shower. She could put the light on in there, I told her, but she had to switch it off before she came out. I locked her in just to be on the safe side. Then I peeled off my socks and trousers, picked up the post, including the letter from Lizzie, and sat down here in the dark.

My phone rang. A number I didn't recognise. A furious voice. 'Do you have my daughter?'

'Who is this?'

'I know she's with you. You've been up at my house. Don't even try to deny it. She's half your age. You filthy, disgusting man.'

Oh, Victoria. Bloody hell. I hung up.

It rang again. And again. And then a text: I hope you feel proud of yourself.

I could still hear the shower, the gurgle of the pipes. I stood up. Beyond the glass, dark shrubs writhed. Rain streaked. I pulled down the blinds, sat on the edge of a chair.

It felt like seconds later when the car slammed into the verge at the bottom. Victoria running, knocking over planters, banging on the door, shouting. 'Onnie. I know you're in there. Come out.'

Her voice right up at the window, under the streaming gutter. 'Jack. I know she's with you. I found the drawing. And your boots.' She was talking under her breath, hissing. She moved away from the window and her voice got louder. She was losing control. 'You sad fuck, Jack, Zach, whatever you call yourself, you talentless arsehole.'

Her footsteps moved around the bungalow and back down the path. I watched her through a crack in the blinds. The old woman came out of the house opposite with an umbrella. Rain glanced off Victoria's coat; her hair stuck to her face. They talked. The old woman looked back up at Gulls and shrugged. Victoria clapped her hand to her head and got back into her car.

A text. Where are you?

I left my boots; of course I did. Annoying, as they were absurdly expensive and I can't see a way of getting them back — not that she'll ever know for sure they're mine. But 'the drawing': that was stupid. Did I sign my name? A stupid slip. I'll have to bluff it out.

On the road from Dartmoor, I wrote. Who is this? Pressed 'Send'.

A banging from the bathroom door. 'I'm ready to come out.'

'Give me a few minutes,' I said.

Next text: You're lying, you fucker. I know it was you. I'm not stupid. Where is my daughter, you pathetic man?

My blood pressure rose at that. I stood to try to recover my composure. I peered through the slats. There she was, mistress of the universe, sitting out there, in that smooth sleek black BMW, with her slew of inherited houses, her politician husband, her stuck-up face and her vile mouth. She thinks she knows everything. She knows *nothing*. I might have followed her down here all those years ago, not for love, of course – though it was satisfying to seduce her that once – but for social admiration, a sense that she was living a life that could belong to me. But it's empty, all that, I realise it now. All that education. She doesn't even know how to look after her own child. It's impossible to state how irritated I felt by her superiority, her sense of entitlement. She thinks she's better than me. Her horror that I had spent time with her offspring. Her noxious combination of snobbery and hypocrisy.

I couldn't stop myself. I wrote, What a lovely girl Onnie is. What a treat to spend the night with her. Oh, the sweet joy of youthful flesh.

The phone rang again almost immediately. I watched it skittle across the table. I realised I was smiling. It rang off finally. And then several texts all at once.

You fucker.

You don't know what you've done.

She's 17.

I was beginning to enjoy myself. If I'd wanted to wait two decades to serve my revenge, I couldn't have planned it better.

Young enough to be my daughter, I replied.

A moment. A pause. And then her last text pinged in. I stared at it, aware of the BMW outside roaring into life and driving off. She'd gone. It was still a few seconds – five or six maybe – before the text reached my brain.

Even then. The words jerked, in and out of focus. They made no sense. A bad joke. A clumsy reiteration of how young Onnie was. A predictive mistake.

They made no sense. What did they need to make sense? The synapses in my brain fired, connections were made. A night years ago. A party at the hotel, gatecrashing some arsehole's twenty-first, flirting with Vic because it was fun to see Murphy, little round tummy in a stiff suit, the youngest MP in the history of the Tory Party, scowling across the room at me. And Vic, not yet bitter, but flexing against the bonds of early motherhood and Important Wifedom, desperate to flirt and be found desirable, dragging me on to the beach. Drunk with the night and the attention, completely off her head with it, letting me fuck her down on the rocks, under the overhang of the cliff.

When was it? Sixteen, seventeen years ago? Maybe. Probably. 1994. The maths could work. It was before I bought Gulls. The next time I saw her, after my mother died and left me the money, Onnie was a toddler, up on the headland, kicking her legs on Murphy's shoulders. It had never occurred to me even to wonder.

I read it again, letting the content settle.

She IS your daughter.

'Let me out!' Banging from the bathroom door.

'Wait,' I said.

My daughter. Her eyes, I suppose, could be said to be like mine, perhaps the shape of our faces. Her restlessness. Her interest in the more obscure aspects of pharmaceutical production. But what else? Nothing. Murphy's large hands clamped those kicking legs, her fleshy knees under his hairy knuckles.

Guilt? Remorse? No, not me. I threw back my head, and laughed. I poured myself another malt, dipped my finger in Kulon's plastic bag.

The delicious position in which I found myself finally dawned. Victoria would never denounce me now. What sweet agony.

Having to watch me carry on as if nothing had happened. Never to be able to tell, for the sake of her own daughter's sanity. And Lizzie would never find out.

I opened the bathroom door and released Onnie, the fruit of my loins, from the bathroom. I gave her some dry clothes to wear, some shorts that she secured with one of my belts, a sweatshirt. She told me she loved me and wanted to be with me. Did I love her? she asked. I prodded around to see if I could find an emotion – a paternal instinct perhaps – but the probe came up clean. 'Yes I do,' I said, wishing the words were true. But it's not in my make-up. Am I to be blamed for that?

The fact is, Onnie was already an inconvenience. I wanted rid of her, so I could read Lizzie's letter in peace.

Could she have something of mine to take with her? Yes, yes, a picture, I said, scanning the room, letting her choose. I put it in a bin bag along with her filthy clothes. (Annoying, actually. It's one of my favourites.) I was running out of patience. 'Where shall I go?' Find Kulon, he'll look after you. 'Will you come and get me later?' she cried, barefoot on the doorstep, clutching her swag. 'Will you leave your wife?' 'Yes. Yes. Yes. I'll come and get you.' 'Do you promise? Whatever happens?' Yes. Yes. Yes. 'Keep the faith!' I shouted after her.

I seem to have got through rather a lot of whisky. More in the car. The plastic bag is looking depleted. I have to wash and change my clothes. Lizzie. She's the only woman I've ever trusted, because I do trust her, despite everything. All the rest – they turn against you in the end. Betray you, tread your heart in the dust.

A love letter: I turn it in my hands. It's all I needed.

Thank God for Lizzie.

It's not about houses, I realise that, or finding the right location. It's not about the sea. It's about love. I'll put the light on now and open her letter, inhale her soft words, and then I'll ring her. I'll think of a way out of the mess I'm in. As long as I have Lizzie, everything will be all right.

Chapter Twenty-four

Lizzie

It's a cold, sharp day. The sky has cleared, blue sky for the first time in weeks, but a bitter wind flaps at the awning above Londis and flattens the long grass on the common. I run as soon as I am off the bus, down the last bit of Trinity Road and left into my street. The disloyalty to Zach has released something wild and unstoppable. It's the final treachery. I feel the fear and freedom of it in the soles of my feet.

I know something bad has happened the moment I reach the house. The front door is open a crack. I push past and into the hall, and stand there, my breath still hot in my chest.

The tiled floor is covered in envelopes and pizza flyers, unopened bank statements, hair ties, a bottle of de-icer and keys. Lots of keys. The pottery pot they were kept in is in pieces on the ground too.

For a moment, I just stare. The shelf where all this lay yesterday is empty but for one thing. A small painting is propped there now. It's of a young woman with dark hair in a doorway. She's looking down at her arms, her face distorted by the angle of perspective. It's an uncomfortable picture, shadowy and lonely. The room looks cold and she's wearing too few clothes. It's hard to look away.

It's one of the best pictures Zach ever painted, the picture you might show if you ever felt his talent was in doubt. It used to hang at Gulls. It's the one that was missing.

A pile of clothes is at the bottom of the stairs. I step towards them, as if in a trance, and pick them up, one by one – his old navy shorts, faded on the seat, the zip bent; a grey sweatshirt, with an ink blot on the hem, a worn brown leather belt. I hold the sweatshirt to my face, rub it against my mouth, run the heavy buckle of the belt down my cheek. There's a towel at the bottom and something falls out of it – a shiny blue photo album. I flick it open with one hand. Each page holds a single photograph. The first shows Zach, smiling, in his charity-shop suit. He is standing outside Wandsworth Town Hall. Our wedding day. You can still see half my arm across his shoulder, but my face has been cut out. Through the jagged hole, a piece of the photograph beneath shows through. A fragment of the slate house sign fixed to the porch in Cornwall: 'Gulls'.

A jolt above my head. A scrape. I drop the album and lay the shorts down on the bottom step. I am breathing so lightly it's as if the air is hardly moving past my lips. I'm so faint I'm not sure I can do it, but I begin to climb the stairs. I put one foot in front of the other. One foot in front of the other: it's what I've been doing all year. One foot in front of the other; it's how you survive. He has come back from the dead, but I am the ghost. I am so quiet, so light, I seem to move sound-lessly, up to the bathroom, and then the final flight of stairs to the two top rooms. A moment of dizziness. I put my hand on the wall to steady myself. The door to the bedroom is open, and I can see the mess inside. The bedclothes are on the floor and the contents of the cupboard emptied on top of that. The bedside lamp, switched on, lies on its side, casting a strange yellow shadow of itself on the wall.

I lean against the bannisters. The study door is closed. He's moving around inside, shifting objects.

I don't know what's going to happen now, whether I hate him or still love him, whether he has come back to apologise or to kill me, whether I'm scared of him or whether – I haven't thought of this before – he's scared of me. I forget he's a killer and a liar. All that matters in this small moment is that I'm about to see his face.

Tears are pouring down my cheeks. I can taste the salt.

I push the door. It catches on the carpet, and I have to push harder to make it budge. I'm not sure if I have stopped breathing completely or not.

I say, 'Hello, Zach.'

Stillness. But a small creak – at once movement and sound, the rasp of fabric against wood. Someone is here, a figure by the desk. I can see the shape of them against the light. Jeans, boots, draped shirt, long hair.

The wave that has been building inside me rises and breaks.

I lean back against the door. Somewhere on Trinity Road, a motorbike squeals.

'You,' I say.

The figure moves towards me. 'Oh. I'm sorry. The door was open.'

I feel myself sink. The muscles in my legs are worn thin, like paper. Perhaps I'm dead. Perhaps I am a ghost.

'Sorry. I don't know what you must think. I . . .'

'What are you doing?'

'I was looking for Onnie. The door was open and . . . I came in. I'm sorry. I shouldn't have.'

Victoria is poised for departure, slinging her bag over her shoulder, pulling back her blonde hair, securing it at her neck with a tie.

'Onnie?' My voice sounds squeezed and odd.

'I've looked everywhere.'

I'm staring at her, but she won't meet my eyes.

318

'Sorry about your photographs,' Victoria says. 'Do you have backups?'

'What?'

I look down. The floor is covered in fragments of torn paper – an arm, a corner of sea. My photographs. The room has been destroyed. The books have been pulled off the shelves. The box that was under the desk has been shredded, stamped on with violence. I've got here too late. He has been and gone. I've slipped to the floor. I think about Zach's anger, how he's kept it down for a year, held it close to his heart, and how it will have grown and intensified in force. How frightening he could be, when he was in control of himself; how much more frightening when he wasn't.

The door is still open and I push it shut with my hand and press my back against it. 'Ring the police,' I say. 'My phone is in my bag downstairs. Could you ring the police? Please?'

Victoria takes another step towards me. She puts her hands out. 'Wait a minute. Let's talk about this calmly, can we? I'm furious with her. She isn't always in control of her actions. But the police – well, if you could just think about my, our position.' She sits down at the table and, removing her bag from her shoulder, pulls out a long leather-encased chequebook. 'A terrible mess and an awful inconvenience for you. Let me pay for all the damage. Up here it's mainly cosmetic, though downstairs there's some smashed crockery and I think the glass in the back door might need replacing. Shall we say £1,000 – just to be on the safe side?'

I stare at her. Her left hand fusses at her neck, smoothing the hair into her ponytail, checking and checking for a loose strand. A nerve is pulsing to the side of her cheek.

'You think *Onnie* did this?' I say. 'Why would Onnie have done this?'

She sighs, spreads her hands again to express hopelessness. But it's fake. She's pretending to be open and honest, but beneath the surface, I can sense panic. 'It's a pattern with her.'

'I don't think Onnie did this,' I say carefully. 'Downstairs, someone's left some stuff – clothes and a painting. The person who brought those things into the house left them there for me to see. And that person—'

'No. No. No.' Victoria stands up and steps towards me. 'That was me,' she says. 'I brought those things. I know . . . they belonged to your late husband. And again, I can't apologise enough.'

I stand up. 'You had Zach's clothes? That painting? You brought them here?'

'Yes. No. Not exactly. Look.' She puts one long elegant hand under my elbow.

'I'm terribly sorry,' she says. Her mouth is stretched in a peculiar way. 'I've handled it all very badly. I've been away all week. I got back last night to an empty house. Alan, when I finally spoke to him, said Onnie was staying in London with the friend whose aunt runs the fashion house.'

'Shelby Pink.'

She glances at me and then away. 'Well, it was lies. Onnie isn't answering her phone, but she hasn't been there all week. So then I went through her bedroom with a fine-tooth comb and that—' she gestures to the door '—is what I found. Now you might be wondering why Onnie had some of your late husband's possessions.' She tries another ghastly smile. High spots of pink have appeared in her cheeks. 'Nothing sinister. It dates back to the time he was tutoring her. I think it was raining once and he lent her some clothes to go home in, and the picture she borrowed for inspiration. So – there. I think I'd better try and find my daughter before she does anything silly.'

She moves towards the door. I can't let her leave.

'I know about Onnie and Zach,' I hear myself say. 'You don't have to hide that from me.'

'You know?' She stares at me in horror. She seems to be having trouble controlling her mouth. 'What do you know?'

'That they had an affair.'

'Oh.' Her head jerks back. 'An affair? I wouldn't dignify it with the term "affair". Perhaps a one-night stand.'

'I think it was more than a one-night stand.'

'I don't think so.' She shakes her head, and then wipes some invisible dust from her cheeks, light sweeping gestures: an attempt at dignity. 'I'm sorry that you had to find out. You didn't know when you came to Gulls. Did she tell you?'

'She did. Yes.'

'Typical. It's just pure destruction. I'm sure your late husband and you were very much in love, that it wasn't his fault at all.'

'Why do you keep calling him my late husband? You knew him well. It's Zach we're talking about.'

She glances at me and then out of the window. 'My daughter . . .' She looks quickly at me again. 'If we made it £5,000, would that go some way to compensate for the hurt and damage my family has caused you?'

I shake my head, baffled. 'Are you paying me off?'

'I wouldn't put it that way.' Her mouth is a firm line. 'Please understand. My husband is about to stand as leader of the Conservative Party. It's a sensitive time for us.'

I stand up and open the door. 'You don't need to pay me for anything.'

I walk down the stairs ahead of her. I want her out of the house now. If Onnie took Zach's holdall, and clothes, and the picture, then *he* didn't. But Onnie wouldn't have added the figure to the painting in the studio, or wrecked it, or left the messages for me in the house. She wouldn't have taken the china houses from the Beeches. It wasn't Onnie I saw in the car park by his studio. It wasn't Onnie who almost killed Sam. He's still out there, violent, out of control, beyond reach. Last night, I slept with someone else. I still have reason to be afraid.

In the hall, I pause. The kitchen door is open. I can see right through, past chair legs and broken china, to Howard's upended bed. Victoria is a few steps behind me. 'She really did excel herself this time,' she says. 'Did the two of you have an argument?'

I don't answer. My eyes are still on the kitchen. I walk into it, full of dread. Howard isn't in his bed. He didn't come to greet me earlier. He isn't here. As I open the back door, a hunk of glass falls out of the frame. The garden is bright under a thin sky, empty.

'At least she hasn't broken your laptop,' Victoria says behind me.

I turn round. Zach's MacBook Air is on the kitchen table.

'My dog's gone,' I say. 'I don't know what's happened. He's not here.'

'The front door was open,' Victoria says. 'He might have just wandered off.'

I'm beginning to panic. 'I'm going to drive round and look for him.'

I grab my keys and go back into the street. I run to where I thought I'd left the car. It's not there. I stand on the pavement. Where did I park it the last time I used it? I run up and down the road, and then back into the house. I have an increasing sense of foreboding. I have started wringing my hands.

'My car's gone,' I tell Victoria. I scoop up all the keys that were on the floor and start sifting through them. The spare car key isn't here.

'I can take you,' Victoria says, hovering.

'No. No.' I'm trying to stay calm. 'My car's gone. Onnie, or someone, has taken my car. And maybe—' my voice is out of control '—maybe they've taken Howard too.'

'OK. Now calm down.' Victoria steers me into the kitchen. 'Where would she have gone?' She's talking to herself. 'I just need to think it through.'

'Not Onnie,' I say. 'It's not Onnie who has done this. It's Zach. It's Zach who wants to punish me. It is Zach who wants to ruin my life.'

Victoria says, 'Can you just think what might have upset her? Why would she have snatched your dog? Where would she have taken him?'

'Not Onnie,' I repeat. 'Zach.'

I'm sitting in front of the laptop. It's open and plugged in. There's a sheet of lined paper in front of me, covered in scrawls. It's the scrap of notebook Onnie was writing on the other night. I focus my eyes. There are various headings. Under '*Pets*', Onnie has written *Howard* and crossed it out. There is a heading for '*Memorable Places*' and crossed out under that, among other random places, are *Cornwall* and *Gulls* and *Sand Martin, Isle of Wight, Marchington Manor, Stepper Point, Blue Lagoon, Wandsworth Common*. The third heading, one that she has added since Thursday, is '*What meant most to him? Who did he truly love?*' Under this, she has written, *Onnie Murphy, Aine Murphy, Zach Hopkins. Glengoyne*. All of these have been scored through.

Only one name remains.

What meant most to him?

Not crossed out.

Who did he truly love?

One name.

Lizzie Carter.

My hand is at my mouth.

I turn the laptop towards me. Across the keyboard, my fingers pick out the letters.

LIZZIECARTER.

The screen vibrates. *INCORRECT PASSWORD.*

I try again, remembering the space.

LIZZIE CARTER.

The screen goes blank and immediately springs back to life. Zach's screensaver still reaches the corners of the space, but in the middle of it is an open file.

My hands fall away. Zach used my name as his password.

'Have you thought of something?'

Victoria is staring at me. I hadn't realised she was still here.

'No. Yes.'

It's a Word file. Small print, single-spaced. Page 119 of 120. '*Lizzie. My Lizzie,*' I read. I move the cursor up, so the page flips. My eyes skit. '*I haven't got a choice . . . Dartmoor . . . You fucker . . . People always . . . What was it Lizzie said?*'

I sit back. 'It's Zach's laptop. We were trying to work out his password and I think Onnie cracked it. I'm not sure what this is. A diary, or a letter maybe. But if she managed to open it, then perhaps she read it.'

'And that's what upset her?'

I turn back to the screen. I move the cursor quickly up and then as quickly down. The document is divided into sections, with separate headings – months, I think, or more precise dates. It's not a letter. It's a diary. I picture Zach tapping away – ideas for paintings, he told me. I hear his voice in my head. '*As long as I have Lizzie,*' I read, '*everything will be all right.*'

I spin down again to the last page. I have pains in my arms. I want to wrap them around myself to relieve the welling that I can feel building inside. I have to read the last page. I know I do. I force my eyes to focus, and my brain to concentrate on what they absorb. '*A fast road and a wall, or a tree: that's all I need.*'

I feel drawn so far into his heart, reading this, I think I will never climb out.

'What's the matter?' Victoria has put her hand on mine. 'You're shaking.'

'The last section of diary,' I manage to say. 'This . . . bit at the end – it's a suicide note. And I made him do it. It was my fault. He died because of me.'

Victoria waits with me for a while. I don't know how long. And then she is standing up and talking. I'm aware of her moving around the kitchen. A glass of water is put before me. She's still speaking, but not to me now. I hear her, still on her phone, leave the room. The sound of her footsteps on the stairs; the bathroom door opens and closes.

Zach is dead. He isn't out there, trying to destroy me. He's dead. And I killed him.

Victoria is back in the room, kneeling next to me. She has moved the laptop to the other side of the table. 'Is there some-one you can call?'

I stare at her with incomprehension. 'Why? Where are you going?'

'Onnie. I've got to find Onnie.'

'Onnie? Yes. Of course, Onnie.' I rest my head on the tips of my fingers and close my eyes. 'Where would she go? She's got my car. What is she planning to do?'

'I don't know. I'm trying to think. She obviously did read whatever's on there.'

'She's blaming me for his death. She's taken my dog.'

'Where would she have gone?'

The screen of Zach's laptop, across the table, has filled again with Stepper Point.

'Cornwall,' I say suddenly. 'She's driven to Cornwall.'

★   ★   ★

In the car, I sit with the laptop, a cold metal sliver, on my lap. Victoria tried to take it off me, to leave it behind, or at least to put it in the boot, but I won't let go of it. I don't want to read any more. Not now. But I know I'll have to. Zach's thoughts. Zach's secrets. The truth behind all his lies. I'll know it all. If that's what I want.

I stare at Victoria's feet much of the time. She has taken off her shoes and is driving in her socks. Thin navy blue socks. Why does anyone drive without shoes? To protect their footwear, I suppose, though you'd have to be the sort of person who had footwear you cared enough about. Victoria was wearing boots. High-heeled and shiny black leather ankle boots. I wonder where they are.

I'm trying to keep the desolation at bay – not a nice clean sadness, but a filthy, murky one. If Onnie thinks I caused Zach's death, she's right. I am responsible. That letter was painstakingly written. I judged the tone carefully, each vapid term. I knew how betrayed it would make him feel. It wasn't just the request for a separation, but the blandness of the phrasing, the way the words avoided any real emotion. It was my form of aggression. I might just as well have attacked him with claws.

I try and remember our last conversation, when everything was still normal. Except it wasn't. He told me he was on Dartmoor. But he wasn't; he was already at Gulls.

'Just catching the light,' he said. 'It's dying on me. There is this run of ancient stone tors stretching into the distance that look like unmarked graves. Not a person in sight.'

'How wonderful,' I said, relieved that at least his work was going well. 'Don't stay too late.'

'I won't get there until after dark.'

'Drive carefully,' I said, suddenly close to tears. I knew the letter was waiting for him. I wanted to wind back time to the beginning. I was beginning to regret it.

What was he staring at when he spoke to me? Was he with Onnie? When I can bear it, the laptop will tell me.

I lift it off my knee and pull it up to my chest.

Victoria casts a quick look in my direction. 'You shouldn't read any more,' she says. 'It never does any good to read someone's diary. It always ends up being hurtful.'

'You're probably right.'

'Did you get to read much already?'

'A little. I didn't really take it in – apart from the last bit.'

'You know what you should do?'

'What?'

'You should throw it out of the window. Now. Just open the window and chuck it.'

She indicates to pull into the inside lane, and slows down. She presses a button on the console between us and my window retracts electronically, filling the car with noise and wind. She gestures to the laptop with her hand.

'I don't think so,' I shout, clutching it more tightly. 'I'm not ready for that.'

She winds the window back up and the car is sucked into silence again. 'Suit yourself.'

I study her for a moment, in case she was joking, but she is grim-jawed. Several strands of hair have come detached from the tie at her neck. She's chewing her lip as she drives.

We've hardly spoken since we left the house, both of us too desperate.

'I hope my dog is all right,' I say suddenly. 'You don't think she would hurt him, do you?'

Victoria doesn't answer directly but after a few minutes of silence, she says, 'Leave her to me when we find her, won't you? Just take the dog and go. You don't have to be involved with the rest of it.'

She begins to talk after this – scraps of information. Onnie was named after Alan's mother, she tells me. It's Aine, really.

She was difficult, even as a baby, fussy and hard to feed, never slept, always reaching for things that she would then hurl to the floor in frustration. She was nothing like her older brother. And then her schooling – it's been 'a catalogue of disasters'. She never seemed to make any friends. Victoria worried about her, 'of course I did', but Onnie didn't make it easy for herself. 'She was arrogant. She was angry all the time, subject to mood swings. She always blamed other people if she failed. It was never her fault. She was always very literal, too. And you could never say the right thing. You were always putting her back up.'

'Sounds like a typical teenager.'

'Well, the various schools didn't think so. She was bullied a couple of years ago and we should have taken her out then. If we had we would have saved the situation. As it was it went from bad to worse. Onnie eventually got her own back on the girl in question. She Photoshopped some pictures and posted them on Facebook. The pictures were actually not at all nice. Cruel. And she got kicked out for it.'

She stares straight ahead now. We are just beyond Bristol at the point where two motorways converge. She concentrates on the signs and getting into the right lane. Finally, she says, 'I hope she hasn't hurt your dog.'

I turn my head so she can't see my face.

A few more miles pass.

'How did you know about Zach and Onnie?' I ask. 'When did you find out?'

'The day before his accident,' she replies shortly. 'I caught them at it.'

'In Cornwall?'

'Yes.' She frowns, concentrating on overtaking a tourist coach. 'It wasn't a pleasant scene, though we tried to forget it

328

in view of what happened to Zach. She was in a fearful state after we heard. I tried to keep it from her. But it was impossible.' She sighs.

'Did your husband know?'

'No,' she says shortly. Then when I think she isn't going to say anything else, she adds: 'That's one thing I did succeed at. One of the reasons I was so keen to pack Onnie off to Switzerland was so she wouldn't let slip anything to Alan. It never fails to amaze me how many secrets couples hold from each other. This liberal idea – tell each other everything. Nine times out of ten someone is hiding something. Even if it's just thoughts, desires, hopes. You can live in the same house, share the same bed, but how much do you ever really know anyone?'

I watch the borders of the road streak by. After a minute, she says grimly, 'Clever of you never to have children. They ruin your life.'

'You don't mean it.'

'I don't know about that.' She smiles briefly.

'I wanted a child,' I say. 'Zach didn't.'

'Oh.'

We are silent for a while. I continue to look out of the window. Eventually I say, 'Xenia. Someone called Xenia left flowers for Zach.'

I don't think Victoria has heard but she says, 'Everybody has a Xenia.'

We leave the motorway behind at Exeter and join the A30. It is mid-afternoon by now and the sun is low. Clouds are gathering, grey streamers across the pale blue sky. Alongside us stretch the purple uplands of Dartmoor where Zach didn't park up to paint, where he didn't leave the car and hike to a point called Cosdon, where ancient stone tors might or might not look like unmarked graves, where he didn't wait for a dying light.

*   *   *

She doesn't take the short cut, the route Zach and I used to take, the one I thought he had forgotten. She sticks to the main road. I watch the turning flash past.

A mixture of anger and panic and unhappiness begins to rise inside me. I've been trying to keep it all down, but now we are getting close I become so agitated I don't know what to do with myself. I start moving about in my seat.

'What's the matter?' Victoria asks.

I don't answer. I can see something ahead and I start shouting. 'STOP. Pull over. Pull over!'

'Fuck. What? What?'

She screeches into the blunt end of a lay-by, the car nosed in at an angle, half up on the kerb. A car horn blares loudly and passes. Behind us, parked squarely to the road, is my grey Nissan.

I'm out of the car before she can say anything, tearing across the gravel back to my own car. It's empty. No Onnie. No dog. Victoria is out, too, struggling to pull on her boots. Her hair is flapping. The top buttons of her shirt have come undone, the wind filling the fabric. I shout above the drone, pointing to the other side of the road, to the site of Zach's accident. I scan the hedgerows. There's a figure over there, with a dog on a lead – just before the corner. I can see the shape of her – long hair, a flash of blue. The dog keeps stopping and she's trying to drag him.

We need to cross but the traffic is constant in both directions. Cars just keep on coming. Pale winter sun glitters on their windscreens. In the first gap, I grab Victoria's arm and run to the middle of the road. The arrowed wires between pylons vibrate above our heads. I search for a gap between the cars coming in this direction. A space larger than most. The glare of lights approaching. I gesture to Victoria and run.

She's a hundred feet or so away from us. I'm not sure if she's seen us. She hasn't turned round. 'ONNIE!' Victoria shouts.

She glances over her shoulder, yells something and turns again.

There's hardly any space between the hedgerow and the road. We start towards her. Onnie begins to run, the lead jerking in her hand, the dog, now he's seen me, pulling against her. Victoria is running, too, still shouting. On the ground are curls of burned-out tyre. The bushes, branches trailing against my face, are greener than they were. As we begin to gain on her, she stops and turns to face us. 'Don't come any closer,' she yells. 'Don't you dare.' She has Howard by his collar now. He is twisting to get away from her.

Victoria and I have both stopped but Onnie is staring at me. Now we're closer, I can see the tears in her eyes, the streaks of blackened mascara, the rawness of her mouth. 'You killed him,' she says to me. 'It's your fault he's dead. You pretended to care, but you didn't. He died because of YOU.'

'No,' I say. 'That's not true.'

'It is. You were leaving him. You broke his heart. You lied to me, pretending you were all sad that he was dead. You made me feel sorry for you. Guilty. Well fuck you.'

She pushes Howard into the road with her knee. An approaching car swerves slightly to avoid him, sounds its horn. Victoria takes a step forward.

'Don't you come near me. You lied too, Mum. You're all liars. You made me feel I was the bad one. I was the failure. *I didn't know.* Why didn't you tell me? How could you have let it happen?'

Victoria lets out a sob. 'It wasn't like that. We'll talk about it. I'll explain.'

'It's too late for that,' Onnie shouts. 'I hate you. I hate myself.'

She turns away and, still dragging Howard, stumbles on towards the bend. Over her shoulder, she yells again, 'You killed him, Lizzie. The only person I've ever loved is dead.' She sounds as if she's choking. We're almost at the point of Zach's accident. The tree is near. It's blocking the last of the sun, dappling the road. She stops again. A container lorry thunders past, its horn sounding. She takes a sideways step out towards the road. She bends to pick up Howard. He's struggling, scrabbling in her arms.

She says, 'I thought you liked me. You turned out to be just like everyone else.'

'Let's go back to the car. Let's talk about it.'

'I'm tired of talking. I'm tired of everything.'

Victoria lets out a cry and pushes past me. 'Don't come near me,' Onnie says. She has put the dog down but she picks him up again and takes another step out. She is right on the edge now, dangerously close to the path of the traffic. A van in the inside lane swerves, sounds its horn, accelerates. 'Are you going to try and save me? Or the dog? Would you give your life for him? You wouldn't for me.'

A black sports car snarls. She is distracted for a moment. And then she stares at me again, with a terrible expression on her face. I know what she's about to do. We're too close to the corner. The cars are going too fast. No time to stop. No room here to swerve. Victoria has started screaming.

I don't think. I just run. Onnie sees me coming, hurls herself forward on to the road. She is spreadeagled, her face down – I see her arms go out, the dog under her. I imagine the screech of brakes, the heat of diesel, the crumpling of metal. I feel a rush of air on the backs of my knees and I am on top of her, pulling her up and backwards, yanking, my arms full of hair and body, my fingers scrabbling at her clothes. She is pushing against me, panting, crying. I don't know where the dog is.

But I don't let go of Onnie. I stumble backwards under the weight, and my feet tangle. We fall. Zach's tree closes in above us. Branches drag at my face. My head knocks against the root. My cheeks are stinging, cuts on my arms. Somewhere I can hear Howard barking, the sound of feet running towards us. But I'm still holding on to Onnie and even though she's fighting and kicking out, I'm not going to let go.

We're straddled across the gully. I can see the trunk of Zach's tree. The lilies are still there, blown aside from the base of the tree, the cellophane yellowed, the flowers brown and desiccated. The note's still attached. I can read it from here. The heart with the name around it. *X E N I A*.

'I'm sorry. I'm really sorry,' I sob in Onnie's ear.

The fight has gone out of her.

My eyes are still on the note with the flowers. From where I'm lying, my head close to the ground, the letters seem to run the other way.

It says *A I N E X*.

Her name, Aine, with a kiss. *Onnie.*

In my ear, she says, 'I did it for Zach.'

'But he's dead,' I say, and the words fill me with relief. 'Zach is dead.'

Zach

I am calm. My emotions have shut down. I'm not angry, or perhaps my own pure anger isn't like other people's. It doesn't flow, like blood, or crackle like fire. It's a heavy, solid object. I clutch it against my chest. It's drawn through my skin and becomes a hard case around my heart.

That letter – every phrase in it was targeted to hurt. She's leaving me and she can't even do it truthfully or honestly. She needs 'space' to fuck her other man. She doesn't love me. End of story.

The house is tidy and clean. That's important. I've removed all evidence of my brief occupancy. The bed wasn't even slept in. We've run out of bin bags. I gave Onnie the last one. I put the empty whisky bottles, my dirty clothes and Onnie's towel in a holdall I found in the cupboard. I have scrubbed the bathroom and polished the chair where I sat to open her letter. I rubbed it so hard I almost gave myself blisters. If I wasn't in a hurry to leave, I would have burned it.

I finished that painting she liked. It lacked something. The dealer in Bristol said my art needed more 'emotional engagement'. Well, I've added a figure. Zach Hopkins – off to face his death. She'll find it after it's happened. She knows me well. She'll understand. Does it represent hope or despair? She can work it out.

It might destroy her, my death, and its aftermath. She loves me enough for that, even if she doesn't know it. Can you kill someone from beyond the grave? A new one on me.

I'm not your average killer. I'm different. My legacy, my life's work: not the pictures in the end. Polly Milton – I didn't mean for her to die. She must have hit her head when we fought, toppled in. I hardly heard the splash. Charlotte, too, an unnecessary accident, if a planned one. I shouldn't have slept with her, but she should have been more careful. Her fault.

I'll find the car in a minute, climb over the back fence and along the alley to where Jolyon said he'd leave it. I'm waiting until the world is in bed, for the roads to empty. The rain has eased off. Heavy clouds are rolling in off the sea. I'll stop for petrol. A full tank. Roof down. A bit of fog: good. A fast road and a wall, or a tree: that's all I need.

The walls are closing in. That confidence I felt earlier, I can feel it slipping. People are always quick to judge – they take the easy moral route. People never look beyond the cliché. Lizzie won't forgive me, even if I sorted the situation. Perhaps I can't forgive myself. I should love that girl. I should feel something. I don't

People always . . . People never . . . What was it Lizzie said? She's right. The rest of the world, all those people lumped together, they're all the same. I am different.

A slight dizziness has come over me. Set off in a minute. Not enough sleep. Too much . . . too much thought.

Lizzie. My Lizzie. I thought you could save me. You've destroyed me instead. It turns out I don't want to live without you. Ironic that. I could say forget me, but I can't. I don't want you to move on. I want us to be together. I want you to remember me, to feel me close to you, every day.

Lizzie – one last gift to show my love, to carry for ever: my death.

Chapter Twenty-five

Lizzie

I did read Zach's diary. I might not have done if it hadn't been for Onnie. I didn't want her knowing any more about him than I did. I grieved for a while, dwelt painfully on my part in his death, and then one night I read it alone, as I planned, in an empty house. I played Elvis Costello. Occasionally I broke off to pour myself a glass of water. At one point I put my head between my legs. I didn't cry, though, even when I read about Onnie. His daughter. I was proud of myself for that.

He wasn't who I thought he was: that's the cliché, that's what I told Jane. He had secrets and his mind twisted in private in a way that was foreign to me. 'We were all fooled,' Jane said, to make me feel better. 'We were all charmed by him. Evil can be attractive. Everyone knows that.'

I showed the diary to Hannah Morrow. Victoria was obviously against it, but I felt I had to. There were too many holes in his narrative, too many disturbing details. She took it to Perivale, and investigations into the deaths of Polly Milton and Charlotte Reid were eventually reopened. No further evidence was unearthed in the case of Polly Milton.

Charlotte Reid's death was a different matter. CCTV footage was discovered of Zach arriving at Brighton Station at eleven on the morning of her death and a witness came forward who claimed to have seen him outside her house shortly afterwards. A new inquest was ordered, but the evidence was deemed circumstantial. Her parents were photographed leaving the coroner's office, her mother hardly able to stand for grief. Nell gave a statement on how sinister she had always found Zach. 'There was something off, if you know what I mean.' It's easy to justify things after the event.

The press got hold of it, despite Victoria's best efforts. The *Daily Mail* went to town on the dangers of Internet dating and there was an in-depth article in the *Sunday Times* about Charlotte Reid's death. In the end, it was Onnie who revealed her own side of events. A piece in the *Guardian* Family section appeared three days after she left the Priory, where she had been treated for 'borderline personality disorder' in tandem with post-traumatic stress. The piece was entitled 'My Father, My Lover' and pretty much ended Alan Murphy's leadership ambitions (he fell at the first ballot). I found it almost unbearable to read, but not for the obvious reasons, perhaps. She was staking a claim on Zach, a claim on his memory.

She wrote me a letter – one of the steps in her recovery programme – saying how sorry she was for sleeping with Zach, and for being so 'annoying' afterwards. She confessed she had rung a few times in the months after Zach died and then hung up. (The other silent calls, the police have assured me, were the result of 'hitches' in call-centre technology. I have been advised to report them to Ofcom.) I don't want to see Onnie again – I am sure that's best – but sometimes I think about her face when she held out her damaged wrists, the vulnerability, the anguished gratitude, and wonder if things might have been different.

People have been very kind to me recently – much kinder than I deserve. Not just Peggy and Jane and colleagues at school, but the police too. Everyone is pretending they understand how I could have convinced myself Zach was alive. No one looks at me as if I am mad. Perivale, muttering about Morrow's 'lack of experience in matters of such sensitivity', was keen to lay out the evidence – specifically the report from the Scientific and Technical Services Unit. This catalogued the chain of evidence: skid marks, vehicle liquid spillage, the scatter pattern of surviving car pieces, road condition readings and a computer chip proving the Fiat had been driving in excess of 80 mph. 'No one parked that car against a tree and lit a match,' Perivale said. He also put me in touch with PC Paul Johns, the missing persons manager for the Devon and Cornwall Constabulary, who said the disappearance of Jolyon Harrison had never been a high-priority investigation. Jolyon was deemed neither vulnerable nor representing high risk and at the Rogue Nightclub in Bude had told several witnesses he was heading off to Cambodia for a business opportunity. It also turned out he owed money to some people in Truro. PC Paul Johns concluded he had 'found himself in a spot of bother and scarpered'.

The diary, Perivale told me early on, is my insurance policy. 'Mr Hopkins wouldn't come back now, even if he could,' he said. 'He'd be arrested the moment he walked through that door.'

'Are you humouring me?' I said, looking him in the eye.

He smiled thinly.

Most of my hauntings have been explained. I already knew it was Onnie who had the clothes and the picture from Gulls, but she had also wrecked the studio in her distress the day after he died. It turns out it was Peggy, irritated at my lack of generosity to Alfie and convinced I wouldn't notice, who took the Rotring pens. She brought the red lipstick back, too, after finding it one day down the back of her sofa. She had just forgotten to mention it. The dead bird – Jane looked that up for me. It's not unusual apparently. Collision with windows is one of the three most common causes of bird death in the UK, along with cats and cars. 'The British Trust for Ornithology says up to a hundred million birds strike windows each year in this country, and a third of them die.'

Sam's attack was one of several muggings to take place that winter. Howard discovered Zach's poisoned marrowbone when the storm blew the shed door loose. The Xanax had deteriorated in the damp, so there was, luckily, only enough to make him ill, not enough to kill him. The man in the bathroom my mother talked about – I think her brain was dredging the trauma of seeing Zach that first time. The two missing china cottages turned up at Peggy's house: 'Really? You were concerned about their disappearance? My bad. If you like them that much you can have them yourself.' I think a nurse at the hospital stole my mother's ring.

When I thought I saw him, across the car park at the grey-hound track – it was my imagination playing tricks, my own obsession catching me out. Because that's been the thing this whole time, my obsession. Jane and Peggy have both sepa-rately said how I was 'the victim', the hapless object of Zach's obsession. But I'm the one who was obsessed. There are passages in his diary that shock me. But when I think about Zach, my heart still beats faster, something deep in my stom-ach clenches. Peggy says he pulled the wool over my eyes – her phrase – but he didn't. Not really. I think I always knew something was deeply wrong. In my darkest moments, I wonder whether I loved him *because* of what he was like, not despite – his anger, his jealous flares, they excited me, made me feel alive. I loved a possible, probable murderer: what does that say about the workings of my own heart? He was wrong about one thing: I would have forgiven him for sleeping with Onnie. He didn't know what he was doing. Perhaps, after all, I would have forgiven him even if he had.

People ask if I wish I'd never met him, but it would be like wishing away the blood in my veins, or stripping my body down to its white bones.

He loved me back. I know that now. That's what shines out of his diary. Sam, who has read it, says Zach wrote for control, to self-justify. 'Duper's delight: a common facet of the socio-path,' he explained, 'an extreme glee in getting one over on others.' It's not how it seems to me. If I close my eyes to certain parts, if I try and forget the other women and Onnie, it reads to me like a declaration of love. His love for me led to his death. It's a simple equation. It's my mind, since he died, that has twisted and manipulated, that has misconstrued, that has dreamt of hauntings and revenge, waited for violence. People stroke and hug. They can talk as much as they like about grief and bereavement, abusive relationships, the mindset of the victim. Sometimes I wonder if I'm not the one they should be worried about.

Lizzie

May 2014

Last weekend we were up in Northumberland. Sam's parents live in Newcastle and we spent a few days with them before driving up the coast to a cottage I had rented through the National Trust website, inland a bit from Berwick-upon-Tweed. We wanted to give Agnes her first glimpse of the sea.

It rained almost continuously, which kept us in or pottering around the local shops. But on Sunday the sun cracked through the clouds and we drove to a clifftop car park we had located on the map. It was a long hike down to the shore, across a high field where two skylarks erupted, to the top of a headland, and then a steep final descent on a zigzagging path in a dip in the cliff. At the bottom, we made a camp in the cup of the sand dunes. Howard chased the seabirds, and Agnes sat on a rug, propped up by the picnic basket, small fists waving.

We had brought sausages and bread and wine and Sam collected driftwood to make a fire. No one else around. Or hardly anyone; a couple of figures in the distance. I remember clocking them; I tend to be aware of strangers. When you lose a person you're close to, whatever the truth of the relationship, you never stop feeling that something is missing – not really. But it was late afternoon; that time on a Sunday when you're normally gearing up for school or work. There was a bank holiday ahead of us and we were luxuriating in the feeling that we were bunking off. The sand stretched, stippled, in all directions. Wind bent the beach grass. You could taste the early breath of summer in the air. It was heaven.

I said I'd go when we realised we'd left the matches by the kitchen stove. I love Sam. I love my daughter. Every day I want to pinch myself; I can't believe how lucky I am. But I still quite often seek out opportunities to be alone.

We'd passed a garage back on the main road. I climbed back up to the car and drove there, parking on the forecourt to one side of the pumps. There were no other cars. Inside, a young woman with heavy bags under her eyes was sitting behind the glass partition at the till. The shop was empty. I was choosing a bar of chocolate when I sensed a presence. The door must have opened and closed without me noticing. A single figure, tall, dark-haired, was picking out a pint of milk from the cold storage.

Something about the shape of him, the gait, lopsided, stooped. He was wearing heavy boots, the kind worn on building sites, jeans and a pale blue shirt. He crossed the shop in front of me and stood at the counter to pay. I waited behind, hardly breathing. What I could see of his face was brown, weather-beaten; hanks of hair hung forward across his brows.

He didn't look at me until he reached the door and then he turned, caught my gaze, trapped it for a fleeting moment in his.

Of course it wasn't. Too tall, his face too angular. But I didn't move an inch until the door jangled shut.

I don't think I'll ever be free. I'll always be looking over my shoulder, despite everything, and half wanting to see him standing there.

I waited, flicking through magazines, until I could be sure the man was gone.

Acknowledgments

Lots of people were very helpful when I was researching this book. My gratitude is due to Sophie Mellor, Karen Robinson, Sophie Hayes, Jo Marchington, Ben Smith, Katie Smith and Ella Hearn. Thank you also to my wonderful agent Judith Murray and to my fantastic editors Ruth Tross, Emily Bestler and Lorissa Sengara. And, as ever, thank you to Giles Smith.

If *Remember Me This Way* has left you desperate for more, why not try Sabine Durrant's brand new psychological thriller, *Lie With Me?*

A few little lies never hurt anyone. Right?

Wrong.

Paul has a plan. He has a vision of a better future, and he's going to make it happen.

If it means hiding or exaggerating a few things here and there, no harm done.

But when he charms his way on to a family holiday . . .
And finds himself trapped among tensions and emotions he doesn't understand . . .

By the time he starts to realise that however painful the truth is, it's the lies that cause the real damage . . .

Well, by then, it might just be too late.

Out now from Mulholland Books.

Turn the page to read the gripping opening chapter!

August 2015

It struck me in the night that it might have started *earlier*. I sat up in horror and, in the darkness, used my fingernail to scratch the word 'BOOKSHOP' on the inside of my forearm. It has gone now: the skin is inflamed due to an infected insect bite, which I must have further scratched at in my sleep. Still, the act of writing did the trick, as it tends to. This morning I can remember well enough.

Hudson & Co: the secondhand bookshop in Charing Cross Road. I have been assuming it began there – that none of it would have happened if my eye hadn't been caught by that silly little shop assistant's red hair. But am I wrong? Were the forces already in motion, in the weeks and months before that? Does the trail of poison lead back, long before the bloody girl's disappearance, to university? Or before then, even – to school, to childhood, to that moment in 1973 when I struggled, puce-faced, into this unforgiving world?

I suppose what I am saying is, how much do we collude in our own destruction? How much of this nightmare is *on me*? You can hate and rail. You can kick out in protest. You can do foolish and desperate things but maybe sometimes you just have to hold up a hand and take the blame.

BEFORE

Chapter One

It was a wet day, one of those grey, drizzly London afternoons when the sky and the pavement and the rain-streaked buildings converge. It's a long time since I've seen weather like that.

I'd just had lunch with my oldest friend Michael Steele at Porter's in the Charing Cross underpass, a wine bar we had frequented since, at the age of sixteen, we had first discovered the discretion of both its location and its landlord. These days, of course, we would both have much rather met somewhere less dank and dark (that chic little bistro on St Martin's Lane specialising in wines from the Loire, *par example*), but nostalgia can be a tyranny. Neither of us would have dreamt of suggesting it.

Usually, on parting from Michael, I would strut off with a sense of groin-thrusting superiority. His own life restricted by the demands of a wife, twin boys and a solicitor's practice in Bromley, he listened to my tales of misadventure – the drunken nights in Soho, the young girlfriends – with envy in his eyes. 'How old's this one?' he'd say, cutting into a Scotch egg. 'Twenty-four? Saints alive.' He was not a reader and a combination of loyalty and ignorance meant he also still thought of me as The Great Literary Success. It wouldn't have occurred to him that a minor bestseller written twenty years ago might not be sufficient to maintain a reputation indefinitely. To him I was the star of 'Literary London' (his phrase) and when he picked up the bill, which he could be depended upon to do, there was a sense less of charity than of him paying court. If an element of mutual bluff was required to sustain the status quo, it was a small price to pay. Plenty of friendships, I am sure, are based on lies.

That day, however, as I returned to street level, I felt deflated. Truth was, though I had kept it to myself, life had recently taken a downward swerve. My latest novel had just been rejected, and Polly, the twenty-four-year-old in question, had left me for some bum-fluffed political blogger or other. Worst of all, I had discovered, only that morning, that I was to be evicted from the rent-free flat in Bloomsbury I had, for the last six years, called home. In short, I was forty-two, broke and facing the indignity of having to move in with my mother in East Sheen.

As I have mentioned, it was also raining.

I trudged along William IV Street towards Trafalgar Square, dodging umbrellas. At the post office, a group of foreign students, wearing backpacks and neon trainers, blocked the pavement and I was pushed out into the gutter. One shoe sank into a puddle; a passing taxi soaked the leg of my corduroys. Swearing, I hopped across the road, wending my way between waiting cars, and turned up St Martin's Lane, cut through Cecil Court, and into Charing Cross Road. The world juddered – traffic and building works and the clanging of scaffolding, the infernal disruption of Crossrail. Rain continued to slump from the sky but I had made it doggedly beyond the Tube station before an approaching line of tourists pulling luggage thrust me again out of my path and against a shop window.

I braced myself against the glass until they had trundled past, and then I lit a cigarette. I was outside Hudson & Co, a secondhand bookshop specialising in photography and film. There was a small fiction section in the back where, if I remembered rightly, I had once pilfered an early copy of *Lucky Jim*. (Not a first edition, but a 1961 orange Penguin with a Nicolas Bentley drawing on the cover: nice.)

I peered in. It was a dusty shop, with an air of having seen better days – most of the upper shelves were bleakly empty.

And then I saw the girl.

She was staring through the window, sucking a piece of long, red hair, her features weighted with a boredom so sensual I could feel it tingle along my fingertips.

I pinched the lit tip off my cigarette, put the remainder in my jacket pocket and pushed open the door.

I am not bad looking (better then, before everything happened), with the kind of face – crinkled blue eyes, strong cheekbones, full lips – I've been told women love. I took trouble over my appearance, though the desired result was to make it look as if I didn't. Sometimes, when I shaved, I noticed the length of my fingers against the chiselled symmetry of my jaw, the regularity of the bristles, the slight hook in the patrician nose. An interest in the life of the mind, I believed, was no reason to ignore the body. My chest is broad; I fight hard even now to keep it firm – those exercises I picked up at Power Pulse, the Bloomsbury gym, over the course of the free 'taster' month continue to prove useful. I knew how to *work* my look, too: the sheepish, self-deprecating smile, the careful use of eye contact, the casual deep-in-thought mussing of my messy blond hair.

The girl barely looked up when I entered. She was wearing a long geometric top over leggings and chunky biker boots; three small studs in the inside cartilage of one ear, heavy make-up. A small bird-shaped tattoo on the side of her neck.

I dipped my head, giving my hair a quick shake. 'Cor blimey,' I said in mock-Cockney. 'Rainin' cats and dogs out there.'

She rocked gently backwards on the heels of her boots, resting her bottom on a metal stool, and cast a glance in my direction. She dropped the spindle of ruby hair she'd been chewing.

I said, more loudly: 'Of course Ruskin said there was no such thing as bad weather. Only different kinds of good weather.'

The sulky mouth moved very slightly, as if vaguely in the direction of a smile.

I lifted the damp collar of my coat. 'But tell that to my tailor!'

The smile faded, came to nothing. *Tailor?* How was she to know the coat, bought for a snip at Oxfam in Camden Town, was ironic?

I took a step closer. On the table in front of her sat a Starbucks cup, the name 'Josie' scrawled in black felt tip.

'Josie, is it?' I said.

She said, flatly: 'No. That was what I told the barista. I tell them a different name every time. Can I help you? Are you looking for anything in particular?' She looked me up and down, taking in the absorbent tweed, the cords, the leaking brogues, the pathetic middle-aged man that wore them. A mobile phone on the counter trembled and, though she didn't pick it up, she flicked her eyes towards it, nudging it with her spare hand to read the screen above the cup – a gesture of dismissal.

Stung, I slunk away, and headed to the back of the shop where I crouched, pretending to browse a low shelf (two for £5). Perhaps she was a little too fresh out of school, not quite my audience. Even so. How dare she? Fuck.

At this angle, I smelt damp paper and sweat; other people's stains, other people's fingers. A sharp coldness in here too. Scanning the line of yellowing paperbacks, phrases from my publisher's last email insinuated themselves into my head: 'Too experimental . . . Not in tune with the current market . . . How about writing a novel in which something actually *happens*?' I stood. Bugger it. I'd leave with as much dignity as I could muster and head off to the London Library, or – quick look at my watch – the Groucho. It was almost 3 p.m. Someone might be there to stand me a drink.

I have tried hard to remember if the door jangled; whether it was the kind of door that did. The shop had seemed empty when I entered, but the layout allowed anyone to hide, or lurk – as indeed I was now. Was he already in the shop? Or not? Do I remember the scent of West Indian Limes? It seems important. But perhaps it isn't. Perhaps it is just my mind trying to find an explanation for something that may, of course, have been random.

'Paul! Paul Morris!'

He was standing on the other side of the bookcase, only his head visible. I took a brief physical inventory: close-set eyes, receding hairline that gave his face an incongruously twee heart shape, puny chin. It was the large gap between the two front teeth that sparked the memory. Anthony Hopkins, a contemporary from Cambridge – historian, if I remembered correctly. I'd bumped into him several years ago on holiday in Greece. I had a rather unpleasant feeling that I had not come out of the encounter well.

'Anthony?' I said. 'Anthony Hopkins!'

Irritation crossed his brows. 'Andrew.'

'Andrew, of course. Andrew Hopkins. Sorry.' I tapped my head. 'How nice to see you.' I was racking my memory for details. I'd been out on a trip round the island with Saffron, a party girl I'd been seeing, and a few of her friends. I'd lost them when we docked. Alcohol had been consumed. *Had Andrew lent me money?* He was now standing before me, in a pin-stripe suit, hand out. We shook. 'It's been a . . . while,' I said.

He laughed. 'Not since Pyros.' A raincoat, pearled with drops, was slung over his arm. The shop assistant was looking over, listening to our conversation. 'How are you? Still scribbling away? Seen your byline in the *Evening Standard* – book reviews, is it? We did love that novel you wrote – my sister was so excited when you sold it.'

'Ah, thank you.' I bowed. His sister – of course. I'd hung out with her a bit at Cambridge. '*Annotations on a Life*, you mean.' I spoke as loudly as I could so the little scrubber would realise the opportunity she had passed up. 'Yes, a lot of people were kind enough to say they liked it. It touched a nerve, I think. In fact, the review in the *New York Times* said—'

He interrupted me. 'Any exciting follow up?'

The girl was switching on a blow-heater. As she bent forward, her silk top gaped. I stepped to one side to get a better view, caught the soft curve of her breasts, a pink bra.

'This and that,' I said. I wasn't going to mention the damp squib of a sequel, the disappointing sales of the two books have had that followed.

'Ah well, you creative types. Always up to something interesting. Not like us dull old dogs in the law.'

The girl had returned to her stool. The current from the blow-heater was causing her silky top to wrinkle and ruche. He was still prattling away. He was at Linklaters, he said, in litigation, but had made partner. 'Even longer hours. On call twenty-four seven.' He made a flopping gesture with his shoulders – glee masquerading as resignation. But what can you do? Kids at private school, blah blah, two cars, a mortgage that was 'killing' him. A couple of times, I said, 'Gosh, right, OK.' He just kept on. He was showing me how successful he was, bragging about his wife, while pretending to do the opposite. Tina had left the City, 'burnt out, poor girl', and opened a little business in Dulwich Village. A specialist yarn shop of all things. Surprisingly successful. 'Who knew there was so much money to be made in wool?' He gave a self-conscious hiccupy laugh.

I felt bored, but also irritated. 'Not me,' I said gamely.

Absent-mindedly, he picked up a book from the shelf – *Hitchcock* by François Truffaut. 'You married these days?' he said, tapping it against his palm.

I shook my head. *These days?* His sister came into my mind again – a gap between her teeth, too. Short pixie hair, younger than him. I'd have asked after her if I'd remembered her name. Lottie, was it? Lettie? *Clingy*, definitely. Had we actually gone to bed?

I felt hot suddenly, and claustrophobic, filled with an intense desire to get out.

Hopkins said something I didn't completely hear, though I caught the phrase 'kitchen supper'. He slapped the Hitchcock playfully against my upper arm, as if something in the last twenty years, or perhaps only in the last two minutes, had earned him the right to this blokeish intimacy. He had taken his phone out. I realised, with a sinking horror, he was waiting for my number.

I looked to the door where the rain was still falling. The red-haired temptress was reading a book now. I twisted my head to read the author. Nabokov. Pretentious twaddle. I had a strong desire to pull it from her grasp, grab a handful of hair, press my thumb into the tattoo on her neck. Teach her a lesson.

Turning back to Hopkins, I smiled and gave him what he wanted. He assured me he would call and I made a mental note not to answer when he did.

You've turned the last page.

But it doesn't have to end there . . .

If you're looking for more first-class, action-packed, nail-biting suspense, join us at **Facebook.com/ MulhollandUncovered** for news, competitions, and behind-the-scenes access to Mulholland Books.

For regular updates about our books and authors as well as what's going on in the world of crime and thrillers, follow us on **Twitter@MulhollandUK**.

There are many more twists to come.

MULHOLLAND:
You never know what's coming around the curve.

HODDER